A QUANTUM OF THOUGHT

THE DISCOVERY

A D QUINTON

First published in 2025
Copyright © 2025 by A D Quinton

Adrian Darren Quinton asserts the moral right to be identified as the author of this work.

ISBN: 978-1-0684842-0-9 (Paperback)
ISBN: 978-1-0684842-1-6 (eBook)

This is a work of fiction.
While real locations such as Oxford University and the Beecroft Building are referenced, all characters, events, and organisations are the product of the author's imagination. Any resemblance to actual persons, living or dead, or to real events is purely coincidental.

All rights reserved. No part of this publication may be reproduced, stored in a retrieval system, or transmitted in any form or by any means—electronic, mechanical, photocopying, recording or otherwise—without the prior written permission of the author, except in the case of brief quotations used in reviews, blogs, or literary analysis.

For more information, visit:
www.adquinton.com
@adrianquintonauthor

With heartfelt thanks to my wife Anita, my daughter Sarah and my dear friends, Jacqui, Gabrielle and Emma for their invaluable time, keen eyes and unwavering encouragement.

Your support and dedication have meant the world to me.

Take a look around you...

How can any part of this be real?

1

'Nothing is created unless first a thought.'

Fog clouded Manisha's mind. Her eyes were tired and sore. The dim glow from the VDUs and desk lamp barely touched the corners of her lab where LEDs blinked on shadowy machines. Endless hours two floors underground in the Beecroft Building, combined with her lack of progress, were taking their toll. The constant hum from the vast array of computers crunching data in the next room only added to her soporific state. She pushed through the haze, clinging to the hope that the breakthrough she desperately sought could unlock the key to human consciousness.

She picked up a scalpel and slit the seal on a fresh box of surgical gloves. Her hand shook and she nicked the side of her index finger with the blade. Blood seeped from the tiny cut. She cursed and sighed before sucking the blood from the wound. The warmth of her mouth dulled the pain but, when she took her finger out, the blood reappeared, oozing in a steady stream from her skin. She grabbed a tissue to stem the flow and mopped up a stray spot of blood from the side of a petri dish. Her patience waning, she tried to switch to a more positive mindset. She took a deep breath and imagined the joy she would feel upon making the progress she so desperately wanted. She visualised it as if the mere thought of success would pull that version of reality towards her.

The security camera in the corner of the lab whirred, refocusing, snapping her back to the present moment. A shiver ran down her spine. She shook her head and scowled at the camera. She imagined an overweight security guard, feet up on his desk, watching TV. 'Watch the game or do your rounds, but stop stalking me,' she muttered in its direction. The camera whirred in response. She glared at it in disgust and reached into a drawer for a square of chocolate from a half-eaten bar. It began to melt in her mouth, and the impact was instantaneous. Calmness and positivity took over as endorphins surged into her brain.

Manisha pulled on the surgical gloves, picked up the petri dish and placed it under an electron microscope. She looked up as the image appeared on one of the large VDUs above her desk. Multicoloured brain cells filled the screen. Their tentacles reached out to other cells as if trying to make a connection. They lay in a base of neuroprotective chemicals and neurotransmitters, which she hoped would support the birth of new brain cells. Going on autopilot, Manisha placed the dish in the dome-shaped scanner. It started its silent process, and the results began to flow up a second screen above her desk. Her tired eyes strained as she copied and pasted the long list of results into her new algorithm. After checking and re-checking the new variables, Manisha sat back in her chair. She raised her hands high, letting out a rasping sigh as a satisfying stretch ran through her shoulders and arms. She lowered her hands, letting her index finger hover over the enter key. Pressing it would set her decryption process in motion. A process that could take anything from a few minutes to a few days to complete and one she had started over a hundred times. Each time her experiments had failed. She stopped, glancing at the black box secured in the corner of her lab. *I need to see it again.*

Manisha eased herself off her chair. The dull ache in her back told her she'd spent too long hunched over the desk. She grabbed her eye protectors, straightened her posture, and made her way to the specialised equipment. Butterflies fluttered in the pit of her stomach. As she slipped on her protective glasses, her surroundings faded into opaque purple tones. An array of fibre optic cables fed into the twelve-inch black cube. It let out a quiet hum, punctuated by the occasional crack of static electricity. Tinted glass on one side of the box gave a faint glimpse of the secret held within. Manisha eased the clasps open, then lifted the lid. A brilliant white light burst through the darkness, filling the room. Her heart skipped a beat, as it did each time she gazed in wonder at the miracle she had achieved. Before her was the physical manifestation of a person's thought.

A glass sphere held captive a bright, swirling, multi-coloured cloud of energy, reminiscent of gases formed in a nebula in the aftermath of a supernova. It moved constantly with a power and life of its own, as if trying to escape the confines of its prison and spread out into the world as it was born to do. She felt an affinity with the light as if it were part of her soul. Manisha had caught a fleeting moment of life, the essence of humanity, and possibly the secret to life and consciousness. If only she could decode it.

Manisha felt the familiar ache in her heart as her thoughts turned to her parents. If only her father were still here to help her. His sudden death still filled her with pain, like an open wound that could never heal. Despite the years that had passed, the image of the last time she saw him consumed her.

And the memory of her mother—her beautiful mother, confined to a wheelchair after a massive stroke. A sharp mind trapped in a broken body, trying to express her thoughts, feelings, and emotions but unable to communicate. This fuelled Manisha's work from early each morning to late into the night. 'I won't let others suffer the way you had to. I will succeed.'

Manisha gently closed the black box, placing the clasps down, ensuring her miracle was safe. The iridescent light in her lab dimmed as she removed her protective glasses, and the room returned to normal. Her teary eyes blurred as they adjusted to the light. Once back at her desk, she wiped her cheek and forced her melancholy aside. She checked the configuration one last time and hit *enter,* starting experiment one hundred and eleven. Within seconds, the tally of attempts to decode the energy multiplied on the screen before her. From the corner of her eye, she caught the wall of flashing LEDs in her machine room, assuring her that all the computing power she had was being put to use.

She switched off the desk lamp and walked into the outer office. Her head pounded and her eyelids were heavy. 'God, I could sleep for a week,' she said to the empty room. Satisfied that she had done all she could for the day, she picked up her coat and rucksack, ready to leave. She started to pass through the glass and steel mantrap security door when an alert sounded. The rhythmic beep cut through the darkness and the hum of the machines. Her heart skipped a beat. It was the sound she'd been waiting for. She threw her coat and rucksack onto the outer office desk and ran back to the main lab.

Her eyes scanned two of the large VDUs above her desk. Lines of data scrolled rapidly up the screen. She was transfixed by a third screen. Her hands trembled, and adrenaline coursed through her veins as she watched an image building, line by line. Her breath caught in her throat as emotion took hold. A tear trickled down her cheek as she stared, open-mouthed, at an image she'd seen hundreds of times before—but until now, only in her mind's eye.

'This changes everything,' she whispered.

RAIN SPLASHED HEAVILY on the tarmac, creating the fleeting illusion of tiny craters in the water. It pooled and drifted before cascading into a drain. A streetlight bathed the pavement in an orange-white glow. Leafless trees swayed in the wind as the rain lashed against the side of the Beecroft Building. The streets of Oxford were quiet; the dedicated students stayed in their dorms to study while others smoked, drank, gamed, or had sex.

Laing sat alone in his Mercedes, windscreen wipers on intermittent, brushing away the water, clearing his view temporarily before the rain blurred and distorted it again. He checked his watch: 22:07. 'Why do you always have to work so late, Professor Williams,' he said, squeezing the bridge of his nose while yawning. He rubbed his eyes, encouraging heavy eyelids to stay open. The view of the building hadn't changed in the last hour. But he knew she was in there, working hard on her discovery—a discovery he knew could change the world. For good or for bad, only time will tell. A power, once unleashed, can never be contained. This was Laing's biggest fear—it kept him awake at night. He looked in the glove box and reached for the pristine packet of Marlboro Red, still in its cellophane. The government health warning screamed at him. The cellophane crinkled as he toyed with the idea of opening them to kill the monotony. Having them to hand brought a sense of security mixed with the familiar lure of temptation. Laing killed the thought before it got out of control and threw the packet into the back of the glove box, slamming it shut with a disgruntled humph. A routine he had gone through countless times over the last two years since kicking the habit. He wrapped his arms around himself and rested his head against the window frame, keeping a steady eye on the main revolving door to the building. He willed the woman he was there to protect to appear and head back to her flat for the night. He would stay and wait as long as he had to—nobody was waiting for him at home anyway.

The darkness of the streets was cut by headlights speeding down Parks Road. A black VW Transporter pulled into the car park, reversing into a space two spots down from Laing—the furthest space from the building's main entrance. The headlights shone through the rain, making the watery craters shine bright until the lights were killed. A man in a dark hoodie exited the driver's side, grabbing a rucksack from behind the seat. A second, stockier man emerged from the passenger side—torch and crowbar in hand. He landed heavily in a puddle, wearing black VANS with faded white trims and closed the door with a muted clunk. Laing switched off the windscreen wipers and kept his head down. His eyelids were barely open, content to give the appearance of a man sleeping off a few beers before driving home. His focus sharpened as he watched the men disappear down the side of the building—the side of the building leading to the lift shaft which provided access to Professor Williams's lab.

Laing opened the car door, his breath slow and calm. Icy rain bounced off the door trim onto his face. He closed the door quietly behind him and took large, hurried strides across the car park, avoiding streetlights; his black bomber jacket camouflaging him in the darkness. He ran down the side of an adjacent building, hiding behind columns which kept him in the shadows and sheltered him from the rain. Picking his approach carefully, he ran past the revolving doors to the corner of the building where the men had disappeared moments earlier. He took a tentative glance around the corner and saw their huddled forms. The men crouched by the building's rear fire exit with their backs to him. One held the torch, filling the space between them with light, while the other rummaged around in a rucksack. Laing glanced at the security cameras—surely a guard would see this, if they bothered to look. Laing ran across the grass and hid behind a tree only ten feet away from the intruders. In the reflection on the side of the building he saw the men look around. They paused, listening, and quickly turned their attention back to the job at hand.

'You picked a great night for this,' the smaller of the two men said with a Middle Eastern accent. 'How do you know she's even in there?'

The stocky man spoke in a condescending tone. 'I checked on the security camera before I left. She's in her lab.'

'Why can't we take her when she comes out?'

'The data is in her lab—we need to secure the data and the woman. Once we're sure we have the data they want, then they will tell us what to do with her.'

'Sure, but we can have some fun with her, right?' he said with a lewd chuckle.

The thought made Laing shudder.

The smaller man continued to dig around in his rucksack and pulled out what looked like a device with an aerial. He stuck it between the camera and the door alarm.

Radio jammer, Laing thought.

The smaller man wiped rain from his face. 'This had better be worth it.'

The stocky man laughed. 'Your brain could not comprehend the uses of this woman's discovery. Just do what I tell you and open this fucking door.'

The man placed a charge next to the lock. 'Five seconds.' They crouched to one side of the door and waited.

Laing moved deftly from behind the tree and landed his foot into the side of the larger man's head. Knocked off balance, the man fell backwards, rolling in front of the door, dazed. The second man plunged his hand into his rucksack and pulled out a knife. The charge popped, and the door flew open, slamming into the side of the stocky man's head. He rolled onto his side, writhing in pain.

The smaller man lunged forward with the knife, which Laing parried away, sending the knifeman crashing into the tree.

Laing's attention switched back to the stocky man who still looked stunned, shaking his head as he tried to make sense of his surroundings. He landed a downward punch onto the side of the man's jaw to keep him down. The man took the blow and laid flat on his back, eyes wide, breathing heavy.

A sharp kick to the back of Laing's leg made him fall to one knee. A blade flashed in front of his face, and he grabbed the man's arm and landed a crunching blow to his stomach. Spit flew from the man's mouth as Laing sprang to his feet and struck him square in the face. The cartilage gave way under his fist as he heard the nose crack. The man stumbled backwards and tripped over his partner, sprawling onto the wet ground.

Laing looked from one man to the other as the stocky man rolled away and stood. The smaller man recovered his balance and knelt on one knee, as blood poured from his nose and over his mouth. He lunged forward, knife outstretched, heading for Laing's gut. Laing grabbed his assailant's wrist and hit the back of the man's hand. The blade clattered against the building. Laing locked his grip, twisting the man's arm hard, bringing him down to the ground. He landed a knee into the man's head, knocking him backwards and he landed heavily on the rucksack. Grabbing the knife, Laing turned to the stocky man who stepped forward, ready to join the fight.

'So here we are, Mr Laing. Face to face at last,' he said, looking out from under his dark hoodie.

Laing stayed quiet. Waiting for the man to make his move. The smaller man staggered to his feet. 'What are you waiting for?'

'We've been told not to kill Mr Laing. He's too important to our game,' the stocky man said. 'But his day will come.'

'He's seen us now. There's no going back.' The smaller man pulled another blade from a strap on his ankle and lunged forward.

Laing stepped to one side, his attacker tripped and fell

onto the steel blade held firmly in Laing's hand. It sank deep into the man's neck and Laing felt the weight get heavier on the knife. The man's weapon slipped from his fingers and splashed onto the grass. His life drained away, blood pooling on the rain-soaked earth.

'I'll see you again, Mr Laing,' the stocky man said, pointing at Laing as he walked backwards before he turned and ran towards the VW Transporter. Tyres screeched as the van sped out of the gates and down the road towards Summertown.

Laing pulled the knife from the man's neck; the lifeless body lay limp, eyes wide, staring into the darkness as the rain bounced off his face. The streets were quiet again, no passers-by, the security cameras jammed—no other witnesses. Laing pushed the boot release on his key fob, grabbed the rucksack and threw the knives in. Heaving the body over his shoulder, he ran to the boot of his car. The suspension creaked as he dumped the body in the boot and threw the backpack against the corpse. Laing pressed the boot's close button and slid into the driver's seat. He held onto the steering wheel, panting, catching his breath. He was torn about his next move—*should I stay and ensure Professor Williams is not under any further threat or leave and dispose of the body?* Seeing a uniformed man hurrying through the reception settled his mind, and he gently pulled away. In the rear-view mirror, he could see the stout security guard with a torch and baton running down the side of the building. 'Better late than never,' Laing said as he turned out of the car park. The VW van had vanished. He hit the microphone button on the steering wheel and said, 'Call Redfern.' The electronic voice responded, 'Calling Susan Redfern.'

'Laing, what do you want at this time of night?'

'Ma'am, there's been an incident.'

'That usually means you've killed someone.'

'I was on surveillance at the Beecroft Building, and two men tried to break in to abduct Professor Williams and gain access to her research.'

'What were you doing there?' The tone of her voice cut deep. 'I told you this level of surveillance was not required.'

'I followed my instincts, Ma'am.'

'Your bloody instincts have got you into too much trouble in the past! Is Professor Williams okay?'

'Yes, Ma'am, she's oblivious. But I have a body in my boot.'

'How do you know they were after Professor Williams?'

'I heard them discuss it, Ma'am. Their intentions were clear.'

'What does this man look like?'

'A small unshaven man with a foreign accent, possibly Middle Eastern. He had a partner, a stockier man who got away.'

'Why did you let him get away?'

'He ran, Ma'am. But he knew my name. Apparently, he'd been told not to kill me.'

There was a long pause. 'Well, maybe he should have,' she said dryly.

Her sense of humour washed over him. 'Ma'am, I need a cleanup team to take care of the body.'

'Yes, yes. I'll take care of it. Do you think this man will be missed?'

'No idea, Ma'am.'

'This is another bloody mess, Laing. From now on, do exactly as I say. Do you understand?'

'Ma'am, Professor Williams could have been abducted tonight.'

'Do you understand?'

Laing paused, clenching his teeth, 'Yes, Ma'am.'

The line went dead.

Laing let her lack of gratitude slide. He'd stopped trying to impress his superiors—he was too long in the tooth for that game. However, he did expect her respect and, most of all, her trust.

2

'Reality is merely an illusion, albeit a very persistent one.'

Albert Einstein – Physicist (1879–1955)

The professor sat in his chair, drooling into a bowl of cold, congealed soup. The late-afternoon sun poured through the windows, casting a comforting warmth in the dying weeks of winter. The nurses had already taken the other inhabitants of the nursing home to their rooms for the evening, but the professor liked to spend the day in his comfortable chair in the communal lounge. He would sit for hours, staring out of the large bay window at the winding, tree-lined drive that led to the home, as if waiting for someone or something. This had been his routine for the last fifteen years.

The smell of wood smoke filled his nostrils as he turned

to scan the room. Drool hung from his chin, swinging from side to side as he moved his head. The old library was empty. Embers in the impressive stone fireplace, combined with the high, wood-panelled walls, evoked distant, comforting memories of his childhood home. He turned his gaze to the window, taking in the view over the landscaped garden, with woods beyond. *Why am I here?* He hung his head in quiet resignation at the enigma he couldn't solve.

His head throbbed as faint memories of his time in this room surfaced. Flashbacks of violent scenes. Times when he had refused to take his medication, and they had forced the pills down his throat. Other times, they tried to move him from his chair overlooking the tree-lined drive before he was ready, and he had lashed out, punching and kicking until they sedated him. An ugly side of himself that made him feel ashamed and angry. Ashamed that he had lost control in such an inglorious way, and angry that no one could answer his simple questions.

He couldn't remember why it was so important for him to sit there, by the window with the view of the drive, but his instinct screamed at him to keep looking, watching, waiting. But for what, he had forgotten. Just as he'd forgotten his life before he was interned, held captive like a convict who could no longer remember his crime. His only consolation was that he had evidently trained the staff to put him there every day, with his view, even if his mind was still smudged and distorted by the drugs.

'Andrew, Andrew!'

The faint sound of the evening nurse calling him drifted into his consciousness, and he became aware of fingers snapping in front of his face. The sound grew louder, drawing him out of his intense daze. He lifted his blank stare to look at her.

'Are you ready to go to your room now?' the nurse asked.

'No, no.' The professor shook his head and the drool swung from his chin. He felt a moist wet wipe wash his mouth and surrounding skin as the nurse cleaned the saliva from his unshaven face.

'You can have another thirty minutes, but no more. I have my rounds to do!' She picked up his untouched bowl of soup, her footsteps fading as she left the cooling room.

The sign at the bottom of the drive caught his gaze. His blurred vision could just make out the words as he narrowed his eyes: *Bletchley Residential Nursing Home for Ex-Service Personnel.* 'I wasn't in the forces, was I?' he murmured, shaking his head in frustration. An object in his dressing gown pocket pressed against his leg. He pulled it out and laid it on the table before him. The stained brown leather wallet contained a faded photograph of a woman and child. He glanced at his left hand—the gold band on his wedding finger told him he was a married man. *I can't remember who you are,* he thought, as he looked at the woman in the photo. His gaze turned to the child. *Why can't I remember your name?* He stared deep into the child's eyes, searching for an answer, as if the photo would unlock his memory. A steady silence filled his mind. He opened each pocket in the wallet, expecting it to contain some clue that would remind him of his past. But there was nothing. No driving licence or any form of ID. He clenched his weak fist in frustration. *Is Andrew even my real name?*

He glanced out of the side of the bay window at the building that confined him. It was Victorian gothic in architecture, with arched mullion windows, and an imposing array of gargoyles that cascaded rainwater away from the building. The style was impressive but dominating. 'It's like being in a bloody prison.'

He looked back to the faded photograph with heavy eyes. 'Why don't you come to visit me?' he asked, as he drifted off to sleep.

Andrew awoke to the faint sound of heels on wooden flooring, growing louder until Angela, the evening nurse, appeared by his side. The evening sky darkened as rain started to tap against the tall windows.

'Okay, Andrew, your time is up!'

'Oh, all right,' the professor surrendered, feeling more lucid as the drugs began to wear off.

The nurse sat in the chair next to him and held his hand. Andrew could see the worry in her deep brown eyes.

'How are you feeling, Andrew?'

'I just want to know why I'm here?' he asked, trying to summon anger, but weakness and a sense of resignation won out.

'Your mind is not well, Andrew. That's why you're here. I know you can't remember, but I've told you this many times before. You're in the best place for your wellbeing.'

'I don't believe you. This all feels wrong.'

'Andrew.' She looked straight into his eyes. 'You're not eating enough. You've lost too much weight. You can't afford to get any weaker.'

'Oh dear. Am I being told off?'

A sympathetic smile passed over her lips. 'No, I'm just concerned for you.'

He caught her smile turn to sadness and he looked down, avoiding her gaze, feeling ashamed that his life had somehow come to this. He sensed he didn't have long to live. But he didn't know what he was living for anyway.

'You deserve better, Andrew.'

'I know.'

Angela helped him into his wheelchair and wheeled him through the residents' lounge. Large table lamps placed equidistantly along the walls provided just enough light to fight back the darkness. They turned down a dimly lit, wood-panelled hall and headed towards the lift.

Andrew looked up at the walls to see a wooden plaque with the names '*Lord and Lady Manton*' written in gold leaf, which sat under a haunting painting of a couple in nineteenth-century clothing. Two paintings of younger men flanked them. Further along hung black and white photographs of doctors and nurses lined up outside the building during the Second World War, with patients in uniforms lying on beds pulled out onto the lawn on a summer's day. A stark reminder that he was in an eighty-year-old hospital for mentally scarred ex-service personnel.

'How are you, Angela?' Andrew enquired, as the fog in his mind started to clear.

'I'm just fine. The world's a wonderful place and I'm just happy to be alive,' she replied whimsically.

The professor smiled. 'Life is precious, you know. You need to make the most of it while you can—because you never know when the illusion will end.'

'The illusion?'

'Our reality is just an illusion. None of us exist in a physical world.'

'Is that right? So, if I don't exist, who's pushing you down the hall?'

'You're just perceiving pushing me down a hall. It doesn't mean you are.'

She pressed the button to call the lift, and the motors droned into life.

'Will I ever get out of here, Angela?' he asked, his voice heavy with quiet desperation.

Angela went quiet for a moment, as if weighing up her response. He caught her stare as she looked deep into his eyes, into his soul, as if she were searching for the right way to let him down gently, without destroying his reason for being. 'Maybe one day,' she said. 'Until then, we need to follow the doctor's orders and maintain your medication.'

'The drugs make me feel so groggy all the time. I don't like them. Can we try reducing them for a few weeks and see how I get on?'

'I'm sorry, but I'm under strict instructions to keep you on this course of medication until the doctor and the government advisors tell me otherwise.'

Andrew vaguely remembered his last visit from the doctor—a tick-box exercise with no chance of a change in medication even if the doctor felt he was getting better. He found himself stuck—stuck in a situation he didn't understand and for reasons he could no longer remember. However, deep down, he knew that someday he would be free from this place. He had seen it.

The lift doors opened, and Angela wheeled the professor in. She pressed button two and the doors closed. Lift motors whirred into life, shattering the silence of the building.

'The doctors know nothing,' Andrew muttered, his frustration barely contained.

'You must take the medication until you're told not to, Andrew. The doctors know best and that's final.'

Andrew sensed an inflection in the nurse's voice that made him doubt she truly believed her own words.

A soft ping announced that the lift had reached its destination. The doors opened, and Angela pushed the professor down the corridor and into his room. A small lamp lit the bed and orthopaedic chair, while a large sash window dominated the wall opposite.

'Do you want some help? Or shall I leave you for a few minutes to get into bed?'

'I'll be all right, Angela. Thank you.'

The nurse walked out of the door and turned before she closed it. 'I'll be back in five minutes.'

Andrew pushed himself from the wheelchair, his thin legs struggling to support his feeble frame. He shuffled to the sink, pulled the cord to switch on the shaving light, and brushed his teeth with trembling hands. The bedrooms were large and airy, with the orange alarm cords next to the bed and sink, reminding him he was in a care home. Andrew looked at himself in the mirror, past his unrecognisable grey, unshaven face and deep into his own light blue, bloodshot eyes. 'I will get out of this place. They will come for me.'

He switched off the shaving light and shuffled to the side of the bed, removing his food-stained dressing gown, which he draped over the chair. He sat on the bed, looking past his reflection and out of the window. Rain started to lash down, clattering against the glass with every gust of wind. He could hear the splashing of the water from gargoyles working overtime on this dark, dank evening, and imagined the ground beneath them sodden. Twin lampposts cast a soft glow across the grounds. Their light fractured and shimmered on rain-streaked walls.

Angela knocked softly before re-entering. She picked up his dressing gown and hung it on the back of the door. 'Time for bed, Andrew. Here's your sleeping tablet and your night-time medication.' She handed him four pills and a cup of water.

A faint cry from another resident reminded him it was a good idea to take his nightly sleeping pill, even if he hated the other tablets. Sleep was his only sanctuary where he could escape this unexpected reality he found himself in. One by one, he swallowed the pills, resigning himself to another drug-induced sleep.

Angela plumped up the pillows and pulled back the covers. 'In you go, Andrew. If you need anything during the night, just pull the orange cord.'

Andrew laid his head against the soft, clean pillow. Angela pulled the covers up to his chin, switched off the bedside light, and walked over to the door.

'Have a good night, Andrew.'

'Good night, Angela, and thank you.'

The door closed, and darkness took over. As his eyes adjusted, he could see a faint white light from outside, which cast shadows on the ceiling as the rain poured down the panes of glass. He lay still, waiting for the drugs to take their course, his mind grasping at fragments of forgotten memories. *The photograph shows I have a family. Where are they?*

Distant cries echoed through the home, swelling into tormented screams. The poor souls relived their worst ordeals, trapped in the dark corners of their minds—never free, not even in sleep. The noises of the night upset him, and he urged the drugs to kick in and take him away.

'I will be free from this place. They will come for me,' he said over and over, as he began to feel his body surrender to the medication.

The screams grew fainter and fainter and the light outside the window faded to black.

3

'Mind is the Master power that moulds and makes,
And Man is Mind, and evermore he takes,
The tool of Thought, and, shaping what he wills,
Brings forth a thousand joys, a thousand ills—
He thinks in secret, and it comes to pass;
Environment is but his looking-glass.'

James Allen – Author / Philosopher – (1864–1912)

The cold spring breeze whipped through Manisha's long, dark ponytail as she completed her second lap of the frost-laden Christ Church meadow. The grass glinted in the early morning sun. She breathed in deeply, allowing the invigorating fresh morning air to fill her lungs. It was Sunday, 7:00 a.m. as she started the last lap of her 5.5km route. Sweat soaked through her T-shirt as she pounded the frozen path next to the River Thames.

The morning was bright and peaceful. Birds sang and squirrels leapt along the path before her. She exchanged satisfied, knowing smiles with fellow joggers who were also enjoying the beauty of the morning. Mist rose from the river, cut by the bow and oars of a two-man racing shell, forming eddies and vortices in its wake. As she ran past, Manisha instinctively pondered the mathematics of the phenomenon—then caught herself. This was time to clear her head and free her mind. Time to zone out of the day job and be at peace. Exercise and meditation, all in one.

Manisha ran farther down the path and recognised a muscular man with tanned features, neatly trimmed stubble, and a shaved head. As he stretched his hamstring on a bench, the bottom of his t-shirt hitched up, revealing tattooed wings spilling down his back, with strange writing underneath them. He smiled as Manisha ran past and called out, 'Beautiful morning.'

His piercing blue eyes locked onto Manisha's, sending a chill down her spine. There was something cold and disconcerting about his stare. She forced a polite smile before darting her gaze back to the path.

For the final kilometre, Manisha focused on her breathing and quickened her pace. The path veered left, away from the Thames, before curving north along the bank of the River Cherwell. The tree-lined trail sheltered her from the worst of the cold breeze, but also took the best of the early morning sun. A young muntjac deer darted across the path in front of her—the beast appearing just as startled as Manisha. She pushed on and rounded the north corner of the meadow. On the home straight, with only three hundred and fifty metres left back to the Meadow Building, she upped her pace again. She gave the final straight everything she had. Her heaving breath, the pounding of her heart, and the sound of her feet hitting the frozen path was all contained within the moment. Nothing else existed apart from this snapshot in time. Her reality.

Her solitary, enjoyable moment was broken by the thud of heavy footsteps behind her. She knew instinctively who it was—the tattooed man from earlier—and the thought gave her goosebumps, scaring her into trying to run faster. Manisha could hear his breath over her shoulder as if he were following in her tracks. She veered onto a wider path along the Broad Walk leading to the Meadow Building, giving him plenty of space to take an alternative route. But the heavy footsteps kept on coming. The muscular man with a bald head sprinted past, as if trying to prove he could run faster than her. She exhaled in relief as he ran ahead to start another lap of the meadow. 'Get a grip, Manisha,' she said under her breath as she crossed the imaginary finishing line parallel to the entrance of the Meadow Building. She pressed the stop button on her Garmin and slowed to a walk —hands on hips, heart pounding. *Calm down, girl.* Her hands were shaking as she looked at her Garmin, which read 26:56. It wasn't her best time, but it was far from her worst.

She took a slow walk to the steps leading into the building, steadying her breathing. After stretching, she sat under the large lancet arched entrance to cool down and enjoy the view.

Manisha looked out over the sun-kissed meadow, reflecting on her life. The dreaming spires of Oxford had captivated her since childhood. The city and university had shaped her, from her years at St Edward's senior school, to her research post in Oxford University's Physics Department at the Beecroft Building. The commitment she gave to her work was absolute, and her efforts were paying off. After the success of experiment one-hundred and eleven, she finally felt she was on the verge of a breakthrough—a significant one. Her work held the possibility of improving the quality of life for millions of people.

Her thoughts turned to her father, who had instilled a love of science in her from an early age. A smile spread across her face, and childlike excitement filled her as she remembered a chilly November evening just after her eighth birthday. Her father had bought her a telescope for her birthday. She had been so thrilled as he'd set it up and pointed it towards the velvet night sky. When she'd looked through the eyepiece and seen craters on the moon for the first time, she had been stunned. She could still remember their conversation.

'The moon reflects the light from the sun; that's why it shines at night,' he'd told her.

'Wow,' Manisha felt excitement bubbling up within her.

'The light from the sun takes eight minutes to reach earth,' he'd explained. 'Light from the nearest star takes four years to reach us and light from the furthest stars takes billions of years to hit our eyes.'

'That's amazing,' she'd said, looking up into the night sky, drinking in the beauty of the universe. 'So, when we look up to the stars, we're looking back in time?'

'Exactly, sweetheart!'

The broadness of his smile at her understanding such an amazing concept at such a young age had been etched onto her mind forever. That single moment had planted a seed she would nurture for the rest of her life. Since that evening, she'd known her calling and pursued her desire to understand life and the universe with relentless passion.

It was the same evening her father had told her a black hole existed at the centre of our galaxy called Sagittarius A*. He'd been so enthusiastic, waving his arms around and making her laugh. She could recall how important the black hole had been to his work, although she had no idea why. From that evening onwards, 'SagAstar' had become his nickname for her. *How I wish I could hear you call me that again.*

As Manisha cooled down, a chill brushed over her, prompting her to head inside the Meadow Building. From the corner of her eye, she saw the muscular man completing his lap of the meadow. Their eyes met and then, to her surprise, he changed direction and sprinted straight towards her. Her heart thumped as she fumbled in her pocket for the electronic key fob to open the wicket gate. He was only meters away, looking straight at her, running at full speed, as if trying to get to her before she disappeared through the door. She retrieved the fob, and the lock buzzed—just as the man collided with her. He towered over Manisha, breathing stale garlic into her face, his piercing eyes looking straight into hers.

'What do you want?' she shouted, shoving against his sweaty, muscular chest.

'I just need to get through. I forgot my key,' he said with an easy smile.

Confused, Manisha stepped back, allowing him a clear path through the wicket gate. She heard him laughing as he jogged through the courtyard towards Tom Quad.

Manisha caught her breath. She had encountered many creeps during her time at Oxford, but this one was quickly climbing the leaderboard.

She climbed the steps, her heart still pounding, and passed through Arch Six, buzzing into the stairwell to the second floor. She ensured the door locked tight behind her and headed up the staircase, which still had the original wrought iron banister and ornate overhead cross supports. However, the blue stair treads made of modern hard-wearing carpet did nothing to complement a building of its age. Her destination was room 6-12, where Matthew, her boyfriend for the last year, lived and studied for his finals of a Philosophy and Theology degree. She only stayed on Friday or Saturday nights, giving them space to focus on their work during the week. They tried to keep the weekend free for play, time away from Matthew's dissertation and time for her to be free of her lab. But her mind always wandered back to her work.

Manisha clicked the door shut and the warmth of the room embraced her. Its familiarity calmed her nerves. The fridge buzzed in the background as she tiptoed through the minefield of clothes and books which adorned the floor. It was a large and peaceful room, with a high ceiling, ornate plaster coving and two simple ceiling lights. The double bed placed in the middle of the far wall allowed a pleasing view over the tree-lined path which cut through Christ Church meadow. Books, used mugs, and glasses covered the desk beneath the triple-arched mullion window. She shook her head and smiled as she picked up a framed photo of the two of them in Paris. 'You'd better be tidier if we ever live together.' As she looked at the photo, her mind recalled their first date in Gee's restaurant on the Banbury Road. For her, it hadn't been love at first sight. Matthew had been entertaining to talk to, tall, attractive, with an athletic build. However, his strong New York accent had done nothing for her. Determined to enjoy an evening away from work, she kept the conversation light and playful—despite being a quantum physicist and he, a philosopher. They had a natural banter around the meaning of life, and the nature of reality. The contrasting views of their chosen educations made the conversation interesting and funny. Matthew's light-hearted nature and mischievous wit pleased her, making the evening unexpectedly memorable. They had met for coffee a few times over the coming weeks, which had grounded their friendship. She felt sympathetic for the difficulties he'd had with his father while growing up; problems which she could see still troubled him even after so many years. As he'd often quote, 'Friends are God's way of apologising for family.' However, it was a surprise call one Friday afternoon and a spontaneous trip to go stargazing at the dark sky reserve in Brecon Beacons in Wales that had won her over. That evening spent looking up at the stars, laughing and drinking champagne, had captured her heart. His kindness, sense of humour, and—most importantly—his unwavering support for her work transformed a dependable friend into a devoted partner. 'You're not bad for a blind date,' she said, as she placed the photograph back on the bedside table.

She docked her iPhone, which flashed 7:25 a.m. Music filled the room as she peeled off her leggings, draping them over a chair. She caught her reflection in the mirror; the bags under her eyes were a reminder she needed to get the work and personal life more balanced. She released her hair from its band, cascading it over her shoulders down to the small of her back. She kept it long in memory of her Indian mother, Attiqa, whose glossy dark hair she'd loved to brush as a child.

Determined not to let her morning encounter unsettle her, she danced into the en-suite, making the most of the endorphins that still pumped around her body. She pulled the silver lever, turning the shower on, allowing the water to warm before committing to enter. The water bouncing off the inside of the glass door absorbed her. She studied the droplets as they gathered, gravity pulling them into rivulets that trickled down the glass, each seemingly following its own random path. *There are no accidents; everything happens for a reason.* She chased a droplet of water with her finger.

Steam poured from the top of the shower cubicle. Manisha slid the door open and embraced the warmth that welcomed her. She clicked the door shut, took a deep breath, and angled her face to the shower of hot water which poured down over her body; the warmth reaching into her core. She ran her fingers through her hair, sweeping it back over her shoulders, and immersed herself in the feeling of the moment.

THE SUN WARMED Matthew's face as he left the Oxford University Boat Club after another tough training session. His arms hurt and felt heavy. However, his commitment was stronger than ever. *This year, I am going to win, no matter the cost. No one can stop me*, was his daily affirmation. The reality of last year's race caught him. He clenched his fists. 'Cambridge can go to hell,' he muttered.

The early morning training sessions had become part of his routine. He had no problem jumping out of bed at 5:30 a.m. on a cold, dark morning to row 10k with his fellow teammates in a chilly, musty gym. Taking part in the Boat Race was half the reason he'd chosen to study at Oxford. His love of philosophy and the tradition that came with life at the university was the other draw. Matthew had started out at Harvard, studying for a degree in medicine. 'Cardiology is the right specialism for you,' insisted his father, trying to enforce his own chosen career on his son. However, medicine had never been a comfortable pursuit for Matthew. The tedium of it did not agree with him—the endless lists of body parts to learn, regurgitating biological facts and figures without room for original thought. He yearned for insights into the nature of reality, to ponder our reason for being and our place in the universe. After years of arguments, Mathew had finally broken free to pursue his own passion. He'd severed ties with his father—who cut him off financially, cancelling his credit cards and stopping his monthly allowance. It forced him to take out several eye-watering loans to fund his education in England.

Matthew pulled the hoodie over his head and started the ten-minute jog from the Iffley Road Sports Complex back to the Meadow Building. He shook his arms, releasing the tension from the pounding he had given them over the previous ninety minutes. He'd taken up rowing as a child as a means to escape the fractious family home, enjoying the isolation on the water of the lake adjacent to his father's estate. The anger he'd felt inside him as a child from the pressures of his overbearing father had been released on those waters. His father had scolded him for not pursuing a place on the school football team and laughed at his obsession with rowing. Matthew had done his best to ignore him, and he'd often Googled the Oxford vs. Cambridge University Boat Race and watched countless videos of the most famous rowing race in the world, dreaming that one day he would take part. Once at Oxford, he'd never wavered from his resolve, even though friends often challenged him, asking if the hundreds of hours of training were worth it for an eighteen-minute race. They didn't understand. This was *the* Boat Race. One of the oldest, hardest, and most prestigious rowing races in the world. Its two-hundred-year history was something he had to be part of, and he had to be on a winning team. Then, he would take great delight in sending his own video clip of him winning the Boat Race to his father.

The Meadow building came into sight as Matthew jogged the final one hundred meters to arrive at the wicket gate, feeling strong and confident. He executed the same stretching routine as Manisha, before tracing her steps up to room 6-12. As he entered the room, he heard music streaming from the speaker and inhaled the sweet scent of Manisha's jasmine body wash.

He removed his hoodie and stripped, throwing his sweaty gym clothes into the nearest corner, and stretched high, releasing the ache from his torn muscles. He looked at his naked body in the mirror and smiled, pleased with what he saw. Tripping over the mess of clothes and books, he made his way to the bathroom. Steam hit his face as he entered the en-suite. Then he saw Manisha's perfect silhouette behind the steam-ridden shower door.

The perks of life at Oxford are better than I could have imagined, he thought with a wide smile.

Without a word, he stepped into the steamy cubicle, wrapped his arms around Manisha, and captured her lips in a deep kiss. Their arms intertwined, hands exploring, stroking, smoothing and caressing as the water poured over them, cleaning away the sweat of their exercise. Matthew turned Manisha toward the wall, his fingers weaving through her hair before giving it a gentle pull. His lips lingered on the nape of her neck, biting and kissing while caressing her breasts.

Manisha put her hands against the shower wall to steady herself as their bodies became one.

4

'How can you prove whether at this moment we are sleeping, and all our thoughts are a dream, or whether we are awake, and talking to one another in the waking state?'

Plato – Philosopher (427BC–347BC)

Acrid smoke blotted out the warm evening sky. Alex choked, gasping for air as he inhaled fumes and sand deep into his burning lungs. Adrenaline surged through his body as golden streaks of light from red-hot bullets tore through the air in a relentless stream of potential death. They whistled inches above his skull, sending shudders down his spine. The stench of death, thick and oppressive in the heat of the desert, was stifling.

Alex was part of a Royal Marine Commando patrol that had been pinned down in a shallow bomb crater for over thirty hours. Their radio was full of bullets, and their water had run out hours ago. One by one, stray enemy bullets had picked them off—more by chance than any worthy marksmanship. Out of a squad of six men, three were dead, and one was badly wounded. Only Alex and his best friend Jason could still fight. Alex had made his wounded comrade comfortable and administered morphine, knowing he wouldn't survive for much longer. They used their remaining bullets sparingly, knowing the enemy's last assault would soon come to finish them. The few bullets they had were their last hope of survival.

An overwhelming feeling that he was going to die consumed Alex. The once-fearless Commando, with an 'anything-is-possible' attitude, sat trembling, certain of his fate. He pulled a blood-stained photo of his wife from his left breast pocket and held it close, studying every detail by the light of flames from a burning vehicle. It was their wedding day. Broad beaming smiles filled the picture, which had been taken on a beautiful spring afternoon. Diane looked stunning, her bright eyes seemed to gaze directly at him from the photograph. *If only I could hold you one more time.* Tears threatened to run down his cheek, the feeling emptying him to the core. *If I'm going to die tonight, I'm going down fighting.* He kissed the photograph.

'Don't go getting sloppy on me,' Jason said, as he looked over his shoulder, watching his best friend put away the photo.

'Piss off. At least I love a woman, rather than my right hand.'

'Remind me to unfriend you on Facebook later!'

'Over my dead body.' They laughed, trying to hide their fear as bullets ricocheted around them.

Alex took a steadying breath, thinking through their

final line of defence. 'We need to conserve ammo. Don't fire until you know you can't miss. It would be better if we split. I can try to get behind the burnt-out truck when it gets darker, then we can cover each other.'

Jason tried to use a mirror to see enemy locations. 'For fuck sake, I can't see anything through the smoke.' He gingerly put his head above the parapet to gain vital intelligence to feed into their final strategy.

Alex looked up at him, silently willing him to pull himself out of danger. Jason raised his head up slightly for a split-second and started to speak, but a bullet struck him square in the face, tearing away the top of his skull.

Blood and brains splattered over Alex. He spat out the pieces of his friend's flesh and stared wide-eyed, shaking in terror at the gruesome sight in front of him where his best friend had been. A coldness shot through his veins as fear gripped him.

Alex took deep breaths, covered his friend's face with a jacket, gathered the few remaining bullets, and focused on staying alive. Dusk turned into darkness as the final assault began. The shadows in the distance taunted him, playing tricks with his eyes. Sweat slipped down his forehead, which he wiped away with his sleeve, keeping his eyes clear. Fear and desperation drove him to let off a few poorly aimed rounds, which did more to give away his location than defend his position.

Alex could see the shadowy forms getting closer and closer. He sat waiting until the last possible moment before firing, until he was sure he couldn't miss. He tried to keep his breathing deep and controlled, steadying his finger on the trigger, ready for his last attempt to cling onto life. The shadow grew larger until it was only a few feet away. Knowing he couldn't miss, Alex squeezed the trigger. The hammer clicked into an empty chamber. He was out of bullets. The dark figure pounced and landed in front of him. Alex flicked on his torch, aiming to blind his assailant. He locked eyes with his enemy—piercing blue eyes that froze him in place. His enemy grabbed his hair, pulled his head back, and drew an eight-inch blade across his neck.

Alex Laing awoke screaming, clutching his neck. He fought the invisible attacker, pushing and punching into thin air, until reality sunk in—the nightmare from over two decades ago had returned to haunt him. Goosebumps covered his body as he lay in a pool of damp, musty sweat.

He sat bolt upright in bed, rubbing his eyes. The white linen duvet had slipped off the bed in the frenzy. After a few moments, the feeling of panic subsided, and he controlled his breath. He was safe. However, the reality of the experience shocked him. It had been so vivid; he questioned whether he was awake or still caught in a dream. His body had reacted as if the experience were real, so what was the difference between a dream and reality anyway? The two worlds were inextricably entangled.

He took a series of deep breaths to steady himself. As the terror gave way to anger, he punched the bed, riled that his mind continued to torment him after so many years. Then, he focused and calmed himself, trying to make sense of his nightmare. The image of the man with bright blue eyes stayed with him. *Where did you suddenly come from? You weren't there that night.*

Laing's body and mind bore scars from the six months of interrogation and torture that followed his capture that night. Healed wounds ran deep covering his back and arms, which pulled his skin whenever he stretched. His mind had been more affected than he ever let on. He wasn't superstitious and read little into his dreams—they were simply hauntings of a tortured soul. However, he trusted his intuition. *Danger is near again. Leave nothing to chance. The risks are too high.*

Laing rose to his feet. He adjusted his blue boxer shorts as he wandered barefoot into the kitchen to make a cup of coffee. Leaning against the worktop, he welcomed the new day with an enormous yawn and rubbed his hand across his unshaven face. The intense feelings brought on by his recurring dream faded, and he focused on the day ahead.

His phone vibrated. It was going to be a challenging day. The only person who would call him at 06:30 on a Monday morning was his boss, Redfern.

'Good morning.'

'Laing,' came the clipped voice on the end of the line. Redfern never had time for pleasantries. 'I read your report and it tells me nothing.'

'I can only tell you want I know, Ma'am.'

'Well, you should know more. I can't just have you going around randomly killing people.'

'It was self-defence.'

'Maybe. You shouldn't have been there in the first place. Do as I tell you, Laing.'

'Yes, Ma'am.'

'Laing, I need you to dig into Professor Doulton's phone records, find out who he's been calling and why. He keeps on coming up with lame excuses for why he hasn't found an assistant to work with Professor Williams.'

'No problem, Ma'am.'

'Let me know what you find. That goes for Professor Williams' calls too.'

'Yes, Ma'am.'

The line went dead.

Laing tossed his phone onto the kitchen counter and exhaled sharply. 'Bitch.' He walked into the living room and grabbed his MI5-issued laptop from his rucksack and placed it on the table. He connected to the secure VPN back at GCHQ to review Doulton's recent calls. There were several morning calls from his PA confirming his itinerary for the day. A call to his wife saying he'd be late home as he was playing squash and a call to his deputy of Physics at Oxford. Laing listened more intently as the conversation went on.

'David, it's Nigel. I have a delicate and confidential situation we need to progress.'

'Okay, how can I help?' David Adams responded keenly.

'I need a student to work with Professor Williams as her lab assistant. Her sponsors are questioning her progress and the use of their funding. Whilst I have one hundred per cent confidence in Professor Williams and her work, they want someone to work closely with her. You know, a second pair of eyes, so to speak, so someone else knows how to conduct her experiments and use her specialised equipment. If we don't sort this out our way, then her sponsors may take a more formal route and we'll have an external auditor crawling all over her work and her funding, and we don't need that.'

'They can't know her very well if they're questioning her progress,' David said. 'She's the most trustworthy person in the department.'

'Yes, indeed. But who pays the piper calls the tune. We have to keep them happy. I'm looking for someone who is bright and has a good level of understanding of quantum theory and the concepts of Biocentrism. But they also need to do what they're told and report back. Anyone spring to mind?'

David paused for thought. 'Jayden Phillips?'

'Not bright enough.'

'Stephanie Wright?'

'I'm not convinced she'd report back honestly.'

'Perkins?'

'Hmm, Perkins.'

Laing heard a change of tone in Doulton's voice.

'Yes, I think Perkins would be perfect. A bit of a loner. Bright when he wants to be. I'd imagine he'd jump at the chance to work with Manisha.'

'She won't like it.'

'I know, but I can convince her. Thanks, David.'

The recording ended.

Laing sat in his kitchen looking out of the window, trying to see deeper into the conversation he'd just heard. 'Why would you worry about auditors? There's no way Redfern would play that card.'

Laing continued to review calls from Doulton. Another call to Manisha grabbed his interest.

'Hello, Manisha, it's Nigel. How are you?'

'I'm fine.'

Laing detected annoyance in Manisha's voice.

'We need to talk about your new lab assistant, Manisha. Your sponsors are concerned that your brilliant work is only in your head. Other people need to know how you conduct your experiments and how your equipment works.'

'You know I like to work alone. I keep records of all my research, and I've documented how to use the lab equipment. Bringing someone new in now will just slow me down.'

'I'm sorry, but this is not a debate. You wouldn't be where

you are now without the funding that's being provided. It would be terrible if it stopped.' There was a pause. 'Help me, so I can help you.'

'They can't stop my funding. I'm so close.' The panic was clear in her voice. But then her tone changed. 'What are you up to, Nigel? This doesn't feel right.'

'I... I just need to keep your sponsors happy, Manisha, and this is one of their conditions. You'll announce you're looking for a lab assistant in your lecture on Monday morning. Okay?'

The call ended with Manisha hanging up.

Laing retrieved his discarded mobile from the kitchen and called Redfern.

'Yes?'

'Ma'am, I've just reviewed all recent calls and there was a call from Doulton to Professor Williams on Friday that concerns me. Doulton is making all the right noises; however, Professor Williams is resisting. Do you want me to take any action, Ma'am?'

The phone was silent for several seconds.

'Pay Doulton a visit. Remind him of the importance of the task in hand and of the entire project. Find out what he knows about the attempted break in and update him on the situation regarding the other organisations seeking Manisha's work. Tell him to keep his eyes open! We've never been in a more critical phase of the operation, nor in more danger. He needs to know if he can't get the job done, we'll find another way.'

'Will do, Ma'am,' Laing replied, gripping his phone tight.

5

'If quantum mechanics hasn't profoundly shocked you, you haven't understood it yet.'

Niels Bohr – Physicist (1885–1962)

Manisha stood at the front of the Lindemann lecture theatre, outwardly composed while butterflies flitted wildly in her stomach. She glanced at the black face of her Tag Heuer as the second hand ticked past 10:00 a.m. Her boss, Nigel Doulton, Head of Physics at Oxford, walked across the front of the room and called for quiet. The warm, steeply banked room, filled with one hundred and fifty first-year students, gradually fell silent. She glanced up at her audience before shifting her gaze back to Professor Doulton as he began his introduction. Her stomach churned as she looked at him—her trust in him was waning daily.

'Today, we have the great privilege of a lecture from one of our brightest researchers, Professor Manisha Williams,' Doulton said. 'Professor Williams is a respected member of Oxford Physics and has been studying and working at Oxford University for over twelve years.'

Manisha bit her lip. *Ha! If I'm so respected, why force me to take on a lab assistant?*

'She started her life at Oxford with the goal of understanding how our reality works. She now has a doctorate in Theoretical Physics and a master's in Neuroscience. She is currently researching the connections between quantum mechanics, consciousness, and how we think. Her research is developing our understanding of the effects our thoughts have on our perceived reality and how these connections can aid stroke victims and people with locked-in syndrome. And one of you may also be lucky enough to help her on her journey. Please welcome Professor Williams for what will be a fascinating and thought-provoking lecture.'

The students applauded warmly as Manisha walked along the front of the room. She felt self-conscious in her black trousers and a white blouse, a stark contrast from the jeans and jumper she normally wore to work. She fiddled with the heart-shaped pendant that hung from her neck. The smooth texture of the silver and glass grounded her as she took centre stage. The applause quietened as Manisha grabbed the presentation remote control and pressed a button to move to the first slide of her deck. The radio microphone switched to Manisha's, and she checked it with a quick tap before proceeding with her presentation.

'Nothing in our physical world is real.'

She looked up and down the auditorium to see that all students were focused on her.

'There are only two things we experience that are truly real: what we think and how we feel. A sweeping statement, I know, especially if you are new to the inner mechanisms of how our reality works. However, this is the truth that is becoming apparent, and accepted thanks to pioneering research over the last one hundred years.

'Since the days of Planck, Bohr, and Einstein, we have understood that nothing we perceive is truly solid. Reality seems to be an illusion happening deep within your brain. This makes the study of consciousness, and the quantum world, so fascinating.'

She paused to let her opening statement sink in.

'The human brain is extraordinary. Atoms and molecules have assembled into entities which are capable of pondering their own origins. Is there a God who created our universe? How do our minds interact with the energy all around us? Do we live in a collective consciousness, or are we living in a simulation? With the collaboration of all the brilliant scientists we have on our planet, I'm confident that one day we will understand our own origin.'

Manisha clicked the button on her hand-held remote. The lights dimmed, and the slide moved to a timeline of significant discoveries in physics and philosophy, which included Aristotle, Descartes, Newton, and Einstein. She discussed the work of the role models she so deeply admired, who had made giant leaps forward in understanding our reality. She soon got into her natural flow and the butterflies in her stomach receded. On completing the historical part of her lecture, Manisha paused and scanned her audience to ensure they were still with her. Many heads were down, typing notes, while others looked eager for her to continue.

'Any questions? Does that all make sense?'

The room fell silent, save for the faint sound of scribbling pencils and keyboards being tapped.

'Okay, good.'

A phone rang. Manisha arched an eyebrow at the offending sound. Rule number one was all phones were off while a lecture was in progress, the penalty for not complying being instant removal from the session. To her surprise and annoyance, Professor Doulton plunged his hand into his jacket pocket, retrieved his phone, and silenced the noise. He dashed down the steps to the front of the theatre with an embarrassed wave of acknowledgment to Manisha, mouthing a silent 'sorry.' He disappeared through the green double doors, uttering the words, 'Professor Doulton…'

'He's barred!' Manisha declared, pointing toward the doors her boss had just exited through. 'Does anyone else have a phone they would like to switch off?'

Students laughed as they rummaged in their rucksacks to double-check their own devices.

'Professor Doulton speaking. How can I help you?'

As Doulton answered the phone, the doors swung shut behind him to the faint sound of laughing students.

'Do you have a name for me?'

The sound of the man's voice filled him with dread. 'Mr Laing. I'm a little busy at the moment. Can I call you back?'

'No. Do you have a name for me?'

'No, not yet. I'm working on it. I'll have someone in place

by the end of the week. We can't rush this. I don't want anyone to be suspicious. Timing and consistency with the way we work is everything,' Doulton said, adjusting his tie.

'Nigel, grow some, will you? We need to talk. I'll be in your office in five minutes. Be there.'

'Mr Laing, there's no need to...'

The phone went dead.

Doulton breathed deeply, controlling his annoyance, as he made his way back to his office.

'Okay, where was I?' Manisha tapped her notes before continuing. 'Ah yes—light! Light is amazing. However, it was a mystery to physicists in the early twentieth century. Einstein's work on the photoelectric effect showed that light behaves as discrete packets of energy, or photons. However, the idea of light behaving as discrete particles seemed contradictory to its wave-like properties, as seen in diffraction and interference patterns. How can light act as a particle and a wave at the same time? This contradiction was something that troubled Einstein for nearly twenty years. In 1923, Louis de Broglie postulated that if photons can behave either as particles or waves, the same should be true of other particles such as electrons, and he was correct. We have since proven that all matter acts in the same way. Quantum mechanics shows that all matter exists as a probability wave until observed or measured, at which point it behaves as a particle.

'But what causes matter, in this wave-particle duality, to be seen either as a wave or as a particle? The famous "Double Slit Experiment" shows the wave-particle duality in action, but with some fascinating and incredible results.

Quantum mechanics shows that particles do not have definite properties until they interact with a measuring device. Instead, they exist in a superposition—holding multiple possibilities at once. Upon measurement, the superposition collapses into a single state, creating the reality we perceive. This implies that our observation, or consciousness, has to be an integral part of creating the world that we observe.'

Manisha took a deliberate pause, sipping water from a glass, giving the students time to process the significance of her words.

'Although we don't yet understand why this happens, some interesting conclusions have been drawn from these results. The Copenhagen interpretation suggests that a quantum system remains in multiple states until a measurement forces it into a single outcome. While most physicists define measurement as interaction with a detector, some interpretations speculate that consciousness plays a role. Does this mean that there would be no reality without consciousness, implying the universe would not exist unless someone observed it?

'The Many-Worlds Interpretation suggests that all possible quantum outcomes coexist but remain separate due to quantum decoherence. While mathematically self-consistent, there is no direct evidence that these parallel realities exist. I find this interpretation very difficult to accept. It's incredible our own universe exists, without the concept of a universe existing for all other conceivable outcomes of an observation or decision.

'I firmly believe that our consciousness plays a role in creating our reality. This is also where my research has taken me. Our consciousness interacts with the energy all around us, solidifying it and creating our reality. We create each second of our reality and record it within us—and this is what my research is close to proving.'

Manisha's heart pounded. She felt alive, standing before so many people, explaining theories of how our reality worked. The excitement of knowing the potential leap forward her work could have for humanity bubbled inside of her. There were so many things she wanted to say and explain; she was bursting with excitement. As she took a sip of water, one student caught her eye. He sat in the third row from the back, legs outstretched in the walkway and arms crossed. Her intuition told her he was trouble. His eyelids hung heavy, and she deliberately took the tone of her voice up a notch to pull his attention back to her.

'Any questions?' She saw him jump and re-engage with the lecture.

A single hand shot up from the fifth row. A bright-eyed, dark-haired woman was eager to voice the first question. 'So, the particles of energy all around us are in a constant state of flux until they're observed?'

'Yes, exactly. Quantum mechanics suggests that reality exists as a set of probabilities until it is measured or observed, at which point a definite outcome is determined, shaping our perception of reality. This may seem inconceivable, as all the objects around us feel solid and seem to exist just like you and me. We go through our daily lives oblivious to the fact that we construct our reality using our minds. Science and mathematics show us that all is not as it seems. As Einstein so eloquently put it, "Reality is merely an illusion, albeit a very persistent one."'

Manisha walked around the desk to the centre of the auditorium to get closer to her audience. 'Many scientists have been ignoring a detail that has been under their noses for over a hundred years—that they are an intrinsic part of the problem they are trying to understand. As Planck said, "We ourselves are part of the mystery we are trying to solve."

'Consciousness is the elephant in the room—undeniably present yet largely unexplained.'

Manisha paused, scanning her audience.

'However, that is about to change.'

6

'The day science begins to study non-physical phenomena, it will make more progress in one decade than in all the previous centuries of its existence.'

Nikola Tesla – Inventor (1856–1943)

A cool breeze caught Laing's hair as he stepped out of his black Mercedes C63 AMG. The car was unassuming, lacking the sports body trim, but it gave the performance he needed, when he needed it. He crossed Sherrington Road, locking the Merc behind him, and made his way through the glass revolving doors at the entrance to the Beecroft Building.

Alex Laing had a slim, muscular frame—unusual for a man in his mid-forties. His short hair was still more black than grey. The passive surveillance work, combined with a poor diet and drinking, would have taken its toll on most men his age, but he counterbalanced the diet of convenience with his early morning training regime, running 10k twice a week and lifting weights three times a week. He missed the camaraderie of active service in the Royal Marines Commandos and had once worn the coveted green beret, or "lid", with pride. Laing would have happily given his life protecting his fellow Royal Marines, and his country. But looking towards his fifties, the opportunity of working on a special surveillance operation with MI5 had seemed like the perfect way to wind down his career. A 'departure lounge' project, as he liked to call it. His personal plans were focused on leaving the service and living the simple life he desired. That's all his pension fund could afford after the messy divorce from his wife. At least there were no children to complicate the split.

Laing enjoyed seclusion and needed to get away from London and the political bullshit that came with his current role. In the time he had off, he spent it on the rugged coast of Cornwall, staying in a cottage he'd inherited from his uncle, north of Sennen Cove. The place he planned to live when he retired.

Laing reached Doulton's third-floor corner office, only to find it empty.

'Can I help you?' Doulton's personal assistant enquired while giving Laing an annoyed stare over the top of her glasses.

'I'm here to see Professor Doulton.'

'Clearly. Is he expecting you?'

'Yes. My name is Alex Laing,' he responded with a courteous smile. 'I'm happy to wait.' He gestured towards Doulton's office.

'Very well. I'll let him know you're here.'

Laing showed himself into Doulton's modern, glass-fronted office and closed the door. He took out his adapted smartphone and scanned the room for bugs. Finding his own bug on the underside of the desk reassured him the app was working. He then found an unexpected bug in the back of Doulton's leather desk chair. He removed the bug and studied it before crushing the device in his fingers until the app no longer sensed life in it. Laing looked out of the office to find Doulton's PA glaring at him. He gave another courteous smile and continued scanning the rest of the office when she looked away. Once satisfied, he relaxed in a green leather chair and studied Caribbean holiday photos of Doulton and his family that adorned his desk and the bookshelves. He looked out of the tall window and across the adjoining Oxford University parks, watching students as they walked past.

Within five minutes, Doulton returned to his office and gave Laing an irritated look before closing the door behind him.

'We really don't need this conversation. I have everything under control.' Doulton made his way to the other side of his desk and sat in his black leather office chair, crossing his arms.

'You're moving too slow. Our superiors are losing confidence in you. We're at a critical phase, and there's no room for error,' Laing said.

'Look, can you please report back to Redfern that there's nothing to worry about? I have the situation in hand.'

'You don't have things in hand, and I don't think you grasp just how vital Manisha's work is to our national security. If her work gets into the wrong hands, it *will* be used against us. If it were anyone else, we would have her working in a secure government location.'

Doulton interjected. 'We've had this conversation a hundred times. If we tell Manisha about our plans for her work, she will stop. We can't afford to lose her. It'll set us back years. I advise you to back off—and that goes for Redfern too. I'll take care of this in my own time.'

Laing's jaw clenched, but he remained calm. 'You need to be smart, and it's critical you stick to our timeline. I don't care how you do it but keep Manisha on-side. Make sure she keeps progressing her research, and once she's found the key, government scientists will step in.'

Doulton frowned. 'Make sure you keep this low-key. I don't want Manisha or myself discredited.'

Laing laughed. 'The way you're dealing with this, you'll be lucky to stay alive.'

Doulton smirked and shook his head.

'You really don't understand the lengths people will go to get hold of Manisha's research, do you? People would kill to get hold of this technology. Make sure you keep to the plan. It's the only way you'll save yourself and Manisha.'

'Why do you always have to be so dramatic? Nobody is going to get killed,' Doulton turned his gaze to the window.

'On Friday night, I put a knife in someone who tried to get Manisha and her work.'

Doulton forced a nervous smile, unsure if Laing was joking. 'Did you kill him?'

'Yes. Two men attempted to break into the rear fire escape to get to Manisha and her research. Do you know anything about it?'

'The security report said it was petty thieves. Probably druggies trying to steal equipment.'

'Petty thieves don't carry radio jammers and military-grade detonation charges.'

'There was no mention of a body, or anyone being hurt.'

'That's because I cleared up.' Laing paused. 'Manisha could have been abducted that night.'

Doulton looked away, his face slightly flushed.

'Let me spell it out to you again.' Laing leaned forward, pulling Doulton's attention back to him. 'Manisha is an innocent in this. She doesn't even know what she's involved in. You need to look out for her and protect her. Her intentions are admirable and the technology she's developing is incredible. However, humanity has a track record of using such technology to help people and also to harm people. The real threat is an organisation called *Heylel*. They're the ghost in the machine, Doulton. An underground organisation that seems to have a never-ending supply of funding. Do not underestimate them. The only way to protect Manisha and her technology is by working together.'

'Ah yes, Heylel. The shining one, the morning star.... Lucifer?' Doulton smiled sarcastically. 'And what is *Heylel* out to achieve?'

'That's classified.'

Doulton laughed. 'How very convenient.'

'Deal with it.'

'I've said it before, and I'll say it again: I don't see how planting an innocent student into this situation is going to help?'

Laing sat back in his chair. 'We need someone else in the mix. Someone we can control and who has direct access to Manisha's work. Someone she will learn to trust.'

'But a student?' Doulton raised his arms and looked at Laing in disbelief.

'Yes, this is how our superiors want it played,' Laing said. 'Unorthodox as it is.'

'I have access to her work. I can get you anything you need.'

'Can you?' Laing raised his eyebrows. 'It seems like her trust in you is fading, and your role as Chief Science Advisor to the government doesn't help. Even a kid could put two and two together. That's why she doesn't tell you everything, and why she has encrypted her research so nobody else can access it. She doesn't trust you, Doulton. We need someone else—someone who has access to her lab and her data.'

An uncomfortable silence hung heavy in the room.

'If you can't get someone in place this week, we'll take control and we'll move her research and equipment to our maximum-security facility at Porton Down.'

'Then Manisha will stop her work,' Doulton said with a shrug, 'and none of your government scientists will come close to matching Manisha's brilliance. She's the only person who can take this technology forward and you know it.'

'Well, you had better keep her on side then, hadn't you? Or else your job, reputation, and the nice monthly retainer payments will be history.'

Doulton frowned at the thought.

'Who do you have in mind?' Laing followed Doulton's eyes, testing his honesty after hearing the telephone conversation with his deputy.

Doulton gripped the arms of his chair. 'I'm considering a student called Simon Perkins. I'll have him in place by Friday. But it has to look like he volunteered for the role. I can't just make him do it. He needs to be convinced.'

'Well, convince him then. Get him on board. Send me his file—I'll have tracking set up within twenty-four hours.'

Doulton shot Laing a concerned look.

'It's for his own safety. Also, be careful about who you let into your office. I found this pinned to the back of your chair.' Laing threw the crumpled piece of electronics onto

Doulton's desk. 'It's not ours, and it's not Russian or Chinese. So, be careful who you trust. In fact, trust no one.'

Doulton's expression turned from one of surprise to one of disdain. 'Not even you?'

Laing smiled. 'Who else can you trust?' He stood and walked to the door. 'Make sure your office and your communications are secure. Anything suspicious, anyone following you, any unusual calls, or indications that Manisha is in danger, call me.' He turned and looked straight at Doulton, 'Sort this out, or we'll sort it out for you. Do you understand?'

Doulton paused, frustration etched onto his face. 'Yes, I understand.'

Laing left, closing the door firmly behind him.

7

'The universe bursts into existence from life, not the other way around as we have been taught. For each life, there is a universe, its own universe. We generate spheres of reality, individual bubbles of existence.'

Robert Lanza – Scientist (1956–)

Manisha sipped her water and took a deep breath. She swept her hair over her shoulder before moving on to the next phase of her lecture, knowing she was about to expand the minds of her audience.

'Since the early twentieth century, quantum theory has shown that consciousness influences what we observe. However, radical approaches have been necessary to take our understanding of reality further. One alternative approach has come from the study of biology and the theory of *Biocentrism*. Biocentrism is a controversial idea that suggests life and consciousness play a fundamental role in shaping the universe.'

Manisha paused briefly while students took notes.

'We think of life as a miracle of the universe. However, physicists have yet to explain how consciousness arises from matter, or if it does at all. There are approximately two hundred parameters which, if changed even slightly, would have meant the universe would not have evolved to support life. If the Big Bang had been more powerful, the universe would have expanded too fast for galaxies and planets to form. If the strong nuclear force was just a little weaker, an atomic nucleus would not hold together. If gravity changed by the slightest amount, stars would not ignite. Depending upon which of the two hundred parameters we consider, the odds of conditions in our universe being compatible with life are several trillion trillion to one. Multiverse theories suggest that countless universes exist, each with different physical laws, which statistically means at least one universe will be in the *Goldilocks Zone,* which is just right for life to exist. However, all the *'theories of everything'* to date, that have come from physics, have been missing one important component—consciousness. Consciousness interprets sensory data, shaping our perception of reality within the brain.'

Manisha paused, using the remote to move on to the next slide. The room hushed as young minds absorbed a field of science that was relatively new and affected them personally. She revelled in watching minds open, seeing her students challenge their deeply ingrained yet misleading perceptions, ones they had held their entire lives.

'Let's go through our senses, starting with our hearing

and an age-old question. If a tree falls in a forest, and nobody is there, does it make a sound? Please show your hands if you think it does.'

The question split the room fifty-fifty, many students looking bemused by such a seemingly ridiculous question. Others gave it more thought and kept their hands down.

'Okay, interesting.' Manisha pointed to the middle of the third row, where the highest concentration of raised hands was.

'Why do you think it does?'

A smug-looking undergraduate with fashionably coiffed blond hair and a pierced ear took it upon himself to respond on behalf of his row.

'Well, it's obvious! Just because nobody is there, it doesn't mean falling trees produce no sound. Branches will hit other branches, displacing air and creating sound.'

'You're half right. The falling tree hits the ground, creating thousands of vibrations through the air, but it produces no sound. If a human is nearby, these vibrations cause the eardrums to move, which then stimulates nerves, but only if the air is pulsing at the right frequency. Any vibration outside of the range of a human ear will not stimulate a human's neural architecture, and so we hear no sound. Other animals such as dogs or dolphins can hear frequencies way outside of our range and so, from a sound perspective, their perception of reality differs from ours. This isn't due to anything external to us. It's all being driven from our senses and how our brains react to the surrounding energy. So, a tree falling in an empty forest makes no sound. It falls silently, creating nothing more than thousands of tiny puffs of air. The fact is, we live in a silent universe.'

Manisha paused for a moment to let her audience take notes before continuing. 'Let's move on to sight.' Manisha pulled a lighter from under the desk and lit it. 'Tell me what you see.'

A female student from the front row answered. 'A hot, yellow flame.'

'Correct, that's what your brain perceives. But the flame itself is purely energy. In this case, hot gas which is emitting photons, or light, in tiny packets of electromagnetic waves. But if we look at electricity and magnetism individually, neither of them has any visual properties. So, it's easy to grasp that there is nothing bright or coloured about the flame on its own. However, if we let the invisible electromagnetic pulses hit the retina, then the energy stimulates the rods and cones which pass electrical signals to the brain. We perceive the energy as yellow light appearing in what we have been conditioned to call *the external world*. But what would a dog see?'

The same student answered. 'A grey flame, as dogs are colour blind.'

'Exactly. The point is, there is no bright yellow flame at all. All there is, is an invisible stream of electric and magnetic pulses of energy. A conscious human being is necessary for the experience of what we would call a yellow flame. Without us, it is just a pulse of energy.'

Manisha walked to the other side of the lecture theatre, letting her hand glide across the desk, and knocking it as she spoke. 'What about touch? When you touch something, it may feel solid—however, this too is a sensation within your brain. The sensation of pressure is caused because every atom has negatively charged electrons in its outer shell and negatively charged atoms repel each other. Nothing solid ever meets anything else solid. Back to basic physics, how much of an atom is empty space?'

'Ninety-nine per cent,' was the collective murmur from the group.

'Very close. An atom is almost entirely empty space, or a vacuum, with a tiny nucleus sitting at its centre and electrons orbiting around it. It's the vibrational force, or energy of an atom, that stops your fingers sweeping through an object like your hand swiping through fog. Your nose detects molecular vibrations, which the brain translates into smell. Your tongue translates vibrations of energy into taste. Our brains take these inputs and translate them into our perceived reality. All these inputs, combined with our thoughts and our reactions to them, dictate how we feel.'

Manisha took a small sip of water.

'When you combine this with what we understand about quantum theory and the fact that the observation of the energy around us causes the wave function to collapse into tangible particles, then you have a basis for a theory of how our reality works that includes consciousness. The universe remains a field of energy—waves of potential—until it is observed. Many materialists would scoff at such a theory. But there are hundreds of scientists around the globe researching variations of this hypothesis. It cannot be denied that the two things we understand least about are quantum theory and consciousness and they must play a big part in how our reality is created.'

Manisha paused and moved the deck on to her final slide.

'If you take away all your senses, how much of your perceived physical universe remains?'

'Nothing?' a collective murmur responded.

'Exactly! Going back to my opening statement. Nothing truly exists apart from your thoughts and your feelings. There is nothing out there, nothing outside of you apart from a swirling sea of energy that your consciousness reacts with and creates the perceived reality you experience every day.'

Bemused faces peered at Manisha as students scratched their heads, trying to bend their minds to this biocentric view of the universe.

'Is it really so hard to believe? The fact that we're here in the first place is a miracle,' she said, trying to free their minds from years of conditioning.

She placed the remote on the lectern and stepped forward, her voice steady as she continued. 'Where do we truly exist? It is plausible that we exist only within our minds, or consciousness, and nowhere else. The hard question now becomes: what is consciousness? How do our brains interact with it, and do we have control over it? This is where my research at our Beecroft Building has been focused for the last three years. And, I'm pleased to say, I've been making progress. Although theories about consciousness and the nature of reality have gained significant attention—both positive and negative—over the past decade, they remain theoretical.'

Manisha paused, letting the tension in the room build.

'Until now!

'I've found a way to tap into a person's thoughts and I'm starting to decode what I have found. At the moment I am only scratching the surface of fully understanding how our reality works. But I believe my research to date will help people who cannot communicate, and so provide a much better quality of life, not only for them but also for their families and friends.'

Manisha took a deep breath, uneasy about what she was being compelled to do next. 'As Professor Doulton said, I am looking for a part-time assistant to help me with some experiments at Beecroft. I will not take too much of your time and this work will not interfere with your lectures, course work or study time. But it will take up to five hours of your free time each week. I work a lot of evenings, so prepare for some impact on your social life. If you would like to join me, please send an e-mail to the addresses on the screen stating your weekly availability and why you would like to be a part of my research project. We must receive applications by this Friday, when we'll be making the final decision. You will need to sign a non-disclosure agreement, which is legally binding, so please take this into consideration. Thank you for coming to my lecture, I hope you've enjoyed it.'

The lecture theatre broke into applause and a hundred and fifty inspired students packed away their pens, notebooks and tablets and prepared to leave the room. Some stayed to discuss the session in small groups, while others went straight to the front to introduce themselves to Professor Williams and ask further questions. The majority made their way towards the green double doors.

Professor Doulton had been hovering outside the lecture theatre for the last five minutes, waiting for Manisha's talk to finish. He was feeling cornered and couldn't risk losing the government funding that he, and Manisha, relied on. The sudden applause and a quick glance at his watch confirmed the lecture had ended. Seconds later, the double doors burst open to reveal a herd of students reeling from their new insight on reality. Doulton saw Simon Perkins shuffling through the crowded doorway.

'Simon, Simon!' the Professor called.

Simon Perkins, a scruffy and unshaven Merton student, turned to the Professor.

'What did you think of Professor Williams's talk?' Doulton enquired.

'She looks amazing,' he said with raised eyebrows.

'And her lecture, Simon?'

'Oh yeah, it was great. She really knows her stuff.'

'She certainly does. You could learn a lot from her. Are you going to apply for the opportunity to work with her?'

'Hmm, I wasn't planning to. I'm sure there would be someone else better suited in the room.'

Doulton felt his stomach churn and put his arm around Simon's shoulder. 'We might surprise you, Simon. Believe me, I think you would be perfect. I would highly recommend you put your name in the hat and see what happens. You might be exactly what Manisha is looking for, and you'll learn so much from her. It's an excellent opportunity and will benefit your studies.'

'Yeah, I guess… maybe.' Simon's lack of commitment was tangible.

'Some of your work with Manisha might even count toward your end-of-year credits—pretty easy work if you ask me.'

A raised eyebrow from Simon, and Doulton could see he was hooked and just needed reeling in.

'So, I'll take it you'll apply?'

'Yes, I will. Thanks for the heads-up, Professor Doulton.'

'Good man. Looking forward to your email.'

Nigel patted Simon on the back as if he were petting his dog and headed back to his office.

8

'Multiplicity is only apparent, in truth, there is only one mind.'

Erwin Schrödinger – Physicist (1887–1961)

Zarek sat cross-legged on the living room floor of his spacious, minimalistic flat. He stared intently at his tattooed back, reflected in the mirrored walls where his gym equipment stood. The piercing eyes of Lucifer met his gaze. Brooding black wings spread across the entire width of his broad shoulders and reached the small of his back. Writing in Hebrew sat at the foot of the image:

כוכב בוקר – מביא השחר

Morning Star - Bringer of Dawn

The ache in his arms and pinch in his legs were signs it had been a good workout. One hour of weights followed by a thirty-minute run was his early morning routine. Now, the meditation would begin. Sweat dripped from his forehead as he tuned in to the sensation of the cool air entering his nose and warm air leaving his mouth, over and over. His heart rate slowed to a rhythmic beat as his attention drifted to the swirling colours behind closed eyes. He allowed the colours to build and fade many times until they developed into an all-encompassing band of pure white light. Then he began to chant.

'I am the saviour. I control the secret to life, consciousness, and reality. The secret is already mine. I am the saviour. I control the secret to life, consciousness, and reality. The secret is already mine. I am the saviour. I control the secret to life, consciousness, and reality. The secret is already mine...'

Visions of the future flooded his mind, each one sharpened by intent. He directed them into the light—into the power that existed beyond the physical world. He had secured the data his masters so desperately sought. His victim lay helpless on a tabletop, hands and legs bound beneath it. Ripped clothes revealed a bare chest. He could feel the chill of the large, razor-sharp blade as he drew it slowly across the exposed throat. A contrast to the warmth of the blood pouring over his hand, escaping the confines of the physical body. It poured across the table and pooled on to a stone floor below. The moment of release—the transition of a life force into another realm—obsessed him. He fed on the feeling of strength and power—seeing his victim's eyes wide, as they choked on blood. He willed them a swift parting from this world as he thanked them for the precious secret they had delivered to him. The smell of their scent filled his nostrils as he heard the blood gurgling in their throat. The image then transformed into a blinding, bright white light. He had experienced nothing like it before in any of his previous visualisations, but it felt peaceful. He took the brightness as a positive sign and continued to smile to himself, confident his visions would soon come to pass. He knew there was little difference between the reality he experienced in his mind and the physical reality he experienced every day. 'Everything is within, nothing is without,' he said as he exhaled and bowed his head.

Zarek opened his bright blue eyes. His mind was wired, enthusiastic, and energised. 'My visualisations will come to pass, just as they always have,' he said. 'My masters will honour me.'

The smell of the sandalwood incense burning in the room transported him back in time. Back to the start of his lifelong journey. His parents had died when he was only five, leaving him, and his younger brother, Dante, alone. He had been afraid and angry that his parents had been taken from him while he was so young. He had provided for himself and his brother by doing what work he could find and stealing food when he had to. At seven, his teacher had entered his life. His saviour. A man who had seen his true potential and put him on the right path. The smell of sandalwood had filled the ancient hilltop monastery in Turkey where he and his brother had been brought up with the other children. They were the chosen few; orphans who had been selected to be indoctrinated in the ways of the monks and wise men that governed them.

One day, in his tenth year at the monastery, his teacher had pulled him aside, away from the other children, and whispered: 'You are the special one. It is impossible for you to fail.' He could still hear his teacher's voice, whispering this belief into his mind, and still see the intense look in his eyes. *You shall bring light into the darkness. You will save humanity.* His seventeen-year-old self had been filled with pride and an unshakable belief in himself and his abilities. Now, after a further three years of teachings and six years of small assignments, his belief was absolute. He was ready for any challenge, determined to succeed in his mission—no matter the cost.

Zarek came out of his trance and readjusted to the room. He felt strong as he stretched his muscular arms up high, before moving from his cross-legged position to standing in one unaided movement. His long grey jogging bottoms hung loose around his muscular obliques; his bare feet felt the warmth of the wooden floor as he made his way towards the locked door of the room dedicated to his work. He opened it and walked in. He looked at the subject of his mission, which dominated the wall opposite the door: a large photograph of Manisha, flanked by pictures of her spanning her childhood to present day. Images of her parents, her lover, ex-lovers and friends surrounded the main image. Photos of Manisha at her parents' funerals, displayed alongside those of Doulton and Laing. An iPhone, placed on a charging mat, blinked silently. Synced with hers, it showed her itinerary for the day and allowed him to see her calls and pick up voicemail without her knowledge. He knew her routine—where she socialised, and with whom. The computer screen beside his desk showed a real-time stream of her lab, allowing him to watch her at work. He was frustrated that he couldn't breach Manisha's own security cameras, though Oxford's standard cameras were laughably easy to crack. He picked up the lock of her thick black hair from the table beneath her picture, smoothing it and rubbing it across his lips. 'It won't be long now, Manisha. You will deliver the key to consciousness to me.'

He turned to the desecrated photo of Laing—his eyes scratched out, blood splattered across it. Zarek pursed his lips at the irritation Laing had caused him. Killing his partner at the Beecroft building was an inconvenience. However, he was more annoyed by Laing finding the bug he had placed in Doulton's office. His partner was replaceable. But missing an up-to-date view of Laing's and Doulton's state of play could set him back weeks. Zarek had followed his master's orders and left Laing unharmed. Having the British Security Service pay closer attention to the assignment would help no one. However, it made the game more interesting—more of a psychological challenge than a physical one. 'When the time is right, I will destroy you.'

Zarek checked his watch. It was 8:30 a.m. His phone vibrated on the desk next to his laptop. He answered it with a sense of anticipation. 'Yes?'

A woman's voice replied, much to Zarek's delight. His master normally called him at 8:30 each morning, but to hear the woman's voice meant important changes were about to come into play.

'Zarek, I'm sorry to hear your partner has been killed.'

'He was stupid. It was his own fault.'

'We need to move forward as planned. Manisha has been assigned an assistant to work with her. Manisha will meet this person later today at Beecroft. Investigate him, follow him, but do not make contact. Timing will be important. I will contact you when action is needed. Do you understand?'

'Yes. Thank you.'

The line went dead.

Zarek switched to the tracking app. The red dot flickered; Manisha was on the move. He crossed the room, pried open a small slit in the blinds, and watched. Across the road, outside her flat, she climbed onto her bike, heading towards Beecroft for her first meeting of the day.

Zarek's lips curled into a smile. 'Go to work, Manisha. Deliver the world—and everyone in it—to me.'

9

'I regard consciousness as fundamental. I regard matter as derivative from consciousness. We cannot get behind consciousness. Everything that we talk about, everything that we regard as existing, postulates consciousness.'

Max Planck – Physicist (1858–1947)

'What's changed?' Manisha said as she looked at the image displayed on the VDU above her desk. The image filled her with mixed emotions: sadness, as it was the last time she had seen her father alive; joy, because she had successfully decoded the image only days before; and frustration, because she had re-run the experiment again and again, only for it to fail. She reviewed her notes and algorithms, and everything seemed to add up. However, the key to why experiment one hundred and eleven had worked eluded her. It was as if the universe was teasing her, giving her a glimpse of success, but without wanting to reveal all its secrets to her.

Six widescreen VDUs sat before her on a central island, alive with real-time graphs updating from ongoing experimental feeds. Powerful lasers fired through prisms, splitting the light into all bands of the spectrum, sending a rainbow of photons across the room. Each laser was mounted on vibration-resistant frames, designed to protect her experiments against mild earthquakes.

Manisha turned her attention to an email confirming that her latest request for equipment had been approved. She smiled. *At least the money keeps coming in.* She added the latest invoice to her accounts, and the balance tipped over three million pounds spent to date. *How deep does the pot go?*

Another e-mail alerted her to check her security logs, to see who had tried to access her lab the night before. Only three passes granted access to the 'man-trap' door, which secured the entrance to her office area. One belonged to Manisha, another to Doulton and the final one to the Beecroft facilities manager. She switched to the evening recordings from her security camera. Doulton had entered her lab at 11:07 p.m.

An unsettling queasiness stirred in her gut. 'What are you up to, Nigel?'

She watched the screen as he rifled through paperwork in her office. Then, he placed his hand on the biometric scanner, granting access to her main lab and machine room. The device flashed green and gave a high-pitched beep, allowing Doulton through her second layer of security. He looked through more paperwork and then tried to access her computer. The security logs showed his access was denied. He walked to the corner of her lab, to the black box that was still running her latest experiment. Bright light shone throughout the room, causing the image to flare, making it difficult for Manisha to see what he was doing. He stayed there for several minutes, before completing a final circuit of the lab and leaving.

'And you wonder why I don't trust you.'

Manisha had doubts about Doulton for some time. For several months, her sixth sense told her he had an ulterior motive. His recent, incessant desire to assign someone to work with her only heightened her suspicions, and his affiliation with the government had always concerned her. He had hinted that her work could be of great use to government departments. However, she was determined that her research would only be used positively, and the security measures in her lab guaranteed it couldn't fall into the wrong hands. Her intrusion detection software would immediately alert her if anyone attempted to hack into the system. She could even remotely wipe all the servers if she needed to. She was far from as naïve as Doulton thought.

Manisha walked over to the corner of her lab and slid on a pair of black protective glasses. She opened the black box which sat bolted to the desk and folded down two of the hinged sides, revealing the small glass sphere with its small, blindingly bright cloud of light. A camera fixed inside the box recorded the energy and magnified it by fifty times on one of the VDUs. Six powerful electro-magnets placed on all sides of the sphere generated an invisible force which held the energy in place. It gently twisted, ceaselessly trying to find a way through. A myriad of sensors and lasers probed the cloud, attempting to map and read the unique properties of every particle. Manisha stood transfixed, staring at the energy, which was only visible to the human eye because of the complex array of lasers. The frequency used reacted with a chemical compound on the surface of the sphere to show the otherwise invisible energy inside.

Once she was satisfied that Doulton had not tampered with the experiment, she secured the black box and checked her machine room. She headed to the far end of the lab and peered through the thick glass. Three racks of IT equipment, stacked floor to ceiling, flashed red and green. These were the artificial brains of her operation, which processed vast amounts of data, day in and day out. Three supercomputers configured for parallel processing consumed half of each rack, with their own cooling and ventilation system. The machines worked tirelessly, recording, analysing and trying to decode the energy using Manisha's algorithm. Everything in the machine room looked normal. She looked at the photo of Alan Turing she had stuck to the glass and tapped the picture. 'I know exactly how you felt, Mr Turing!'

She walked back to her desk and sat, mesmerised by the image of her own thought energy on the screen before her.

My quantum of thought—reveal your secret to me.

A tap on the glass brought Manisha out of her daydream. She saw Doulton swipe his pass as he walked through the man-trap door, a nervous smile on his face. A student followed in his wake, looking very impressed at the security system he was walking through.

'Hello, Professor Williams, I would like you to meet Simon Perkins. He will be assisting you in your research over the coming months.'

Manisha didn't even acknowledge Simon and just glared at Doulton. 'You said we would select someone together, Professor Doulton!'

'Simon is perfect for what you need, Professor Williams; he's bright, intelligent, and enthusiastic. He's studying Particle Physics under Professor Adams at Merton.'

'This is not what we agreed,' Manisha raised her voice. The reference to Doulton's deputy had only fuelled the fire.

Simon stood there, not looking particularly bright, intelligent, or enthusiastic. 'Ah, I'll go.' He pointed behind him and tried to reverse towards the door.

Doulton put an arm around his shoulder. 'Let's not be too hasty. We can make this work for all our benefits.'

'We need to talk about this, Professor Doulton.' Manisha ushered them out of the side doorway, sealing her lab behind her. She walked to the lift, signalling to Doulton and Simon to enter. 'Let's go to your office, Professor Doulton. Alone.' She shot a glance at Simon, who looked bemused, as if he were already planning to make himself scarce.

They entered the lift and Manisha hit 'G' and '3' before Doulton and Simon had a chance to touch the silver buttons. The lift was small, and they filled it with an uncomfortable silence. It announced its arrival at 'Ground Floor' and the doors opened.

Simon fidgeted with his jacket zipper, clearly itching to escape. 'See you later?' he said, more question than farewell.

Manisha stared at him. 'Sorry for the misunderstanding, Simon.' She wanted to appear calm, but she knew the annoyance in her demeanour was palpable. The doors slowly closed, and Manisha couldn't hold back. 'What the bloody hell do you think you're doing, Nigel? We agreed we would jointly decide who was going to work with me!'

'Manisha, Manisha, he's a great kid. And he's perfect for what you need.'

'I don't need anyone. He'll just be a hindrance. I'm so close now—I don't need the distraction of someone looking over my shoulder, asking questions.'

The lift doors opened, and Manisha stormed out towards the corner office, followed by Doulton. She could feel Doulton's PA stare as the whirlwind passed through the open area. On entering Doulton's office, Manisha slammed the door behind them. 'What the hell are you playing at, Nigel?'

Doulton stood behind his chair. 'Manisha, your work is very important, and I respect the fact that you are getting close to a breakthrough. However, we agreed three years ago that your work needs to benefit the whole university. You represent Oxford; this is not just about you. I have given you everything you wanted over the last few years. You have the best lab in Oxford and a salary worthy of a professor twenty years your senior. You've been given a lot of trust and free rein. What more do you want?'

The room fell silent. Manisha knew Doulton was right. She wouldn't be as advanced in her research if it wasn't for him and the funding he'd secured.

'Your research will bring a massive change to our world, and that change will be associated with Oxford forever. Please, work with me!'

Arms crossed, Manisha gave an annoyed glance to her side. She didn't trust him and couldn't put into words the frustration she felt at being held to ransom.

'Our investors have spent millions on your research, Manisha. Part of the conditions for their investment is evidence that the research is benefitting the whole university, which is something that has been lacking lately. Having Simon work with you will tick a box and you will find him useful. Do some experiments on him. Do anything that will help you take your work forward. Adding another dimension to your research may lead to a happy accident.'

Manisha shot Doulton a look of contempt. 'Who are the investors, really?'

'You are mostly funded by the National Health Service,

but some of your funding comes from the university and some from other private investors. You already know this, Manisha.'

'When you say the NHS, you mean the government is funding my work. And to what end?'

'You know the government dictates how NHS funding is spent. Are you still hung up on this fixation that the Ministry of Defence are involved?'

'So, are you working for them?'

'I advise the government on scientific matters. But there is no connection between your funding and the MoD.'

Manisha could see the lie in Doulton's body language. 'I will not allow my research to be used against people. Do you understand?'

Doulton looked unconcerned by Manisha's conviction. 'Manisha, I am one hundred per cent with you. The moral and ethical argument for how your research is used is of utmost importance to me. You have my word on that.'

Manisha pursed her lips, shaking her head in disbelief. The more Doulton spoke, the less she trusted him. *All I can do is play along, keeping my research secure. Everything is encrypted. Everything.*

Manisha breathed deeply. 'Okay, this is not helping anyone. All I can do is trust you, Nigel.'

'Good.' Doulton exhaled, his shoulders relaxing as he sank into his chair.

'If I ever find out you've been lying to me, I will destroy all my research. No one will ever get it.'

'Fine, but you'll be in breach of contract with the university. As long as you remember that.'

'I'd rather break my contract than betray people's privacy.'

An awkward silence filled the room.

'Are we done?' Doulton asked.

'Yes.'

'Good. I'll ask Simon to come to your lab when he's free and you can set up a schedule for him.'

Manisha opened the door to go but stopped. 'What were you doing in my lab at eleven o'clock last night?'

Doulton looked sheepish. 'I was just looking for some paperwork I thought I left in there.'

'What paperwork?'

'Er, my notebook for meetings. I'm always leaving it places by accident,' Doulton said with an uncomfortable smile and a hint of a flush on his face.

Another lie. Manisha glared at him and walked out of the door, leaving it open.

'Oh, Manisha, I have a review meeting with the board later this week, so get your monthly report to me by end of today,' Doulton called after her.

Manisha didn't look back.

10

'The greatest discovery of my generation is that a human being can alter his life by altering his attitudes.'

William James – Philosopher (1842–1910)

The sun shone through the trees, creating a dappled pattern of light that danced on the road beneath Manisha's bicycle. She pedalled hard, still irritated by the argument with Doulton. She had left work early in an attempt to lighten her mood and enjoy the sunshine, but she could still feel the deep frown etched upon her face. Her mind gravitated to the conundrum: *what is Doulton up to and why?*

Manisha cycled off the road, across the pavement, and onto the gravel drive of a large Edwardian house, which had been divided into flats. A black Labrador with a grey muzzle greeted her, almost wagging himself in half with the joy at seeing his neighbour.

'Hi, Max.' Manisha smiled at the animal, which only made him wag and whine even more. His warm welcome instantly eased her tension. Manisha parked and locked her bike in the rusty bike stand before petting and hugging Max, who reciprocated with a lick across the cheek.

'Hello, Manisha.' Julie Pemberton, who lived in the flat below Manisha's, and was the owner of Max, stood in the doorway of her flat. 'You're home early.'

'It's not been a good day.'

Julie's soft, smiling face took on a frown of concern. 'It sounds like you need to unwind. Glass of wine?'

'Ah, sounds lovely.' Manisha surrendered to the temptation, even though it was a school night. They walked in through the small porch to a hallway with black, red, and cream geometric floor tiles and intricate coving around the ceiling. Max led the way, followed by Julie and Manisha, and lay on the rug in front of the large, open fireplace adorned with photos of family and friends.

'Red or white?'

'Red, please.'

Julie poured a generous glass of Rioja for Manisha, taking only a small one for herself. She took the seat opposite Manisha, each woman having a large cream two-seater sofa to themselves, scattered with sumptuous, colourful cushions. Max was already asleep on the rug between them.

'So, what's Doulton done now?'

'Ha, you have impeccable intuition, Julie. Where do I start?' Manisha shook her head at the impossible situation. 'We had a massive argument today. He's making me work with a lab assistant when all I need is peace and time to focus. He's forced me into a corner, and I have no choice but to go along with it. I'm sure he has a hidden agenda, and I certainly don't feel I can trust him. But what else can I do?'

Julie frowned. 'He's always had his own agenda. It frustrated your father too.'

'His death was strange, wasn't it, Julie? I have a constant feeling that there's something I wasn't told about the way he died.'

'It was so sudden. That's what shocked me. He was in good health—stressed—but in good health all the same. They said he slipped and fell down the stairs at work. The only person who formally identified his body was Doulton. Your mother was too ill, and you were so young and upset.'

'I remember you saying he and Nigel had argued before he died. But I thought Nigel had learned from his mistakes and that he'd changed.' Manisha fiddled with the stem of the wine glass and frowned. 'Can you tell me again about the last time you spoke with my father, in case I've missed anything?'

'Well, I remember he was so annoyed with Nigel, almost exploding with rage, which was most unlike him.' Julie raised her eyebrows. 'He sat where you are now, his knee bouncing out of frustration at the situation Nigel had put him in. As you know, your father had made a huge discovery in his research, but what it was, he wouldn't say as he didn't want to burden me with his secret. So, I can't even imagine where his research had taken him.'

'But Nigel knew everything, right?'

Julie took a small sip of wine. 'Yes, since their days as undergraduates together, your father and Nigel shared everything. They had absolute trust in each other. But this trust had been severely broken because Nigel was adamant your father's discovery had to be shared with someone else. But who exactly, he couldn't say.' Julie shook her head.

'I remember. And you said you thought there were no notes or files left from his research? That he destroyed them all?'

'That's right,' Julie said. 'When your father left that evening, he told me he was going back to his office to destroy all his research so that nobody could ever use it.'

'So, not even Nigel had copies of it?'

'Not as far as I know. Nigel knew what he was working on, but he didn't know how he had made his breakthrough. After his death the police and some guys in suits ransacked his flat, almost gutting it. Nigel was with them. I asked him what they were looking for as they made so much noise upstairs, even pulling up floorboards. They left looking very annoyed, so I assumed he had managed to keep his work safe.'

A chill ran down Manisha's spine. 'They must have really wanted his research.'

'I know. I only wish I could tell you why.'

'I've asked Nigel for my father's notes, and he said they were lost. He goes very quiet when I ask him how far he progressed and patronises me, telling me to just focus on my own research.'

'And is your work secure, Manisha?'

'Yes, it's secure. Nobody can get hold of my data but me. But it shouldn't be like this. I should be able to trust my colleagues. Perhaps I'm trying to uncover a secret that people aren't ready to learn. If humanity isn't mature enough to use this technology wisely, then perhaps I should stop. Is it worth the risk?' Manisha let out a big sigh and held her head in her hands at the impossible situation.

'I understand your concern, Manisha, but you have a gift. Your father would be so proud of you. You're too far on your journey to give up now. Especially when you have so much positivity you can bring to the world. Remember, you don't have to reveal all your discoveries. Just share what you want.' Julie paused. 'Unfortunately, this is where your father went wrong and shared too much too soon with Nigel.'

Julie stood and walked to her mantelpiece and picked up a photo of Manisha's father with Max as a puppy. 'I still miss putting the world to rights with him over a glass of wine or two.'

Manisha joined her and looked at the photo of her dad. Her eyes brimmed with tears. 'I wish he were still here.'

The photo was taken in his office in Oxford. He had a wide smile, and his eyes sparkled, like a man who was in control of his work and enjoying life. As Manisha studied the picture, she noticed an image of a two-headed figure on the wall behind him. 'What's that?' she asked, pointing to the photo.

Julie smiled. 'Do you remember your father's fascination with ancient gods? He used to give his projects secret code names after them. Actually, that's how we got to know each other. When I was teaching Religious History at Oxford, he would ask my advice on a suitable god for his latest research project. His last project we dedicated to the god Janus.'

'What does Janus represent?' Manisha asked.

'Janus is the Roman god of new beginnings, time, and duality.'

'Do you know why he chose Janus?'

'I'm so sorry, Manisha. I can't remember now, but he obviously felt it was appropriate to what he was trying to achieve.'

Manisha stared into space, thoughts spiralling as she tried to understand why her father had chosen this Roman god for his last research project.

Julie put her hand on Manisha's arm and squeezed.

'Look, if you need to get away for a break, you can use my holiday home in Venice. It would be good for you to have some down-time. It's free for the next few weeks, and you're welcome to use it. *Vita* is in the centre of Venice, only about five minutes' walk from St Mark's Square. The city is amazing—and it's very romantic. It might do you and Matthew some good,' Julie said with a twinkle in her eye.

Manisha smiled at the sweet gesture. 'Thank you, but I have so much work to do. But maybe later in the year, if it's free?'

'Of course, just let me know. Make sure you put yourself first, Manisha. Take care of yourself, and your work, at all costs.'

'Thank you, Julie.'

They hugged, and Manisha drained the remaining wine from her glass. She took one last look at the photo of her father on the mantelpiece. The memory of the last time she saw him flooded into her mind. The recollection of him holding her head, his eyes boring into hers as he said the last words she would ever hear him say.

'Manisha, don't fear the world. It isn't there.'

MANISHA WALKED BACK through the black door of the Edwardian house and up the stairs to the flat above Julie's, which she had inherited from her father. He'd used it as a place to stay while working in Oxford and would return to the family home in Wiltshire on Friday evenings for the weekend.

Once inside, she closed the door and went into the living room. The afternoon sun had warmed up the space, making it feel stuffy. She walked to the window and opened it slightly. A cool breeze floated in and she breathed deeply. She gazed out of the window at the passing traffic when a man sitting on a bench opposite caught her eye. Large, mirrored aviator sunglasses hid his eyes. A black cap covered his head, and his muscular arms hung outstretched over the back of the bench, as if arrogantly proclaiming ownership of everything he surveyed.

The man removed his glasses and their eyes met. She instantly recognised him. It was the same man she had encountered on her morning run two days ago. He stared straight at her, his smile wide and unnerving, as if daring her to realise she was being watched.

Manisha stepped behind the curtain, peering around it. The man kept on staring. Manisha's heart pounded as she grabbed her phone and tried to discreetly take some photos. She switched the camera to video mode as the man stood up and laughed, his gaze still fixed on Manisha's flat. He put his glasses on and pointed at her, silently mouthing something before he turned and followed the path into Park Town Crescent and disappeared behind the trees.

She watched the video repeatedly, dread knotting in her stomach. Then she saw it—his lips forming four silent words.

'I see you, Manisha.'

11

'We have these words 'space' and 'time,' but you can't touch them. They're not objects, they're not things, they go forever. Space and time are really tools of animal sense perception, the way we organize and construct information.'

Robert Lanza – Scientist (1956–)

'Here's to our first year together, and to many more,' Matthew said, raising his glass of Champagne.

The glasses clinked and Manisha smiled, pleased that Matthew had at least one eye on their future. 'The first step is for you to complete your degree. Then I'll consider if you're worthy of the next stage!'

'And what's the next stage?'

'Children, of course!' Manisha kept her poker face until an unmistakable moment of fear swept across his face.

'God, you had me for a second.' Matthew held his chest. 'But given a few years, maybe,' he added as a counter.

Manisha laughed.

'I will ask you to marry me one day, Manisha Williams—so be prepared.'

'Well, time will tell. I may say yes, or I may say no. But until then, let's enjoy our time in Oxford.' They clinked glasses again just before their main courses were served.

The romantic setting of Gee's restaurant had always been their favourite place to eat, particularly on special occasions. The wrought iron and glass framework of what used to be an old Victorian greengrocer's made a perfect setting for a restaurant, especially with its contemporary interior, ambient lighting and mellow music.

'How's your training going?' Manisha asked as she picked up another fork full of porcini risotto.

'I'm ready!' Matthew said with a full mouth and a confident shrug of his shoulders.

'I can't believe the race is this weekend. It's come around so quickly.'

'I wish it were tomorrow, so I could get on and win.'

'And have you been doing the visualisation training I suggested, even though you were so negative about it?'

'Yeah, we're doing that, twice a day, every day. It's good, and it has given us so much more confidence. The whole crew knows how they want to row the race and exactly how they will feel when they finish. I actually enjoy it now.'

Manisha smiled with a raised eyebrow, knowing she didn't need to say the words: *I told you so!*

'I know, I know, I was a little sceptical to start with. But I think it works,' Matthew responded.

'I'm glad you're finding it helpful. The mind doesn't know the difference between an imagined and a real event. It's like working out a muscle. Once you train it for the outcome you want, that's all it will expect, and that's what will happen.'

'But how does it work?'

'Not sure yet; I'm still working on that.' Manisha grinned.

'And how is your research progressing?' Matthew frowned as if he knew he were pushing a big red button.

'Ah, Doulton! Would you believe it? He's now put a weasel in my lab to spy on me. An undergraduate who will be of zero use to me, except as a lab rat. I just don't know what he's thinking. He works too closely with the government for my liking; he must be trying to pass my work on. I can't let him use my work immorally. I just won't have it!'

'Okay, okay, I only asked…'

'The amount of money I'm paid, along with the endless budget worries me. I know I'm good at my job, but the amount of money being thrown at me is ridiculous.'

'Well, that's a really nice problem to have, Manisha. I wouldn't worry about that one!' Matthew raised his eyebrows.

'I've also got this strange guy following me. I've seen him a few times, and it's starting to worry me. Here's a photo.' Manisha passed her phone to him.

'This is just a guy standing by a bench, Manisha.' Matthew dismissed her concerns. 'How can you be sure he's following you?'

'But he's looking right at me.'

'He was probably thinking, *why is that weird woman looking at me from that window?*'

'But look at this.' Manisha played the video. 'I think he's saying, "*I see you, Manisha.*"'

'Are you sure? I can't make out what he's saying. It's really poor quality. He could be saying hello to a person on the other side of the street.'

Manisha continued to study the video; concern etched over her face. She hid the hurt she felt of Matthew not taking her seriously.

'Look, if you see him again, call me. I will come immediately and we'll confront him. Is that okay?' Matthew said, holding Manisha's hand.

'Okay.'

'But my guess is, you'll never see him again.'

'Oh, I don't know any more. Perhaps I am being paranoid, but my instinct tells me not to trust anyone!'

'Even me?' Matthew put on his best puppy dog eyes and held his arms open.

'Especially you!' she threw her napkin at him, smiling broadly.

'Well, you know what they say, keep your friends close and your enemies closer!'

'Yeah, you're probably right. Perhaps I should embrace Doulton and the Weasel!'

'Yeah, embrace the Weasel!' Matthew's loud American accent and laughter echoed through the restaurant, while he held his glass in the air.

Looks of disgust from other patrons didn't go unnoticed. 'Shush!' Manisha laughed, rolling her eyes. 'It's a good thing you can make me see the funny side of this.'

The waitress came over to the table. 'Is everything okay with your meals?'

'Yes, thank you.'

'And can I get you more drinks?'

'Yes please. Another glass of Champagne for me and a glass of water for him,' Manisha said, looking at Matthew who sat there, with the pout of a petulant child. 'You're still in training, mister. Keep focused for the last few days!'

'Yeah, I know, I know.'

'I've been offered an escape from the stresses of work if I need it,' Manisha said, returning to their original conversation.

'Really? Who, how, where?'

'Julie's place in Venice. She said I'm welcome to use it if I want to.'

'Which part of Venice?' Matthew looked interested.

'It's a small flat called *Vita* near St Mark's Square. She spends around six weeks there every year, and the rest of the year she lets friends and family use it.'

Matthew picked up his phone and started to type. 'I've always wanted to see the Basilica.'

'Who said you were invited?' Manisha said with a smile. She stood and kissed the top of his head as she made her way to the ladies.

LAING SAT IN HIS MERCEDES, with two wheels on the pavement, watching Gee's restaurant closely. The interactions and laughter between the young couple caused him mixed emotions. He thought of how he was at their age, when dating Diane. The strange ache in his heart was a powerful reminder of how positive and invincible he'd once felt in their relationship. They had been so optimistic about life, and he missed the lovely couple they had once been. He recalled the excitement of their first date—swiftly followed by the pain of their broken marriage. He watched the rain trickle down the windscreen and thought again of Manisha and Matthew. He wished the very best for the couple he protected, but he struggled to see how the current situation could end positively.

Instinctively, he completed a 360-degree observation check. There were no threats to Manisha and Matthew's safety. *How lovely to live a life unaware of how much danger you're in.* 'Bliss in oblivion.'

After another hour the couple left the restaurant, laughing and giggling, huddled under a single coat to stay sheltered from the rain. Laing hid from view, leaning into the passenger footwell, as if looking for something. The footsteps faded before he looked up. 'I don't know how much longer I can live like this.'

He watched the happy couple start their two-minute walk back to Manisha's flat. He pulled away slowly and drove past them before pulling into the far end of Park Town Crescent. He stopped in front of a driveway, providing clear sight of Manisha's flat. Suddenly tired after a long day, Laing massaged his face and sighed deeply. He waited until he could see they were home safely, praying that the outcome of the assignment would be good for Manisha.

ZAREK'S LAPTOP was open before him, the screen illuminating his face. A red dot moved closer to his location on the display as he heard Laing's car pull up outside. Another red dot moved slowly across the screen. The rain clattered against the window and the glow from the streetlight created patterns on the ceiling. He stood up and walked to the window. Peering through a slit in the blinds, he could see the black Mercedes parked on double yellow lines to the right of his drive. Only Laing's hands on the steering wheel were visible from his elevated position. To the left, through the trees, he spotted Manisha and Matthew walking in the pouring rain. There was a definite spring in their step as they approached her flat. He smiled to himself, watching the pawns of his game play their part outside his window.

Manisha and Matthew disappeared through the black door of 85b Banbury Road. The upstairs light came on and the curtains were quickly drawn.

The V8 engine of Laing's Mercedes purred into life and Zarek watched it pull away before taking a left turn out of Park Town and disappearing down the road at a steady pace.

He stepped back from the window, retreating into the shadows. Tomorrow, the game will continue.

12

'Quantum physics really begins to point to this discovery. It says that you can't have a Universe without mind entering into it, and that the mind is actually shaping the very thing that is being perceived.'

Fred Alan Wolf – Physicist (1934–)

Manisha sat in her lab, her eyes glued to a double eyepiece microscope as she blindly wrote notes on an A4 pad beside her. A loud buzz from the main door broke her concentration. She looked around to see Simon, a stupid smile on his face, which quickly vanished as Manisha shot an unmistakable look of disappointment. She slumped, silently wishing he would go away, but when she looked up again, Simon was still there, forcing a pathetic smile and giving a half-hearted wave through the glass. He gestured for her to open the door, while silently mouthing, 'Can I come in?'

Manisha sighed. 'Embrace the Weasel,' she muttered, unlocking the door.

'Hi…Professor Doulton told me to come down and see you,' Simon said sheepishly.

'Come in,' she said, trying to hold back her annoyance. 'Leave your coat and bag down there.' Manisha pointed to a spot next to the main door.

Simon dropped his bag and threw his jacket on top before walking through the outer office and into the main lab area. The doors hissed shut behind him.

'The rules in my lab are quite simple: one, touch nothing unless I tell you; two, take nothing from my lab; three, anything you learn about my work is confidential. You do not tell anyone —not even Professor Doulton. Any information passed to Professor Doulton comes from me only. Remember, you are legally bound under the non-disclosure agreement which you are about to sign.' Manisha pulled the three-page document from her desk drawer and a pen from the top pocket of her lab coat, slamming them on the desk before him.

Simon, slightly stunned, gave the document a cursory scan before signing on the dotted line at the bottom of the last page. He gave Manisha a look of concern. 'Look, Professor Williams, it's clear you don't want me here. But I'm genuinely interested in your work, and I don't want to get caught in the crossfire between you and Professor Doulton.'

Simon's maturity caught Manisha off guard. 'Okay, just guarantee you won't let me down, Simon.'

'Why would I do that?' he said with a Gallic shrug.

Manisha stared hard at him. A stare that told him he would regret it if he ever betrayed her.

'Can you explain how far you have progressed with your research and how I can help?' Simon asked.

'As you know from my lecture, I'm researching a way of communicating with people who appear unreachable, stroke victims for example. To cut a long story short, I've discovered a way to capture a person's thoughts. To capture the energy created and transmitted by the brain during the thinking process.'

'Wow, that's amazing!' Simon shook his head in disbelief.

'Yes, it is, isn't it!' Manisha gave a nod of her head. 'Have you ever thought about someone, and they suddenly call you on the phone?'

'Yeah, that's happened to me a few times. Kinda freaks you out. I believe Carl Jung referred to it as synchronicity.'

Manisha looked at Simon with surprise. 'Absolutely. People think it's just a coincidence. But there are many examples of synchronistic events that science cannot explain. However, I believe some of them are down to the power of our thoughts and our ability to communicate at a subconscious level. Capturing thought energy is one thing, but decoding it is another.'

'Is that what these screens are showing?' Simon asked, nodding at one of the six screens in front of him.

'Yes, I've had many experiments running over the last few months trying to decode my thought energy. However, there's only one image which makes sense to me, which came from an experiment last week.'

'Image? Surely you want to see text; words that can be read?'

Manisha realised that Simon wasn't as enlightened as perhaps his 'Carl Jung' reference had led her to believe.

'We don't think in words, Simon—our minds work in images. If I say the word "elephant", you see an image of an elephant in your mind's eye, not the letters spelling it out. You see images through your eyes. You imagine things in your head, maybe recalling something you've already seen or imagining what something or someone may look like. The person on the end of a phone, the hotel you're going to stay in on holiday—or your perfect woman,' Manisha said, finishing the sentence with raised eyebrows.

Simon gave a cheeky smile and an understanding nod.

'Even when you're asleep, your mind sees images. You dream, and they feel real. You may have physical reactions to nightmares and scream out or wake up in a cold sweat. The language of humankind is thoughts, feelings and images held within our minds, and this is the way it's been since the dawn of time. Theories say that early humans may have used telepathy to communicate, which is something we still observe in animals today.'

'Do you think you can help people to communicate that way again?'

'Yes and no. I don't know of a way of enabling telepathy in a person, but what I want is to create an artificial portal into someone's mind to enable communication. However, I do believe we already have this telepathic capability buried deep within us. We've just forgotten how to use it.'

'Interesting.'

'We think in images. Whether an event is real or imagined, it feels exactly the same to us. The world is perceived through our senses. However, quantum physics tells us nothing is tangible, until it's observed. So, our reality may only exist in our brains. Do you understand why I say nothing is real except for what you think and how you feel?'

'I think so. Do our dreams count as an observed experience?'

'Our bodies can react as if the dream experience is real. But whether we're creating a reality in our dreams, like we do when we use our senses, I do not know. The point is, dreams can feel real to us, just like our everyday waking existence. However, they both only exist in our brains.'

Simon rubbed his chin. 'I think I get it. I'm still grappling with the fact that if you're right, everything around us exists only within our minds.'

'That's right, Simon. It could all be an illusion.'

He grabbed the pen he'd used moments earlier to sign the NDA and held it up. 'Okay, so if this pen exists within my mind, how can you see it?'

'I'm a long way off proving this, but I believe this could be part of how our collective consciousness works.'

'Hmm, okay.' Simon looked at the screen in front of him. 'What's this image showing?' He pointed to a slightly blurred image of a man standing outside a building.

'This image is amazing, Simon. This is the first image to be decoded from a human thought.'

Manisha could see the reality of the situation hit home in Simon's eyes.

'Okay, this is getting a little freaky. You really are making progress, aren't you?'

'Yes, but this image seems to be a happy accident.' She let out a long sigh. 'I can't explain how this single image decoded successfully, when all other thoughts I've captured cannot be decoded.'

'It sounds a bit like Sean Connery in the film *The Medi-*

cine Man, when he discovers the cure for cancer and then loses it,' Simon recalled.

'Did he find it again?'

'Yeah, I think so,' Simon said with uncertainty, while scratching his chin. 'Where's the source of this image?'

Manisha paused, trying to gauge how much she should trust him. 'Okay, put these on.' She handed him a pair of dark glasses and put on a pair herself.

Simon, looking slightly bemused, slipped on the glasses and followed her to the corner of the lab. Manisha slowly opened the outer casing of the black box, revealing the minute, swirling cloud of energy.

Manisha looked at Simon. The look of astonishment and wonder that spread across his face excited her.

'This is incredible!' Simon said. 'Is this really...?'

'Yes. This is my thought energy. The one that produced the image you can see on the screen.'

'How can... what... really?'

After another minute of staring at the tiny cloud of energy in silence, Manisha closed the box and took off her glasses.

'So, there you have it. A summary of what I've achieved so far.'

Simon regained his ability to speak. 'This is amazing.'

Manisha let him take a moment, as she watched the cogs whirring in his head, processing what he had just witnessed.

'Can I ask, why?'

'Why what?'

'Why are you doing this, Professor? What's your motivation?'

Manisha was momentarily taken aback by the question, feeling a gentle tug at her heartstrings. 'My mother had a massive stroke when I was fifteen. It left her paralysed down one side and unable to speak. You've heard of locked-in syndrome?

'Yeah.'

'There was the famous book—The Diving Bell and the Butterfly—by a French journalist, Jean-Dominique Bauby, who had a stroke, and wrote the whole book by blinking his left eyelid. A transcriber recited the alphabet and Bauby blinked whenever they got to the correct letter. Can you imagine that kind of frustration?' Manisha's voice lowered, growing quieter. 'I can. I watched my mother live it.'

'I'm sorry,' Simon said.

'Her quality of life would have been so much better if she'd had a way to communicate freely. Now imagine if, using my technology, someone like my mother—like Bauby—could just transmit their thoughts to be read by their loved ones instantaneously. Faster than articulating them in words. Imagine the joy of it. That is why my father and I vowed to find a way to help future stroke victims.'

Manisha forced her melancholy to one side, not wanting to show Simon her vulnerable side.

'So, what can I do to help?' Simon asked.

'Well, I do need to run my experiments on someone else. So, you can be my lab rat.'

'All right, what does that involve?' Simon asked.

'Come over here.' Manisha led him to a large reclining chair in the corner of the lab.

Simon followed, looking nervous.

'Jump in.' Manisha pointed to the chair, her tone leaving no room for discussion.

'This device picks up the frequency of your brainwaves,' Manisha pointed to a glass face mask which hovered over Simon's head. 'The fibre optic cables are connected to sensors that detect your thoughts. The LEDs indicate the frequency your brain is working at and when it reaches a certain frequency, and sustains it, the LEDs will glow white. At this point you are emitting your thoughts out into the world around you. Do you have any questions before we begin?'

'Is there anything that can go wrong?'

'Nothing has gone wrong so far.'

'How many people have you experimented on?'

'Just one. Me. Any other questions?' Manisha asked, with raised eyebrows.

'No,' Simon said, looking no less concerned.

'Lie back, place your head on this headrest, and relax.' Manisha pressed a button and the glass mask lowered to within a foot of Simon's face.

A faint tingling spread across his forehead as the mask lowered. He wasn't sure if it was real or just his nerves. A flicker of light behind his eyelids, then a strange, almost magnetic pull deep inside his skull.

The array of tiny LEDs flashed into life, giving a wave of blue light, pulsing three times across the glass, indicating it was recalibrating. The LEDs started flashing different colours: red, green, blue and white.

'I need you to stay still, Simon. You don't want to know how much it cost to build this sensor. If you need to come out, raise your arm.'

'How long will it take?' Simon asked, looking even more anxious.

'As long as it takes for you to relax and send your thoughts out to the world. Just lie back, clear your head and think calm thoughts while I set up the equipment.'

'It's difficult to be calm when you feel like you're at the dentist.'

Manisha loaded a visual representation of the face mask

on the VDU next to Simon. A percentage indicator progressed past ninety-five per cent as the calibration neared its completion.

Manisha closed the armrest on the right side of the chair and reclined it further, aligning Simon's face with the mask. The equipment hummed as a dark blue wave of light pulsed from one side of the mask to the other, signalling it was ready for the experiment to begin. Manisha pressed another button to manoeuvre the mask down further, covering Simon's face. The holes near the mouth and nostril areas ensured he could breathe comfortably.

'I hope you're not claustrophobic,' Manisha joked.

'Err, I don't think so.' Simon gripped the armrests firmly.

'Okay, here we go. Relax and follow my instructions,' Manisha looked at Simon, seeing the grimace on his face through the glass and myriad of cables. 'Just close your eyes and relax,' she said soothingly. 'Imagine the glass is not even there. It won't hurt you.'

Simon closed his eyes and waited for further direction.

'Clear your mind, Simon; just focus on your breath and my voice. Close off all other senses and pretend nothing else exists. Take deep breaths, in through your nose'—Manisha took a deep breath in—'and out through your mouth'—and exhaled.

After a couple of minutes, the LEDs monitoring Simon's brainwaves turned from dark blue to a light green, showing he was relaxing.

'That's good. Keep on breathing deeply. Focus on a happy memory; a place or event that you enjoyed.'

The edge of Simon's mouth curled into a smile and the LED lights temporarily went back to flashing deep blue.

'Keep it clean, Perkins!' Manisha said on seeing his smile.

Simon's smile soon disappeared and he visibly relaxed.

'Focus on the image in your mind. Make it real for you, as if you were there.'

The LEDs on the face mask started changing from light green to an increasingly brighter and brighter white light. The indicators on Manisha's VDU displayed how close the equipment was to triggering the thought capture process. Excitement filled her as she watched her equipment capturing another person's thought for the first time.

'Okay, that's good, Simon. Keep it going.' Manisha focused on the status displayed on the VDU, her eyes wide. 'Okay, make sure you keep your eyes shut tight, Simon.' The LEDs let out a brilliant white light for two seconds, then faded.

Simon's eyes opened just as the LEDs went out. 'Was that it?'

'Yes, that's it,' Manisha pushed a button which raised the scanner, allowing Simon to move.

'That wasn't difficult.' Simon half sat up in the chair. 'But it's not quick.'

'This is an experimental prototype. Once I've refined the process, I'm planning to reduce the equipment to a hand-held device which will be much easier to use. Well, that's my goal, anyway.'

'That would be amazing. You could help so many people, not only in the UK but all over the world.'

'That's my plan. As long as I can get this technology working reliably.' Manisha shrugged. 'Okay, I just need you to describe or draw the image you were thinking of. Don't tell me what it was. Just write it on this piece of paper and seal it in the envelope.'

Simon scribbled an image on the paper and jotted down some notes while Manisha powered down the equipment.

'Here you go.' Simon handed over the sealed envelope.

Manisha took the pen from her lab coat and wrote his name and the date on it.

'So, can I see it?' Simon nodded towards the black box next to the reclining chair.

'Sure, it's literally your "intellectual property" after all.'

Manisha slipped her glasses on and handed a pair to Simon, then slowly opened the black box with the same configuration of wires, lasers, and magnets around it as the box she'd shown him on the other side of the lab.

'That... that is my thought?' Simon's fingers twitched, as though tempted to reach out and touch the swirling cloud—despite knowing it was impossible. 'I mean... this is real, right? You're not...this isn't just some illusion?'

Manisha smiled. 'No, it's not an illusion. This is where science meets the spiritual side of the human experience.' She closed the box, and they took off their eye protectors.

Simon blinked as his eyes adjusted. 'So, when do you want me back?'

'This weekend is out, as I'm away in London.'

'Really? So am I. Well, Sunday at least. It's the Boat Race and I'm meeting up with a few friends in Chiswick to support our guys and have a few beers.'

'Matthew, my other half, is rowing for Oxford. I'll be there supporting him and either celebrating or commiserating.'

'Well, I may see you there,' Simon walked towards the door.

'I'll contact you next week,' Manisha confirmed as she turned to her keyboard and brought up the control panel for her lab. She clicked the door release, to allow her lab rat to leave.

Simon stopped and looked back a thoughtful expression on his face.

'Professor Williams, this has the potential for all sorts of uses, hasn't it? Not just for helping people.'

'Yes, it has. Now do you understand why I need your absolute trust, Simon?'

'Yeah, I understand. It's very sobering.'

An uncomfortable silence filled the room.

'I think it's best you go now, Simon.'

13

'We are what we think. All that we are arises with our thoughts. With our thoughts, we make the world.'

Buddha – (6th–5th Century BC)

Outside the window, dawn broke over a misty London. Susan Redfern's desk in Thames House was bare, save her laptop, dual screens, and a lamp. She treasured the early mornings for their calm, which gave her time to deliberate on her long-term objectives and focus on the details of the day ahead. She sat in silence, watching the headlights of commuters crawling over Lambeth Bridge. Each mind fixated on its own path—love, career, wealth, fame—fragile, fleeting. None of it mattered to her. She was one hundred per cent focused on the future. Not her own future, but that of the UK and humanity. She would sacrifice anything to keep humanity safe—even the risk of death wouldn't deter her from her goal. Redfern listened to her instincts and set her sail, allowing a fair wind to take her to her destiny.

She swivelled her chair away from the window and back towards her desk to scan one of her two touch-sensitive screens, which displayed her packed schedule for the day. Her priority was operation 'QUANTUM II' and had been for some time. She logged into the finance system to check the accountants' updates. The long list of specialised equipment purchased for the lab in Oxford ran down the page. Only five million pounds had been spent on the operation to date, which was a drop in the ocean compared to the three-billion intelligence budget under her control. *The smallest operation, but with the biggest potential.*

Redfern knew if the research was brought in-house too soon, costs would go through the roof and attract unnecessary scrutiny. The idea would seem insane to the Home Secretary and the Secretary of State for Defence, who often slated the Americans for their 'weird' defence projects—his favourite being Project 'Stargate'. Two decades of research and tens of millions of dollars spent on using remote viewing, the ability to psychically see places from a distance, to gather military intelligence. She often wondered if the project had been more successful than her American colleagues let on. However, it was irrelevant. She was on the verge of having a superior technology for a fraction of the cost.

But how should it be used? She tapped her fingers on the desk, thinking through a decision that, once taken, would change the course of humanity. *What's more important, the status of the UK on the world stage, or the status of the world itself?* Her frown faded. She realised the answer was obvious.

The sun broke through the mist, sending a shaft of bright light into her otherwise dark office. A quiet knock at the door told her it was already 8:00 a.m. Her PA entered with her morning coffee and croissant.

'Put it there.' Redfern nodded.

The middle-aged woman put the tray on the side of Redfern's desk. 'Will there be anything else?'

'No,' Redfern said, without even glancing away from her screen.

'Very good, Ma'am.'

Redfern cleared her e-mails, sipped her coffee, and teased her croissant apart as she read through Laing's weekly report. Once satisfied she had all the updates, she put on her wireless headset and dialled Laing's mobile.

'Morning, Ma'am.'

'I see Doulton finally put someone in place. What's he like?'

'Your average Oxford student, very bright, wealthy parents, and he likes to drink. He's had one misdemeanour for public intoxication when he climbed on a statue of a horse and screamed "charge" for an hour. He paid a small fine, and he was very embarrassed about it. He seems to have a chip on his shoulder about his parents being in the "new money" set. He gets a little grief from the toffs and that's about it. He's clean. Your average bloke in his early twenties. I think he'll be easily manipulated to give us what we want.'

'Good,' Redfern said. 'We need some progress on this operation.'

'Do you want me to lean on him?'

Redfern hesitated, then said, 'Just observe him. Do not

make any contact; I don't want him spooked before he's done anything useful.'

'Yes, Ma'am.' Even though Doulton has bent over backwards to get him in place?'

Redfern frowned. 'Do not question my judgement. Even if he appears to be in danger—just leave him alone. He's not important. Do you understand?'

'Yes, Ma'am.'

Redfern clicked her mouse and ended the call.

She spun around to look out the window again. The sun had now broken through the clouds, casting bright patches of light over the rooftops and river in an otherwise grey landscape.

Removing her headset, she walked to the corner of her office. Bending down, she opened the lower cupboard containing her private safe. The eight-digit code was quickly entered on the keypad and the door sprung open. The safe was almost empty, apart from a large brown envelope, a data DVD, and a basic pay-as-you-go phone. She removed the phone and walked over to the window. She typed, *'I'll do the call today'* and sent it to a number she had memorised.

At 8:30 a.m. she dialled a second number she had also committed to memory.

'Yes.'

'Good morning,' Redfern said in a measured tone. 'I have an important task for you. It's very delicate, but I know you will do well.'

'Thank you.'

'Professor Williams' assistant, Simon Perkins, is now working in her lab. Do whatever it takes for Simon to give you her work. All of it! I want him to download all the data on her research, especially her algorithms. He needs to do this without raising Professor Williams' suspicions. She cannot find out. Make sure he understands—failure is not an option.'

'Of course.'

'Well done. Your time is near.'

Redfern hung up the phone.

14

'The distinction between the past, present and future is only a stubbornly persistent illusion.'

Albert Einstein – Physicist (1879–1955)

Matthew sat in position six of the eight-man racing shell, his oar buried deep in the water, ready for the red flag to drop. His heart pounded. The Thames was calm, a cool breeze stirring the water as sunlight wove bright patterns through shifting shadows. Hundreds of hours of training were behind him. All that mattered was the next eighteen minutes. *I will be victorious. This will be the start of my new life.*

Oxford had won the toss and started on the more advantageous Surrey side. The Cambridge cox lowered their hand, shortly followed by the Oxford cox. They were ready to start.

The umpire dropped her red flag. 'Attention... Go!' And they were off.

Adrenaline coursed through Matthew's body as he dug deep, pulling hard to get the boat in motion. The sprint start got them up to speed before they settled into their race pace for their battle over the next six and a half kilometres.

SIMON JOSTLED through the packed crowd in The Ship at Mortlake, trying to find the best TV to watch the race. He and his friends had got there late and missed the start, already a little oiled from drinks they'd had on the train. Simon went up on tiptoes and surveyed the room, looking to see if Manisha was in the pub. Spotting a woman with long dark hair, he squeezed his way through the crowd, ensuring he didn't spill his pint. He gave her a sideways glance before committing to speak. 'Who's winning?' Simon asked while sipping his beer and looking at the screen.

Manisha looked round. 'Cambridge, but it's close!'

'Which one's Matthew?' Simon asked, keen to know what Manisha's other half looked like.

'He's in position six, third from the cox,' Manisha said, pointing at the screen.

Simon studied his contorted face. 'Looks like he's suffering!' he said, and then took a couple of large gulps of his beer.

'He's doing great,' Manisha said, her eyes glued to the screen.

The graphic displayed on the TV screen showed Cambridge had a mere three-second lead.

Manisha glanced at Simon. 'Look, I'm sorry I was so direct with you yesterday, Simon. My work means everything to me.'

'I understand, Professor Williams,' Simon said, unsure of whether he should call her Manisha in such an informal setting. 'You can trust me.'

'Can I really? Doulton's been pressing you, hasn't he? If you're here to dig for him, just say it now. I don't have time for games.'

'He was persuasive. But he hasn't asked me to spy on you. I enjoyed our first meeting. You can trust me.'

Manisha looked at him as if challenging his words.

'You can trust me!' Simon looked purposefully into Manisha's eyes, hammering home his resolve.

'Okay. Thank you.'

Simon drained his glass. 'This is thirsty work,' he said nodding at the screen.

'I'm going to get another pint. Can I get you anything?'

'No, I'm fine thank you,' Manisha said, raising her glass of diet coke as she turned her attention back to the screen.

Simon kept an eye on the TV as he edged past Manisha, hoping he had enough time to get his drink before the race ended. The boats were neck and neck. The footage flicked from crew to crew, showing the pained expressions on their faces. 'They can't be far away now,' Manisha said over her shoulder and punched the air on seeing a close up of Matthew, his sports sunglasses covered in spray and his face twisted in pain.

'Same again, please.' Simon handed his glass to the barman, who seemed more interested in the screen than his order.

'I can see them!' a shout from the pub door marked the mass evacuation to see the race finish outside.

'Are you coming, Simon?' Manisha shouted as she headed out to the riverside.

'Yeah, I'll be out in a minute,' Simon shouted, and turned towards barman, willing him to hurry up. Simon hugged the bar as the crowd, including his friends, rushed past him, leaving the once-heaving pub almost empty.

MATTHEW BREATHED IN DEEPLY, his heart pounding, his arms and legs on fire. The cox screamed words of encouragement: 'Dig deeper! We are Oxford, we will win!'

Matthew could see they were gaining on Cambridge. The boat dipped into the water with each stroke.

'Forty-one,' the Oxford cox shouted. With only two hundred metres to go, the time was right to summon all their strength and increase their stroke rate for the final push. Matthew heaved harder than he knew was possible, his muscles screaming with pain. With both crews' stroke rate now even, the boats were neck and neck—each boat surging forward in alternating strokes. Nausea rose from the pit of his churning stomach, threatening to overwhelm him as his vision blurred from lack of oxygen and sheer effort. He summoned every ounce of energy for the last strokes of the hardest race of his life.

As the cheers reached fever pitch, the boats crossed the finishing line simultaneously. It was a photo finish. Matthew released his oar, letting it glide across the water. He could do no more and hunched over, his body pushed to its limit. He gasped in air, taking as much breath into his lungs as he could. It was not the finish he'd imagined. He looked over at the Cambridge boat as it drifted, the blades skimming across the water while the crew members fought for breath.

Some of the crew lay back, others clung to the side of the boat, utterly exhausted. Every muscle in Matthew's legs, arms, and shoulders burned as a thin veil of steam rose from his shattered body.

SIMON HAD MISSED the race's dramatic conclusion. The barman had taken forever with the world's slowest-pulled pint of lager. Simon tapped his foot in frustration, watching the race on TV while listening to the roar of the crowd outside on the riverbank. He may as well have stayed in his flat and watched it there. Annoyed, he placed his pint on the end of the bar and searched for a sign for the lavatories. He followed a path to the back of the pub where a man courteously stepped aside as he approached. Once past, Simon felt a firm hand grip his shoulder and a hard prod in his back.

Simon twisted around. 'What the fuck are you doing?' He tried to push the man away, but he was too strong.

'Keep quiet and come with me if you want to stay alive.'

A cold metal point pressed into his ribs. His heart pounded. 'Whatever I have on me is yours,' he stammered. 'I have an iPhone 13 and a nice watch.' He held up his left arm.

'Be quiet. I don't want your watch.' The man held his shoulder in a vice-like grip and guided him towards the exit.

Once outside, Simon desperately searched the crowd for a face he recognised, only to be met with the backs of people's heads, all engrossed in the spectacle on the river. Simon scanned the road, trying to figure out where he was being taken. His breathing quickened, and his heart raced as he was pushed towards a large black van. The street was empty. His throat was dry, and he was too scared to shout out for help anyway.

The stranger opened the back of the van and pushed Simon in with a force that smashed his head against the solid metal interior. Simon landed hard, flailing on his back; the metal ribbed floor dug into his shoulders, and his feet slipped as he tried to get up. Through blurred eyes, he looked up at the man in anger—but his anger turned to terror as he saw a gun being pointed at his face. 'What do you want?' Simon asked, his voice trembling.

The man jumped into the back of the van and slammed the door shut. Simon saw the side of the firearm heading towards his face and tried to jerk his head away. The crack echoed through his head as metal hit bone. Pain shot through his nose, followed by a warm torrent of blood. The man grabbed him by his hair, forcing his face against the side of the van. Simon could feel the cold steel of the gun's barrel thrust firmly into the back of his neck. The blood tasted metallic as it ran from his nose across his lips.

'Listen carefully,' the man hissed, his mouth close to Simon's ear. 'You're going to get a copy of Manisha's work. All of it. I want her algorithms, her plans, and results of her experiments. Everything. Manisha mustn't know anything about it. If you fail, I will find you—and I will kill you. Do you understand?'

Simon stared out of the corner of his eye at the man's mouth. Saliva seeped through his teeth as he spoke, and the sour smell of his breath crept into Simon's bloody nose. The man moved his grip and Simon cried out as his powerful fingers bore into the back of his neck, squeezing it hard as he thrust the gun firmly under his chin.

'Do you understand?'

'Yes, yes,' Simon said, shaking in fear as tears mixed with the blood under his nose.

'You have forty-eight hours. I'll be in contact.'

The door of the van opened. Simon felt a hard shove in his back as he was pushed out. He landed heavily on the hard, gritty tarmac. The van door slammed shut, leaving him dazed and bloody.

I MUST HAVE WON. I had to. If I lost... no. The shame, the look in my father's eyes—it would break me, Matthew thought. He couldn't get the image out of his mind. The realisation that his father still had a hold over him only made his anxiety build.

The boats drifted towards Chiswick Bridge, the cool shade providing relief from the bright, warm sunshine. Matthew looked at the Cambridge crew. They looked annoyingly confident.

A loudspeaker announcement came from the bank of the Thames. 'The winners are...' Matthew's heart pounded as he sat, trying to hear the voice over the noise of the crowd... '...Oxford, by a foot!'

Matthew felt the slap of his crew member's hand on his back. He looked behind at his teammate, who grabbed his uncomprehending face. 'We won!'

'Yes!' Matthew roared. He reached both hands up high before slamming them down into the water. The echo of his celebration ricocheted off the arch of the bridge. 'Screw you, Dad,' he said under his breath, before letting out another triumphant cry. An overwhelming feeling of freedom washed over him.

No one can stop me now.

He regained his composure, wiping sweat and tears from his eyes, and grabbed his oar. The crew slowly edged their boat towards the Mortlake boat club on the north bank of the Thames. He looked back towards The Ship, where he knew Manisha would be cheering for him.

Manisha stood in the crowd outside The Ship feeling elated. 'Well done, Matthew,' she shouted as she watched him disappear towards the other side of the Thames. She headed towards the bridge, keen to get to Matthew, only to meet Simon coming out of the pub, walking unsteadily, eyes wide and blood covering his nose, chin and shirt.

'What the hell happened to you?'

'I... ah... got into a fight. But I'm okay. You should see the other guy,' Simon said. The joke was at odds with the shocked expression on his ghostly face. His hands shook as he dabbed at his bloody nose with a bundle of tissue.

'Are you sure you're okay? Do you need an ambulance?' Manisha asked.

'No, no, I'll be fine,' Simon said as one of his friends joined him.

'Have you been in the wars again, Perkins! Don't worry. I can get him home,' Simon's friend said, looking at Manisha.

'Why would someone have done this to you, Simon?'

'It all happened so fast; I don't really know. I'd rather not talk about it,' he said, looking down towards his feet to avoid eye contact.

Manisha continued to look concerned. 'Are you sure there's nothing I can do?'

'No, I'll be okay. I'll get home and get cleaned up. Enjoy your evening, Manisha.'

Simon hobbled away but turned suddenly. 'See you at the lab tomorrow?'

'Yeah, I'll be there first thing. But don't come in if you're not up to it.'

As she walked away, she looked back at Simon. Blood covered his hands, and he walked with a limp, using his friend for support. His friend was laughing and asking, 'Who have you upset this time, Perkins?'

Manisha walked on, her arms crossed, her instinct causing doubt to creep into her head as she made her way towards Chiswick Bridge.

15

*'We don't just passively perceive the world;
we actively generate it.'*

Anil Seth – Neuroscientist (1972–)

It was 8:00 a.m. Simon sat in the cool reception of the Beecroft Building in a navy and white varsity jacket. Unshaven, he bit his nails. The occasional sound of the receptionist answering the telephone echoed around the hall, breaking the silence in an otherwise cold and quiet space.

His sleep had been fitful, and his jaw ached from yawning. His nose still throbbed from yesterday's beating. Try as he might, he could not make sense of the situation he found himself in. The memory of a gun at his neck felt surreal.

The thought of what he had to do made him feel sick. *I can't betray Manisha. Can I?*

The sound of heels on the marble floor reverberated through the atrium as Manisha arrived to escort him down to her lab. His heart raced, hands clammy.

'You certainly have a shiner there. How are you feeling?' Manisha asked.

'I'm fine.' Simon attempted a grin. 'It looks worse than it is.'

They stepped into the lift in silence. As they stood face to face, Simon could see concern written all over Manisha's face. He looked into her eyes, trying to control his trembling hands, as a thin layer of sweat began to build on his brow.

'Why are you here so early?' Manisha asked, breaking the awkward silence in the confined space.

'I want to see if you can read my thoughts,' he said, his second attempt to smile causing him pain. He cringed inside. *That's the last thing I need you to do right now.*

'The scan is still running; it could take days before we know if the experiment has worked. Your job today is to review my notes from the experiment where the image was decoded successfully, to see if I've missed anything.' The lift pinged, the doors opened, and Manisha walked to the outer door of her lab and swiped them both in. Simon took off his rucksack and jacket and left them in the outer office before they made their way through to the main lab. Manisha handed him a black folder. 'Here are my notes from the successful experiment. You can sit there.' She pointed to the end of the central island. The fact it was as far away from Manisha as possible was not missed by Simon.

He sat down in front of the large VDUs, the soft buzz of the equipment in the lab swimming around his ears.

Manisha sat at the end of the island in front of her laptop in silence. He could feel her watching him from the corner of her eye as he hunched over the desk, a frown across his face, his bruised eyes drawn into a squint. He loosely scanned the folder's contents, while his mind agonised over how he could control the situation and come out unscathed. He checked the lab for PCs. There was only one: Manisha's. He felt in his right pocket for the flash drive. It was still there, ready to receive Manisha's work. *How do I distract her long enough? How do I even find the right files?* He sighed, held his head in his hands, and looked blankly at the contents of the black folder.

Manisha looked over the top of her laptop screen. 'Are you sure you should be here?'

'Yeah, I'm fine.'

Minutes passed without another word. Manisha's gaze bored into him.

'You have the weight of the world on your shoulders, don't you?' Manisha said. 'Do you want to talk?'

Simon desperately wanted to tell Manisha what had happened and what he was being asked to do, but his survival instinct won out. 'I've been thinking about what we discussed last week. Later on—as the technology evolves—do you think you would still need the subject's cooperation to capture a thought? Or could someone —like —scan a mind and take a thought without permission? Without them even knowing?'

'Possibly. That's why I'm so secretive about how the technology works, Simon.' She looked at him coldly. 'Don't take it personally, but I don't trust anyone. Governments around the world have spent billions on defence projects designed to spy on their enemies, and I know many governments will be interested in my research. But I'm determined it won't be used in that way. This technology needs to be used to help people. I will not allow it to be used as a weapon of war to gather intelligence without a person knowing about it.'

Simon felt sheepish as his mind spun out of control. *'That must be what the man with the gun was after? He wants to turn Manisha's technology into a weapon.* His thoughts raced through the repercussions of the options before him. Tell Manisha everything, and risk being killed, or betray her, and risk being responsible for the creation of an instrument of war. At times like this, he wished he had a backbone.

Manisha looked warily at him. 'Simon, you can talk to me.'

'Ah, no, no, it's okay,' Simon said, shaking his head before looking back at the folder he'd been given.

Manisha continued with her work, touch-typing on her laptop while reading from a printed document.

After several minutes Manisha eyed Simon trying to discreetly massage his temples. 'Are you in pain?' Manisha asked.

'I'm okay. I just have a banging headache.'

'Do you want some painkillers?'

'No, it's okay. I'll be fine.'

A few seconds passed.

'Actually, I will have some tablets if you have some, please?'

Manisha stared at him over the top of her laptop screen. She walked abruptly to her outer office.

Simon watched her through the glass, searching through her handbag and desk drawer before she leaned around the door. 'I don't have any tablets down here. I'll need to go up to my locker. I'll only be a few minutes. Do not touch anything!'

'Okay.'

As soon as the door closed, Simon nervously rushed

around to Manisha's laptop, keeping an eye on the door. He looked up at the security camera, turning his back to it in an attempt to conceal his crime. His distraction had worked; Manisha had left her machine unlocked. With his hands shaking, he slipped the USB flash drive into her computer. He scanned the connected network drives to determine which would most likely contain Manisha's work, clicking frantically to find anything he thought would denote her research. On finding a folder that contained file names depicting the experiments she had completed, he dragged and dropped the folder across to the flash drive. A countdown of the copy started. There were ten minutes remaining. Simon massaged his temple with his thumb, his stress levels rising as the time to complete the copy slowly reduced.

MANISHA RETRIEVED the tablets from her locker. As she turned, she jumped—Doulton had appeared beside her. His mere presence irritated her. She stepped into the lift without greeting him, hoping to get away, but he held his hand high against the lift door, keeping it open.

'How's it going with Simon?' Doulton asked.

'It's like looking after a child,' she said, waving the headache tablets in the air. 'He got into a fight yesterday and he's in pretty bad shape.'

The lift alarm started ringing, telling Doulton to either get in or step away and release the door. Manisha stood still, leaving him with little choice if he wanted to continue the conversation. He stepped into the lift, allowing the doors to close, and they started their descent.

'What happened to him?'

'He's not saying much. In fact, he's being very secretive about the whole incident. I think there's more going on than he wants me to know.'

'You're being paranoid. He's probably just upset the wrong people,' Doulton shrugged.

Manisha shot him a look of disdain. 'I'm not being paranoid. I'm being forced to work with Simon; he's been attacked for reasons he's not willing to discuss. I'm finding the whole situation very uncomfortable and your attitude to all of this is not giving me any confidence.'

'Oh, thanks Manisha. I've fought to secure your funding, and all you can do is doubt me.'

'Nigel, I don't trust anyone.'

'You've got to trust me, Manisha. Can't you see I'm on your side?'

Manisha turned back towards Doulton and looked him straight in the eyes. 'I don't know whose side you're on.' She stood with hands on hips. 'In fact, it all feels a little too easy. Whoever is funding my work has a bottomless pit of money. That doesn't sound like the NHS, now, does it?'

'Manisha, calm down. The money spent on your research may seem like a lot to you, but it's a drop in the ocean to the government. Look, let me talk to Simon. I'll try to find out what really happened.'

Doulton's reference to 'the government' rather than the NHS compounded Manisha's unease. 'Do not tell me to calm down. I want to see evidence of who is funding my research, Nigel. And if you want to talk to Simon, use your own time, rather than wasting mine.'

～

SIMON HEARD the faint ping of the lift doors. Stretching his neck as far back as he could without leaving his tilted chair, he could see the outlines of Doulton and Manisha through the frosted glass. The file copy countdown still showed it had forty-seven seconds remaining. Simon felt panic rising within him, wondering if he should he cut his losses and just remove the USB drive, or wait until the outer lab door opened. He stood, keeping his hand on the device, his hands clammy, his fist shaking. He kept one eye on the shadows outside the office door, listening to the muffled exchange of angry voices. 'Keep on arguing, keep on arguing,' he said, willing the delay to continue.

The copy showed it had twenty seconds remaining. He moved to the side of the desk, ready to remove the device and run back to his seat the moment he heard Manisha's footsteps enter the outer office. He looked back towards the outer office to see Doulton peering into the lab through the clear strip of glass on the upper part of the lab window. Doulton pulled a puzzled expression on seeing Simon standing in front of Manisha's computer. Simon held his nerve and waited for the first click-clack of Manisha's footsteps. Each second felt like an eternity, before Simon heard Manisha swipe her key card, making the door open.

AS MANISHA WENT to enter the lab, she was shocked to feel Doulton firmly grip her shoulder.

'Manisha, I cannot tolerate this attitude or tone. You need to sort your act out and focus on delivering results, else your funding may dry up.'

Manisha looked back at him, his body language tried to hide his false threat, but she could see the truth in his eyes.

She shrugged his grip from her shoulder, ushered Doulton backwards and she made her way through the mantrap security door. She stood for several seconds in the outer office, taking deep breaths to compose herself. The lift opened, and she watched through frosted glass as the dark figure disappeared.

Walking back into the main lab, she found Simon looking white, sweaty, and out of breath.

'Are you okay?'

'No. I think you're right Manisha. I'm not feeling too good. I'm not going to be much help to you today,' he said, between breaths. 'I'll go home and come back tomorrow.'

'Do you think you should see a doctor?'

'No, I'll be fine. I'll just go home and get some sleep.'

Simon got up to leave and brushed past Manisha.

'Hang on, what are you doing?' Manisha asked.

Simon froze.

'Your painkillers,' Manisha said, holding them out.

'Oh, thanks,' he said. He turned hesitantly to leave, but then turned back. 'Professor Williams…' he started.

'Yes,' Manisha said.

'Ah, no, nothing. It's okay. I'll see you tomorrow.'

Simon put his jacket on, slung his rucksack over his shoulder and walked through the exit. The door softly clicked shut behind him. Moments later the lift motors sprang into life.

Manisha stared at her laptop. The position of her computer and the windows on the screen had changed. Her stomach twisted. 'Simon…what have you done?'

16

'It will remain remarkable, in whatever way our future concepts may develop, that the very study of the external world led to the scientific conclusion that the content of the consciousness is the ultimate reality.'

Eugene P. Wigner – Physicist (1902–1995)

Heavy rain splashed on Laing's windscreen as he watched a bruised and battered Simon leave the Beecroft Building. Officially, he was there to watch over Manisha's movements. However, upon seeing Simon's condition and the fact he was leaving the lab less than an hour after he'd entered, Laing knew something was awry. Simon's stride was hurried, his stress evident. He checked his phone twice within the same minute and he kept glancing over his shoulder. About twenty metres behind, a man followed, dressed entirely in black, carrying a rucksack and wearing familiar Vans with faded trims. It was the same man with piercing blue eyes who had suddenly appeared in his nightmare a few days earlier. From his gait and worn Vans, he was certain it was the same stocky man who had tried to break into Beecroft. He watched as he held his phone, appearing to send a message.

Laing logged into his tablet and accessed the monitoring service he'd set up on Simon's phone. The messages exchanged were brief and to the point.

> Do you have my data?

> Yes

> I'm watching you. Go straight to your house

> Ok

Laing started the engine, turned his car, and slowly drove past both men, following the route to Simon's student house. He parked opposite in a "Permit Holders Only" carpark on Cobden Crescent. Only a few minutes passed before Simon came into view, turning the corner, looking wet, miserable, and scared. The man dressed in black followed, his cold gaze fixed on his quarry. Laing looked on as Simon walked up the path to the blue front door of the Victorian terraced house.

SIMON FUMBLED FOR HIS KEY. His hands shook so much that he couldn't get the key into the lock. *How did he get hold of my phone number? What's going to happen now?* As the door clicked open, a hard shove in his back sent him crashing through the door and onto the hallway floor. Fear and dread overwhelmed him as he got to his feet, using the door frame to steady himself, only to be pushed into the lounge. Simon landed in an armchair and the thickset, muscular man sank heavily onto the sofa, pulling a laptop from his rucksack, ready to inspect the spoils of Simon's betrayal.

The man's merciless eyes landed on Simon. 'Give it to me. Now!'

Simon gingerly took the USB drive out of his coat pocket and passed it over at arm's length. Once the handover was completed, he sank back into the chair. He drew his feet up onto the cushioned seat and hugged his legs close, cowering behind his knees.

He watched as the man quickly slipped the flash drive into the laptop and jabbed the keyboard feverishly. After just a few seconds the man's sharp gaze was on Simon. He swallowed hard as his guts turned to ice.

'Is this your idea of a joke?'

Simon edged away, pressing himself further into the seat.

'What do you mean? Aren't they the files you want?' Simon asked. His thoughts went into a tailspin. *How can it be the wrong data? It can't be.*

'Do not treat me like a fool. Of course they aren't—it's just rubbish. Look!'

The man turned the laptop towards him, and Simon stared at the jumble of hashed characters on the screen in desperation. 'Perhaps it's encrypted?' Simon said, as he forced himself to his feet and hovered over the laptop, his hands shaking.

Instantly, Simon felt the full force of a punch in the face, which sent him crashing into the armchair. He let out a howl of pain.

'I know when data is encrypted. Do you think I'm an idiot?'

'No, no. I thought I took the data you wanted,' Simon said in desperation.

He pushed himself further into the chair as the man took a single stride over the coffee table. He was cornered, with no escape. Simon braced himself, instinctively cupping his hands over his bleeding nose whilst peering at the man through half-closed eyes. He could feel the man's breath on his face as he leaned in, towering over him. Terror rose in his chest as the man levelled his gaze to stare intently into his eyes.

'Are you left or right-handed?'

'What?'

'Are you left or right-handed?' the man shouted.

'Right,' Simon winced, almost in tears.

The man grabbed the index and middle fingers on Simon's left hand and in one quick movement snapped them both backwards. The sharp crack was followed by a searing pain shooting through Simon's hand as he let out a primal scream. Tears ran down his face.

'Be grateful you still have your right hand for typing. Get the real data to me by tomorrow afternoon, or else I will break your neck.'

Laing sat opposite Simon's student digs as the man in black stormed out of the house, his face like thunder, leaving the door wide open in his wake. Several minutes went by before Simon came to the door, pale faced, clutching his left wrist, pain etched across his brow. Simon looked each way down the road before he closed the door and headed towards the river path.

Laing quickly considered his options. 'This is getting out of hand,' he muttered. He pulled out of the parking space and followed the injured student. As Simon approached the footpath to the Thames, Laing pulled alongside and lowered his passenger side window. 'Hey, do you want a lift? I can take you to the hospital.'

Simon looked both cold and frightened. 'No. I'm fine, thanks.'

'It's an hour's walk and I can get you there in fifteen minutes.'

Simon stopped and hesitantly walked over to the car. Laing registered the shocking change in the young man's appearance. He'd obviously taken a beating, and the cocky looking student from a few days earlier was gone. He had the haunted eyes of a child caught in a game he could neither understood nor ever hope to win.

'Who are you?' Simon asked, his voice trembling.

'I'm just a good Samaritan trying to do my good deed for the day. I can see you're in pain. I don't think your fingers are supposed to bend like that. Can I help? If not, I'll leave you in peace.'

As Simon glanced up at the sky, a couple of drops of rain splashed off his face. He looked at Laing as if resigning himself to the offer of help. 'Take me straight to A&E please,' Simon said with as much control as he could muster.

'Okay, no problem.'

Laing waited as Simon got in the car and watched as he pulled the door closed with his right hand. He winced in pain as he tried to put on his seat belt without knocking his broken fingers.

'What happened to you?' Laing probed his captive as he pulled away.

'A disagreement with a friend.'

'A friend wouldn't do this to you. Are you in trouble?'

'No, I'm fine.'

'It looks like you're in trouble to me. I can help.'

'Who the fuck are you?' Simon asked, looking directly at Laing.

'You just need to know I won't break your other fingers. I'm on your side.'

Simon stared at him, wide-eyed. 'Just let me out. I want nothing more to do with this.'

'What did he ask you to do, Simon?'

'How the hell do you know my name?'

'That's irrelevant. Just tell me what he's asking you to do.'

'I can't, he's threatened to kill me,' Simon said, on the verge of tears, fear written all over his face.

As Laing turned the car on to Abingdon Road, Simon tried to duck down in his seat, tangling his broken fingers in the seat belt, causing him to cry out in pain again.

Laing spotted who Simon had seen: the man in black, walking at pace beside the road. 'He's not a nice man,' Laing said, nodding towards him.

'Who do you work for?'

'That's irrelevant.'

'How do I know I can trust you?'

'Who else can you trust?' Laing said, turning his solemn face to Simon's. 'Believe me, you need all the help you can get.'

Simon seemed to weigh up his options. Finally, he caved. 'He's after some data from where I work.'

'Manisha's algorithms and experiment results?' Laing asked, looking for absolute confirmation of the situation.

'Yes! How do you know about Manisha?' Simon asked, pressing his back against the car door, his eyes wide and hands shaking.

'Don't worry about that. Have you given him any of her research?'

'I thought I had, but he said he couldn't read the files.'

'So, he has no data at all. None of Manisha's work is in this man's hands? Correct?'

'No. I thought I had given him hundreds of files. But he said they were unreadable.'

'Manisha let you take the wrong data.'

'She doesn't know what I've done,' Simon said with a look of dread. 'How could she know?'

'Manisha is cleverer than you think, Simon. You've been played, in more ways than one.'

'She knows?'

'Of course she does. She let you take the wrong data to see if she could trust you.'

Simon looked crushed. He sat in silence for the rest of the short journey.

Laing pulled up outside the John Radcliffe Hospital and scribbled his telephone number on a small notepad and ripped out the page. 'Here's my number. If you get into any more scrapes, call me.'

Simon grabbed the paper and opened the car door with his right hand, slamming it behind him without saying a word.

What game is being played here? Laing wrestled with the dilemma until a sudden clarity washed over him.

I need to speak to Redfern.

17

*'Consciousness is never experienced in the plural,
only in the singular.'*

Erwin Schrödinger – Physicist (1887–1961)

Manisha sat in Doulton's office, a picture of calm and composure, waiting for her boss to arrive. She'd settled herself into the green leather chair just before 8:00 a.m., expecting him to be in work early. However, an hour had gone by, and she was still waiting. She entertained herself by watching the sun shifting shadows across the park. She gazed in awe as its rays filled the clear morning sky, trying to imagine how much human life would change if our senses were tuned differently. What would the world look like if all frequencies of light—microwave, radio waves, and X-rays—were visible to her?

How would the world sound if she could hear sound waves of higher or lower frequencies than human ears allowed? What realities existed all around her that she was unaware of, purely because she was trapped in a human body tuned to a human experience?

Her childlike curiosity remained boundless. In this moment of calm, she surveyed the room and thoughts raced through her mind: *How can any part of this be real? How can any of this exist externally to me? This incomprehensible amount of matter that forms all we can see in our universe cannot come from nothing. Life is a neurological projection shaped by consciousness and its interplay with the boundless energy surrounding us. We create our own reality within our minds, based on our interpretation of the input from our senses, combined with our own beliefs and expectations about the world. But how can you prove you're in a box—a projection of your own creation—when you can never touch the sides?*

She smiled, pleased the spark of wonder and curiosity was still alive within her. Manisha knew who to thank for that. During the few quiet moments she had in her busy life, her thoughts always turned to her father. She embraced the inquisitiveness he had instilled in her and felt gratitude for having time to find that side of herself again, even if it were only for a moment as the dawn of a new day unfolded before her. In a life overshadowed by the politics of a modern world, where humans were obsessed by their own self-importance and the desire to accumulate wealth and power, these fleeting minutes were precious. They brought her back to her purpose in life — to help humanity understand itself.

The years working for Doulton had flown by, with many good times, some bad, and some just plain weird and confusing. The funding she received for her work was astonishing. Her grade and salary were more than she could have imagined so early in her career. She'd always put this down to Doulton, doing his best to take care of his friend's daughter. However, the recent events with Simon's beating, the attempted theft of her research, and her discussion with Julie about the circumstances around her father's death, had cast more doubt in her already confused mind. Her funding compounded her concern. If it wasn't the NHS funding her work, then who was? Her research was secure, she was sure of that. However, what worried her more was her inability to trust Doulton. Manisha knew a change was necessary, and that it had to happen sooner rather than later.

Her thoughts were interrupted by Doulton casually strolling into the office, looking bemused to see her. Manisha glanced at the clock. It was five past nine.

'Good morning, Manisha. Do we have a meeting today?'

'No, but I wanted to talk with you.'

Doulton gave a wry smile. 'You don't need to apologise for yesterday. I know you're stressed at the moment. Just forget about it.'

Manisha kept her cool. Doulton's arrogance had pushed a button, but she gracefully smiled through it.

'I'm not here to apologise to you. I have nothing to apologise for, and you know it.'

'What are you talking about?'

'Simon, that's what I'm talking about. He tried to steal data from my lab yesterday.'

Doulton sat down at his desk and sighed. 'Here we go again!'

'Nigel, I have the evidence. When I left the lab yesterday to get his headache tablets, I left my PC open with a screen capture program running. I can see exactly what files he tried to find, and I can see which files he copied to a USB device. So, don't give me the '*you're paranoid*' speech. What game are you playing and why?'

'I don't know what you're talking about, Manisha,' Doulton said, shuffling papers on his desk.

'Nigel, you planted Simon in my lab. You delayed me getting back into my lab yesterday by keeping me talking and then physically held me back. Are you honestly going to sit there and deny any involvement? How can you lie to me after everything we've been through?'

'I know nothing of this, Manisha,' Doulton said, clasping his hands together in front of him on the desk, attempting to mirror her peaceful demeanour.

Manisha caught a hint of deceit in Doulton's eyes. 'Who's really funding my work, Nigel? Just come clean with me, show me the evidence, then maybe we can come to an arrangement we're both comfortable with.'

'I'm not going over this again. I've told you who is funding your work and, as you know, you're under contract. So, whatever you discover on this project is the intellectual property of your sponsors. Your work is owned by them.'

'And who are the sponsors?'

Nigel sat in silence, clearly not prepared to repeat himself. Several seconds went by as Doulton attempted the intimidating stare of a manager looking down at an inferior member of staff.

'Well, perhaps I need to rethink my options,' Manisha said, sitting upright in her chair, as if ready to get up and leave. 'This situation is becoming untenable. People are getting hurt and I'm not convinced they even know why.' She paused, looking suspiciously at Doulton. 'What are you involved in, Nigel?'

'I have no idea what you're talking about.'

Manisha stared at him, her face filled with disappointment and disbelief.

'Look, you know I work as an adviser to the government, and you also know I cannot discuss any details of this work with you. However, your research is not on their agenda. There's nothing more I can say,' Doulton said, unclasping his hands and spreading his arms in an open gesture.

'What about my father? What really happened to him, Nigel? Was he just another innocent victim of your egotism?'

'Manisha, you're on very thin ice. Your father and I were the closest of friends. I was devastated when he died. It was a very unfortunate accident. He was tired and careless; it could just as easily have happened to me.'

Manisha clasped her hands and stared at him coldly. 'He was only careless with his friendship with you. He trusted you and it cost him his life.'

'I'm sorry you feel that way, Manisha. I valued your father's friendship deeply.'

For once, he sounded like he was telling the truth.

LAING sat in his car in the Beecroft carpark, listening intently to the conversation taking place in Doulton's office. He was impressed with the way Manisha was confronting Doulton, concerned that they were at risk of losing Manisha's input into the project and interested to see what Manisha would do next.

He took a sip of coffee and wrote down some notes. It was obvious Doulton knew nothing about the man who threatened Simon. All he knew was the government's interest in Manisha's research via Redfern. Laing's thoughts turned to his boss. *Why are you happy to sit back and watch events unfold?* This question circled in his head as the conversation unfolded.

Manisha was almost drawn in by the look on Doulton's face as he remembered his friendship with her father, but then she caught herself. 'I'm sorry, Nigel, but I'm not going to be fooled by you anymore. Why does everybody trust you? How do you bring people under your spell and get them to do exactly what you want? Is it the promise of money, success or just your innate charm?'

'Manisha, I'm not going to dignify that with a response. I work hard for this organisation. I think you should get back to your lab.'

'I'm not allowing Simon into my lab again. I can't trust him,' Manisha said, getting to the point of her impromptu meeting.

'Did Simon get any of your data in this supposed theft?'

'Of course not. The only network drive I had connected to my PC looked like it contained my research, but the files were fake. The fact that he didn't get any of my research is irrelevant. It's the fact that he tried in the first place. He's not going anywhere near my lab again.'

'Talk of the devil and he doth appear,' Doulton said, raising his eyes to the glass door behind Manisha.

Simon peered into the office, like a tied-up dog outside a shop, trying to see when his master was going to return.

Manisha turned and waved through the glass at him, summoning him in.

Simon awkwardly opened the door and Manisha eyed his newly bandaged fingers.

'Sorry to disturb, but are you going down to the lab soon?'

'Come in and sit down,' Manisha said, 'and close the door behind you.'

A look of concern swept across Simon's face as he sat down in the green leather chair next to Manisha's.

'Another fight?' Manisha calmly asked, looking at his fingers and hand which were now in a cast.

'Ah, yeah. I mean no. I trapped them in a door,' Simon said, clearly not having thought through his story.

'You trapped them in a door,' Manisha said with raised eyebrows while looking at Doulton. 'You're having your fair share of bad luck, aren't you?'

An awkward silence filled the room for a few seconds as Doulton and Manisha exchanged glances.

Doulton sat back in his chair, enjoying the theatre of what was about to unfold.

'Why did you try to steal my research data, Simon?' Manisha asked.

'I... I didn't,' Simon said, his hands trembled and his face blushed as he avoided her gaze.

'I have the evidence. I told you yesterday—no one touches my work without my consent. I have video footage of you using my computer while I was out of the lab. I recorded the mouse movements on my PC, so I know exactly which files you copied. The only thing I don't know is why.'

Simon sat like a rabbit in headlights.

Doulton leaned over his desk. 'Well?'

Simon swallowed hard, his hands shaking as the blood drained away from his face.

'What's happening, Simon?' Manisha asked, trying to be

sympathetic, but barely hiding her anger bubbling under the surface.

'He's threatening to kill me if I don't get the data he wants. He's threatened to kill me if I even tell anybody about this,' Simon said. His trembling hand passed across his clammy forehead.

'Who's threatening you?' Manisha asked.

'A bald-headed man. I don't know who he is, but he's going to kill me.'

'He's not going to kill you,' Doulton interjected.

'This sounds like a man who's been following me,' Manisha said, her eyes boring into Doulton's. 'Do you still think I'm paranoid?'

Doulton pawed at his chin, his smug look fading to concern as if a penny had dropped.

'Do you know this man?' Manisha asked, looking at Doulton.

'No, I don't,' Doulton said, frowning.

'What am I going to do?' Simon asked, with desperation in his voice.

'I suggest you go home, Simon,' Doulton said.

'I can't go home, he knows where I live,' Simon said in a high-pitched tone.

'Okay, okay, calm down. If you two can leave me, I'll make some calls,' Doulton offered.

Manisha shot an angry look at Doulton. A growing sense of nausea filled her stomach, while a question spun in her mind. *Who could you call to protect Simon, other than the police?*

Rising smoothly, she maintained her composure. For the first time in a long while, she felt she had finally broken through to Doulton. 'I'll leave you to clean up this mess, Nigel.'

As Manisha opened the door, she turned back towards Simon. 'I'm sorry you've got mixed up in all this.' She closed the door quietly behind her.

DOULTON LOOKED AT SIMON, who looked back with a mix of desperation and expectation.

'Take a seat outside, Simon.'

Simon complied and sat outside Doulton's office.

Doulton leaned back in his chair, deep in thought, tapping his fingers on his desk, before he grabbed his mobile and made the call.

'Good morning, Professor Doulton,' Laing said.

'We have a situation...' Doulton started.

'Oh, really. What's happened?'

'Have you or Redfern asked Simon to steal Manisha's research?'

'No, of course not. He's hardly had time to get his feet under the table.'

'Well, someone is forcing Simon to try and steal her work.'

'Do we have a data breach?'

'No, thankfully not. Manisha is far too shrewd with her security. However, Simon's life has been threatened. He's outside my office right now.'

'Who's threatened him?'

'Some bald-headed guy. That's all I have.'

'Do you know who this man is?'

'No. I don't know who he is or who he's working for, but he's hurting Simon. I told you we shouldn't get a student involved.'

'Is there anything else you can tell me?'

'Manisha is not happy. I'm even starting to believe that her paranoia is based on some kind of truth. She also thinks she is being followed by the same man.'

'Okay, leave it with me and I'll sort something out. Tell Simon to wait in reception.'

LAING HUNG up and immediately called Redfern.

'Yes,' the icy cold voice pierced Laing's ears.

'Ma'am, I have an update for you. The boy, Simon Perkins, is in danger. His life has been threatened. He needs protection.'

'Laing, I don't care. I told you to leave him.'

'Ma'am, we can't sit back and watch him being threatened. He's already had his nose and two fingers broken.'

'Who's threatening him and why?'

'I believe it's someone that is part of the Heylel network. I'm not sure who else it can be. They want Simon to get a copy of Manisha's research.'

'How's the girl taking all of this?'

'Naturally, she's not happy, Ma'am. She confronted Doulton, probing to see what he knows. She is also questioning him again about who her sponsors are and suggested that she may need to consider her options. What that means, I have no idea.'

'She's a clever woman. We can't underestimate her resolve,' Redfern said. 'Okay, you focus on Simon. Protect him for as long as you need to.'

'Are you sure, Ma'am? I should focus on protecting Manisha with this new threat in play. We can get the police to protect Simon.'

'Do not question my authority, Laing.'

Laing paused for a second. 'It feels like there's something you're not telling me, Ma'am.'

'I will tell you what you need to know when you need to know it. Until then, do exactly as I tell you and stop being so obstinate.'

The call ended, and Laing frowned. He'd never been ordered to take his eye off Manisha before.

He grabbed his jacket and left his car to babysit Simon.

REDFERN LEANED back in her leather and chrome office chair and turned to look out over the Thames. Like a game of chess, she had to keep control over all the pieces and think three steps ahead.

She walked over to her safe, retrieved the mobile phone, and dialled the now familiar number. A voice answered—a voice she'd become strangely attached to.

'Yes?'

'Your mission has changed. Focus on tracking Professor Williams twenty-four-seven. Like a cornered animal, she's now unpredictable. Do not lose her, even for a minute. Do you understand?'

'Yes, of course.'

18

'The mind is its own place, and in itself can make a heaven of hell, a hell of heaven.'

John Milton – Poet (1608–1674)

Manisha glanced at her watch as she left the Beecroft Building. It was 11:00 p.m. She'd spent most of the day indoors, underground, in artificial light. She breathed the fresh night air, welcoming the contrast to her stuffy lab. A cool breeze swept through her hair as she walked onto the moonlit streets, to where she'd locked her bike earlier that day. She turned on her bike light, which flickered before fading to darkness. She pushed the switch on and off several times before she gave up. 'Oh, great!' She looked up at the night sky. The afternoon sun had been replaced by a beautiful blanket of stars, which seduced her into taking the short walk back to her flat.

The beating Simon had received had unnerved her. She slung her rucksack over one shoulder and looked both ways down Parks Road. All was quiet, apart from a student staggering home from an evening at the pub, bouncing between a wall and a bus stop. She walked at a steady pace, keen to get home. The moonlight cast bright patches on the pavement, interspersed with the outlines of spring trees. Caught in her own thoughts, she deliberated over who would want to get hold of her research so badly. There must be an insider informing them of her progress. How much did they know? Could it be Doulton? She felt sick knowing that someone she trusted could betray her.

As she walked past the park entrance, she became aware of multiple footsteps. She looked into the park, only to be blinded by two men wearing head torches. They rounded the corner and ran towards her. She let out a shriek and clutched at her chest.

'Sorry,' the late-night joggers said as they glided past.

'For God's sake, girl. Get a grip.'

Manisha kept her head down and quickened her pace towards the Banbury Road. Her eyes were sore, and her head throbbed as she started the home stretch towards her flat. The stresses of the day weighed heavy on her mind. She had an overwhelming feeling that things would get worse before they got better. *Just get some sleep, Manisha. You'll feel better in the morning.*

In the distance, a man in a black hoodie stood at a bus stop. She considered crossing the road, but a stream of oncoming cars held her back.

His gaze followed her as she walked past. 'Evening,' he said, as he exhaled a thick cloud of smoke towards Manisha.

The distinct smell of weed filled her nostrils, making her cough. She shot him a look of disgust and peered into a void; his face hidden by a veil of darkness. Only his lips and high cheekbones were visible in the moonlight.

She quickened her pace. Her flat was only a few minutes' walk away. She looked over her shoulder and saw with a lurch of her stomach that the hooded man was following her. He flicked the remains of his spliff into the hedge, put his hands in his hoodie pockets, and took on a determined stride. Her heart pounded as she heard his footsteps gaining on her. She crossed the road, and half stepped into a jog to avoid a car. She considered waving it down but hesitated. *Just get home!*

Manisha took several purposeful strides before looking over her shoulder again. The man was still there, but he wasn't alone. She could see another figure, a distance behind, wearing similar clothes. Apart from the three of them, the streets were empty. Her breath was shallow and sharp. A thin layer of sweat began to form on her brow and her laptop bag hung heavy on her shoulder. As she neared Gee's she looked through its windows in desperation, hoping it would provide a refuge, but her heart sank as she saw the restaurant in darkness. She could hear her stalker getting closer and opened her rucksack, desperately rummaging for anything she could use to protect herself. Her fingers brushed against her can of body spray.

'Hey pretty, what's the hurry?'

Fear gripped her. 'Leave me alone,' she choked. Her right hand closed on the body spray, and she pulled it out. Throwing the rucksack back over her shoulder, she upped her pace.

'Where's the fun in that, my lovely?'

Footsteps got closer and she gripped the spray, her

hands trembling, hoping she wouldn't miss his eyes should she need to defend herself.

Her flat was only forty metres away. As she approached Canterbury Road, a hand grabbed her shoulder. She lost her balance as someone yanked her toward a black van, forcing her left arm behind her back. The back doors were slightly open. She let out a sharp scream, which was quickly smothered by a hand covering her mouth. Her fingers pressed down frantically on the body spray, desperate to make it work. Nothing happened; she'd forgotten to twist it to unlock. The van door was pulled wide open and a shove in her back sent her flying into the back of the van. Her hands shot out to save her fall, and she dropped the body spray, which clattered across the metal floor. She tried to scream again, but fear caught her voice, leaving only a whimper.

'What do you want?' Manisha said, mustering all the courage she had.

'I want what you have,' the man said as a wide smile spread across his face. He pulled his hoodie down revealing an unshaven face. 'Don't scream or struggle, else I'll make it worse for you.'

Manisha hurled herself at him, punching as hard as she knew how, her knuckles slamming painfully into his large frame. His firm grip held her wrists while she writhed, trying to escape, and then pushed her further into the van. He ripped some gaffer tape with his teeth and pasted it tight across her mouth, forcing her to breathe heavily through her nose. He turned her over and knelt on her, his knee digging hard in her back, making it even more difficult for her to breathe. She felt coarse rope wrap around her right wrist, stinging and burning as she tried to kick hard with her heels.

Manisha heard the van door open suddenly, and the van rocked as another person climbed inside. The man tying her hands shouted, surprised that someone else had entered the van, then Manisha felt the pressure of her attacker's knee release as a fight broke out between the two men. Fear drowned her. She was helpless. She used her free hand to push herself up and untie the rope, pulling and fumbling until she was free. Then, she ripped the gaffer tape from her mouth. Dark shadows in the van fought each other, causing it to sway. Fists flew as a series of heavy blows rained down on one of the men. In the darkness she was now confused as to who was her attacker and who was her saviour. One of the men kicked the other hard in the stomach, causing him to fall out of the van and land heavily on the tarmac. The second man jumped out after him and continued the fight.

Manisha grabbed the body spray and twisted the top. She edged out the door, past the two fighting men, avoiding flying fists, and tried to make her escape. Every fibre of her body screamed at her to run, but her legs were like jelly. As she turned, looking back to make sure the men were not following her, the dominant figure delivered a decisive blow, leaving his victim silent on the ground. Manisha remained frozen as he turned and began to approach her. Shivering, she tried to make out the man's features in the moonlight, hoping it would be a friendly face—only to find herself face to face with the bald man with piercing blue eyes she had seen from her window only a few days before. She gasped, but there was no hesitation: the body spray flooded his face. He cried out in anguish and screwed his eyes up tight as he blindly grabbed Manisha's wrist, trying to stop the torrent of pain. Instinctively, she clawed at his face with her left hand, leaving two deep, bloody wounds, as her nails sank deep into his skin. He released his grip, and his hand shot to his wounded cheek.

With both men now disabled, Manisha grabbed her rucksack and ran towards her flat, sobbing and fumbling for her key. Her shaking hand struggled to slide the key into the lock, but eventually it found its home, and the door opened. She stepped in and closed the door behind her, pressing her back against it, panting in the darkness, preying they had not heard where she had escaped. She checked all the locks on the door, hands shaking, as she tried to catch her breath. Adrenaline coursed through her body and her mind reeled, hoping neither man would try and follow her. She ran upstairs and peered through a gap in the curtains. Muffled voices were followed by the sound of an engine starting. She heard the screeching of tyres as a vehicle sped off and she saw a lone shadowy figure run across the road, clutching his face as he entered Park Town. He disappeared into the night, leaving the street quiet, as if nothing had happened.

She closed the curtains tight and switched on her bedside lamp. On her left hand, she could see blood and strands of skin caught deep under her fingernails. She ran into the bathroom and washed her hands, scrubbing hard, wanting the filth of her attacker removed from her body. The blood and skin made her retch as she thought of what might have been.

Manisha walked back to her bedroom, bouncing off the doorframe. She sank to the floor, with her back against her bed, trembling, as she tried to calm her racing mind. Had that been an attempted rape or an abduction? The face of the bald-headed man filled her mind. If he'd also attacked Simon, then he must be after her research. Should she call the police? But what could they do now the moment had passed—and she'd just washed away the DNA evidence.

She wanted to call Matthew. But there was nothing he could do as he was in Barcelona, celebrating his boat race win with some teammates. She would only worry him and spoil his trip. *Perhaps I should be working with the government. Then I would have protection, wouldn't I?* She put her head in her hands. 'Don't be stupid, Manisha. You can't risk this happening again.'

Manisha sobbed in the dimly lit room; her blouse stained with teardrops mixed with eyeliner. She thought through her options when a sudden moment of clarity gripped her. She glanced around the room, looking for her suitcase. She calmly stood up, pulled the suitcase down from the top of her wardrobe and started to pack enough clothes for a few days. If she needed more, she could buy them in Venice.

19

'Mind and intelligence are woven into the fabric of our universe in a way that altogether surpasses our understanding.'

Freeman Dyson – Physicist (1923–2020)

Manisha stood at the back of the water taxi, drinking in the beauty of the scene before her. The speed of the craft made her hair fly behind her as the sun glistened off the crests of a million tiny waves in the shallow lapis blue waters of Venice lagoon. The channel to the ancient city stretched into the distance, marked by large weathered wooden posts that guided her through a view millions of travellers had admired over hundreds of years.

The taxi slowed before entering a small canal on the edge of the city. It meandered along the narrow waterway.

Manisha gazed upwards, captivated by the unique architecture of the city. The tall Venetian buildings provided welcome shade from the heat of the sun as she admired the houses, churches and palaces, all built on a billion logs thrust into the soft lagoon bed. Small boats moored next to narrow entrances bobbed up and down in the taxi's wake, as passing gondolas gave couples a romantic tour of the city.

They left the warren of tiny canals and entered the Grand Canal. The magnificent and busy waterway, cutting through the heart of the city, opened up before them. Ornate buildings commissioned by long dead merchants dominated the waterfront, ensuring their presence was still felt through their architectural legacy. Most buildings were faded by hundreds of years of weathering and decay, but some still displayed the extraordinary gold exteriors and lavish mosaics that had adorned many merchants' houses when the city was in its prime.

Manisha breathed in deep, trying to put the fear and anxiety she had felt in Oxford behind her. She looked out over the Grand Canal, knowing that escaping from Oxford had been the right thing to do. However, she could hear her mother's voice saying, *'You can escape your troubles for a while, but you always have to confront them.'* The dilemma she would have to face was when and how to return to Oxford safely. Suppressing her trauma, she focused on enjoying the peace and embracing the unique atmosphere of Venice.

The boat approached the Rialto Bridge: a stunning white structure which linked the two sides of the canal in one magnificent, ornate span. Manisha looked up and caught the eye of a bride, full of smiles and tears, posing for photos with her new husband. She thought of Matthew and looked forward to talking to him once she had settled into her flat.

'Which stop, *Signorina*?' the pilot asked.

'Near St Mark's Square, *grazie*,' Manisha said, using her rudimentary Italian.

He smiled back at her. '*Prego.*'

Manisha took photos on her phone of the hustle and bustle of the Grand Canal with countless gondolas, water taxis and vaporettos ferrying people along the ancient waterway. Ornate buildings covered in bright and colourful banners advertising the Venice art scene captivated her. Manisha's eyes were wide, absorbing the breath-taking views. 'Your city is amazing!' she shouted to the pilot.

'*Grazie, signorina,*' he said with a wide smile.

The aroma of spices and garlic from nearby restaurants mingled with the putrid stench of a passing garbage barge—an assault on her senses. The city was alive. Alive with tourists and locals, who were easy to distinguish; the tourists with their phones out, snapping everything in sight, and the locals, stern faced and stylish, wishing they could take their precious, overpopulated city back to the way it had been forty years ago.

St Mark's Campanile, the columns of The Venice Lion and St Theodore, and the bright white facade of the Doge's Palace, welcomed Manisha to the city she had wanted to visit since being a child.

The water taxi dropped her outside the Doge's Palace, and she paid the pilot his one hundred and twenty euros. She stood, taking in the sights, before using her map to find her way to *Vita*.

She headed over a bridge which provided a perfect view of the Bridge of Sighs. Stopping at the highest point amongst the crowds, she studied the ancient construction. The bridge before her dwarfed its counterpart back home in Oxford, being bigger, more solid, and more secure, with its purpose being far more poignant—connecting the Doge's Palace courtrooms to the city's dungeons. She imagined the thousands of prisoners who would have had their final view of the beautiful Venice lagoon through the decorative holes in the bridge. Their last glimpse of sunshine before they were condemned to the darkness of the dungeons, and their inevitable fate.

Manisha made her way down the other side of the bridge, struggling with her suitcase through hundreds of tourists jostling to get their photo trophies. Thousands of images, destined to be uploaded to social media by excited travellers proving to their friends back home that "they were there," before quickly moving on to the next photo opportunity.

On the other side of the bridge, she was met by groups of sightseers—Japanese, German, American—each with a tour guide holding up their own recognisable object. A green umbrella, a red and gold flag proudly showing the Venetian Lion, and the American stars and stripes, each followed by eager tourists listening to their tour guides on a radio earpiece.

Manisha pulled out the map that Julie had given her and continued along the Venice waterfront.

Laing had received the alert from GCHQ the previous day, confirming Manisha had booked a flight from London to Venice. Redfern hadn't instructed him to follow Manisha, which was unusual. Normally she led efficiently, without delays. Laing felt he had to protect Manisha and, preferring to ask for forgiveness rather than wait for permission, had booked a seat on the same flight. He'd put a call in to MI6 in Venice, knowing local knowledge and support would be essential, Venice being a maze of narrow streets and waterways and his Italian being almost non-existent.

The flight had been uneventful, and Laing was through airport security in no time. He met up with his MI6 contact, James McCray, on the other side of Customs. McCray was a small Scottish man with a thin frame but muscular build, wearing tan chinos and a navy Harrington jacket. They shook hands and quickly went to the dock side. Travelling by boat was the most logical way—and for some people, *the only way*—to get into the heart of Venice. As soon as they had met, McCray had given Laing a small box containing a radio mic and earpiece, so they could stay in contact easily and inconspicuously.

They had followed Manisha into Venice at a distance and watched her jump out of her water taxi near St Mark's square.

Laing looked through binoculars at the Venice pontoons. Thousands of tourists lined the seafront. 'Following her is going to be interesting,' he said.

'We should be fine.' McCray said. 'Based on her internet access, she only looked at one flat in Venice. I'm quite sure she's booked to stay in a flat called *Vita*.'

McCray pointed to the shoreline. 'That large building with arches along the bottom is the Doge's Palace. We'll talk more about its significance later.'

McCray took his boat a further thirty metres across the Venice seafront from where Manisha had been dropped off and landed at the San Zaccaria pontoons, keeping Manisha in sight.

Laing jumped from the boat while McCray secured it. Instinctively, they took up the double surveillance relay.

'I'll head into the San Zaccaria Square; that's the route I expect Manisha to take,' McCray said over his radio mic.

Laing walked along the pontoon and lost himself in the masses opposite the pink exterior of the Danieli Hotel. He kept his calm as he momentarily lost Manisha in a crowd of tourists, flags and umbrellas hampering his view. 'Where are you, Manisha?'

~

Manisha weaved her way through the chaos, past the Danieli Hotel, over another packed bridge and through a small archway, past a police station and on towards San Zaccaria church. The quiet square she found herself in was a stark contrast to the hustle and bustle of the main thoroughfare.

She stopped and studied the printed map. Finding her position, she got her bearings and continued across to the left corner of the square, under an ancient archway and past *Trattoria da Nino.* The smell of freshly cooked pasta made her realise how hungry she was. 'Just find the flat, Manisha. You can get some food later', she murmured, as she walked through the back streets and over a small bridge.

~

McCray stood in the shade, leaning against a water fountain outside San Zaccaria church, sunglasses on, smoking a cigarette. It was a habit he had tried to give up many times, but he used it as a convenient excuse to blend in and look like a local. He was excited to be working with a partner for the first time in a long time. He had heard a lot about Laing from other colleagues who worked for MI5 and knew he had a reputation for being open and direct; a character trait he admired, and which was useful in this instance, as they wouldn't have time for normal pleasantries.

He watched Manisha as she stopped, reviewed her map and continued across the square under the archway opposite, just as he'd expected. Laing walked through the square and followed Manisha past Nino's on the left. McCray followed in turn, watching Laing slip past Manisha on her blind side outside *da Roberto's* restaurant, and onto a small stone bridge.

'Look right now and you'll see an ochre stone balcony with brown chairs, about a hundred feet down the canal. That's *Vita*,' McCray said through Laing's earpiece. 'If you take the next three right turns, you'll be at the front door. However, go past the third right, as it's a dead end. Otherwise, you could end up face to face with Manisha and she'll wonder why there's someone standing outside her door.'

'Okay, great,' Laing said. 'You've done your homework.'

'MI6 are renowned for it; haven't you heard?'

McCray heard a laugh in his earpiece. He continued to follow Manisha at a safe distance while Laing found a secluded spot further on from the alleyway leading to *Vita*.

McCray watched Manisha looking at every door and down every alleyway, trying to find her way. 'I think she's lost,' McCray murmured into his mic.

'I'm not surprised. This place is like a rabbit warren.'

'Okay, she's read her map and she's back on track and coming towards you,' McCray warned Laing.

'She's overshot her turning.'

'I'm on it.' McCray sped up, dodging the crowds to catch up with Manisha who had stopped again to review the map.

'*Buonasera, Bella,*' McCray said, '*Si è persa? Posso aiutarla?*'

Manisha stood, clutching her chest. '*Buonasera*,' she said as she studied McCray. 'Sorry, do you speak English?'

'Sorry, *Bella*, I didn't mean to scare you. Are you lost? Can I help?' McCray switched to an impressive Italian-English accent, while nodding to the map Manisha was studying. He felt her eyes pierce him, as if trying to work out if she could trust the stranger before her. He smiled and her gazed softened.

'I'm trying to find a flat called *Vita*,' Manisha pointed to the map. 'I know it's close, but I just can't find it.'

McCray looked both ways down the narrow alleyway, making out he didn't know exactly where to go. Looking at the map and scratching his chin, he led Manisha away from Laing, taking the first left into the passageway which led to *Vita*.

'I think this is the place you're looking for, *Bella*.' McCray grinned and bowed to the beautiful woman before him. He looked directly into her eyes, weighing her up.

'*Ah, grazi*. Thank you,' Manisha smiled nervously.

'*Prego*. Enjoy your time in Venice,' McCray walked off down the alleyway and turned left, in the opposite direction to Laing.

'She nearly jumped out of her skin,' McCray said to Laing over his radio mic. 'She's on edge.'

'She got every reason to be. That's why we're here,' Laing said.

MANISHA PUSHED the key into the solid oak door and turned it. The lock clunked, and the door opened, revealing a blend of modern and historic—a contemporary leather sofa and glass table set alongside an ancient stone floor and wooden beams. A small kitchen and dining area lay to her right, and a comfortable seating area with large soft cushions and a TV to her left. Looking up, she saw a balcony leading to a bedroom. Through the middle of the flat she could see a double-height ceiling with ornate wooden cornice, showing the opulence of centuries gone by.

A note had been left on the kitchen table under a bottle of red wine, with a sourdough loaf and cheese under a napkin. The message from Julie, written by Vita's caretaker, read:

Dear Manisha,

Enjoy Vita, and the wine! The flat is yours for as long as you need it.

Love, Julie x

Manisha smiled at her friend's lovely note and the gift of wine, which she immediately opened, pouring herself a glass before continuing to explore the flat. The scent of flowers and sea salt filled the air.

A door led from the kitchen onto a spacious ochre stone balcony with brightly coloured mosaic floor and wooden seating. She walked out onto the balcony and looked over the canal below towards a small bridge beyond. It was swarming with tired tourists making their way through Venice as dusk approached, bringing the end to another long day. Tired feet in search of food and a place to sleep for the night.

A gondola drifted past, the gondolier skilfully guiding the majestic craft through the narrow waterway with minimal effort. His passengers were a young, happy Western couple enjoying the Venice experience. A beaming smile shone from the woman's face as she smelled her red rose and cuddled close to her lover.

Manisha took a sip from her glass, then went back inside to explore the upper level of the flat. The ancient wooden staircase creaked as she carried her suitcase to the bedroom. She opened the door to a spacious and lavish room, with red silk-lined walls and a Murano glass chandelier. An outside balcony, directly above the one from the kitchen, shared the same pleasing view, only from a higher elevation. She unpacked the limited supply of clothes and put her toiletries into the marble-tiled en-suite.

Once back downstairs, she poured another glass of wine, cut some bread and cheese, pulled her laptop out of her rucksack and switched it on. Vita's information pack provided the Wi-Fi code as the machine booted. Within minutes, Manisha was online and connected to her lab back in Oxford—the VPN she'd installed without Doulton's knowledge proving its worth.

She checked the security logs and could see Doulton, and the Beecroft caretaker, had both tried to enter the lab within quick succession. No doubt Doulton would be spooked by no longer having access to one of the physics department's greatest assets, and at feeling he was no longer in control.

Another log entry showed they'd tried, unsuccessfully, to circumvent the security she'd put in place. She smiled, pleased her security measures were holding firm.

Manisha switched to another app and hooked into the security cameras she had installed in her lab; additional to the ones the Oxford security team had already installed. These monitored her experiments twenty-four-seven and gave her a view of her lab door, her main lab area, the rack of computer equipment and the equipment used to capture thought energy.

She checked her monitoring system to confirm it was configured to text her newly purchased pay-as-you-go mobile, should anyone attempt to change any security settings.

Finally, she opened an app on the remote system within her lab and sent a text, hiding her true location. The simple text went to Julie:

I have arrived safely. Thanks for everything. Love Manisha x

'Very good,' Laing said as he saw McCray come out of the alleyway.

'The Italian lessons do come in useful,' McCray switched back to his Scottish accent. 'I also took the opportunity to slip a tracker into her rucksack.'

Laing went silent, not sure whether he was happy or annoyed with McCray's improvisation. 'What does it look like?'

'It looks like a Euro. Even if she finds it, she won't know what it really is. The worst that can happen is she spends it. I'll give you the code for your tracker app and we can both keep track of her.'

'Okay. I guess it will be useful around here. I have no idea where I am.'

Laing caught up with McCray, and they retraced their steps over the bridge opposite *Vita* and saw Manisha sipping her wine and making her way back into the flat as a gondola drifted past.

At that moment Laing spotted someone who was of

concern. 'Split. You carry straight on,' Laing said, giving the command quietly to McCray over his earpiece.

Laing took a sharp right, and McCray went straight on.

'What just happened?' McCray asked.

'In front of you, there's a man in aviator mirrored glasses and a black baseball cap. He has a deep scratch on his right cheek. It's no coincidence he's here. I've seen him several times in Oxford and even outside the building where Manisha works. I don't want him to know I'm here as he will recognise me. It'll remove our element of surprise. You follow him; but keep your distance.'

'Okay,' McCray confirmed. 'It's good to have a bit of action to keep me on my toes.'

Laing peered around a corner as McCray walked past the suspect and stood outside *da Roberto's*, inspecting the menu. Laing slipped behind an archway as the man in the black cap walked past.

McCray glanced over his sunglasses to see which direction the man had headed. 'He's stopped on the bridge overlooking *Vita*. He's staring straight at the flat, grinning like an idiot,' McCray said.

'Then there's no doubt. He's our biggest threat.' Laing frowned, concerned how anyone else could have known Manisha was in Venice so quickly. 'We cannot lose him. Manisha is in real danger,' he said, trusting his intuition with a growing sense of unease.

20

'Art has a double face, of expression and illusion, just like science has a double face: the reality of error and the phantom of truth.'

René Daumal – Author (1908–1944)

After checking that all doors and windows were locked, Manisha sat down on the double-seated brown leather sofa to deliberate her next move. It was surreal to find herself in Venice at such short notice. She let out a long, deep sigh, relieved to feel safe and hidden away. Manisha looked through her photos of her trip through Venice, and one picture in particular jumped out at her. A multicoloured double helix on a twenty-foot-square banner advertising the Venice Biennale was paired with the slogan:

Art for Life...

> *Dynamic*
> *Natural*
> *Art*

> *... it's in your DNA.*

She became engrossed in the banner as if her sixth sense were telling her that the image was important. She'd learned to trust her intuition over the years and sat fixated on the photo she'd taken advertising the Biennale. 'Why is this so important? DNA, DNA, deoxyribonucleic acid?' She sat upright, her heart beating with excitement. 'Surely it's not that easy?'

She connected her PC to the soft phone in her lab and called Simon. 'Where are you?' Manisha asked, without wasting time with the usual etiquette.

'I'm staying at a friend's hous...'

Manisha heard Simon's sentence cut short, as if the penny had dropped.

'Don't ask me to do anything for you, Manisha, I'm scared enough as it is.'

'I need you to go to the lab and run an experiment for me.'

'Manisha, I'm a terrified, paranoid wreck. I'm sure that nutter is still stalking me. I don't want to be involved in this anymore, and that's final.'

'I think I've found the answer, Simon. I just need to prove it. You want to know, don't you?'

'Of course I do. But staying alive is at the top of my priority list right now.'

'Well, if you don't want to be part of a life-changing

discovery, and for your name to go down in history, that's your choice.'

The conversation fell silent for several seconds while Manisha chewed her lip, silently willing Simon to agree to help.

'Argh, what do you want me to do?'

'I need you to go to my lab and run a fresh experiment. But first we will need to analyse your blood.'

'My *blood?* How much?'

'Don't worry. Just a few drops. Then we can run another experiment.'

'So, it's my blood you want now? You don't ask for much, do you? I guess you want that immediately?'

'Yes,' Manisha confirmed. 'I can get you into my lab. When can you be there?'

'Bloody hell, Manisha. What if that nutter sees me? Where are you, anyway?'

'Where I am is not important, Simon. Just go over to the Beecroft Building. I'll call you at 7:00 p.m. and let you into my lab. Okay?'

'I'm just a bloody lab rat to you, aren't I?'

Manisha could hear the lilt in his voice. 'Thank you, Simon.'

SIMON SAT on a secluded bench outside the Beecroft Building, hoodie covering his head, waiting for his phone to ring. He looked out cautiously from under his hood, hoping he wouldn't see the man in black. His mind wandered, excited about the possibilities of what this discovery could mean, but also scared at risking his life to help Manisha. He thought about leaving and heading back to his friends flat, when his phone rang, making him jump.

'Are you at Beecroft?' Manisha asked.

'Yes. Can we just get this over with before I change my mind?'

'Do you have your pass to get in?'

'No, Doulton took it off me so I wouldn't be tempted to go back to your lab.' Simon laughed nervously. 'Like that would ever happen! It's fine, I can tailgate someone.'

'Fair enough. Stay on the line and get into the building. I'll do the rest.'

Simon lingered outside the Beecroft Building, waiting for his opportunity. A couple of students made their way towards the entrance, talking and laughing. 'Here goes,' Simon said, holding his bank card in his hand, pretending to swipe through, as the out-of-hours security guard looked on from behind the reception desk. 'I'm in,' he said, as he walked across the main entrance hall, through a single door and down the staircase to the Beecroft labs. 'I'm probably going to lose you soon as the signal will drop.'

'I'll let ... in and call ... landline...' Manisha's voice crackled, and the line went dead.

Simon approached the lab door, which opened on cue. He walked into the office and the desk phone in the main lab rang immediately. Simon rushed through, picked it up, and pressed the receiver to his ear.

'Put me on speakerphone and I'll talk you through what I need you to do,' Manisha instructed.

Simon pressed the speakerphone button and put the handset down. 'So, what's your big idea?

'Well, it's a theory that's been playing on my mind this evening.' Manisha's voice echoed around the lab. 'I can't tell you what it is, Simon, you know that.'

'Yeah, yeah, I guess.'

'I don't like putting you in this situation, especially after everything you've been through, but you can't even tell anyone we've run a new experiment.'

'I know I can't. I'll blank it out and forget it ever happened. I'm good at that,' Simon said, feeling nervous about the mess he was involved in, only to be pulled back to reality by Manisha's instructions.

'Okay, first I need you to get a clean petri dish from the fridge behind you. On the shelf above you'll find sterilised needles.'

Simon clumsily got the items as requested and then looked up at the camera, his stomach churned as he knew what he was going to be asked to do next.

'You just need to prick your finger with the needle and put a few drops of blood in the petri dish.'

Simon felt queasy as he opened the petri dish and took the needle from its packet. He stood, the needle shaking in his right hand while pointing it at his two uncast fingers on his left hand.

'What's the matter?' Manisha asked.

'I hate needles. Hang on, can you see me?'

'Of course. I'm dialled into the lab, and I have cameras everywhere.'

Simon looked around the lab, picking out the cameras and waved at one.

'It's okay, you'll hardly feel it,' Manisha said, urging Simon to get the job done.

'I hate blood, too.' His hands shook as he tried to summon the courage to pierce his finger with the sharp point. 'Arrrgh, why am I doing this?'

'The longer you spend thinking about doing something, the harder it is to do it,' Manisha said.

'Bloody hell.' His hands shook as he got close to piercing his skin—and then his hand holding the needle backed off again.

'Oh, for God's sake, man up and prick your finger.' Manisha's voice bounced around the room.

'Arrgh...' Simon pulled the needle back slightly, closed his eyes, and then thrust the needle into his finger. 'Ouch! Oh, that wasn't as bad as I thought,' Simon said, smiling at the camera.

He looked back at his hand to see a big droplet of blood forming on his finger. Blood drained from his face.

'Put the blood in the petri dish and grab a tissue from the box in front of you.'

'I need to sit down...' Simon slumped into the chair and squeezed his finger over the petri dish. His face screwed up as he looked out the corner of his eye at the blood dripping from his finger. He grabbed some tissues, covered his finger, and sat willing the room to stop spinning. He held the tissue tight and looked down at the floor.

'Well done, Simon. If you want some chocolate to get your sugar level up, there's some in the drawer on your right.'

Simon took the chocolate, feeling like a child being rewarded for good behaviour.

'Behind you on the right is a white dome-shaped machine. Place the petri dish in the opening.'

Simon got up, feeling a little unsteady, and placed the petri dish in the scanner. 'Okay, done.'

'I'll run the scan from here.'

The machine's lights flashed as it silently scanned Simon's blood.

'Great. Now sit in the large chair, like you did last time, and relax. You'll have to place the energy scanner over your face yourself, and I can do the rest from here. I've done all the preparation. The vacuum chamber is clear and tested to ensure there is no residual energy left from the previous scan.'

'Do you treat your boyfriends like this?'

Manisha ignored the question. 'Make sure you don't get any blood on my equipment.'

Simon lay on the 'dentist chair' as he called it, feeling relieved that he could lie down. He got comfortable before reaching up for the equipment with his right, unbloodied, hand. The chair automatically reclined further as he pulled the energy scanner down, ensuring his face was parallel to the device.

'That's great,' Manisha said. 'You know the drill: take deep breaths, relax, and start to focus on a single image. Make it clear and obvious to me.'

Simon closed his eyes, his finger pulsing, as the blood started to return to his head. The equipment went through its calibration tests in readiness to capture the energy his brain was casting out to the world around him. He achieved a relaxed state far quicker than the first time, and the scanner responded, only taking two minutes to complete the scan.

'Excellent. You're getting better at this,' Manisha said.

'A lab rat knows its way out of the maze faster the second time around. When do you think you'll know the result?'

'I need to enter the details from your blood scan into the algorithm and then start the decoding process. There's a massive number of combinations. It could take five minutes or several days to unlock that mind of yours.'

'Okay, I won't wait up. Is there anything else you want me to do? Or are you going to set the lab rat free?'

'No, that's it. Thanks for your help, Simon. I'll let you know when, or if, I get a result.'

'I'll let myself out.' Simon waved at the camera. 'Bye.'

MANISHA WATCHED Simon leave and secure the door behind him. She entered the results from Simon's blood scan into the system and set her algorithm running. She breathed in deeply and looked on as the attempts to decode the energy steadily increased. 'All I can do now is wait.'

She poured another small glass of wine and rummaged in the freezer, where she found a pizza to cook. Lost in her own thoughts, she suddenly realised, for the first time in weeks, she felt relaxed and safe. No one knew where she was, apart from Julie. The sense of freedom at being away from prying eyes and the scrutiny of management filled her with joy. The thought of being close to a breakthrough elated her even further. She watched the number of combinations tested increase, knowing an alert would sound when an image with form was detected.

Midnight came and went. After nearly five hours of her computer systems running at full stretch, only seven per cent of the possible combinations had been processed. She grabbed her phone and did the maths to extrapolate how long this process could take. 'Three days!' She slumped back into the sofa and drained her wineglass, her elation turning into momentary dejection. 'What will be, will be. I'll find a way.'

Manisha set her laptop volume as high as it would go, before taking herself, and the laptop, upstairs to the bedroom. She stripped off and climbed into the shower. The warm water splashed her face, relieving her tired eyes. She relaxed, finding welcome relief from the stresses of the last few weeks, and her terrifying ordeal only twenty-four hours ago. She'd escaped to a sanctuary. A place where no one could find her, and where she could progress her work in peace.

After drying herself, she put on a long, baggy T-shirt, switched off the lights and opened the door to the balcony overlooking the canal. Warm air had accumulated in the room during the heat of the day, and she longed for a cool breeze. She slid into bed and lay there, stunned by how quiet Venice was at night. No traffic, no motorbikes, no noisy students staggering home from a night out. Just the gentle lapping of water from the canal outside and a cool breeze caressing her face. 'This is so lovely.' She turned on her side, clutching her smooth, clean pillow, and stared at her laptop. The soft glow from the screen lit her face. She hung on to her optimism, knowing this could be the answer she needed to take her work forward. Closing her eyes, Manisha drifted into a peaceful, deep sleep.

McCray had followed the man with the black cap around Venice for several hours while Laing familiarised himself with the maze of alleyways around Manisha's flat. He watched their suspect eat in a restaurant and drink a non-alcoholic beer before he headed back to a pontoon outside the Danieli Hotel. The man climbed on board a small boat and made a short journey to the side of the Doge's Palace. The boat was moored under the Bridge of Sighs, next to a door which led directly into the palace. He checked the moorings and walked through the door, the lock giving a solid clunk as it closed behind him. Then, everything was quiet.

'All the lights are off in Manisha's flat,' Laing said through his earpiece.

'That must be it for the night,' McCray said. 'We know everyone's location.'

'Yeah, now I just need to find somewhere to stay.'

McCray sensed a weariness in Laing's voice. 'That's been taken care of.'

'Great, where?'

'You're in *Hotel Fontana*, top floor with a view of the bridge that looks over Manisha's flat.

'Perfect,' Laing said. 'That's a relief. I've found three routes to *Vita* so far. Are there any more?'

'The main route is over the bridge, but don't worry about other routes. I've already installed a wireless infrared camera so we can see if anyone approaches her door.'

'Ha, well done.'

'The camera is accessible via your phone. I just need to install the app with the camera's code. I'll do it when we get to the hotel.'

'Okay, thanks.'

'You'll have company tonight, I'm afraid. I booked a twin room so we could monitor Manisha and take turns sleeping.'

'Excellent, I didn't know MI6 were so capable.'

'Piss off.' McCray laughed, enjoying the traditional banter between their sections.

'Is there anything you haven't thought of?' Laing asked.

McCray's Scottish accent took on a more mischievous tone. 'Well, I thought of arranging a few bottles of red wine and a couple of lovely Venetian masked women for the night, but I thought that would be too much of a distraction.'

Laing laughed. 'That would have been a good way to end the day.'

∽

LAING MET McCray in *San Zaccaria* square. They made their way to their hotel room and checked the video surveillance equipment. McCray sat at the window with his phone charging. The ghostly screen displayed an image of the alleyway leading to Manisha's door. All was quiet.

'Your man dressed in black. He's definitely part of Heylel,' McCray said.

'How do you know?'

'The Doge's Palace is one of Heylel's strongholds. It's been a hub of Heylel activities for a long time, centuries even. The Doge was the military leader, or Duke, of Venice back in the day. So, it makes sense that it's a seat of power that Heylel would want to occupy and influence.'

'Makes sense,' Laing replied.

Heylel had been born from a desire for power—a coming together of influential figures from powerful and wealthy dynasties around the world, whose sole purpose was to secure yet more power and wealth through the influence and control of human progression. The Doge's Palace, with its rich history and domination over trade routes, was a place Heylel naturally wanted to control in the fourteenth and fifteenth centuries. In the twenty-first century Heylel had more modern ways of expressing global power. Laing knew from his briefings that Heylel owned companies and organisations across the globe, with the ability to influence billions. Venice, and the Doge's Place, was just one of the strategic locations for the organisation. It was the bridge between Eastern and Western Europe. In the modern era, it was not as critical as some other locations, such as New York, London, Brussels, and Beijing, but it was still high up there.

'So, this lady and her work,' McCray glanced and nodded out of the window, 'she seems harmless enough. Why doesn't the government just ask for her cooperation and fund her research?'

'If she found out her work is going to be used by the government for intelligence gathering, she'd stop. Unknown to her, the government are already funding her work. Until she gets her technology fully operational, I've been instructed to observe and protect. No interaction. She's a very smart woman. However, an incident in Oxford when her lab assistant was threatened has really spooked her.'

'No wonder she's trying to lie low,' McCray said. 'She's a very beautiful woman too,' he smiled.

'Indeed.' Laing said, keeping his thoughts to himself. 'I'll get showered and take the first stretch of sleep and take over at 2:00 a.m. Sound good?'

'Sounds good.'

ZAREK LAY ON HIS BED, happy that Manisha was exactly where he expected her to be. His room was small and basic, with a stone floor and a wooden bed in what used to be a prison cell. Moonlight flooded through a small, barred window at the top of the cell, casting a shadow of a cross on the floor. Much of his teaching had been completed within the Doge's Palace and he knew Venice intimately. Many would have expected more refined accommodation for someone of such importance to Heylel, but Zarek was just happy to be back in one of the organisation's strongholds. He felt at home here, knowing he had the run of the palace should he need it.

He grabbed his laptop and hooked into the Oxford security cameras, reviewing the day's activity recorded by the camera in Manisha's lab. He put the playback on 8x speed, expecting to see nothing of interest. But his attention was gripped as he saw Simon enter the lab, and he changed the playback to normal speed. Although there was no sound, he could see Simon answer the phone and talk on speaker phone.

Zarek watched the playback twice before switching to the real-time view of the camera. He could see the lights in Manisha's machine room lit up and flashing furiously. He smiled, knowing Manisha must have progressed her research to allow Simon to enter her lab again.

He switched off his laptop and tried to drift off to sleep. However, his mind raced as he realised what achieving his goal after so long would mean. *The secret will be mine, and my masters will honour me.*

Zarek closed his eyes and practised his visualisations. Imagining his deepest desires in precise detail, he allowed sleep to take him away to a world of subconscious dreams.

21

'Through conscious beings the universe has generated self-awareness. This can be no trivial detail, no minor by-product of mindless, purposeless forces. We are truly meant to be here.'

Paul Davies – Physicist (1946–)

Manisha awoke to a cool morning breeze drifting through the open window. She lay still, watching the assortment of shadows and bright patches dance across the bedroom floor as the curtains flapped gently. She stretched her arms to the heavens, took a deep breath, and smiled, happy to see the rooftops of Venice outside the window. She stared at the large, wall-mounted clock in disbelief. It was five past ten, and she hadn't slept this late for months.

She tapped the mouse on her PC and entered her password. The progress tracker on the algorithm running back in Oxford had only reached twenty per cent, confirming her calculations were correct—just seven per cent progress every five hours.

Manisha pulled on her jeans and a white blouse, tying it loosely at the waist. She slipped into a pair of dark-blue deck shoes, found her sunglasses, and locked her PC. The cool morning breeze beckoned her onto the balcony, and the warmth of the sun kissed her face. The waters of the canal reflected the surrounding buildings like a mirror. Stepping back inside, she closed and locked the balcony door, then checked that her heart-shaped pendant was around her neck. Satisfied, she left the flat in search of food, locking the door securely behind her.

The streets of Venice were starting to get busy with tourists keen to make the most of the beautiful day. Manisha retraced her steps from the previous afternoon, walking over the bridge with a view of *Vita* and on to *da Roberto's*. She took a seat outside overlooking the bridge, and a waiter promptly arrived to take her order.

'Cosa posso portarti, signorina?'

'Can I have an orange juice, a black coffee and a croissant, *grazie*?' Manisha asked, assuming the waiter had just requested her order.

'Certo, signorina,' the waiter said and hurried off into the restaurant.

People-watching was a luxury Manisha hadn't enjoyed in a long time. The combination of Venetians and tourists made for interesting viewing. The Venetians were outnumbered by at least ten to one, trying to stride through the crowds with a definite purpose, whilst being openly annoyed at the meandering tourists who stopped suddenly, taking in the sights.

Although Manisha enjoyed people-watching in a new city, deep down she felt alone and afraid. Her thoughts drifted to her father, wondering how different life would be if he were still alive. She imagined what he would be like now, longing for his fatherly wisdom to guide her through her challenges at work. Often, she dreamed of working alongside him, so they could progress their research together. She missed him deeply and had resigned herself to feeling this way for the rest of her life. The injustice of losing him so young fuelled both her grief and her growing distrust of Doulton. Now, more than ever, she was determined to uncover the truth about what had really happened to him.

Her breakfast was quickly delivered as she continued to watch people meandering by; the unceasing crowd getting larger and larger. She imagined thousands of thoughts being cast out by the minds of the individuals. Each person crafting a unique experience of life, shaped by their own perceptions and emotions. No two realities were the same. Each individual observed a different version of Venice, their own personal lens colouring the ancient city's streets.

She could tell what some people were thinking just by their expressions—eyes wide and smiling, captivated by the stunning architecture or their beautiful lover. Others drifted into daydreams, oblivious to their surroundings, their minds elsewhere; a work e-mail that had stressed them, a hunger for food, a longing for an absent lover or the void of someone they had loved and lost. Regrets of the past and dreams of the future consumed them, leaving little room for the present. *The only thing that truly exists is the here and now. Nothing else is real*, Manisha thought. *Mindfulness should be taught in schools*, she concluded.

As Manisha watched the crowd, she imagined all the

invisible thoughts filling the air, bouncing off the surrounding people. She considered how a strong emotional bond, like those purported between twins, close family members and lovers, seemed to unlock the capacity to feel, instinctively, what the other person was thinking or experiencing. Manisha still *felt* a close connection with her father. *Is it possible to feel the thoughts of someone who has died?* she wondered.

Her own thoughts were drawn back to her goal: to help people who had lost the power to communicate to regain their quality of life. Her mother had been a very active woman with a large circle of friends whom she had loved to talk to. Manisha and her father had watched as one by one her friends had slowly drifted away because it was so difficult to communicate with her after her stroke. When her mother had died, soon after her father, Manisha had known she needed to make a difference in the world. The person who would enable future stroke victims to communicate with loved ones, ensuring they no longer lived in a lonely world. They would finally be able to express their love to the loyal few who still took the time to see them, even though the conversation had been entirely one-sided.

Doulton and whatever was motivating him troubled her. She had to find a way of protecting her technology, once it was ready for medical practice. Unless the code was encrypted, a specialist in the military could reverse engineer her equipment. *Slow down, Manisha. First, you need to have something to protect!*

She finished her breakfast and left a twenty-euro note as payment and a tip. '*Grazie*,' she said as she handed the waiter the silver bill tray.

She walked through the crowds she'd spent the last hour

watching, unaware that she had been watched the entire time.

LAING stood in his hotel room, looking out of the window with a perfect view over the restaurant where Manisha had been enjoying her breakfast. McCray sat inside the restaurant and watched Manisha through the window as she walked away in the direction of *Vita*.

'It looks like our scar-faced friend has also joined the party,' Laing said to McCray.

'Where is he?'

'He's standing outside *Trattoria da Nino*, the restaurant to the left of our hotel, behind a tall revolving menu stand.'

'I can see him,' McCray said as he left his breakfast table.

Laing watched as Manisha stopped outside a shop selling hundreds of multi-coloured Venetian masks.

'You follow Manisha. I can keep an eye on both her and our friend from here.'

As she walked on, Laing's eyes followed her, instructing McCray when to follow and when to hold back.

'It looks like you've got company,' Laing warned McCray. 'Our scarred friend is on the move.'

'I'll hold back and let him pass, so I can keep an eye on them both. Hopefully she'll just go back to the flat.'

'She's on to something,' Laing said. 'While you've been enjoying your breakfast, I've reviewed her calls.'

'I thought she'd stopped using the mobile you tapped?' McCray said.

'She has, but yesterday evening she called her lab landline, which is also tapped. She spoke to Simon Perkins, a student who's assisting with her research.'

'What was the call about?'

'It looks like she may have discovered how to progress her work. Tests are running on her system back in Oxford as we speak. If this is the key to advancing her work, then we'll have something of importance to protect.' He narrowed his eyes as Manisha turned a corner. 'Manisha's taken the turn back to *Vita*, and she's out of my line of sight,' he said, 'and our friend is just about to pass you.'

Laing watched as McCray stopped and looked in the same shop window as Manisha had. 'I can see him in the reflection,' McCray whispered.

The man dressed in black walked past at pace, his black baseball cap standing high in the crowd.

McCray turned to follow him and took a right down the next alleyway. 'I can see them both,' he said. 'It looks like she's heading back to the flat. I would expect our friend to peel off as soon as she goes down her alleyway.'

'Agreed. If he doesn't, stick to him and protect Manisha.'

'As predicted, she's gone back to her flat and our friend has stopped further down the alleyway with a view of the path to her flat.'

'I can see her opening the door,' Laing confirmed as he studied the live feed to his phone.

MATTHEW'S PHONE rang with the caller ID withheld. 'Hello?' he said with a bemused tone.

'Matthew, it's me.'

'Manisha! Where are you? I've tried to call you at work and at home.'

'I've decided to get away for a week or two after all.'

'Are you okay? Why didn't you tell me?'

'Don't worry, I'm fine. I'm sorry I didn't tell you, Matthew, and I'm sorry I missed your calls. It was a spur-of-the-moment decision. I just need some time away from the politics in Oxford.'

'I've been worried about you, babe. Are you sure you're okay? Do you need me to come and see you?' Matthew asked, just as a tannoy announcement blared.

'I'm fine. Please don't worry. I just need time alone. Time to think. Anyway, where are you? It sounds like you're in an airport.'

'Oh, I'm just on my way back from Barcelona. We've had an absolute blast.' Matthew said. He grinned while looking up at the departures board.

'Okay. Well, have a safe trip. I'll be in touch again soon.'

'Just know, Manisha, the next time I see you, I've got a big surprise for you. You will not believe it!'

'Okay,' she laughed, 'what is it?'

'If I tell you, it wouldn't be a surprise, now would it?'

'Okay. I'll look forward to it, whatever it is. I must go. I'll be thinking of you, and I'll be in touch soon. I love you.'

'See ya, Manisha.'

Matthew hung up, checked his flight number, and headed to his departure gate. Another tannoy announcement gave a final call for his flight, forcing him to quicken his pace. He handed over his first-class ticket just before the gate closed.

22

'Mind and intelligence are woven into the fabric of our universe in a way that altogether surpasses our understanding.'

Freeman Dyson – Physicist (1923–2020)

As evening approached, the progress counter on Manisha's PC tripped to thirty-three per cent. She'd spent the afternoon planning how to protect her work. Formulating ideas to ensure her technology could not be reverse-engineered and making notes on the legal agreements and patents she would need when the time was right.

The sound of lapping water and the thinning crowd were the only sounds drifting into the flat. She turned on a lamp and sat back on the sofa, taking time to relax. She picked up the TV handset and flicked through the list of channels, trying to find an English-speaking channel.

Just then, her PC emitted a repeating beep. She sat bolt upright before jumping to check her laptop screen. The system back in Oxford had decrypted a form—something which could be interpreted as an image. She switched to another window—and there it was. An image she'd never seen before. An image deciphered from the thought energy captured twenty-four hours earlier, from Simon's mind.

The image showed an attractive woman with dark hair wearing a red jumper, standing outside a well-known student haunt in Oxford called The Bear. The black and white exterior of the pub with gold lettering was familiar to Manisha. However, she had never seen the woman before. Astonished, she stood up, holding her face in her hands, overjoyed that her algorithm had worked. Her mind ran wild with the possibilities before her. There was still a lot of work to be done; testing, verifying, and re-testing. However, this was the moment she had been waiting for.

She sat down at her computer and switched to another window. It showed the exact sequence of Simon's DNA that had unlocked the image, and all the other parameters running through her algorithm at the time of decryption. Just one thing didn't add up. Although she was amazed at the clarity of the image, the size of the image file was only a fraction of the size of the data that had been analysed and unlocked.

'What other secrets are hidden in here?' she murmured.

The first thing to verify was whether this was the image Simon had held in his mind during the experiment. She called Simon's number, guarding her excitement.

'Hello,' Simon said.

'It's me, Manisha.'

'I'm not doing anything else for you. I've risked enough.'

'No, it's okay. I just wanted to know what the image was that you were focused on yesterday.'

'I thought you didn't want me to tell you till the experiment was complete?'

'It'll save time later,' Manisha said, playing down the situation.

'Okay, there's a girl I really fancy called Anita. She's part of the group I hang out with from time to time. We were out last week, and I was thinking of her as she stood outside the pub.'

'Yeah, give me more details of the image. What was she wearing, which pub?'

'She's wearing black jeans and a red top. She has long, dark curly hair and looks gorgeous. She was standing outside The Bear on Alfred Street.'

Simon described the scene perfectly; Manisha struggled to suppress her excitement.

'Okay,' she said calmly, as if taking notes.

'You asked me to focus on something important to me, so I did. Beer and women.'

'I should have guessed.'

'So, has it worked?' Simon asked.

'No, no...it's only run through around thirty per cent of the possible combinations. It could be days yet.'

'Okaaay,' Simon said.

'I must go. Thanks, Simon.'

After hanging up, Manisha jumped around the room, laughing and crying. 'I told you I would do it,' she said, as if her mother and father could hear her. Then she refocused and ensured all parameters were safely recorded.

She took off her necklace and pulled the heart pendant in two, revealing a hidden USB drive which she slid into the

PC. She copied all relevant data, ensuring it was encrypted before reattaching the two pieces. Placing the pendant on the table, she reviewed the additional data that had been decoded. There were hundreds of pages, which looked like a continuous stream of numbers, letters, and other strange characters. The first page was in a different format, like metadata for the hundreds of pages which followed. Most of the information was meaningless. However, a set of numbers jumped out at her, which looked like a grid reference:

$$5.16807E+19, 51.751507, -1.2556992$$

Manisha couldn't determine what the first number referred to. She punched the second and third numbers into Google on the off chance the numbers would reveal a position. To her astonishment, a map appeared showing the exact location of the memory Simon had cast out during the experiment. An arrow pointed to Alfred Street, directly in front of 'The Bear'.

Manisha sat back in disbelief. Could Simon's memory hold information from all his senses—what he saw, heard, and smelled—as well as the sensations of his nervous system? The way he felt? His location—perhaps not only in space but also in time? Her mind raced as she tried to gain a perspective on how deep the rabbit hole could go. What if all the memories of every human being were recorded? Every single second of our existence—thoughts, feelings, where we were, who we were with, what was said, what was heard, how our minds reacted, how we felt—a snapshot in time, saved in its entirety for future recall? Simon had purposely cast this energy to the world around him. What if this information was stored in the mind of every human, ready to be accessed at any time, by any means?

She imagined the playback of a single moment in a crowd, each conscious being reacting to input from their senses and to the surrounding people. Each person experiencing the moment from their own perspective, each reacting in their own unique way to the situation they found themselves in, and that moment being recorded.

Slow down, Manisha. One step at a time.

She ensured everything was saved and secured back in Oxford before she let the importance of the moment sink in. A big smile broke out on her face, overjoyed with her success after only being in Venice for two days. Finally, she had the breakthrough she desperately wanted.

At dusk, Manisha went out onto the balcony, breathed in the cool evening air, listened to the gentle lapping of the water below, and looked along the canal towards the bridge. The crowds were quieter now and shadows drifted to and fro across the bridge in the distance. A lone figure stood motionless on the bridge, looking in her direction. She strained her eyes as he shifted slightly, the nearby lamppost illuminating his features momentarily. She gasped, her heart leaping in her chest. Staring back at her was the man in the baseball cap who had attacked her two nights before in Oxford, the same man who had been following her. The dark lines down his right cheek left no doubt.

She regained her composure, stepped back into the flat, and calmly locked the window as if she hadn't noticed his eyes scanning her every move. Once inside, she switched off the downstairs light, grabbed her laptop and made her way up to the gallery. Turning on the upstairs light, she drew the curtains as if turning in for the night. Then she sat bolt upright on the bed, her chest heaving, as she tried to figure out what she should do next.

Moving quickly, Manisha thrust her laptop into her rucksack and grabbed a scarf from her suitcase. She rushed downstairs and went back to the balcony door to peel back the curtains, just enough to see if her stalker was still on the bridge. He was gone. She knew she had to leave now, before he cornered her. She ran to the main door and opened it slowly. Peering through the small gap, she confirmed the coast was clear. Quickly wrapping the scarf around her head, she closed the door. She ran down the alleyway, slowed to a walk to cross *Calle Sacrestia,* and then broke into a run.

23

*'The cosmos is within us. We are made of star stuff.
We are a way for the universe to know itself.'*

Carl Sagan – Astronomer (1934–1996)

It was early evening, and dusk had set in, casting the unmistakable profile of the city in umber and inky blue shadows. McCray had claimed a table outside *da Roberto's* from which he had a clear line of sight to the man dressed in black. He'd ordered a Diet Coke and pizza, picking at it while maintaining radio contact with Laing. A blinking red dot on his phone confirmed Manisha's location.

'What's he doing?' Laing asked.

'He's just grinning like an arse,' McCray replied. 'He seems like an arrogant prick who enjoys playing games. It's as if he wants Manisha to know he's here.'

'Do not underestimate him. He's confident for a reason. We need to understand why.'

'He's on the move,' McCray said, 'walking away from me to the other side of the bridge.'

'It looks like Manisha's been spooked,' Laing said. 'I can see her leaving the flat on the CCTV and she's in a big hurry.'

McCray checked the tracking app and saw the flashing red dot moving rapidly.

'Keep close to him. I'm right behind you,' Laing said.

McCray dropped forty euros on the table and hurried after Manisha's stalker. He ran over the bridge opposite *Vita* and took the first right. He caught a glimpse of a black cap in the distance. McCray picked up his pace, arriving just in time to see a woman with a silk headscarf cross the alleyway two hundred feet ahead. Her stalker sped up, briefly stopping at the alleyway to *Vita,* before looking down the alleyway opposite.

'He's on to her,' McCray said.

'Don't lose sight of them. I'm leaving the hotel lobby now.'

ZAREK SPRINTED. If he lost Manisha now, he might never find her again. He pushed past several tourists, knocking them to the ground. The shouts of protest from angry victims behind him made the crowd part before him. At the end of a long, narrow street, Manisha disappeared from his sight. At a crossroads, he looked all around and spotted the red and orange silk headscarf in the distance. Zarek charged, trying to predict Manisha's next move and where she was headed. He couldn't believe he had been so stupid as to spook her. He knew his masters' would punish him if he failed. The shame would be unbearable. He had to recover the situation.

MANISHA LOOKED over her shoulder and could see the black cap of her stalker still on her tail. She tried not to panic, knowing she needed to get out of the narrow alleyways and back into a wide-open space with plenty of people. Scanning her surroundings, she spotted an old yellow sign pointing towards *'Per Rialto.' Perfect!* She struggled through the narrow alleyway with shops open, still busy with tourists. Her laptop bag felt heavier with each step, making it difficult for her to run at her usual pace.

She ran across several squares and over three small bridges before turning again to see if the man was still there. He was. Glimpses of light reflecting off the Grand Canal through several alleyways, confirming the Rialto Bridge couldn't be far away. She ran on and suddenly burst out onto the main thoroughfare leading to the bridge. Even though it was evening, the bridge was crowded with tourists browsing shops and posing for photographs. Manisha ran as fast as she could up the wide central steps, grabbing a white cartwheel hat from a display outside a shop as she went.

Out of the corner of her eye she saw the keeper run out, waving his fist. 'Fucking tourists!' she heard him shout, followed by a long list of expletives in Italian.

Manisha looked back to see the man in the black cap pursuing at speed and pushing anyone who got in his way. She ran to the top of the bridge, turned left through the central arch, then cut right down the path behind the Rialto

Bridge shops. Knowing she'd be out of his line of sight, she took off the scarf and donned the stolen hat.

'She can run, this one,' McCray said, trying to keep up with Manisha and the black cap of her pursuer.

'Where is she?'

'She's on the Rialto Bridge, heading for the crowds.'

'Can you see her?'

'No, but I can see the man's black cap. I'm more concerned about keeping track of him. We can follow Manisha on the tracker.'

'Agreed,' Laing said.

The man in black spun around at the crest of the bridge, clearly trying to see where Manisha had gone. He stopped as he looked back from where he had just come, staring directly at McCray.

'He's clocked me,' McCray said.

'Be careful. I'm not far behind you. Just keep them in your sight.'

Zarek instinctively took a left at the top of the bridge, hoping to keep Manisha in his sights. He was aware the hunter was now being hunted. He looked down the bridge but could no longer see the brightly coloured scarf. However, he could see Manisha's unmistakable frame and her long black hair hanging under a white hat. He picked up the chase and made his way down the other side of the bridge. He ran past an alfresco restaurant, colliding with a waiter and knocking a large glass of red wine from the tray, splattering it over the waiter's crisp white uniform. He cursed as he found himself back in the maze of dark, narrow alleyways and side streets of Venice.

Manisha had started to run out of ideas and out of breath. Her body just wanted to stop, but fear pushed her on. She headed down a side street towards the Grand Canal, hoping the crowds would be bigger there, giving more opportunity to shake off her pursuer. Or at least offering some temporary safety in numbers.

She ran along the canal's edge and could see a vaporetto docking at *Rialto Mercato* in the distance. *This could be my chance, if the timing is right.* She looked behind her and could see the black cap of her assailant in the crowd. Upping her pace, she ran through the arches of a wine merchant. She got to the vaporetto stop in time to tailgate a large man through the barrier, just as the crew closed the metal gate to prepare for departure.

The vaporetto glided away from the quayside just as the man in black reached the gate, slamming his fist against a notice board in frustration. Manisha looked straight at him, breathing hard, her unblinking, determined stare meeting his frightening gaze.

Zarek smiled through gritted teeth. However, he could now take a chance to turn his disappointment and rage into an opportunity. The hunted would now turn his focus on his pursuer's elimination.

He walked quickly towards a darkened doorway overlooking the vaporetto stop, waiting for his adversary to catch up. Keeping his black cap low and his jacket zipped up tight around his chin, he watched the short man he'd seen following him on the Rialto Bridge run past, looking confused that he could not see him or Manisha. Opening a large switchblade knife, Zarek silently walked up behind him. He smiled. The man's head barely reached his chin—an easy kill if it came to it. He pressed the blade into McCray's side and placed a firm grip on his shoulder.

'Do as I say, and you might live.'

McCray moved to defend himself, but Zarek pressed the blade harder into his side, piercing his skin.

'Who do you work for?' Zarek demanded as he guided McCray down a quiet alleyway, away from the crowds.

'Piss off,' McCray said.

'So, you're Scottish. UK government I assume? MI6?'

'Why are you following her?'

'I think we both know the answer to that,' Zarek said with a smug smile. 'Is Laing with you?'

'Who's Laing?'

Zarek laughed at his audacity.

'Who are you, anyway?' McCray asked.

'My name is Zarek, and soon, everything will change. Too bad you won't live to see it.'

'You're a deluded idiot. You're just a low-life gun for hire. You can't be very important if you're running around Venice after an innocent woman.'

Zarek gritted his teeth, trying to keep his cool, knowing he was being baited. He'd already made one mistake today. He wouldn't make another.

'Oh, so are you taking me for a drink at *Barcollo*?' McCray said. 'How romantic. I'm flattered, but you're really not my type. These wannabe revolutionaries do nothing for me! You're nothing but trouble, I've heard.'

Zarek smiled and pulled the wire from McCray's ear. 'So, Laing is with you,' Zarek said. He shook his head as he pulled the mic towards his mouth. 'Your friend is history, and you're next,' he said before throwing the device to the ground and stamping on it. 'There goes your lifeline.'

Zarek felt his knife hand twist and a punch land in his face. McCray had taken the opportunity to defend himself while Zarek was distracted. Shock and confusion momentarily took over as McCray made the most of the element of surprise. Zarek grunted as his hand smashed against the rough brick wall. His fingers loosened their grip for an instant. It was enough to dislodge the knife from his hand and he heard it clatter to the ground. McCray kicked it away into a side alley.

Enraged, Zarek picked up McCray and threw him onto a table outside a small restaurant. He followed through with a hard kick to the stomach, to ensure McCray stayed down. An elderly couple looked on in shock and quickly edged past the man and hurried away from the scene.

'You're not built for this game, are you?' Zarek said, annoyed that the fight was over so easily. He retrieved the knife and stood over McCray in triumph.

In an instant, McCray lashed out, sweeping Zarek's legs out from under him. He toppled to the ground with a hard thud, the knife slipped from his grip. He watched McCray claw his way along the cobbles, desperate to get the knife. Zarek heaved himself up using a table and chair and grabbed McCray's legs, pulling the man back, away from the weapon. However, McCray's fingertips secured the knife, and he lashed out. Zarek cried out in pain as the blade landed deep into his right thigh. Warm blood oozed from the wound. Rage boiled in his gut as he landed a crushing blow on McCray's shoulders. McCray's grip failed, leaving the knife buried in Zarek's leg. Zarek grinned through the pain. He was back in control. He had the weapon, and his opponent was still down. With a firm grip, he pulled the knife from his limb, flinching in pain, adrenaline pumping through his body. Extending his hand, he grabbed a fist full of McCray's hair, pulling the man's head back to angle his neck towards the sky. In one swift, decisive move, Zarek thrust the knife into the side of McCray's neck. The blade stopped at the guard and blood poured from McCray's carotid artery, filling his throat. Zarek looked on, smiling, as the man gurgled and choked on his own blood. Zarek pulled the knife out and forward, cutting McCray's throat from the inside. He let go and watched as McCray slumped backwards, wide eyed, reaching for his bleeding neck. Zarek bent forward, looking into the dying man's eyes and grabbed the fabric of McCray's jacket. Slowly and carefully, he wiped the blood from the blade and closed it before slipping it back into his pocket. He straightened, looking down at his vanquished foe. McCray twitched on the cobbles, bright red blood spurting from his throat, forming a glossy pool around his body.

Zarek leaned over the man again, stepping in his blood as he searched his pockets. While McCray lay choking, Zarek's fingers closed around what they were searching for. He pulled out his mobile phone, tapped the screen and pointed it at McCray's bloody face. The tracker app was still active.

'Thank you,' Zarek smiled at McCray in his dying moments. 'This will be very useful.'

Laing found *Barcollo* on Google maps and ran to McCray's last known location. The earpiece, now useless, hung from his ear. He hoped to hear the sound of two men fighting, but looking down the dark alleyway, his worst fears had come to pass. He saw legs and feet jutting out of a doorway, below a dim light which reflected in what looked like a puddle. He ran towards the body and his heart stopped as he found McCray laying in a pool of blood, his eyes wide and lifeless. Laing knelt on one knee, blood seeping through his trousers as he checked for a pulse. He was too late. His newly found colleague was gone. He gently closed McCray's eyelids, a cold rage settling over him. Another partner lost. Another friend gone. And now, he was alone. Laing searched McCray's body. His ID and keys were quickly pocketed, but he couldn't find his phone anywhere. Laing shivered, realising the gravity of the situation—Zarek could now track Manisha, and he was alone in an unfamiliar city.

24

'As far as the laws of mathematics refer to reality, they are not certain; and as far as they are certain, they do not refer to reality.'

Albert Einstein – Physicist (1879–1955)

Manisha stood on the vaporetto, deliberating her next move. Knowing she couldn't go back to *Vita*, she needed to find somewhere safe for the night where she could consider whether to leave Venice in the morning. On impulse, she got off at the next stop, *San Stae*, and walked down the wide alleyway, away from the Grand Canal.

After one block, she spotted a brown-and-yellow sign pointing to a hotel. She walked down a narrow alleyway and found the entrance to *Al Ponte Mocenigo*, which looked like a Venetian residence rather than a guesthouse. The lobby was small and ornate. A young man sat behind the reception desk.

'*Buonasera, signorina, mi chiamo Antonio. Benvenuta nel mio hotel.*' His questioning facial expression showed he wasn't sure he'd chosen the right language.

'Do you have any rooms available?' Manisha asked.

'Ah, English! Welcome, *signorina*. My name is Antonio. Let me check for you.' Antonio tapped at the keyboard as he looked through a list of rooms. 'You're lucky, we have one room vacant tonight. A first-floor superior room is available at one hundred and thirty-one euros per night. How many nights would you like it for?'

'Just for tonight,' Manisha said, keeping one eye on the main entrance.

'Perfect. Will you be paying by card or cash?'

'Cash,' she said as she rummaged in her rucksack. She pulled out one hundred and thirty euros in notes, found a single euro coin, and handed the money to the owner.

'*Grazie*,' Antonio said with a satisfied smile as he placed the money into the till. 'Let me take you to your room.'

Room fifty-three had two living areas and an en-suite bathroom. The first area had a wardrobe and a day bed, with a balcony overlooking the main thoroughfare towards *San Stae* vaporetto stop. The second, much larger area, contained a king-size bed, a writing desk, two comfortable chairs and a corner window with a view down to the Grand Canal. The gold silk cloth adorning the walls, combined with the large glass chandelier, gave the room an opulence far above the hotel's two-star rating.

'Will this be okay for you, *signorina*?' Antonio asked.

'Yes, thank you.'

Antonio dropped her bags on the luggage stool. 'I shall

leave you in peace. Please let me know if there's anything you need.' He shut the door quietly behind him.

As soon as he'd left, Manisha flipped the door guard across so no one could force their way in. She switched off the lights and looked out the corner window towards the vaporetto stop. It was quiet outside. A solitary streetlamp provided the only light in an otherwise dark alleyway. Lights from boats and houses illuminated the Grand Canal in the distance.

Manisha drew the thick, gold ceiling-to-floor curtains across the windows and switched on the bedside lights. She sat on the bed and took a deep breath. The last forty-eight hours had been a whirlwind, and she had to ensure she kept herself and her work safe. Seeing the man in black had shaken her. *Who are you and how did you know I was here?*

She picked up her laptop bag and walked over to the desk. Her reflection in the mirror caught her eye, making her gasp. 'Oh, shit!' Clutching at her chest, she confirmed that her heart-shaped pendant was missing. Frantically, she hunted through her laptop bag, pulling everything out onto the bed, attempting to find the pendant which held her secret. *I must have left it on the table in the flat*, she thought, swearing through gritted teeth at her stupidity. After checking her bag and pockets one final time, she knew there was only one choice—she had to go back to *Vita*.

She coiled her hair into a bun, covering it with her scarf, and grabbed her coat. She checked she had the keys to Vita and her hotel room, then crept out onto the dark streets of Venice.

~

Laing switched on his tracker app. The blinking red dot showed Manisha's location. She was only eight minutes away. His brisk walk changed into a jog as he followed the signal through the dark alleyways. He had to get to her before Zarek.

As he got closer, the phone display zoomed into the map. He could see her location was the *Al Ponte Mocenigo* hotel. Laing walked across a narrow footbridge and lifted the latch on the ornate iron gates. They swung open with a metallic squeak. He passed beneath the brick archway and through a small, well-lit courtyard with water fountains leading to the reception lobby. At the reception desk, his phone let out a quiet, steady beep, informing him Manisha was within one metre. However, she was nowhere to be seen.

Antonio smiled at Laing. '*Buonasera*, how can I help you?'

'I'm looking for a guest, Manisha Williams?'

'Ah, yes. She checked in, but she went out again only a few minutes ago, *Signiore*.'

'Did she pay in cash?'

'*Si, Siginore*.' Antonio said with a frown.

Laing started to make his way to the exit but turned back. 'Can you change a note for some Euro coins?'

'*Si*, how many do you need?'

'How many do you have?'

Antonio opened his till and laid the Euros on the counter.

'I have eighteen in the till, but I have more out back if you need them?'

'I'll take all you have in the till,' Laing said, putting a twenty Euro note on the counter. He took the coins, loaded them into his pockets and used the exit.

'*Grazie, Signiore,*' Antonio said, smiling at his two-euro tip.

Laing walked away from the hotel. His tracker app confirmed the token was now in his pocket. He stayed alert, knowing Zarek would now be tracking him, and walked away from the hotel fast, keen to protect Manisha's newfound sanctuary. Instinct told him Manisha must have gone back to the flat. *Why would you put yourself in danger again?*

Laing ran through the dark alleyways and across several bridges, heading south-west away from *San Stae*, in the opposite direction to *Vita*.

The city was quiet. The alleyways were dark, punctuated by the occasional streetlight which cast yellow pools onto the ancient cobbles. He was grateful for the lack of people, which would have hindered his progress. His phone rang, its shrill tone cutting through the quiet street. He silenced it mid-ring by pressing the green button.

'What the hell is going on, Laing?' Redfern barked.

'McCray's been killed, Ma'am. A Heylel agent, who goes by the name Zarek, got to him before I could provide backup. I've lost Manisha, but I have her tracker. I'm sure she's heading back to the flat. From the telephone conversations she's had today, I believe she's made the breakthrough we've been waiting for. She knows how to decrypt the energy.'

'This is a bloody mess, Laing. Get your act together.'

'I have two choices, Ma'am. Lure Zarek in, as he's got McCray's phone and will be tracking me. Or ditch the tracker and protect Manisha.'

Redfern went quiet for a few seconds.

He could hear her breathing as she weighed up the

options. To Laing, the answer was obvious. Protect the asset at all costs.

'Lure him in and detain him,' she said before hanging up.

Laing stared at his phone, incredulous. *Why would you say that?* He ran a short distance into a large square, where a faded street sign read *Campo S Giacomo da L'Orio*. It was flanked by restaurants full of holiday makers enjoying their evening. Laing scanned the square and spotted the tell-tale sight of a tattered hat laid on the paving stones. He walked purposefully towards the darkened recess of a closed shop doorway. Digging deep into his pocket, he dropped the fistful of Euros in the hat.

'*Grazie mille, Signiore,*' the stunned rough sleeper said.

Laing moved on, trusting his instincts.

ZAREK MADE his way through the side streets of Venice, following the red dot on McCray's tracker app. He'd bandaged his leg and taken pain killers, but still winced with each step as he entered the large square, where the tracker app told him Manisha would be. He walked towards a darkened doorway, his heart beating with anticipation, when a text flashed on McCray's phone.

The tracker has been compromised. She's heading back to Vita. Bring her to the palace.

Zarek smiled as he slid McCray's phone into his pocket and changed direction. He was happy to limp through the pain. His prize was in sight.

Manisha hid in the shadows at the back of the vaporetto she had caught from *San Stae*. It was a long trip through more than half the Grand Canal around to *San Zaccaria*, but she knew this would be the safest route back to *Vita*. She kept hidden and kept an eye on all new passengers who boarded the water bus. She was afraid, but her underlying conviction gave her the confidence to push on.

The vaporetto drifted past the Doge's Palace and on to the *San Zaccaria* pontoon. Manisha scanned every figure on the shoreline to ensure she wasn't walking into a trap. The coast appeared to be clear. She left the water bus, keeping her head low as she checked the people around her.

Crossing the bridge, she headed under the dark archway leading to *San Zaccaria* church. The square was dark and quiet, with too many shadows for her liking. She strode on with an inner resolve, telling herself she would get the help, or luck, she needed, when she needed it.

As she made her way towards the dark archway leading to *Trattoria da Nino*, she felt a presence behind her. She tried to quicken her pace, but it was too late. A hand grabbed her around the waist, and another clamped over her mouth as she was dragged into a quiet, dark corner.

'I'm here to help you, Manisha. You must trust me,' a male voice said.

Manisha tried to kick and scream, but her captor was too strong.

The man turned her around, still with a firm hand covering her mouth. To her surprise, she was not met with the piercing blue eyes of her stalker, but met with caring eyes, looking at her intently, without malice. He slowly released his hand from her mouth.

'Manisha, my name is Alex Laing. I work for the British Security Service. You're in more danger than you realise.

There is someone here in Venice who wants your work and is prepared to kill for it.'

'The man in black?' Manisha asked.

'Yes, he's already killed someone tonight. You must trust me. Where are you going?'

'I need to get back to my flat. I've left something there that I need.'

'Is it really that important?'

'Yes. If you're here, you know why it's important,' Manisha said.

'Your work?'

'Yes. There's some data I need to secure.'

'Okay,' Laing said, keeping a calm head. 'What is it? Give me the key and I'll get it.'

'Do you really think I'm going to trust you?' Manisha asked.

'Do you need to go there now?'

'Yes. And I'm going with or without you. If you come, you will not be coming into the flat with me. Do you understand?'

'You don't know the danger you're in, Manisha. I'll be right behind you whether you like it or not.'

'Fine! Let's just get this done, shall we?' Manisha wrenched herself free from Laing's grip, setting off with a determined stride towards *Vita*. Secretly, she felt relieved she had Laing to protect her from the man in black. He was the lesser of two evils. Even though her head told her not to trust him, her gut told her otherwise.

They walked over the small stone bridge and navigated through the alleyways towards *Vita*. She could feel Laing close behind, his breath shallow and controlled, giving her confidence in her stride.

Laing opened his phone. 'Wait.'

Manisha stopped and looked at the CCTV image displayed on his phone. 'You've been spying on me too,' she said. 'We've got a lot to talk about.' Anger boiled inside of her, knowing so much of her privacy had been compromised. That said, she could see from the image the path was clear, and she confidently headed towards *Vita*, her key already out, ready to open the door.

'Wait here,' Manisha said. 'If I need you, I'll scream.'

Laing stood outside, as instructed, with the look of a man tolerating a difficult wife.

Manisha went into the flat and headed straight to the table where she'd been using her laptop that afternoon. She could see no sign of the pendant and scrambled around on the floor, trying to see the object containing her life's work. Catching a glint of something from the corner of her eye, she dropped to her knees and felt around the floor under the sofa. Her fingertips landed on what felt like a coiled metal chain. She pulled it, and to her relief, her heart-shaped USB jewel slid into view. She quickly put it on, covered it with her scarf, and made her way to the door.

'Did you find it?' Laing said, looking her up and down.

'I have what I came for,' Manisha said. 'Let's go.'

'Where is it?'

'None of your business. Now let's go.'

Manisha strode purposefully down the alleyway but before she reached the end, she felt Laing's firm grip on her arm. She stopped in her tracks and felt herself being turned around again to face him. 'Manisha, you need to trust me. A man died tonight trying to protect you.'

Manisha levelled her gaze and looked straight into his eyes. 'You need to earn my trust. Until then, I will not trust you—or anyone. And don't ask me anything about my work. You're a part of the organisation I'm trying to protect my research from.' Manisha pulled herself free and walked away at a pace, leaving the sound of Laing's exasperation behind her.

Moments later, Laing caught her up, holding her arm with his large hand as he fell into step beside her. 'I don't need to know about your work, Manisha, but I am here to protect you. If we get into any trouble tonight, you do exactly what I tell you. Do you understand?'

Manisha stayed quiet. Laing's firm hold on her arm gave her an unexpected sense of security.

'I have a boat moored near *San Zaccaria* pontoon,' Laing said. 'We can use that to get back to your hotel. It has a Union Jack flag on the back. You can't miss it.'

25

'Nothing exists; all is a dream. God—man—the world—the sun, the moon, the wilderness of stars—a dream, all a dream; they have no existence. Nothing exists save empty space—and you!'

Mark Twain – Author (1853–1910)

Streetlights lit their way as Laing led Manisha across the small stone bridge and past the restaurant where she'd had breakfast that morning. They walked under the dark, ancient archway and into *San Zaccaria Square*. As they stepped through the square, Laing tensed as he heard the click of a switchblade being locked into an open position. He pulled Manisha behind him, away from the direction of the sound. 'Stay back,' he said.

Zarek emerged from the shadows, his large, muscular

frame moving with a slight limp. 'I believe you have something for me.'

'There's nothing for you here,' Laing said, knowing any attempt to defuse the situation with words would be futile.

He saw a smirk cross the man's face as he began to speak. 'The number of times I could have killed you—but she told me not to, not wanting to risk the might of the British Secret Service finding out how close Heylel was,' he said with a sneering smile. 'But here we are, and you're the only thing standing between me and what I want. You're going to die tonight.'

Laing stayed silent. He was in for a tough fight, but Zarek was no match for him. He was too self-assured. The blood dripping from his leg told Laing he was injured and wouldn't be nimble on his feet. That said, in a knife fight, Laing never underestimated anyone.

Laing pulled the keys to the boat from his pocket and threw them over his shoulder towards Manisha, whose swift reaction caught them in one hand. 'You know which one, Manisha. Carry on, I won't be long,' Laing said, keeping his focus on the eyes peering at him from the darkness.

Light from a lamppost caught Zarek's face as he laughed and adjusted his grip on the knife. Laing lunged forward but purposely held back, attempting to goad Zarek into making the first attack, knowing the injured man would be easy to defend against. Zarek stumbled backwards slightly but regained his balance. The two men moved slowly in a circle, each trying to draw the other in. From the corner of his eye, Laing saw Manisha quietly slip away under the cover of darkness. Relieved that she was out of any immediate danger, he switched his full focus to the fight.

Zarek took an overstretched lunge forward. Grabbing his shirt, Laing yanked him forwards, using Zarek's imbalance to his advantage as he slammed Zarek into the wall behind him. Zarek quickly recovered his footing and used his hand to wipe the blood from his brow where the stone had grazed his head. The sight of his smug grin made Laing's gut twist with anger, but he couldn't let emotion take over. Suddenly, Laing caught a flash of metal—Zarek lunging, blade flashing, fully committed. He raised his arm to block Zarek's knife hand and delivered a powerful punch to the man's kidneys, followed by an uppercut. The smack of Laing's fist against Zarek's chin—and the clash of teeth meeting teeth—confirmed his punch was on target.

Laing breathed in deeply as Zarek stumbled back, looking slightly dazed, but the injured man stayed on his feet. Before he could move to defend himself, Laing received a direct punch to his face and grappled with Zarek to fend off another attempt to stab him in the gut.

With his head still reeling, Laing grabbed Zarek's knife arm and twisted it back behind his muscular frame. He used all his strength to push him, pinning him against the wall. There was a stab of pain in his foot as Zarek stamped down hard, then shock waves vibrated through his skull as Zarek delivered an elbow to the side of his head and another to his face. He blinked hard to clear his vision. Temporarily stunned, he released his grip and breathed hard as he rebalanced himself. A metallic taste lingered in his mouth. He raised his arm and wiped the blood from his split lip. Zarek was stronger than he expected.

Laing spat blood from his mouth as he watched Zarek switch knife hands and lunge forward. His decades of military experience were more than a match for Zarek's overzealous attack. Reading Zarek's stance, he moved to one side, easily taking control of Zarek's knife arm. Turning the weapon, he used it to stab Zarek in the arm, then followed with a solid punch to Zarek's wounded leg. The pain was clear to see on the man's face as Laing pushed him to the ground, ready to go in for the kill. He bent over Zarek, about to make the decisive cut, when Zarek twisted like a snake and delivered a full-force kick to Laing's face. Another kick to the stomach sent Laing sprawling backwards. He landed awkwardly on the uneven cobbles, winded and gasping for breath. Laing looked up, expecting to see Zarek come in for another attack. Instead, he heard Zarek's retreating footsteps fading as he disappeared under the archway leading towards Hotel Fontana. Laing considered following but getting back to Manisha was his priority.

Pulling himself to his feet, Laing folded the knife, left San Zaccaria Square and ran towards the pontoon. He found the boat untethered and being held in place by Manisha's piloting skills. A mixture of relief and concern was etched on her face. Neither of them spoke as Laing jumped into the boat and took the controls, manoeuvring the boat towards the Grand Canal.

As the craft pulled away from the pontoon, Laing looked back toward the shore. Zarek was hobbling across the bridge towards the Doge's Palace. He disappeared into the darkness. Laing hoped he would take refuge for the night and give them the opportunity to go to ground.

As they motored slowly across the quayside past the Doge's Palace, his hopes were dashed. Behind them, a Tagliapietra water taxi burst out at speed from the quiet backwater—Zarek looking defiant at the helm.

Laing opened the throttle as they entered the waters of the Grand Canal. With their boats evenly matched, he knew survival depended on the skill of the helmsman. Laing could hear Zarek's engine roaring behind him as he pushed his craft to full throttle in an attempt to catch up. Laing glanced over his shoulder to see Zarek stretching down below the cockpit.

'He's got a gun,' Manisha shouted over the roar of the engine, her hair whipped back in a long train behind her.

'Get down,' Laing commanded, focusing on the path ahead as he navigated through a multitude of slower craft.

Two shots echoed through the Venice night, but the bullets failed to find their target. The slower craft in front of them started to part, clearing the way for the deadly chase. Onlookers watched from the canal edge in disbelief as the two boats flew past.

Laing could see Zarek was gaining on them. He gripped the throttle and increased his boat to full speed, the tachometer pushing thirty knots. 'Look in the compartments. There must be a gun on board somewhere,' Laing shouted, knowing McCray would have kept spare weapons.

The wind rushed through Laing's hair, and water sprayed over the front and sides of the boat. Ahead, he could see a gondola directly in his path and deftly steered his craft around the obstacle, drenching other boats in his wake. Laing looked back and seconds later, saw Zarek take the more direct approach, passing straight through the middle of the sleek black craft, breaking it in two. The gondolier went down flailing.

In the back of the boat, Manisha frantically pulled cushions off seats and opened compartments. As they sped down the Grand Canal, Laing saw two Venetian traffic officers on light blue jet skis. They immediately fired up their engines and joined the chase. Laing hoped they would help by slowing Zarek down but feared they would only become victims of Zarek's rampage. As diners at the waterside restaurants crowded forward in astonishment at the scene unfolding before them, Laing glimpsed the first of the officers skimming over the surface of the choppy water, gesturing to Zarek to pull over. A loud crack followed by a collective scream from the onlookers told him Zarek had taken a shot. He craned his neck to see Zarek swerve his boat, forcing the jet ski to take evasive action. There was a sickening crunch as the officer slammed into the back of a lumbering green rubbish collection barge. Laing ducked as the jet ski exploded on impact. The resulting ball of flame lit up the canal for hundreds of feet in each direction, the sound reverberating throughout the city.

'I've found a gun,' Manisha said, handing the weapon to Laing with shaking hands. She looked stunned to see a man's life taken so casually.

'Keep your head down,' Laing said, checking the gun was loaded. He looked over his shoulder to see Zarek only twenty metres behind, his arm raised with a gun aimed in Laing's direction. Laing clenched his teeth and swerved to his right. A bullet whistled past his ear, and a second later, another smashed through the windscreen in front of him. He pulled hard on the steering wheel, placing a vaporetto between him and Zarek.

Laing glanced at the shocked faces of the passengers on board. The sight of a madman tearing through Venice covered in blood, waving a gun, was like something out of a movie. Some passengers instinctively ducked, while others foolishly grabbed their phones to record the scene unfolding before them.

Once Laing cleared the vaporetto, he had Zarek in his sight. Laing fired two shots, struggling to aim as the boat pitched beneath him. Zarek ducked down low and swerved sharply. The resulting wake drenched couples enjoying their evening meal on the canal side and sent confused diners screaming for cover.

Laing glanced back at Manisha. She looked small, almost childlike, her eyes wide with fear. He felt a compulsion to protect her, but her expression changed to one of resolve as she searched other compartments in the boat and found another handgun. He glanced at her as she pointed the weapon in Zarek's direction and pulled the trigger frantically. Nothing happened.

'It's not loaded,' Laing shouted. He pulled open a small compartment under the helm of the boat and grabbed two spare magazines. Manisha held the course of the boat steady while Laing reloaded both weapons and returned two more shots at their assailant.

'Do what you can, Manisha,' Laing said, handing the second loaded weapon to Manisha. Her face had a look of grim determination as she took the gun and got into position at the back of the boat. The violent pitch and roll made it impossible to aim with any accuracy. Cracks like fireworks exploding ricocheted off buildings as she let off a couple of wild rounds, her aim way off target. Two more rounds followed. Laing saw Zarek duck, and his boat swerved momentarily before the unmistakable pop signalled return fire. Splinters of wood flew in the air as a bullet embedded itself in the highly polished woodwork of the cockpit, and Laing cried out in pain as an agonising burning sensation ripped through the side of his calf muscle. One of Zarek's bullets had found its target. Laing grabbed the helm firmly as his leg buckled under him. Acting on adrenaline, he clawed his way back up to his feet and fired two more rounds at Zarek. He saw a mass of tousled hair as Manisha scrambled back on to the seats and let off a few more rounds.

'Keep your head down,' Laing shouted. He breathed

hard to control the pain in his leg, guessing it was a flesh wound, as he could still bear weight.

Ahead, Laing's attention was taken by the sight of two police boats. They'd positioned themselves strategically at the narrowest part of the Grand Canal, with a vaporetto stop on one side and a pontoon filled with boats opposite. Searchlights blazed into life. Laing raised his arm to shield his eyes, momentarily blinded by the white lights which were mounted on the bows of the craft, one pointing at Zarek's boat and a second directed at Laing and Manisha.

More shots came from Zarek's boat. Suddenly, the light trained on Zarek faded to darkness, as a lucky shot struck home. The remaining searchlight switched its position to train its beam on Zarek. Laing took advantage of the situation and raised his gun, letting off two more rounds at his blinded hunter.

Laing knew he had to try to get the upper hand and get Manisha away from the man. Delivering her into the hands of the police wasn't an option as he suspected Heylel would have them in their pocket. As the two speeding craft approached the police vessels, a volley of shots was aimed in their direction but neither man let up on their speed. Laing looked up and swerved his boat to the right of the police, squeezing through a small gap as guns were emptied in their direction.

Looking back, Laing saw Zarek ram through the middle of the two police boats. *What the hell is he doing?* Seconds later a grenade exploded, sending deadly shrapnel into the two police officers on board.

Sirens screamed behind them as the remaining police boat turned and quickly accelerated in pursuit of Zarek. 'They're catching up with him!' Manisha yelled.

Laing turned to see Zarek throw a small, dark object into

the police boat. Zarek's boat swerved violently, forcing his pursuers into the canal wall. A loud explosion echoed through the night air, lighting up the Grand Canal. Their chase was over.

Laing looked back at the chaos. He could just make out a lone officer on a jet ski drawing parallel to Zarek. He was a sitting duck. Zarek fired a single shot, killing him instantly. Laing looked on as the man crashed into the Rialto vaporetto stop. The officer's lifeless body hurtled over the jet ski, smashing into the white and yellow panelling. Horrified bystanders screamed. Crowds of tourists looked on as the two boats roared under the Rialto Bridge at thirty knots, shattering the usual tranquillity.

Laing looked back to see Zarek's boat was gaining on them. With only ten metres between them, Laing heard a shot and then felt the impact of a bullet, as it grazed the flesh of his left shoulder. He lost control. The boat crashed with a roar into the crumbling stucco of an ancient building opposite *Bancogiro*. He heard Manisha scream as she was hurtled forward by the impact, dropping her gun, her hands shooting out instinctively to break her fall. Laing had the wind knocked out of him as he felt the helm dig hard into his stomach, then he fell backwards on to the hard deck.

ZAREK PULLED alongside Laing's stricken craft and tied his boat to it. He jumped on board to find Laing struggling to his feet. Raising his gun, he brought the butt down hard on the back of Laing's head, knocking him out cold. Turning to deal with Manisha, he caught her scrambling towards the gun. 'I don't think so,' he said, before kicking her hard across the jaw. The impact jerked her body backwards, and she smacked her head on the side of the craft. She slumped in an unconscious heap in the bottom of the wrecked boat.

Zarek, energised by his victory, heaved the bodies into the cabin at the back of his boat. He took the flick knife from Laing's pocket and, with satisfaction, bound their unconscious limbs with rope. Then he secured all doors, making escape impossible.

Returning to the helm, he pulled away gently and took the craft through the quiet backwaters, away from the chaos of the Grand Canal. He knew more police boats would eventually follow, so went at a slow and sedate pace, keeping to the speed limits and avoiding any unnecessary attention. Even if the police were to catch up with him, his leaders at the palace would provide a believable story, blaming the carnage on mafia drug runners and throwing the police a sweetener to look the other way.

Zarek's focus was broken by murmuring from the back of the boat. He took the boat out of gear, allowing it to drift, and made his way back to the cabin. On seeing Laing conscious, he pulled two lengths of cloth from a compartment and gagged both of his captives. As Laing struggled and moaned, he took satisfaction in placing hessian hoods roughly over their heads. They would see nothing and say nothing for the rest of the journey.

The night was tranquil again. Zarek took a deep breath, relieved to be back in control. Nothing could stop him now, and his superiors would be pleased. The visions he had focused on with such dedication were about to become reality. He looked up at the starlit sky and smiled as a feeling of elation spread through him. He took in the surroundings as the boat slowly drifted past the tall, dark buildings, where residents switched off their lights and turned in for the night.

Zarek steered onto the waterway leading to the Doge's Palace. The high, imposing walls on either side of the canal increased the depth of the darkness. He moored the boat outside the moonlit side entrance, under the Bridge of Sighs. The night was just beginning. Zarek smiled as he thought about what lay in store for Laing and Manisha within the confines of the palace. In silence, he pulled his captives to their feet and pushed them out of the boat, up the steps and on through the door into the fortress. The ancient wooden doors closed behind them with a heavy, ominous clunk.

26

'But science and technology are only one of the avenues toward reality; others are equally needed to comprehend the full significance of our existence. Indeed, these other avenues are necessary for the prevention of thoughtless and inhuman abuses of the results of science.'

Victor Weisskopf – Physicist (1908–2002)

The damp, musty smell of an old building filled Manisha's nostrils. She pushed the poorly tied gag from her mouth with her tongue, allowing her to breathe more freely. The hessian hood still covered her head. Only the occasional flicker from the dim lights illuminating the stone archways managed to penetrate the weave. She inhaled deeply, the hessian's earthy fibres clinging to her tongue, her breath loud in her ears. Adrenaline coursed through her body as she struggled to comprehend what was happening. Fear, and her inability to see, made her unsteady on her feet.

'Keep moving,' the man in black said as he nudged Manisha forward. She shivered as she felt cold, hard metal touch her back. She could hear multiple footsteps on the stone floor. 'Alex?'

'I'm here.' Laing's muffled but calm voice came from her left.

'Quiet!' their captor shouted.

Manisha heard the slap of a fist land on Laing's back, then the tripping of feet and a groan. She could just see Laing through the weave as he crashed into the ancient corridor wall.

LAING STEADIED his footing and continued to walk, concentrating hard to commit their route to memory. They turned left and came to a flight of stone steps. Laing stumbled before his legs grew accustomed to the climb. The ground levelled out briefly before the climb resumed. As they went on, he could sense the walls closing in as the stairs narrowed. Then the steps opened out on to what Laing took to be a corridor. A cool, salty breeze made its way through the weave of the bag covering his head and lightly touched his face. Laing breathed in deep. *We're near the outer shell of the building.*

It soon became impossible to keep track of all the turns as they went further into the labyrinth. There were several flights of stairs—some made of wood, many of stone. Some were rough underfoot, some smooth. As they were taken deeper into the heart of the palace, Laing could make out marble flooring through the gap between his chest and the hessian hood. They passed through what appeared to be light and opulent staterooms before walking onto wooden flooring again and back into dark corridors. For simplicity, he only counted the number of flights of stairs they'd gone up and knew they had turned left more than right.

Laing had endured capture and interrogation before. The thought made his gut churn, but he knew he could withstand torture. But could Manisha? This wasn't a military capture, and he had no idea what Zarek had planned or how brutal his interrogation would be. The pain from the bullet grazes in his shoulder and leg pinched with each step. He felt a trickle of blood down his calf and wondered if there was enough blood to leave a trail to guide him back to the entrance. He felt another shove against his back.

'Move faster,' Zarek barked.

If I get out of here alive, there'll be no mercy, Laing thought.

They entered the next corridor, and the sound of distant voices, talking and laughing, caught his ear. His senses were heightened as they were pushed towards a room where, presumably, more assailants were waiting.

Laing's injured leg felt like lead. His foot dragged, catching the lip of a step, causing him to trip. He staggered and leaned heavily against the wall. As he approached the top of the flight of steps, the voices hushed. The dimly lit room opened out before him. Through his hood, he could just make out two shadowy figures sitting in silence behind a large table, faintly illuminated by candles. Laing's stomach twisted as he caught sight of Manisha's slight frame, struggling as Zarek shoved her to her knees. The sound of her breath was loud and trembling.

'Stay down,' Zarek hissed.

Laing felt the force of Zarek's well-placed shove in his

aching back, which propelled him further into the room. A kick to the back of his legs followed, causing them to buckle, bringing him to his knees.

Zarek yanked Laing's bound wrists, forcing him forward until his face was pressed against the floor. Laing was aware of a thicker rope being bound around his wrists. He clenched his jaw hard, biting down as his anxiety grew. Zarek's strong hands grabbed his shoulders roughly. The pain in his shoulder was nauseating as he was jerked up to a kneeling position again. Rough cloth scratched his face as the hessian hood was ripped off.

Laing blinked hard, trying to adjust his eyes. He felt the sting of Zarek's slap to the back of his head as he removed his gag, before stepping away to pull the hood from Manisha's head.

In the dim light, Laing could see Manisha's gag hanging loose around her neck. Zarek casually took a seat at the table beside the two figures in the shadows, his rucksack already draped on the back of the chair.

Laing's eyes swept the space. The centuries-old room was adorned with red marble flooring and rich wooden panelling. Three figures now sat behind a large table: Zarek, another man and a woman, judging by their silhouettes. There were two exits, one on each side of the room. The most obvious weapon was the pistol in Zarek's hand. Laing was sure the others would have their own. Large metal candlesticks sat on the table ten feet before him. Old wooden chairs lined the walls. He looked up and became aware of a single spotlight suspended up high, its beam focused on something behind him. He glanced over his shoulder to see an island of three wooden steps leading nowhere. Returning his gaze upwards, his eyes squinted past the spotlight. He could make out a high wooden ceiling in the centre of the room. A pulley system dangled from the beams above, sending a shudder down his spine. He shook his hands behind his back. The rope looped through the pulley system moved in response.

Time was of the essence. Laing knew he had to act swiftly.

MANISHA BLINKED, adjusting her watery eyes to the dimly lit room. Her wrists were sore where the rope which bound them rubbed her skin.

'Welcome to the torture chamber of the Doge's Palace.'

Manisha peered into the darkness, searching for the source of the voice. It sounded like... But surely it couldn't be...? It was impossible... 'Matthew?'

One of the dark shadows leaned into the candlelight, revealing Matthew's familiar face.

'I told you I had a surprise for you!' Matthew said, grinning from ear to ear, as he pushed back his chair to step out from behind the table.

Manisha looked on, incredulous as he stood before her in a crisp white Oxford shirt, the top two buttons undone, with tails tucked into brown chinos, wearing his familiar, highly polished leather brown shoes—the ones he wore on special occasions. The ones he had worn on their anniversary evening only a few nights before.

Matthew laughed, any trace of former affection gone. 'Now, that is a surprised face. It's amazing what you can learn over a romantic meal in Oxford.'

Manisha felt sick, as if an icy hand had gripped her heart as the reality sunk in. She swallowed hard, the weight of his treachery sinking in. 'You bastard!' She choked on her tears.

Matthew smiled. 'You even told me the flat you would be staying in.'

A deep emptiness consumed Manisha as she realised the person she loved had abandoned her. 'I trusted you. Why would you betray me?'

'Why do you think?'

A thick and heavy silence fell between them.

'Money!' Matthew exploded, as he threw out his hands. 'Money, of course.' He nodded towards the man in black. 'Zarek made me an offer I couldn't refuse. I had no choice. The thought of breaking free from my fucking domineering, overbearing bastard of a father, was an opportunity too good to miss.'

'What have you told them?' Manisha asked, as she desperately replayed their conversations in her head.

'Oh, simple stuff. What you've told me about your research, your daily movements, your weaknesses, and strengths. It was easy money. Simple information for a great reward.'

Manisha watched as Matthew walked towards her, hatred rising through her body, driving away every trace of the tenderness she'd once felt. In that moment, she hated him with more intensity than she had ever felt before.

Matthew stopped and knelt on one knee before her. She could smell the musky tang of his aftershave as he raised his hand to stroke her face. 'I can finish my degree, travel the world, buy my first house, and not have to speak to my idiot father again. You made the whole task so easy, and so very pleasurable. Thank you,' he said as he leaned in to kiss her.

Manisha swung her head back and rocked forward,

head-butting Matthew full in the face. A stab of pain shot through her head as an audible crack echoed around the room. She watched from under her brow, through her hair, as blood gushed from his broken nose and poured down his white shirt.

'You have no idea what you've done,' she said.

'You bitch.' Matthew raised an arm to strike her. Manisha readied herself for the blow.

'Enough!' a stern female voice said from the shadows.

Matthew dropped his arm, obeying the command, and made his way to the other side of the table. Blood dripped through his fingers and splashed onto the marble floor.

'I knew something wasn't right about you, Ma'am.' Laing's calm voice cut through the atmosphere.

Manisha's perplexed face turned to Laing. 'Who is she, Alex?'

'This is Susan Redfern, Director General of MI5.'

'You should have listened to your instincts.' Redfern got up and walked into the light. She leaned against the table in front of Laing, chic and collected in her green two-piece suit and cream blouse, as if she were pausing against the table of a board room.

'It all makes perfect sense.' Laing chewed his lower lip and smiled bitterly. 'Why you told me not to bother monitoring Matthew's calls. Why you asked me to track Zarek rather than secure Manisha tonight. I suppose Simon is just another pawn, which is why I was told to leave him alone?'

Manisha's mind reeled at the mention of Simon. *If Simon's involved, did he say anything to them? How much do they know?* Her resolve strengthened.

Redfern smiled. 'Well done. I knew you'd get there, eventually. I was surprised at how long it took you. You're too institutionalised, Laing. You take orders, and you follow them without question, even if your instincts tell you otherwise. There were many times I thought you would push back and investigate me. But you're too stupid to do that. You were the perfect puppet.'

Manisha caught a fleeting glimpse of Laing's gritted teeth, but he maintained a calm tone.

'Whatever your plans are, you won't succeed,' he said with a shake of his head as he held Redfern's eyes in his gaze.

'An excellent segue, Laing. Let's talk about our plans,' Redfern said, as if chairing a corporate meeting. She walked towards Manisha, looking down on her with contempt. From the corner of her eye, Manisha could see Laing reach for the heel of his right shoe. Fingers stretched, he slowly opened a hidden compartment and removed a small, folded knife. He quietly opened the knife and started to cut through the ropes which bound his wrists. Manisha held Redfern's stare as she spoke.

'We know you've made a breakthrough, Manisha. Would you care to enlighten us?' Redfern asked.

'Go to hell! I'm not telling you anything.'

'That's a pity. Someone is going to get hurt tonight, and more blood will be spilt.'

Zarek stood and walked towards Manisha, who rose and stepped back from him, ready to kick out if she needed to.

'No, Zarek. We don't want to damage the asset,' Redfern said. 'However, I'm sure she wouldn't want to see anybody else hurt due to her inability to share information.'

Zarek grabbed Manisha, his powerful fingers digging into her shoulder as he forced her to kneel again. 'Stay down!'

Manisha looked at Laing compassionately, knowing he would take the full brunt of her silence.

'You can't hurt me,' Laing said. 'I would never lower myself to your traitorous depths and you know I'd happily die for my country.'

Manisha watched Redfern take one step closer to Laing, as nausea rose in her stomach.

'You call me a traitor, but you have no idea why I'm doing this.'

'Why, then?' Laing asked, keeping Redfern talking.

Manisha kept one eye on Laing, cutting through the rope which bound him, while Redfern took centre stage.

'The Earth is dying. The human population is exploding, accelerating the climate crisis, and the damage we're doing to our planet will be irreversible without urgent intervention. In the meantime, unnecessary wars continue to pollute the planet, pandemics threaten our survival and famines kill millions. The time for change is now!

'Much of the human population waste trillions of hours in their own personal power struggles, addicted to TV or social media, or in a drug-induced haze. They don't understand that their habitual life of convenience is destroying our world. People are shocked by the impact of climate change, but very few are prepared to do anything about it.'

'What's your grand plan to fix humanity, Ma'am?'

Redfern walked closer to Laing. 'People believe that money and military might are the true source of power. However, control of the money markets, flexing of political muscles, and posturing with nuclear weapons is not the way to dominate. The only way to save our planet, and create a peaceful, sustainable future, is to control human consciousness. When we tap into human consciousness, we're inside a person's head. We can influence people without them even knowing it. We'll have the ability to focus human thoughts on the common goal by stealth and stop the wasteful pursuit of their own personal ambitions—or their mind-numbing drug of choice.'

Manisha shook her head, incredulous. She could see from the corner of her eye that Laing's hands were desperately trying to free themselves. 'What's your ultimate ambition?' she asked, hoping to keep Redfern talking for as long as possible.

'Oh, my dear, it's not just my ambition, it's Heylel's ambition. I'm just another cog in Heylel's well-oiled machine.'

'Who are Heylel?'

'Heylel have been silently manipulating humanity for centuries. Financing world leaders who support our cause and opposing those who don't. However, time is running out and we need to take a more direct approach. Which is why we are here, Professor Williams.

'Our long-term goal is quite simple. Our leaders think on an elevated level, deeper than geographic egotism. Imagine the world coming together as one. A borderless world, with a single government and a single faith. A world where the common people look up to and obey their leaders without question. War will be eliminated overnight. The trillions of dollars spent on defence budgets will be redirected to the new focus of saving the planet and saving humanity. We will eliminate famine and accelerate technology to create sustainable, eco-friendly commerce and industry across the globe. Heylel's leaders will guide us towards this strategic, utopian vision while the population will focus on advancements to save our planet, rather than wasting their precious lives on trivial pursuits.

'Heylel has cohorts in positions of power within all

governments and major organisations across the globe. They are ready to step up and use their influence when the time is ripe. Heylel will rule. We will save the planet—this little human life raft we call Earth—and secure the future of humanity. However,to achieve this, the human race will need to work together as one. Only then will we realise the unlimited power of the human consciousness.'

Manisha shook her head. 'How can you control something humanity doesn't even understand? My work will help people to communicate. But it will not help you control people or save the planet. You're deluded.'

Redfern walked over to Manisha and looked down at her with an unnerving fire in her eyes. 'Your research is just the start. Once you unlock the door, the possibilities will be endless. Our scientists believe control over human consciousness will become a reality. They just need the key. The key which you hold, Manisha. With your expertise, you can play an important part in our vision.' Redfern held out a limp hand of friendship.

Matthew stepped forward. 'Come and join us, Manisha. Heylel's vision of the future is incredible.'

'You've been brainwashed, Matthew. I thought you were stronger than this.'

Matthew held out his bloodied hands. 'Brainwashed? Humanity has been conditioned to conform to the dysfunctional reality we've been trapped in for decades.'

'You need to open your eyes, Manisha. Your work is more important than you realise,' Redfern said.

'I won't help you. I'd rather die.'

Redfern looked at the floor, disappointment etched on her face. 'Someone may die tonight,' she said, looking back at Laing.

'You've been led astray,' Manisha said. 'No one can influence consciousness; it's not technically possible.'

Redfern continued, ignoring Manisha's attempt at grounding the conversation with scientific truth.

'We will advance our technology so power production, farming and transportation can be made one hundred per cent carbon neutral. We'll rebuild Earth's atmosphere and return it to a healthy, pre-industrialisation state. It only takes a small tweak in people's thinking to nudge them in the right direction.

'You make it all sound so easy,' Laing said sarcastically.

There was a cold, inhumane tone to Redfern's retort. 'We have a strategy that's been modelled and simulated—we know it will work.'

'You've been deceived. It's impossible,' Manisha said.

Frustration washed over Redfern's face. 'Nothing is impossible, and we can't sit back and wait until it's too late,' she said, shaking her head. 'Too many governments are happy to take a light touch to the climate problem, while ensuring their GDP remains high. The time to act is now!' Redfern breathed deeply, controlling her anger. 'But first things first. Let's get back to the objective of this gathering.'

Manisha edged away as Redfern moved closer to speak to her. She saw the woman's face looming above her, as she delivered each word slowly, as if trying to convince a child. 'You hold the key to change the world, Manisha. You hold the key to save our planet. Are you going to help us—or not?'

For a split second, Manisha could see credence in Redfern's desire to change human behaviour in such a way to save the earth and humanity. But she caught herself; the ethics directly opposed her moral beliefs.

'Never,' Manisha said, feeling a determination born from

the knowledge she was in control, even though the situation showed otherwise. She held the bargaining chip, and she was prepared to die to keep her secret.

'That's a shame,' Redfern said, chewing her lip in disappointment. 'Let's see how much compassion you really have for another human life.'

She gave the nod to Zarek.

Manisha glanced at Laing, horror tightening her chest as he was dragged to his feet. She glimpsed him folding the knife away, holding it tight in his fist so Zarek couldn't see it.

Zarek pushed Laing backwards up the three steps until he was standing on the top of the small wooden platform. Laing's shoulders were bathed in light with his face in dark shadow. His silhouette looked like a man about to be hung.

A sob caught in Manisha's constricted throat. Zarek was standing behind Laing. Her eyes followed the rope from Laing's bound hands towards the ceiling. It ran through the pulley system and back down to the floor. Fear rose in Manisha's chest as she watched Zarek's large, powerful hands grab the loose end of the rope and pull hard, lifting Laing six feet above the steps, his arms stretched out behind him.

She watched helplessly as Laing cried out in pain. His arms shook as he summoned all his strength to prevent his shoulders from being dislocated. His breath came in short, sharp bursts as he tried to maintain his position. As Manisha looked on, she could see the growing agony Laing felt in his wrists, arms, shoulders and back. Ten to fifteen seconds passed before relief washed over her, as Zarek let the rope slowly slip through his hands, lowering Laing gently to the floor.

Manisha's breath came in waves. She felt totally helpless, shocked that Redfern would torture one of her own loyal people. She wanted to scream and beg them to stop, but her resolve was too strong. She could not reveal her secret.

'Next time, I'll drop him,' Zarek said to Manisha.

Manisha watched as Laing got to his knees, quietly unfolding the knife. He looked desperate, and she doubted he could stomach such torture again.

'Do you have anything to share with us, Professor Williams?' Redfern asked, her eyebrows raised.

Manisha could see no remorse in Redfern's eyes but knew she had only one option. 'No,' she said, as she bowed down her head.

'Very well.' Redfern gave the nod.

Zarek pulled the rope swiftly, and more vigorously than before, hoisting Laing up high. Laing cried out in pain. A primeval, sickening cry that shot straight to Manisha's heart. She caught a glint from the knife behind Laing's back, which he had no time to conceal. The knife cut into his hand and blood dripped as he held it tight. Zarek's focus on the rope saved his secret.

Tears clouded Manisha's eyes as she watched in horror. Laing's shoulders shook as he used all his strength to support his weight, and he breathed sharply through the pain.

'Very impressive,' Zarek said.

Laing held his position for thirty seconds before being dropped to the floor. Manisha flinched as she watched his body crash onto the wooden steps, his face smacking against the cold marble floor. He rolled around, writhing in agony.

'Next time, I'll rip your arms out of their sockets.'

Laing was angled with his back to Manisha. She looked on as he continued hacking at the rope, already halfway through.

Manisha felt Redfern's icy gaze.

'I can do this all night, you know,' Redfern said. 'During my career, I've often had to question people using conventional and unconventional methods. I've never known a person who hasn't cracked. We rarely kill. We find inflicting pain, maiming, and psychologically destroying a person's will is far more rewarding. We always get what we want. The question you need to ask yourself is: how long can you play this game for? Do you want to be responsible for destroying this man's life?'

Manisha knelt in silence. *What can I say to make them stop?* She frantically searched for a solution, but her mind went blank with panic. 'I will tell you nothing,' she said, as tears spilled from her eyes.

Redfern stood above her, smiling. 'It's ironic, isn't it? If we had your technology now, we wouldn't be having this conversation. No one would be getting hurt. I would simply hook you up to a machine and probe your mind to get what we wanted.' Redfern shook her head and sighed. A subtle nod was given to Zarek, who smiled in delight.

Manisha could barely bring herself to watch as Laing was lifted off the ground, his feet dangling as his arms were ripped up behind his back. Zarek pulled harder on the end of the rope, taking his victim ten feet above the floor. Manisha knew what was coming next. She watched him breathing through the pain, his expression changing to resignation, preparing himself for the agony that was about to come.

Zarek let go of the rope, and Laing dropped five feet. Zarek caught it again and Laing stopped with a jolt, his arms ripping upwards behind his back. He cried out as his arms fought to hold his weight—but there was no dislocation.

Only a sudden free fall as the rope snapped, sending Laing crashing to the floor.

Zarek looked on, open-mouthed. His prisoner was free.

Laing got to his knees, his knife still in his hand. In one seamless move, he sent it flying, blade over handle towards Redfern's head, missing her by millimetres. It embedded itself into the wooden chair behind her.

Zarek yanked his gun from behind his back, aiming it straight at Laing.

With her hands still bound, Manisha charged at Zarek, ramming her shoulder into his ribs. He staggered back, losing his grip on the gun. It skidded across the marble floor as she scrambled into the shadows. Laing reached for the gun, rolling along the floor as a barrage of poorly aimed rounds flew over his head from Redfern's pistol. He swept the weapon into his hand, rolled in front of Manisha, and stood, protecting her behind his frame. She cowered behind his broad back as Redfern and Laing pulled their triggers in the same instant. Laing's shot found its target. The bullet hit Redfern square in the chest. She slumped backwards, bounced off the table, and slid to the floor, her eyes staring blankly.

Redfern's bullet grazed Laing's shoulder and carried on its trajectory towards Manisha. Pain shot through her head as she felt the bullet scrape the side of her temple. The impact reverberated through her skull, stunning her. She fell backwards, her vision blurred, her body limp, unable to break her rapid descent. A loud smack was the last thing she heard as she struck her head on the marble floor.

∼

Zarek stood wide-eyed. Regaining his grip on the situation, he kicked the back of Laing's legs to bring him to his knees. He then executed a perfect roundhouse kick to Laing's head, which sent him crashing to the floor. He heard the skidding sound as the gun slipped from Laing's fingers. Zarek looked down at Laing as he lay on his back, dazed. He bent over and retrieved his firearm. A shot rang out as a single bullet, delivered at point-blank range, hit Laing's chest. Zarek looked on as Laing's body shook with the impact, then lay still, devoid of life.

'What do we do now?' Matthew asked, a tremor in his voice.

Zarek turned to look at Matthew who stood behind the table, white with fear. As he walked towards the table, the gun felt heavy in his hand. '*We* are doing nothing,' he said. 'You are no longer required.' Zarek raised the weapon and shot Matthew in the head. He watched dispassionately as the young man's body fell to the floor with a heavy thud.

Quiet and stillness surrounded him. Zarek's head spun as he tried to comprehend how his vision for the future could have ended so abruptly. Everything he had worked tirelessly for had come crashing down around him in seconds.

He walked over to Manisha's lifeless body. He felt her neck and wrists, desperately looking for signs of a pulse. There wasn't one.

'You can't be dead,' he whispered as he stroked her hair, willing signs of life to appear. Slinging his rucksack over his shoulders, he slid his arms beneath her slight frame and gently lifted her lifeless body, knowing this fragile shell contained the secret that could propel Heylel to mastery over the human race.

He carried Manisha's limp body down several flights of

stairs, trying not to bang her head on the solid stone walls. Raising his boot, he kicked the door to the Doge's Palace medical room open. It banged loudly as he passed through. His eyes searched the room and landed on two women in white uniforms, who jumped up from their seats as he entered. Seeing Manisha's limp body, the nurses rushed to her.

'You have to keep her alive,' Zarek said.

27

'I could not possibly be of such a nature as I am, and yet have in my mind the idea of a God, if God did not in reality exist.'

René Descartes – Philosopher (1596–1650)

Everything was impossibly still.

Manisha felt relaxed in her body and mind, like a pond's surface with a crystal-clear reflection on a beautiful summer's day. Her body felt weightless, warm and cosy, as if a million soft feathers were supporting her. Quiet surrounded her. Nothing could spoil this moment; it was absolutely perfect.

She lay with her eyes shut, not wanting to open them, afraid the sensation would pass once she allowed the reality around her to seep in. She hung on to the feeling, with positive thoughts of love and compassion filling her mind. She couldn't remember the last time she had allowed herself to relax so deeply. She always had deadlines to meet or something to achieve. None of that seemed to matter now. She was happy simply being.

Manisha had no recollection of how she'd got here, but she was filled with love and joy and without a care in the world. Her memories of her ordeal in the Doge's Palace seemed distant, and were not strong enough to pull her from the sanctuary she now found herself in. They were mere recollections of what had been; dreamlike shadows of the past that were now insignificant. They were what they were and nothing more. She felt no fear, no pain, worry, or stress. Just a deep sensation of peace.

She knew she'd been shot and remembered the enormous wave of pain which had engulfed her. It had happened so quickly. She had no idea how bad her injuries were, or if she would ever be the same again. However, she felt no fear or worry about the future.

How can I feel so good after everything that's happened? She was aware of feeling totally objective and removed from the situation. It was as if the answer to the question was insignificant and wouldn't change anything, anyway.

Whatever drugs they've given me, they're amazing... But then she stopped, as if answering her own question. *There are no drugs. Your mind is pure and clean.*

This sudden lucidity stunned Manisha. *I must be dreaming.* But again, her mind answered the question with such absolute certainty that it took her aback. *No, you're not.* She knew the answer to her own question before her mind had even finished asking.

Manisha lay for an indeterminate amount of time, relaxing and soaking up the moment. She allowed the warmth and peace to penetrate deep into her being, healing her.

Eventually, curiosity took over, and she allowed herself to become aware of her surroundings. The orangey-pink hue in her unopened eyes hinted she was in a bright room with the sun pouring in through a window, providing a glorious warmth. She blinked and slowly allowed them to open, like a baby using its eyes for the first time. Through her blurred vision, she could see she was in a white room with light flooding in. But she could not tell where the light was coming from.

A woman appeared next to her, bringing her vision into focus. Manisha looked up, and a broad smile greeted her. Deep blue eyes returned her stare.

'Hello, Manisha. How are you feeling?'

'I feel amazing. Very relaxed, thank you.' Manisha said, mesmerised by the woman's gaze.

'Good, I'm glad to hear it.'

'You are so beautiful,' Manisha said, hypnotised by the deep look of love and compassion in the eyes of her carer. Her own directness shocked her. It was as though her filter had been switched off, and she'd said what she was thinking without knowing it.

'Thank you.' The woman smiled broadly and sat beside Manisha, perfectly still, relaxed and composed.

'How long have I been unconscious?'

'Not long. But you're going to be fine. Relax and be at peace for a while longer. When you're ready, we can talk.'

'Okay.' Manisha smiled and let the feeling envelop her again.

Silence filled the room. Not an awkward silence, but a peaceful one. Manisha could feel the woman beside her and felt safe knowing there was no time pressure for her to decide when to get up and have an examination, or whatever was to happen next.

Manisha moved her hand to her head, searching for a wound or a bandage covering it. However, she felt nothing. No dressing, no scar. It was as if the events of the evening had never happened.

Keeping her eyes closed, she reached out for the woman's hand, wondering if she was real or part of a hallucination. A soft hand was placed on hers. Manisha felt a warm, fluid-like sensation, as though the woman was caressing her palm.

'Who are you?'

'I'm here to care for you, Manisha. You've been through a horrific experience. But you're safe now, and I'm sure you'll be back to your work before you know it.'

'I'm not sure I want to return to work,' Manisha said. 'It's too lovely here.'

The woman's laughter gently echoed around the room, filling Manisha's head.

'You can't stay here. You have important work to do. But you already know that, don't you?'

Manisha wanted the feeling to last forever. However, she knew it could not. *Do all good things have to end?* she thought. But again, a voice in her head responded.

This peace will never leave you, Manisha. It is your gift to cherish—but this peace is not where your journey ends.

Manisha slowly opened her eyes and sat up. A warm breeze caressed her skin as it floated through an open window. A sea of turquoise waves flooded the view with sunlight bouncing off their crests. She breathed deeply, and the salty sea air filled her lungs.

All her senses seemed exaggerated. Everything she looked at, heard, smelt, tasted, or felt seemed to be a hundred times more intense than before. However, it wasn't overwhelming. It was perfect.

'Are we still in Venice?' Manisha asked.

The woman smiled. 'Just rest.'

Manisha was captivated by her carer. She was more beautiful than any woman she had ever seen. A simple white linen full-length gown covered her shapely body. Her blond hair hung loosely over her shoulders. A light pair of sandals protected the soles of her feet. However, it was her eyes Manisha found most remarkable: blue eyes that looked out from above the broad cheekbones, full lips, and sculpted chin which complemented her face perfectly.

'You make me feel so relaxed. You're very good at your job,' Manisha said. 'I can tell you have been doing this for a long time.'

The woman laughed. 'I've been doing this longer than you can ever imagine. But there is no place I'd rather be than by your side, Manisha.'

'What's your name?'

'You can call me Sarah.'

'Thank you for looking after me, Sarah.'

'It's my pleasure.'

A wave of anxiety crashed over Manisha. 'Is Alex Laing here?'

'No, Manisha, he is not.'

'Is he still alive?'

'Don't worry, it's going to be fine.'

Manisha lay back, closed her eyes, and let herself relax, trusting her new friend completely.

'I was having an amazing dream before I woke up, Sarah. I was flying, and pure white light surrounded me. I felt an amazing sensation of speed, but I could hear no wind rushing past my ears or through my hair. In fact, there was no sensation of sound at all,' Manisha paused, reflecting on the experience she'd had. 'Then, the bright light closed behind me, and I felt safe. It was such a lovely feeling.'

This must be why I feel so relaxed now, she thought. *I've woken up still immersed in the feelings from my dream.*

I'm glad you enjoyed the experience, Manisha.

Manisha turned her head towards Sarah as she heard her voice, but was amazed to see her lips were not moving.

Manisha looked intently at Sarah. *What's happening?*

It's always strange the first time you see it, Sarah said, answering the question Manisha had only asked to herself, within her mind.

Can you read my thoughts? Manisha asked silently in her head.

Yes, I can.

Have you advanced my research? Manisha looked down at her body for wires and glanced around the room for some form of equipment she could recognise. But she could see nothing—no technology, no computers, just a simple room with simple furniture.

This is the way we have always been able to communicate, Manisha. However, humans have developed verbal language and technology, and have forgotten how to use a gift they are born with.

How come I can use this gift now?

Sarah leaned closer and placed her hand on Manisha's arm.

Manisha, you've passed over. Your body is dead.

28

'Perception is not a window on objective reality. It is an interface that hides objective reality behind a veil of helpful icons.'

Donald D. Hoffman – Cognitive Psychologist (1955–)

The smell of propellant hung in the air from the multiple rounds fired. Laing lay in silence. He stared up at the wooden rafters, wondering how he was still alive. The intense burn in his chest was all the evidence he needed to prove he'd had a lucky escape. The bulletproof vest had done its job.

He stayed still, kept his breathing shallow, and strained his ears for any sign that Zarek might be waiting to discharge a fatal round. He could hear no movement or breathing apart from his own and let out a painful sigh. Lying on his back, he lifted his head. Redfern's dead eyes stared blankly ahead. Matthew's body lay slumped at her feet. Behind him, a spray of blood splatter snapped his attention back to Manisha. *Where is she?*

He propped himself up on his left elbow. The movement brought intense pain to his chest, and he let out an uncontrollable groan. He found the used slug, pulled it from the body armour, and held it between his finger and thumb, studying it. His gut lurched, knowing it could easily have been the one that killed him.

He threw it across the room and pushed the thought from his mind. As he eased himself up to scan the room further, he rubbed his sore chest and touched his shoulder. The wound where the bullet had grazed his skin left a faint smear of blood on his fingers. Pain shot through his arms as he stretched them, releasing the tension after the torture they'd been through. Several drops of blood on the marble floor caught his eye. He followed the path to the nearest doorway, convinced that it would lead to Zarek and Manisha.

Laing knew a fistfight in his current condition would end badly for him. He needed weapons. The knife which had aided his escape came away from the chair with ease. Redfern's pistol still felt heavy, and on checking the magazine, four bullets remained. He gave his ex-boss a final look of disdain and limped towards the door.

A discreet check confirmed the coast was clear before Laing entered the corridor. He hobbled as quickly as his injuries would allow, following gleaming crimson droplets down to the lower levels of the palace. Pain gnawed at his limbs, fatigue dragging him down. He stumbled, crashing clumsily against the stairwell corners. Each time he breathed deep to collect himself and peered down the next flight of stairs, his gun outstretched. He followed this routine for four flights until he saw a guard positioned at the end of a long corridor to protect the next flight of stairs. It was then the muffled sounds of people shouting from the level below reached his ears.

Bullet or knife? Laing couldn't handle more guards coming, so a silent approach was the only option. He crouched in a doorway, out of sight, with his eyes firmly fixed on the guard's shadow. He coughed, hoping to draw the guard down the passage. The guard's shadow moved slightly, but he didn't take the bait. Laing coughed louder. The guard's shadow grew larger as the man stood. Laing heard a button pop and the scrape of a gun being unholstered as the guard walked slowly towards him.

Laing crept back into the shadows of a small room and hid in the darkened recess, leaving the door ajar. The guard walked past the doorway, gun aimed and ready. He looked around the corner of the corridor but saw nothing. He shook his head, re-holstered his weapon, and turned to walk back to his post.

Laing slipped from the shadows and seized his prey. His fingers clamped over the man's mouth, jerking his head back to expose his throat. The blade sliced deep—one swift, lethal stroke. Warm blood gushed, seeping between Laing's fingers as he steadied the guard's weight. His body felt heavy in Laing's arms; it twitched as he dragged it through the doorway into the cold stillness of the darkened room. The guard lay lifeless on the floor, the flow of blood from his neck slowing. Laing stepped across the body and into the corridor, closing the door behind him. The crimson pool momentarily reflected what little light there was.

A rapid flow of adrenaline coursed around Laing's body, suppressing his chest and leg pain. The sound of anxious voices grew louder as he made his way down another flight of steps. He inched forward to listen.

'Give her adrenaline and shock her,' Zarek demanded.

'It's not as simple as that,' a female voice said. 'Give her chest compressions while I cover her body with blankets. She needs to be kept warm.'

Laing stood back and looked through a side window, which housed a grid of metal bars. Manisha was laid on a table covered in blankets. Zarek performed chest compressions while a nurse rhythmically squeezed and released the bag valve mask, covering Manisha's nose and mouth, forcing oxygen into her body. Another nurse quickly wired up a defibrillator.

Laing's breath caught in his throat. Manisha deserved to be saved; the thought of losing her cut deep. For the first time in what seemed like forever, he had met someone he could trust—someone with morals. A stark contrast to the long line of people who had betrayed him over the years. He fought to stop himself bursting through the door and killing Zarek. He knew that any intervention would waste precious time. He needed to leave the nurses to do their jobs. He stared intently at Zarek. *You had better keep her alive, you bastard.*

Keeping his emotions calm, Laing moved back into a doorway. The door creaked open, and he found himself inside a storeroom. Cold. Empty. Another barred window offered a glimpse into the room where Manisha's life hung in the balance. He felt helpless. The continuous flatline sound of the heart monitor plagued him. He stood in the darkness, willing it to spring into life with the steady beep of an active heart. He continued to glare at Zarek. *Whatever happens, you're going to die tonight.*

The sound of a defibrillator charging diverted his attention to the nurse who held the paddles up high, ready to position and discharge them when the time was right.

The nurse leaned over Manisha's lifeless body. 'Charging —two hundred—CLEAR!'

Zarek stood back, his eyes wide. Manisha's tiny body shook as the current shot through her chest.

The heart rate monitor continued to flatline.

29

'The kingdom of God is within you.'

The Bible – Luke 17:21

Manisha sat in silence, struggling to comprehend the truth she'd just been told.

I'm dead?

She felt no anxiety at being given such news; her peace and tranquillity continued. However, her perspective had changed.

She opened her eyes. Everything looked and felt so real. She spread her fingers on the smooth white sheets, trying to understand the sensation of touch she was experiencing. *How can I see my hand if my body is dead? I have no eyes to see with, no fingers to touch with, no body at all. It's dead. But my mind lives on?*

Manisha asked the question, hoping Sarah would give a decisive answer. But her companion remained silent.

Manisha studied her surroundings from her new viewpoint: the room, the bed she lay on, the view from the window, and the sea air she inhaled. The truth suddenly dawned on her. The reality she was experiencing was created in her mind. She didn't need a body in which to live.

Is this life in its purest form?

Sarah smiled. *Yes, Manisha. This is our true nature.*

Manisha extrapolated further and realised the discoveries from her research overlapped with the experience she was having. *The thoughts filling my mind and memories of events throughout my whole life were not being recalled from my brain. They were coming from the energy that creates who I am.*

Manisha, the space you have lived in during your physical life has been created by the way your brain responds to input from your senses. This builds your thoughts, feelings, and the reality you experience every second of your life. You have lived in a virtual bubble created by your mind.

Then, my theory is correct. Nothing truly exists, apart from what you think and how you feel.

Sarah smiled.

Manisha tried to comprehend how her earthly reality worked. She understood her mind created her interpretation of the world via the input from her senses. However, she couldn't understand how other beings interacted with her version of reality. *Do all other beings only exist in my mind?* She attempted to solve the conundrum for some time before Sarah offered a clue.

Remember, Manisha, we are all one. A single consciousness.

Another piece of the puzzle slipped into place for Manisha. *The reality created within the single consciousness is there for every mind to access. Consciousness forms one environ-*

ment, and the energy around us is just information. The location of every atom is stored so when another conscious being comes along and alters that space, the changes are recorded, ready for the next mind to interact with the energy in that space. Like a 3D version of pixels on a VDU.

Manisha worked through a simple scenario. *A cup is moved by a person and placed on a table in a room. The room doesn't physically exist, the same way the table and cup do not exist. They are energy moulded into the shape of a room, table, and a cup within the single consciousness. When that person leaves the room, the room and its contents no longer physically exist, as they are no longer being observed, and they return to the background sea of energy that creates the universe. However, the configuration of the room, including the location of the cup, is recorded. When another conscious being experiences that space, the cup is where another person left it. Everything we experience on Earth is the manifestation of energy, moulded and recorded within the single consciousness.*

Manisha smiled. It was elementary and sophisticated beyond belief; the universe was one sea of energy that could be transformed into whatever our minds wanted it to be. *The world is not out there; it exists within us. We create our own virtual bubble.*

She recalled the times she had looked into the night sky, pondering the existence of extra-terrestrial life in distant galaxies. However, now she understood, when she gazed into the night sky and saw the light from the stars, she was looking at other life. This was evidence that the single consciousness had created something else out there—evidence of something that other minds had created, observed and experienced within the single consciousness. *Where there is light, there is life.*

Yes, Manisha. The only difference between life and death is that you're taken back to your purest form of energy when you die. The energy that creates everything in the universe. Every experience you've had during your life, every thought, every feeling, can never be erased. A record of life is taken for every conscious being. Review your life, Manisha.

Manisha found she could go back to any moment in her life and recall each second with absolute clarity: what she saw, smelled, tasted, who she was with, and how she felt. Her life review started in her mother's womb when the first spark of her life was ignited, and she was given a body in which to live. She raced through childhood, adolescence and through her years at Oxford, stopping to explore the moments that exposed the most substantial feelings. The good memories outweighed the bad. But every memory was filled with a deep recollection and clarity of pure water. Manisha had a sense of being, observing and reflecting simultaneously. Gratitude welled up inside her as she remembered the happy times she'd had and the good she'd done for others in her life. The time she had run the London marathon and raised over seven thousand pounds for *Save the Children* which helped orphans in Turkey. Sarah showed Manisha the positive, life-changing effect she had on people she had never even met. Regret flooded her consciousness for the times she had mistreated people. The time she had teased a school friend to the point of making her cry, for not being able to solve a simple algebra equation. And the time she had fallen out with her mother and said words in anger that she could never take back. Tears of happiness and sadness pricked behind her eyes.

The impact of Manisha's reflection didn't go unnoticed by Sarah. *Our actions and the way we make other people feel are so important. You cannot make another person happy, as happiness comes from within. But you should never be malicious towards another being and make them feel unhappy. As an adult, you have come to know this, but you had so much to learn as a child. I can feel your shame. Through your actions and decisions, you can touch the lives of people you've never met and transform them beyond recognition. Never underestimate the difference you can make in the world, Manisha.*

The final seconds of her life were played back in slow motion. Manisha could see Laing in front of her and caught a glimpse of Redfern raising her weapon on the other side of the room. Shots were exchanged simultaneously, with the rounds crossing in the middle of the room. Manisha saw the bullet speeding towards her and could see the air being displaced as it approached Laing, a sonic wave created in its wake. The shot clipped the top of Laing's shoulder, grazing it. A small stream of blood seeped from the wound. The shot kept coming towards her head, and she felt the impact as the bullet clipped the side of her skull, throwing her backwards to where she smashed her head against the marble floor.

Manisha's life review faded to black.

She opened her eyes and felt sad that her life had been so short.

This is not the end, Manisha. This is just the beginning.

Manisha let Sarah's words bounce off her as she thought logically about what she'd just experienced. *Every moment of every life is captured, retained, and stored forever. The technology I have used to capture a single thought, a single moment, is a split second of life. When combined with the millions of other seconds which have been recorded, we have the memories of a lifetime. Our lives are created within our minds. A quantum of thought is a snapshot of our reality within a moment. We are energy experiencing life, thoughts and feelings, pure and simple.*

I'm pleased you understand, Manisha. You have looked over

your past life. Now let's look to the future. We use our intuition to know if our path is the right one during our lives on Earth. In this place, your intuition is heightened and more accurate. The future is never certain, but you can see the possible outcomes of decisions and events. Look to the future, Manisha. Ask a question and trust the thoughts and feelings that come back to you.

Manisha focused on her research and the effects it could have on humanity. The future she planned for her work and its ability to help people was one of many possible outcomes. She could see this path clearly with the profound and positive impact it could have on the quality of people's lives. Seeing people communicate for the first time in years, decades, filled her with pride. The joy it brought families and friends was immense.

But with every great discovery comes responsibility. Science has always been a double-edged sword, capable of healing or harming. Could she trust humanity to use her work wisely?

Manisha's thoughts shifted to the other extreme. A vision where her greatest fear became a reality. A future where humanity would repeat history and use science as a weapon. Heylel had developed the technology to interface with human consciousness and implant thoughts. They had created propaganda by stealth and used it to control minds, making humanity slaves without free will. Billions perished, slaughtered in a calculated frenzy disguised as climate salvation. Friends and families turned on one another. The streets reeked of blood and decay as mountains of bodies were carted away, some burned, others left to rot. The new global order was unprepared for the famine and disease that followed, unintentionally condemning millions more to an agonising fate. Those who lived suffered an existence in abject misery. Manisha could take no more and stopped her future projection.

There are many possible outcomes from your discovery being used by weak and power-hungry human minds. The visions you've seen are the very best and the very worst. The reality will fall somewhere in between these extremes. We are the guardians, Manisha. We must protect your discovery and ensure it is used wisely by humanity.

Manisha wiped tears from her face, shocked at the suffering humanity could inflict on itself. She looked at the moisture on her hand. *How can I cry? How can I experience this place, these surroundings, without a body and senses?*

Manisha, you can imagine any surroundings in this place and make them real for you. Right here, right now, you are seeing what you expected to see. A simple room with a view over Venice lagoon. The body you can see is created by your mind's residual self-image and nothing more.

Manisha turned her focus to her breath, breathing deep, in and out. However, she now accepted she had no lungs to breathe into. There was no air to breathe anyway. As the realisation took hold, Manisha's breathing started to shallow and slow until it stopped. She felt no different, as if she had kicked a habit she no longer needed. Without a physical body, there was no reason to breathe.

Manisha raised her hand and studied it. *My hand doesn't really exist; it is created in my mind.*

Free yourself, Manisha. Free your mind.

She studied her fingers, becoming acutely aware of every line and pore as if looking at her skin under a microscope. The light falling on her hands began to shift and move. Breaking up and recreating itself, as if her mind was caught between the reality she now found herself in, and the reality she had been grounded in for over thirty years.

As she relaxed further, the light altered and fluctuated. The energy that formed her hand began to glow and break up into thousands of tiny stars. They ran in rivulets and joined in pools of bright light on the bed. She was transfixed as she watched her hands slowly disappear into a glowing stream of light radiating from the end of her arms, which transformed into orbs of energy. She held them up in wonder, sending the rivers of light shooting out in all directions, which re-joined into a minute, dense ball of energy.

She smiled and felt pure joy as liquid light dropped onto the bed and spread out, disassembling, and consuming everything in its path. The speed of change gained momentum as Manisha relaxed. The snaking lines of pure, bright light ran up the room's walls and across the ceiling, making the room dissolve, revealing an even background of energy.

The light spread up her arms towards her shoulders, creating a warm glow where there had once been an idea of cloth, skin, and bone. Manisha surrendered herself to the sensation willingly, encouraging her body to disappear. Overcome with a feeling of ecstasy, Manisha turned her gaze towards Sarah, who was now also fading from view, as the whole room and everything in it became one intense pool of energy. The radiance spread, dissolving into the very fabric of existence, interwoven with the cosmos, leaving two blinding, bright lights. Two stars representing human lives in their purest form.

Manisha no longer needed a physical world. She felt no need to project a familiar reality around her. She dissolved into her original essence, a radiant force beyond form. Space and time as she had known them ceased to exist. She perceived everything at once. All the universe's past histories, and possibilities that were yet to come, were hers to know. She could experience her previous lives, going back through countless millennia, sensing everything as though she were there, reliving her past lives in perfect detail. She went back to her true birth, the birth of the universe and the cosmic force that shaped the stars, the distant galaxies, and all conscious minds. Everyone, everything, came from the one true source. The one true beginning that ignited the universe into life and created consciousness. Everything that can be seen and everything that cannot be seen—matter, dark matter, dark energy, and light—came from this. She understood and could feel its presence all around her. *We are all one. We are all connected. We share a consciousness of pure, ubiquitous and unending energy.*

Manisha's thoughts turned back to her life and the family and friends she had loved and lost. She followed the life of a man most dear to her. A man she would give anything to talk to again. She hoped in this place, she could connect with him. Then Sarah spoke.

He's still alive, Manisha. He will be there to help you. He will stand by your side again.

30

'If science could get rid of consciousness, it would have disposed of the only stumbling block to its universal application.'

Brand Blanshard – Philosopher (1892–1987)

Manisha's perception had changed. She hovered above her body, watching the nurses attempt to perform their miracle. The room around her glowed. Every atom that made up her surroundings radiated its energy in the form of silver and gold light, shimmering and glistening.

Her floating, elevated self was also glowing. Her reformed body, created by her mind, glowed with the same translucent energy. A bright, shimmering aura surrounded her. Manisha looked down on her dead body but felt removed from the experience, as if it were not her corpse lying there.

The thoughts of the people in the room filled Manisha's head—some loud and aggressive, others muted and considered. She could tune in to an individual's perspective and experience what they saw and felt. She was amazed at the passion and intensity in the nurses as they worked to bring her body and soul back together. Their beating hearts glowed brightly with positive, kind, and pure energy. A stark contrast to the dull red glow from Zarek's chest. A heart full of narcissism and darkness.

Zarek stood with his hands on his head, distress etched on his face. Manisha took a moment to glimpse into his version of reality. He had spent his whole life being told and believing that his destiny was to change the world. He had followed the orders of his superiors blindly and adopted the ritual of daily meditation and visualisation, believing this would ensure his success. Manisha knew that his aggressive outer confidence was overshadowed by a deep-seated fear that had eaten away at him since he was a child. A fear of abandonment and loneliness. He felt overwhelmed that his future, and everything he had worked for, now hung in the hands of two nurses he had only just met. He felt no remorse for what he was doing or the people he had killed. His life mission—to help manipulate and control humanity—was the only vision of the future he'd been taught. His foolish beliefs and the evil Manisha could feel in his misguided mind, made her pity him. *Were you a victim of circumstance or the perpetrator? Either way, your life will be reviewed, judged, and you will be put back on the right path.*

Manisha came down to ground level, standing, observing, unseen by anyone else in the room. She looked on as the nurses continued to work hard. However, she already knew what the outcome would be. Within her mind, the right path had already been mapped out. She had seen it. She knew what would happen tonight and that she would be guided throughout the rest of her existence. There was nothing to be afraid of.

She instinctively knew the earthly plane was a learning ground which provided an understanding of the impact of being kind, or harmful, had on humanity. The never-ending cycle of 'life—death—review' that a person goes through until enlightenment is reached—until an individual understands how the gift of life should be used to benefit all and not just the self. Protecting this learning ground was of the utmost importance. Manisha would allow no one to interfere with the natural evolution of consciousness.

She walked towards the doorway, and her hand accidentally passed through the wall. She stopped and played with the energy that formed it. Mathematically, she knew that such a phenomenon was possible at a quantum level, but witnessing it in action intrigued her.

She moved into the corridor and into the storeroom where Laing was waiting. He held a gun in one hand and a knife in the other. Manisha stood in front of him, studying his face carefully. She tuned into his inner self, to feel how he felt inside. The contrast to Zarek was striking. Laing's heart was strong and positive but tinged with an underlying sadness—the result of years of personal heartache and self-imposed berating borne from the regret of the lives he had taken. The years of active service had taken their toll. His rough face bore deep scars from previous conflicts. The blood on his clothes was evidence of how hard he had fought to protect Manisha that night. *For a man trained to kill, you have a kind face and a gentle soul.* She knew him as he knew himself. His genuine desire to do good, and his willingness to die to protect her secret, made her trust him completely—now and forever. She touched his chest, took away some of his pain, and watched as he physically relaxed, as though a weight had been lifted.

Manisha drifted back into the room where her body lay and prepared herself, knowing the moment was now close.

'Take over the compressions,' the nurse shouted at Zarek.

Zarek stepped towards Manisha's body, his eyes wide as he placed his hands on her sternum. Sweat dripped from his brow as he continued to massage Manisha's heart.

'How long has she been gone?' a nurse asked, looking to Zarek to provide the answer.

'Ah, at least ten minutes.'

The defibrillator charged for a third time, its rhythmic beep echoing around the room.

'This is our last chance. Charging—three hundred—CLEAR!' The paddles found their target and the charge was released.

Manisha saw her body shake violently as the current swept through her heart. The reality she found herself in started to disassemble itself and created a bright tunnel through which an invisible force pulled her. The speed of transition stunned her as she was thrust back into her body. A rush of pain coursed through her, as electrical impulses fired within her brain. She could feel the searing ache in her chest from the compressions and the excruciating headache where the bullet had grazed her skull. She tried to sit up, choking on the pipe used to keep her airway open during resuscitation.

One of the nurses stepped forward and pushed Zarek out of the way as she placed her hands on Manisha's shoulders. 'Just relax. You're going to be fine.' She laid her down and slowly removed the pipe.

The sensation made Manisha gag. She coughed and took deep, gasping breaths until her breathing settled back to a normal rhythm.

The room around Manisha was different. It had changed from its shimmering form of energy to the false reality she had lived in all her life. It felt strange, knowing this reality was just a construct used to enable the human experience. No matter how much pain she was in, or how strange it felt, she was grateful to be living a human life again.

The nurses placed a cannula into Manisha's hand and attached it to an intravenous drip to rehydrate her. An injection in her right arm provided pain relief and the wounds on her head were bandaged.

'Leave us,' Zarek said, without a word of thanks to the women for saving Manisha's life.

'Let her rest,' one of the nurses said.

Zarek stared at her as he waited for them to leave the room.

A cloud of morphine filled Manisha's brain, easing the pain. Through her blurred vision, she saw Zarek leaning over her and instinctively felt for her heart-shaped pendant.

A SURGE of elation raced through Zarek's veins. His world was back on its axis. The dread and incredulity he felt at Manisha's death had been replaced by a renewed positivity. He grabbed her hand and prised her grip from her pendant. He tied a length of rough rope around her wrist, then tossed the other end under the table. Walking around her, he picked it up and secured her other wrist tightly beneath the table. There was no chance of escape. Confident she was secure, he looked down at the scene before him. He took in every detail: her blouse, which hung loose; the smooth skin of her chest, still partly exposed. He walked behind her and gently pulled her hair out from under her. Her long black hair cascaded over the edge of the table, nearly touching the floor.

A glint from Manisha's necklace caught Zarek's eye. He gently picked up the pendant and caressed it between his finger and thumb. 'What's so important about your heart, Manisha?' He ripped the jewel roughly from her neck and she moaned. He looked at her face and back at the pendant. He studied the pendant closely, fiddling with its edges and pulling at its centre. A shiver of excitement ran through him as the two halves came apart, revealing the hidden USB stick. He looked around for his rucksack and, spotting it thrown down in the corner, he grabbed it and pulled out his laptop. His fingers felt large and clumsy as he plugged in the small stick to see what data was stored on the device. A banner appeared on the screen, prompting for a password.

Zarek bowed his head and laughed in frustration. 'Of course it's encrypted.' He tried a few obvious passwords. Each time the prompt changed, showing a decreasing number of attempts left, until it finally flashed, *'Final password attempt ... another incorrect password will wipe the device.'*

Zarek turned to Manisha and placed his large hand around her throat, squeezing it tightly. Her eyes opened wide as she struggled for breath.

'Tell me the password,' Zarek demanded. He released his grip, felt in his pocket and replaced his hand with cold, razor-sharp steel. He pressed his knife firmly against her throat. His hands were sweaty, and his voice wavered. 'Tell me now!'

Zarek watched as the fear in her eyes flickered, then hardened into unwavering confidence. 'I've been sent back for a reason,' she said. 'Whatever I do now, you will not succeed.'

Anger burst through him. 'Do not test me!' he shouted. 'Tell me the password.'

He couldn't quite believe it when Manisha spoke, her voice quiet but perfectly clear.

'SagAstar2025'

Zarek set the knife on the table and placed his fingers on the keyboard. 'Upper case or lower case?'

Manisha croaked, 'Upper case S, lowercase a...'

He carefully punched in the password, following her instructions precisely, but paused before hitting enter. He turned to Manisha. 'If you're lying to me, you'll wish you had died.'

He hit enter, his chest tight with anticipation, his breath catching as he watched and waited to see if he had been deceived. The screen went blank for several seconds and then filled with data. Documents, algorithms, formulae, and diaries of experiments with the more recent entries showing how a DNA sequence had been used to decode Simon's thoughts. Zarek smiled and then laughed. A feeling of control filled him. 'This information will give our scientists all they need to continue your work.' He turned to Manisha. 'All that effort to save your life for a single password. Now you're surplus to requirements.' He retrieved his knife and leaned over her, his grip tightening, his excitement growing.

'You're being used,' Manisha said. 'You're an irrelevant pawn in a much bigger game.'

'I may be a pawn, Manisha. But I'm a very important pawn whose success will change the world.' Zarek gently glided the blade across her neck, enjoying the sensation of power. 'You've left your mark, Manisha Williams. The scar on my face will be a permanent reminder of the good deed I did for you.'

'Good deed? You were trying to abduct me.'

'I was saving you from being raped. I should have left you to fend for yourself.'

'I don't believe you.'

'Whether you believe me or not is irrelevant. The fact is, we are finally here, and I have your research.' Zarek took a deep breath. 'I have visualised this moment hundreds of times, and now it's unfolding exactly as I predicted. There is nothing that can stop me now, Manisha. Thank you for your help.' He smiled in satisfaction. He reached out and smoothed Manisha's hair, his touch strangely tender. Then, locking eyes with her, he raised the knife—ready to deliver the final cut.

31

'You are today where your thoughts have brought you; you will be tomorrow where your thoughts take you.'

James Allen – Author / Philosopher (1864–1912)

A hand appeared over Zarek's shoulder and quickly clamped over his mouth. He tried to twist to defend himself, but it was too late. He felt his head jerk back hard as a knife came into view. It glinted in the light before it slipped from view under his chin. The cold metal cut deep as it sliced his throat from side to side. Blood gushed from his neck, splattering over Manisha's face and neck. She choked and coughed as she spat the crimson fluid from her mouth.

Zarek's final image was exactly as he had visualised. His synapses fired in his brain, summoning his final thought, his final realisation. The blinding bright light he had experienced during his visualisations was his own dying moment. The blood splattered across Manisha's face and neck was his own.

ZAREK'S BODY slumped to the floor as blood continued to pump from his neck. Laing wiped Manisha's face with a towel and cut the ropes that bound her. He gave her water to rinse the taste of iron from her mouth.

Manisha spat out the pink mix and wiped her lips. 'Thank you,' she said as she sat up and supported herself on Laing's shoulder.

'We need to get out of here. The exit is just down the corridor. Can you walk?' Laing asked as he removed the cannula from her hand.

'I think so.' Manisha lifted her legs over the side of the table and gently lowered herself to the floor. Staggering to Zarek's laptop, she retrieved her USB stick. She reconnected the two halves of her pendant before thrusting it deep into her pocket.

'We'll take the laptop too,' Laing said. 'It may give us some insight into Heylel.' He turned to a wall-mounted cupboard and rifled through the contents, searching for medical supplies to dress their wounds. Bandages, Steri-Strips, antiseptic spray, antibiotics, painkillers, tweezers and a case of scalpels were all thrown into a white linen bag, along with Zarek's laptop.

Laing turned his attention to Zarek, searching his pockets for the keys to the boat that had brought them there. He checked his back pockets and heaved Zarek's corpse over, eventually finding the keys in a front pocket.

Looking towards Manisha, a new wave of concern washed over him. She was leaning against the table, holding on tightly to keep herself upright. She looked deathly pale, and he could see her hand tremble as her fingers touched her bandaged head. She was bloody and bruised. Laing readied himself as he saw her rock back slightly. She tried to support her own weight, but her legs buckled. Laing shot out a steadying arm and caught her, feeling her warmth as she leaned into him for support. He held her with one arm while clutching the linen bag in the other.

'We need to get out of here before anyone finds us,' he said.

'Okay.' Manisha draped herself on Laing's shoulder as they limped towards the door.

Laing peered left and right to ensure the path was clear. 'Let's go. It's not far.'

They made their way down the corridor, passing under the lights Laing recognised as the ones he'd seen through the hessian hood earlier that night. Just one door stood between them and the main gates where Zarek's boat was moored.

As they approached the door, Laing felt Manisha growing heavier. He gripped her tightly around her waist, pulling her close and giving her more support as they ventured the last forty feet to freedom. Suddenly, Laing saw a shadow through an open doorway to their left. He paused, lowering Manisha to the floor. She slumped against the wall; eyes closed, but still conscious. Laing placed the linen bag in her lap, all the while keeping a watchful eye on the open doorway. He reached behind him and pulled the gun from behind his back. He looked at Manisha, placing a finger over his lips, signalling to her to stay quiet.

Laing flattened himself against the wall and felt the

damp, cold stone against his back. He crept to the doorway and peered in. A lone, thickset figure in a black coat sat at a desk reading a news website on his computer. Images of the high-speed chase through Venice filled the screen.

The movement in the doorway reflected in the black edge of the VDU. Laing's reflexes kicked in as he saw the guard stand and turn. He tightened his grip on the heavy gun, stepping forward for a decisive shot at point-blank range. However, the guard was too fast and lunged forward, knocking the gun from his hands, sending it flying in an arc through the open door. Before he had time to react, another sickening blow hit home, radiating waves of pain and nausea through his stomach. As he doubled over, his stocky adversary landed a well-aimed punch to his jaw. Gritting his teeth and curling his body, Laing took the blows. As his mind cleared, his instincts took over. He raised one arm and then the other, blocking the next two punches with his elbows.

Next, he delivered a heavy punch to his opponent's kidneys and a jab to the face. Striking out, he grabbed the guard's hair and summoned all his strength to throw the man against the desk and into the VDU. Sparks flew as it shattered against the wall.

Amid the wreckage, the guard scrambled back to his feet, smiling, as though he were enjoying the fight. Laing tensed in anticipation as he watched him toss a knife from hand to hand. Suddenly the guard committed and lunged.

Keeping the blade in his sights, Laing twisted and bent his body backwards to avoid the cut. Rage exploded in Laing's gut. He grabbed the guard's arm and slammed him against the wall, winding him. Making the most of the opportunity, Laing forced the guard back across the desk and used all his strength and weight to turn the guard's knife towards his own chest. Trembling hands fought each other. Laing tried to drive the blade home and finish the struggle, but in a desperate surge of energy the guard overpowered him, sending him crashing to the floor.

A heavy boot slammed into Laing's wounded calf, sending pain shooting through him. The guard stood over him and, in an instant, Laing wrapped one leg around the guard's calf and the other around his thigh, twisting and toppling him. The guard hit the stone floor with a heavy thud, his head landing face-up on Laing's stomach. Laing grabbed a polished baton lying close by, slid it across the guard's neck and pulled down hard with both hands, biting his lip with the effort. The guard thrashed his legs in desperation, trying to free himself. He tried to push the baton from his neck, but Laing pulled down harder, grunting with the effort. The man switched tactics and found the knife, lashing out wildly, repeatedly trying to stab Laing, but missing each time. In a frantic attempt, he stabbed behind him, but slammed the knife into the stone floor. Laing heard the clatter of metal on stone as the blade slipped from the man's fingers.

Laing watched the guard's hand desperately trying to retrieve the weapon. It was just a matter of time until he took his final breath. His long fingers stretched out and touched it tantalisingly several times. Then, in a last-ditch attempt, the guard flung his body to one side. The effort paid off. He had a solid grip on the recovered knife.

Laing tightened his hold, knowing the guard had one last chance to live and would try to use it well.

The guard took a decisive swing and stabbed Laing in his thigh. The searing burn as the blade hit home made Laing recoil, momentarily loosening his grip on one side of the baton. The guard freed himself and clawed his way to standing.

There was movement in the doorway. Laing glanced past the guard to see Manisha standing there, looking scared and dazed. She looked down at the gun and bent to retrieve it. Laing barely had time to catch his breath before the guard stepped towards her and struck her. Manisha cried out in pain as she landed in a crumpled heap on the uneven floor.

A wave of frustration and guilt washed over Laing as the guard turned his attention back to his prey. He didn't know how much more he could take. The excruciating pain from his leg threatened to overwhelm him. He felt sick. His breathing was heavy and laboured, but he had to keep fighting. He tried to stand, using his left arm to push himself up against the desk while gripping the baton firmly in his other hand. But as he dragged himself upright, a heavy kick landed painfully in his stomach. Saliva flew from his mouth as the air was forced from his lungs. Struggling to breathe, he coughed violently, as a fleeting feeling of resignation passed through his mind. He had no more strength to defend himself, let alone Manisha.

He looked up, panting and coughing, bloodied and bruised. The guard was standing over him. He lashed out weakly with the baton.

The guard laughed. 'You're pathetic.' Leaning forward, he ripped the baton from Laing's hand and threw it behind him. It landed with a hollow clatter on the floor.

Laing slumped backward, panting with total physical exhaustion. The guard towered over him, and he watched, resigned to his fate as the guard gripped the knife and raised his arms high in readiness to drive the blade deep into Laing's chest. *So, this is how I die.*

Blood and bone burst in a pink cloud from the guard's

head as a shot reverberated through the room. Laing lay motionless, watching as blood poured from the guard's mouth. The man's body slumped to the floor, revealing Manisha, quivering with the smoking gun in her hand.

'Easy,' Laing said. He raised his hands and pushed himself to his knees. 'Give me the gun.'

Manisha let the gun fall into his outstretched hands.

Laing pulled himself to his feet and held Manisha close, steadying her. 'I think that makes us even,' he said. He looked into Manisha's eyes and held her gaze for a split second.

With each step, pain shot through Laing's leg. He looked down to see blood oozing from his leg, soaking in a growing dark patch on his trousers, leaving a trail across the floor. Scanning the room, he spotted a piece of rope discarded in the corner. He tied it firmly around the top of his thigh as a tourniquet. A wave of nausea rose with the pain as the blood flow reduced to a trickle.

'We need to be quick. The gunshot will bring more guards.' He grabbed a set of rusty iron keys from a hook by the door, hoping they would open the entrance to the palace. In the corridor, he picked up the white linen bag and supported Manisha on their final twenty-foot shuffle to the next doorway.

Laing found the correct key within seconds. To his relief, it twisted with ease, but as he heaved open the door, the sound of several sets of footsteps running towards them reached his ears. He bundled Manisha through the door, slamming it behind them, then thrust the key into the lock and turned it, just as the heavy thud of a solid shoulder hitting the other side of the door echoed in the night air.

Laing urged Manisha on, supporting her as they scrambled through the giant water gate, as gunfire rattled through the wrought iron slits in the door. He helped Manisha climb into the back of the craft. Consciousness left her and she fell limp, her body sprawled across the leather seats. He threw the linen bag onto the seat beside her and discarded the old iron keys into the inky water.

The engine purred into life. Laing steered the boat into the quiet backwaters, avoiding the stage of death and destruction. Leaning against the pilot's chair, he felt the cool Venetian breeze wrap itself around him as he slowly manoeuvred the craft through the narrow canals. Now they were free, the numbing effects of adrenaline started waning, and his body screamed as pain took hold. He glanced back to see Manisha curled up on the seat inside the boat. Despite her ordeal, she somehow looked at peace.

Laing instinctively navigated the craft to the terrace under *Vita*. He moored the boat by the bridge opposite *Hotel Fontana*. Moving to the back of the craft, he secured the rear door and then made his way back through the vessel to kneel by Manisha, gently sweeping the hair away from her face. 'We'll be out of here soon.'

She gave a quiet moan of acknowledgement.

Laing continued through the boat, locking Manisha in, hoping it would be enough to keep her safe, before making his way past *Da Roberto's* and through the doors to the hotel.

Laing could see the concern on the receptionist's face as he entered the marble hallway covered in blood. '*Buon giorno*,' Laing said and smiled as if nothing was wrong. He walked as well as he could through the foyer and up the stone steps. Once the door to his room was closed behind him, he let his guard down. He leaned against the door, breathing hard through the pain and exhaustion. Then he pulled on his black bomber jacket before putting all his, and McCray's, possessions into a large holdall. He made a final sweep, searching for any other equipment, and left the room.

Laing made his way through the reception, dropping the blood-stained key on the front desk. 'I'm checking out. The account has been pre-paid. Grazie.'

The receptionist stood in open-mouthed silence.

Laing made his way back to the boat, looking round him before boarding. Dropping the holdall beside him, he checked on Manisha. She was warm and sleeping. As he started the engine, he looked at his watch. It was 4:00 a.m. He took the backwaters as far as he could towards Manisha's hotel. The map on his phone showed the most efficient route to *San Stae* without using the Grand Canal. He had little choice but to use the wide waterway for the last four hundred metres of the journey.

It was quiet as he approached the end of the narrow canal opposite *Rialto Mercato* vaporetto stop. He held back, putting the engine into a slight reverse as a police boat went past, its spotlight scanning water taxi numbers; the light reflected in the choppy water. Once the coast was clear, he eased out, keeping to the five kilometres per hour speed limit.

On the approach to *San Stae*, Laing took a sharp left down *Fondamenta Rimpeto Mocenigo* and moored the boat alongside the entrance to *Hotel Al Ponte Mocenigo*. Its green doors welcomed them.

Laing gently shook Manisha. 'You need to wake up. What room are you in?' he asked.

'Fifty-three,' she said. She searched her pockets for the room key and handed it to Laing. He grabbed the key and stuffed it in his jacket pocket. Manisha got to her feet, bumping her head on the low roof of the boat as she struggled to gain her balance.

Laing grabbed a rain cover stowed under one of the rear seats and spread it out over the back of the boat. He placed it as though the wind had caught it, covering the boat's number plate. He made his way to the front of the boat and helped Manisha climb through the water door into the hotel. Everything was quiet. The low-level lighting glowed behind the reception desk, but there was no one in sight. Laing helped Manisha up the stairs as they quietly made their way to room fifty-three.

Closing the heavy door behind them, Laing hoped they'd reached a sanctuary—if only for a few hours.

32

'Let's say that everything is thought. Now, what IS a thought? And what is the consciousness that allows us to think?'

Klee Irwin – Director of Quantum Gravity Research (1965–)

Laing threw the holdall and linen bag onto the daybed and helped Manisha into the main bedroom. He gently lowered her onto the king-sized bed and pulled the covers over her shoulders, leaving her to sleep.

He ached all over. His mind was wired, reeling from the events of the last twenty-four hours. The new priority was to get patched up and out of Venice as soon as possible. Crossing the polished marble floor, he double-locked the door. After ensuring the windows were secure, he peered outside, searching for any signs of movement. He knew

Zarek could have communicated the whereabouts of Manisha's hotel to someone within Heylel. They would still pursue Manisha's research and seek vengeance after losing so many of their people. However, all was quiet. In the distance, police boats patrolled the Grand Canal. Spotlights worked overtime, trying to find the perpetrators who had caused so much damage to the ancient city.

Laing sat on the day bed, wincing in pain. He knew they'd been lucky to get through the night alive. He checked the gun—only six bullets remained. Laing unzipped the holdall, found his phone, and dialled the emergency evacuation number. There was no tone to show the number was ringing, but a beep told Laing the line was secure. The call was answered immediately.

'ID?' an assertive female voice asked.

'Alpha, Delta, Quebec, Alpha, Kilo, Quebec, Two, Zero, Two, Five, Sierra, Lima, Bravo.' Laing imagined the woman in London, sitting in a darkened room with a bank of VDUs around her. An image of him on the screen would inform her who the phone belonged to. The woman followed the security script unique to Laing's profile.

'How's your day been?' she asked.

'Very pleasant, thank you, but I'm sure you can make it better.'

'What's your location?'

'Wembley Stadium, section 549, row 7, seat 9.'

'How's the weather there?'

'Hot and sunny, but rain is expected later.'

'Thank you,' the woman said. 'Identity confirmed, Major Laing. I can see you're in Venice, what is your condition?'

'A couple of bullet grazes, what feels like a cracked rib, a stab wound to the leg and a thumping headache.'

'Are you in immediate danger?'

'No, but I would like to get us out of here within a few hours.'

'How many of you are there?'

'Two. I have a UK national with me, Manisha Williams. She has head wounds, but she's stable.'

'Okay, let me find the best way to get you back to the UK.'

The line went quiet for several seconds.

'We have three Royal Navy ships in the Adriatic on a NATO exercise with the Italian Navy. They're currently one hundred miles off the Venice coast. Do you have access to a boat?'

'Yes, we have a boat, but not with that range.'

'Stand by while I confirm arrangements.'

Laing went into the main bedroom. Manisha was still sleeping. He checked outside, pulling the curtains back while covering the glow from his phone by pressing it against his chest. There was no one outside.

'Okay, a helicopter will pick you up at coordinates 45.351125, 12.482177 in two hours—06:30 Central European Time. It's approximately seven miles outside of Venice Lagoon. I'll send the coordinates to your phone now.'

'Perfect, thank you,' Laing said, as relief washed over him.

'The Italians will form part of the rescue, so expect to see UK and Italian helicopters approach you.'

'Okay, thanks for letting me know.'

'Call if your situation changes.'

'Will do.'

The line went dead, leaving him in silence and darkness.

Laing plugged in his phone and tablet to charge, then went to the bathroom, closing the door quietly behind him. He removed the tourniquet, blood-stained clothes, and the bulletproof vest and inspected his battered body in the mirror. Most of the wounds were superficial grazes and scratches. The stab wound in his thigh worried him the most. It still oozed a steady trickle of blood. It wasn't deep enough to cause any permanent damage and had missed all major blood vessels, but it needed attention. He stepped into the double-width shower and turned the lever. The cold water slowly changed to hot. The water cascaded over him, washing away the blood, sweat, and dirt from his aching body. His wounds stung as the warm water hit them, but he considered the pain a minor inconvenience, compared to what could have happened. His head fell forward, surrendering to the warm water as he planned how to escape from the city unseen.

THE FAINT SOUND of the bathroom door closing caused Manisha to stir. The haziness in her mind started to clear, but the morphine still provided pain relief. She looked at the high ceiling as twilight flowed around the curtains, ruminating on the life-changing events of the night. The horror and betrayal still shocked her, but a feeling of calm and confidence dominated. Knowing that life would go on when she died filled her with joy. Her heart still felt the euphoria of her life after death experience. However, the high was overshadowed by the truth she'd learnt at the end of her time with Sarah. A truth that caused her pain and confusion. *Someone knows what really happened to him.* And she knew who that someone was.

Manisha tuned in to the sound of splashing water and the occasional wince of pain she heard coming from the bathroom. She had to ensure Laing was fit enough to get them back to the UK safely. She got out of bed, steadying herself against the bedside table, her head pounding. She knocked on the bathroom door and opened it slowly. Peering in, she saw Laing in the shower, blood still seeping from his open wounds.

'We need to get you patched up,' she said.

He turned off the shower, stepped out and stood in front of her, blood trickling from his injuries. 'I'm fine.'

'You're not looking good.' She glanced up and down at him, looking at his wounds. 'Dry yourself and I'll patch your wounds.'

Manisha turned, suddenly a little embarrassed by his nakedness, allowing Laing time to make himself decent.

He smiled as he dried himself and wrapped a towel around his waist. 'Not looking good! That's just what I needed to hear.'

Manisha took some alcohol wipes from the linen bag and cleaned the blood away from the bullet and stab wounds, making Laing wince. A squirt of antiseptic spray readied the wounds for dressing.

'You're a lucky man. If these wounds were a few inches further into your body, you may not be alive.'

He glanced towards the ceiling. 'We've both had someone looking out for us tonight.'

Manisha nodded silently as she stuck the final Steri-Strip to Laing's thigh wound and bound a dressing around his leg. A faint spot of blood appeared on the cream bandage as she tied the ends off.

'Thank you.' Laing touched Manisha's shoulder lightly while giving an appreciative smile.

His tenderness surprised Manisha. He was a stranger to her, and part of her still fought against trusting him.

However, he was the only reason she was alive and the only chance of a safe passage back home.

'Anyway, you're the one who died tonight. How are you feeling?'

'I'm okay. My head is thumping, but I'm just grateful to be alive.' Manisha hesitated, trying to process her life after death encounter. 'It was an incredible experience,' she said, looking Laing in the eyes, looking for the connection again that told her she could trust him.

'What happened?'

Manisha did a final check on his wounds. 'I'll save that story for another day.'

Laing nodded at Manisha's head wounds. 'Do they need any attention?'

'No, I'll be fine.' A small patch of crimson appeared on her fingers as she touched her head. 'I'll take a shower and redress them. You get some rest.'

'Okay. I'll take the day bed,' Laing said as he walked towards the door. 'You try and get some more sleep. I'll wake you at 5:45. We'll need to be ready to go at 6:00. We should be home in twenty-four hours, assuming everything goes to plan.'

Manisha waited until Laing closed the door and then stripped, removed her bandages, and climbed into the shower. The warm water cascading over her body was a pleasant relief. She breathed in deep and immersed herself in the heat, feeling grateful they were both still alive. She thought about the look in Laing's eyes and how she felt when she was close to him. His eyes were deep and kind. She felt safe with him, as though their paths in life were meant to cross.

~

Laing searched the holdall for some clean clothes and got dressed. Zarek's laptop lay on the day bed, its presence making Laing inquisitive. He sat with the computer on his knees and took it out of standby. The machine sprang into life, displaying an error about the USB stick having been removed incorrectly. He closed the error message and started to browse through the open windows.

One window contained documents showing all the information Zarek had collected about Manisha and her work. Another showed financial information. Vast sums of money in offshore accounts that had enabled Zarek to work autonomously. 'Now that's stupid,' Laing said, as he found a file listing logins and associated passwords. Also, e-mails from Heylel's internal operations. Plans, and names of people in leadership positions were displayed. 'The chaps in GCHQ will be very interested in this,' he said, starting to close the laptop. But a thought stopped him.

How could you do it, Susan?

A realisation dawned on him: he could trust no one. He felt alone—but liberated. For the first time in his career, if not his life, he felt a desire to put himself first. Making a decision he would probably regret later, he spent a few minutes tapping at the keyboard and finished with a smile. He cleared the browser's cache and closed the laptop down. 'What will be, will be.'

05:45 — Laing limped into the main bedroom to wake Manisha. He paused and watched her sleeping peacefully. He gently swept her hair away from her face. Feelings churned in his stomach, and he thought how good it would have been to explore Venice with Manisha under different circumstances.

Get a grip, Alex. She's nearly twenty years younger than you!

He shook her shoulder gently. 'Manisha, it's time to go.'

'Okay,' she murmured, coming out of her brief sleep.

Laing gathered their blood-stained clothes from the bathroom and rammed them into the holdall, along with the linen bag and Zarek's laptop. Picking up Manisha's bag containing her belongings, he gave the room a final sweep before guiding Manisha downstairs towards reception.

Halfway down the stairs, a trio of loud voices reverberating around the lobby rose to meet them.

'Are you sure she hasn't returned this morning?' an angry male voice asked.

'No, she went out yesterday evening and she hasn't come back,' Antonio said, shrugging his shoulders. 'I cannot allow you to go to her room and that's final.'

Laing held Manisha back and whispered. 'It's either the police or Heylel operatives.' He crept further down the stairs, trying to see who was in reception.

Two men dressed in black stood at the desk with their backs to Laing. They continued to argue with Antonio as they barged their way behind the desk and forced him to his knees. 'Stay down and put your hands behind your head,' the larger man said, holding a gun to Antonio's temple. The second man took control of the computer.

'Move fast and quietly,' Laing said. 'At the bottom of the stairs, go through the glass sliding doors and onto the boat.'

Laing watched as Manisha crept down the stairs and made the six feet to the doors undetected. The automatic doors slid open with a shuffling, rolling sound that was enough to draw the attention of the men at reception.

Laing fired a shot towards the reception desk, forcing the

men to duck. He limped through the open doors, firing a shot at the control box. The doors closed and locked behind him, disabling the mechanism. Jumping onto the boat, he winced as he hit his wounded thigh against the pilots chair. 'Are you okay?' he called to Manisha as he started the engine.

'Yes. Let's go.'

He pushed the boat into reverse as the pursuers crashed into the glass. Closing his grip around the polished throttle, he pushed it forward. The engine roared as the boat sped towards the Grand Canal. Two shots fired in quick succession, followed by a tremendous crashing of shattered glass, were just audible over the sound of the engine and churning water. Laing saw one of the men lean out over the canal, hanging from the mooring post by one hand. He raised his gun in the other hand and fired. There was a crack as two shots flew over the boat. Laing gritted his teeth and steered onto the Grand Canal. Looking back over his shoulder, he spotted the men emerging from the alleyway, running towards their boat shouting, '*Seguili! Seguili!*' Two scruffy-looking, unshaven men in a second boat moored next to *San Stae* vaporetto stop kicked their engine into life and took up the chase.

Laing squinted, shielding his eyes from the early morning sun as he looked at the two speeding boats on their tail. 'Shit!' he said, as all hope of a quiet exit from Venice evaporated.

Shifting to full throttle, he turned his wrist to check his watch. His heart dropped as the reality of their situation hit home. They'd have to outrun the two boats for a full twenty-five minutes to reach their pickup point.

Laing turned to gauge the situation, catching Manisha in his gaze. She looked afraid, but defiant. He looked beyond

Manisha and guessed the pursuing boats were two hundred metres behind. He checked the fuel indicator set into the veneered control panel. They had half a tank. Chewing his lip, he wondered if it could take them the distance at their current speed.

The early morning sun glistened off the Grand Canal, the beautiful scene before them a stark contrast to the threat of death that followed. Three hundred metres ahead, Laing could see a blockade of police boats and garbage barges. He looked right and left, seeking an alternative path through Venice. With time running out, he instinctively took a left turn down a narrow waterway and glanced behind him. His swift manoeuvre looked like it had paid off. The first boat turned sharply, but it was too late. He watched as it smashed into the iconic 16th-century building, *Palazzo Corner Contarini*. The second boat made the turn, avoiding the debris and mayhem while drenching the occupants of a delivery barge with their wake.

'Keep your head down,' Laing yelled as they approached a low, iron bridge, signalling for Manisha to duck. He gripped the wheel as he weaved the speeding boat around several corners and past ancient houses, ignoring the incredulous occupants shouting abuse as homes were flooded in the wake of the speeding boats.

He clenched his jaw, his eyes beneath furrowed brows fixed on heading due south. *If I keep the sunrise on my left, we should come out near the end of the Grand Canal.*

Seconds later, Laing's strategy paid off, and the boat burst out onto the wide-open vista. Laing chanced a look behind him. Their pursuers were only a hundred metres behind.

Shots were fired, and bullets whistled past their boat.

Manisha appeared by his side, holding on to the edge of

the boat, her knuckles as pale as her face. 'Give me your gun.'

'We only have four bullets left. We need to be careful how we use them,' Laing shouted over the engine's noise. 'If you can find any other guns on the boat, fill your boots.'

Light spray flew over the bow as Manisha turned. She leaned forward, arms outstretched to steady herself as they bounced across the surface of the water. He heard her determined and desperate search as she pulled off cushions and ransacked cupboards, looking for anything she thought could help them. Laing sensed her near his feet as her search returned her to the storage space at the front of the boat. She pulled out a weapon, removing it from an oily cloth before handing it to him.

'A Beretta assault rifle,' he said with raised eyebrows. 'Are you sure you can handle this?' He readied the weapon for firing. 'Dig the butt firm into your shoulder before you fire as she has a kick.'

'Okay,' Manisha looked nervously at him.

Laing looked behind as Manisha went to the back of the boat and crouched. She aimed at the pursuing boat and squeezed the trigger. The look on her face and the jerk of her body told him the kick was more than she expected. She repositioned herself, keeping her body further forward and lower than before. As he kept on course, Manisha unleashed shots in short bursts. The spray of bullets had the desired effect. He turned to see the chasing boat swerve and decelerate.

Laing faced forward to keep the boat on course, the sound of gunfire from behind was evidence Manisha was not giving up. She gave a triumphant shout, and he looked back to see a plume of smoke pouring from their adversary's boat. The damaged craft began to drift, the pilot punching the steering wheel in frustration.

'Well done,' Laing said, surprised Manisha had hit anything, given the swell. He felt a faint glimmer of hope stir in his gut and started to slow the craft to conserve fuel. He kept his eye on the path ahead, feeling confident they now had a chance of getting to the pickup point on time.

'We're not out of danger yet,' Manisha shouted, 'look!' He followed Manisha's outstretched arm as she pointed across the stretch of water. Several hundred metres off their port side, Laing fixed his gaze on another three boats which were coming towards them fast.

Laing glanced at the fuel gauge. 'Shit!' He shoved the throttle to full power.

He took the most direct path across the open waterway, passing between the islands of *Giudecca* and *San Giorgio Maggiore*. Falling silent, he focused on their course. Once past the islands, he manoeuvred the boat around the Venice Lido.

Reaching into his pocket, his hand closed around his phone. With deft fingers he fired up the GPS app with the pre-configured coordinates. He looked at the screen. The exact pickup point was indicated by a red dot. The time was 06:17. They had to last a further thirteen minutes. His eyes flicked to the fuel dial. It showed less than an eighth of the tank was left. Looking back, he could see the pack were gaining on them fast.

Heading out to the deeper waters, the waves grew larger. Spray poured over the bow of the boat. Laing clung on to the wheel as the boat's bow lifted high and crashed down onto the next wave with uncomfortable regularity. Frowning hard, he tried to adjust his speed to get the most efficient cut through the waves. After several attempts, he gave it up as a bad idea. The chasing boats were gaining. Laing gripped the throttle and opened it up. The boat responded as he grappled with the wheel to steer his way through the growing swell.

Manisha stood close, holding a new magazine in her outstretched hand, concern and apology written across her face. 'I tried to change it, but I think it's jammed.'

Laing took the gun and Manisha took the helm. 'You're doing great. I'm amazed you've hit anything in these conditions.' He reloaded it in seconds and passed it back to Manisha. He continued his battle with the waves. Looking around, he saw her make her way unsteadily towards the back of the boat.

A knot tightened in his belly as he scanned the horizon in the hope that support would not be far away. They had agreed on a pickup time of 06:30, and military precision said they would be there on the dot.

Looking back, he could see the boat leading the pursuit was only fifty metres behind. Laing knew they couldn't outrun them. He watched as Manisha resumed her firing position, spraying the boats with short bursts of bullets. There were splashes as the bullets peppered the water around the boat. Suddenly the figures in the boat ducked. Manisha must have hit it. However, it kept on course—and kept on gaining.

'Manisha, look for some flares.'

Manisha stopped firing and scrambled through the compartments. 'I can't find any,' she shouted over the engine and churn of the sea.

Laing felt a twinge as his worst fear was realised. His heart raced as he watched one of the crew pull out a Beretta grenade launcher. He inhaled deeply and logic kicked in. The chances of them getting a shot on target were slim.

Instinctively, he took evasive action and zig-zagged randomly as a last line of defence.

Suddenly, the sea to the side of the boat frothed and boiled as a grenade exploded, showering them in sea water. Laing stayed calm and redoubled his efforts. He could hear the intermittent short bursts from the assault rifle, and the faint crack of return fire. Looking round, he saw Manisha hunched with her head low over the gun.

Laing heard a yell. One of Manisha's bullets had found its target. He caught sight of the pilot of the leading boat clutch his shoulder and fall backwards. The craft turned sharply, temporarily slowing its progress. Within seconds, the other crew member grabbed the helm. The chase was back on, and the boats continued to gain.

Laing looked at his watch. It was impossible to keep their distance until they reached the pickup point. A glance at the fuel gauge confirmed his fears—they were running on fumes, still a mile from the pickup. The three boats closed in, side by side. Laing gritted his teeth, calculating their odds.

Two grenade launchers were pointed at them. He looked again at Manisha, crouched, and doggedly continuing to fire. He had to keep going.

Two dark objects fell from nowhere and landed in the water close by. There was a loud explosion, followed in quick succession by another. Laing ducked as water shot up in a violent plume in front of them, and then again ten feet off the port side. A direct hit had only been prevented by the rise and fall of the waves. They couldn't last much longer.

Moments later, the boat started to cough as the last dregs of fuel were drawn into the engine. Smoke spewed from the boat as it struggled with the imbalance between fuel and air intake. Before dying, the engine gave one final splutter, leaving the craft to drift.

Laing took stock of the situation. He had to face facts; they were outnumbered, outgunned, out of fuel and they would be surrounded in seconds. 'Throw your gun down and put your hands up,' Laing said to Manisha. 'We need to surrender and hope they don't shoot us anyway.'

Manisha rushed to the front of the boat, and Laing pulled her close. He raised his hands, nodding at her to do the same. Her eyes were huge, dark, and frightened.

Laing watched as the three boats surrounded them: two in front and one to the rear. Seeing the grenade launchers and automatic weapons aimed at them made any thought of escape impossible. Death or torture over the coming hours was inevitable.

'Throw your guns into the sea,' a bearded man shouted with a thick Italian accent. Laing reached behind him and slowly retrieved a pistol between his finger and thumb and threw the gun over the side. Manisha followed suit. He watched as she picked up the assault rifle and gently slipped it into the deep blue of the Adriatic. He stood in silence as he watched it sink and drift away, caught in the currents.

'Show me the laptop!'

'What laptop?' Laing called back, trying to stall for time.

The bearded man raised his weapon and Laing heard the crack, followed by a searing, burning pain in his left shoulder as he was thrown backwards on to the hard, polished boards of the deck.

'Do not play games with me. That was meant to kill you.'

Laing was aware of Manisha crouched by his side. He winced in pain as she grabbed a cloth from a compartment and held it firmly against the wound. The strong northwesterly wind swept through her hair, blowing it in horizontal waves as she knelt by his side.

'Keep the woman alive,' the bearded man said to the men in the other boats, 'and kill the Englishman.'

'Don't be afraid,' he said, looking up at Manisha.

'I'm not,' she said.

Laing placed his hand on Manisha's wrist as she maintained the pressure on his wound. He held her gaze and gave her a weak smile. He could hear their hunters' approach. Laing glanced at his watch. It was 06:30 on the dot. They were three-quarters of a mile from their pickup point. He had done all he could, but it wasn't enough.

Steeling himself for what was to come, Laing was pulled from his thoughts by a very faint sound that gave him hope. A second later, three Hydra rockets screamed through the air. Manisha's weight fell across his injured body as their boat rocked violently from side to side. Plumes of water shot up and cascaded over them like freezing rain. Laing held Manisha close, pulling her head against his chest. The missiles had found their targets. All three boats were destroyed and sinking around them.

A Royal Navy Merlin thundered overhead, its rotors slicing through the dawn. On either flank, two Apaches hovered like birds of prey—one British, one Italian. Waves of relief washed over Laing as his eyes fixed on their rescuers flying overhead, machine gun trained to ensure all danger had been eliminated. He watched the Apache helicopters circling around the destroyed craft as the Merlin hovered overhead. Laing pulled Manisha's head close, shielding her from the downdraft. He shut his eyes tightly as water swirled wildly around them, kicking spray high into the air. Squinting, he held one hand up to shield his eyes and could just make out the snaking form of a line which had been thrown down. A large pair of heavy boots appeared as a Commando abseiled onto the boat.

'Take Manisha first—I'll sort the bags,' Laing shouted to the uniformed man.

Laing watched as Manisha was winched up to the helicopter. He let out a shuddering breath and felt a wall of tiredness hit him. Fighting against it, he made one final effort to pull the bags close.

Before long, he was strapped into a stretcher, feeling the weight of the bags on his shins. He'd checked and double-checked that they had been securely attached in a black sack tied to the stretcher. He watched as the commando standing on the side of the stretcher gave a single wave of his hand. He kept his eyes fixed on the helicopter above, growing steadily closer, as they were winched up to safety. The stretcher bounced off the fuselage once, then glided into the helicopter. The swirling wind had stopped, but the noise was deafening.

Laing looked around and saw Manisha strapped into her seat. She was silent and still, clutching a red blanket that had been thrown around her.

A figure in a large helmet with a microphone and earpiece loomed over him to put headphones and a mic on his head.

'Are you okay, Major?'

'Yes. Order the Apache to destroy the boat.'

Laing heard his command being given. Within seconds another Hydra rocket was fired, and Laing looked down just as the boat's stern turned and sank into the depths of the sea.

'How did you know to come for us?' Laing asked.

'Our radar had picked up the boats pursuing you. We knew which one you were on based on the GPS signal from your phone. The long-range camera also confirmed you were under fire.'

Laing looked out of the side door to see an Apache flanking them on their return trip to their carrier.

He rested his head on the pillow and started to relax for the first time in over thirty hours. The view over the turquoise sea made him think of his home in Cornwall; he longed to be there again soon. Relaxing and drinking a beer.

Feeling a soft touch on his hand, Laing turned. Manisha leaned over him, her eyes filled with something unspoken. She mouthed a silent 'Thank you.' In that moment, nothing else mattered.

Laing felt the helicopter bank right. Through the open door, he saw the outline of HMS Queen Elizabeth, shimmering in the early morning mist, brimming with F-35 fighters. He closed his eyes confident no one could harm Manisha now.

33

'There is for me powerful evidence that there is something going on behind it all... It seems as though somebody has fine tuned nature's numbers to make the Universe... The impression of design is overwhelming.'

Paul Davies – Physicist (1946–)

Doulton sat at his desk in the Beecroft Building, his computer logged into his banking website. He smiled broadly as he completed the final transaction.

From his window, he could see a vast expanse of glorious blue sky stretching out over University Parks. The early morning sunrise transformed the dew-soaked grass into a carpet of diamonds. However, dark, distant clouds loomed, threatening a storm.

His hand hovered over his mobile, torn between his desire to call Manisha to put things right and her request for privacy and downtime. He pushed the phone away. *You'll be back when you're ready.*

Doulton had known Manisha since she was a child. She was just like her father and his logic told him that her passion for her work and her desire to finish it would be enough to bring her back. Completing her work was good for her, good for him, and good for the university. She wouldn't want to let anyone down. This was her Achilles' heel. The contract she had with Oxford University was his fail-safe. The university had facilitated her funding, and she'd be foolish to walk away now. She had nowhere else to complete her work, and besides, all her research and data belonged to the university anyway.

The shrill ring from his mobile phone brought his contemplations to an abrupt halt. It vibrated and twisted on the polished surface of his desk. *Is that you, Manisha? Ready to apologise?*

The mobile display read 'No Caller ID' as it vibrated across his desk. He touched the green button and pressed the phone to his ear. The momentary silence that followed made him expect to hear a call centre buzz and crackly line, followed by a heavily accented guy called 'John Smith', trying to sell him the latest scam. The voice which greeted him took him by surprise. It wasn't Manisha or a foreign call centre operative, but a man with a very well-spoken English accent. An accent which betrayed the type of expensive education only a privileged background afforded.

'Good morning, Professor. How are you today?'

'Ah, I'm fine, thank you. How can I help you?'

'Professor Doulton, you don't know me, but I worked

closely with Susan Redfern. I regret to inform you that she was killed this morning.'

Doulton sat back in his chair in shock. 'I'm... I'm so sorry to hear that. What happened?'

'I can't go into details, Professor, you know that. However, Redfern's death has left us with a problem. Or, as I like to see it, an opportunity.'

'What do you mean?'

'I'm aware of the very special arrangement you and Susan had regarding Professor Williams's research at Beecroft. My organisation is very keen to see evidence of the progress she has made with her project. We hear she's made a major breakthrough.'

Doulton stood and walked to the window, trying to work out how best to play the situation.

'Our concern is that Professor Williams has suddenly left the country, and no one seems to know exactly where she is. You'll appreciate our mounting unease, as we have no way of knowing the status of her work.'

'Sorry, but who am I talking to, and which organisation do you represent?'

'My name is irrelevant. However, you can call me 'Moros' if it pleases you.'

Doulton felt the blood drain from his face, and his stomach lurched at the sound of the stranger's pseudonym: the Greek mythological being of impending doom.

'You won't know of my organisation, Professor, as Redfern never spoke to you about us. However, I know all about you and this is where the opportunity comes into play. We suddenly have a new position within our organisation that you may be able to fill. The benefits are very lucrative. Far more lucrative than the monthly retainer you get from the UK government. However, to show you are willing to pursue this opportunity I need to test your capability.'

Beads of cold sweat swelled from Doulton's forehead. 'What do you mean?'

'It's quite simple,' the man said in the same measured tone, 'we need Professor Williams's research. The data which sits five levels below you in her lab.'

'I can't get to her data. She has too much security around it,' Doulton said.

The man laughed confidently. 'Professor Doulton, do you really expect me to believe you? You're the head of Physics at Oxford University. I'm sure you can lay your hands on any of Oxford's intellectual property if you wanted to. You can't be running a very tight ship if you can't even access your own data.'

Doulton felt the criticism bite.

'I know Redfern gave you the benefit of the doubt. In fact, she was far too soft on you. However, that is going to change.' The man paused. 'Now, Professor, here's your choice. You either get the data or you suffer the same fate as Redfern.'

'How dare you threaten me!' Doulton said, gripping the back of his leather chair, his palms sweating.

'Professor, Professor, we all have choices in life. Intelligent people learn to make the right choices, which keep them alive. And I know you're a very intelligent man. So, I'm going to be very generous and give you twenty-four hours to get what I need.'

'This is unacceptable. I will not be threatened by you. Nor will I give the university's data to an unknown person.'

'Professor Doulton, I know you have delivered a lot of great work for Redfern in the past. So, as a gesture of goodwill, I have deposited twenty thousand pounds into your bank account. Take a look. I know you're logged into your bank.'

Doulton walked back to his desk and sat down, shocked. He refreshed the screen. The last transaction showed twenty thousand pounds had been deposited only seconds earlier. 'How the hell do you know I'm logged into my bank account?'

'I know everything about you, Professor,' the man said. He paused. 'And your family.'

Doulton's eyes darted towards the family photograph on his desk, his gut twisting with fear.

'Another twenty thousand will be transferred once I have what I need.'

Doulton clawed at his tie, loosening it so he could breathe more easily.

'Oh, just one more thing to mention, Professor. Any contact with Laing will terminate more than just this arrangement. I do hope you understand. I know you will do what's right for you and your family. I'll be in touch at the same time tomorrow.'

The phone went dead.

Doulton sat motionless, cold sweat beading on his skin. He was alone with an impossible task. Redfern was gone, Laing was clearly out of bounds, and he had no idea where Manisha was. He leaned forward, his elbows resting on his desk as he raked his fingers through his hair.

'Shit! Shit! Shit!'

His mouth was dry, his throat tight. He felt sick. In desperation, he raised his gaze to the heavens before his eyes settled on the sweeping second hand as it glided around the smooth white clock face.

34

'We're all hallucinating all the time; when we agree about our hallucinations, we call it "reality".'

Anil Seth – Neuroscientist (1972–)

Laing opened his eyes. The white-panelled ceiling, the unmistakable smell of antiseptic, and the gentle tremor of a large ship in motion told him all he needed to know.

He lifted his head, the pain in his shoulder caused him to wince. The intensive care unit was empty of patients, except for Manisha in the bed to his left. Three white Steri-Strips held the wound in her head together. He smiled, relieved he had managed to get Manisha and himself out of Venice alive.

A nurse, sitting at a desk opposite him, stopped tapping

on her keyboard, looked around, and walked over. 'How are you feeling?'

Laing took in her smile and dark curly hair as she came into focus. She looked both friendly and efficient in her scrubs. 'A few aches and pains, but I feel fine. How long have I been here?'

'About eight hours. You've got multiple wounds, none of them life-threatening. The bullet has been removed from your left shoulder, the stab wound in your leg has been stitched, and other cuts and grazes have been dressed. You're a lucky man!'

'You're not the first person to say that. So, it's still March 31st?'

'Yes. That's saved me asking you a question.' She reached for the folder at the end of his bed, found the right page in his notes, and ticked a box. 'You know what day it is. Do you know where you are and how you got here?'

'We're on HMS Queen Elizabeth. A helicopter picked us up just outside of Venice.'

A few more boxes were ticked, and notes written. The nurse pulled a small torch from her scrub pocket. She moved in close and held each eye open in turn, momentarily blinding him.

'Your eyes are a little bloodshot, but you'll be fine. Keep your arm up and rest.' The look she gave him told him she meant it.

The radio attached to her belt crackled into life. 'How are our guests, Lieutenant Saunders?'

'They are both doing well. Major Laing is awake and talking coherently and Professor Williams is stable and sleeping, sir.'

'Excellent, I'll be down shortly.'

'Very good, sir.' She turned her attention back to Laing. 'Captain Richards will be down to see you soon.'

'Is Manisha okay?' Laing asked before the nurse had the chance to ask another question.

'Yes, she's fine. She's had head trauma, but she's stable. She's through the worst of it.'

'Good to hear.'

Lieutenant Saunders took heart rate and blood pressure readings from monitors attached to Laing and Manisha. 'Lie still and relax. Shout if you need anything.'

Laing stared at the white ceiling, trying to make sense of the last forty-eight hours. Too many people had died. He felt he should have saved McCray. McCray was a good man and the pain of losing another partner cut deep. But what could he have done differently? He knew it was a question that he would ask himself time and time again. Matthew had simply been stupid, greedy, and easily misled. He shouldn't have died, but his own stupidity and disloyalty wrote his fate. Laing felt no remorse for Zarek's death; one less lowlife in the world was a good thing. Redfern deserved her fate. He knew things weren't right with her, but how could she lower herself to the depths of betraying her country? Gone are the days of fighting an enemy who wore a different uniform. Living in a world with faceless enemies, he wondered how he could trust anyone if his own boss had been part of Heylel.

Laing looked across at Manisha. At least her research was secure. He knew they would come for her again. He had won the battle, and they would live to fight another day. But the war was still raging.

He hoped Zarek's laptop would give some insights into Heylel. Who belonged to the organisation, where they were located and how far their influence reached. He chuckled to himself, wondering why anyone would leave their banking login ID and security code in a plain text document. He knew what he had done was either a moment of pure genius or utter stupidity. Only time would tell. Twenty-five million pounds would go a long way, enabling them to hide safely and allowing Manisha to continue her research independently—if that's what she chose to do. The government would have a field day if they found out. He knew it was also another reason for Heylel to track them down. But they're going to do that anyway! 'Nothing ventured, nothing gained', he said to himself.

The sound of swift, purposeful footsteps on the metal deck drew Laing from his thoughts. A tall, smartly dressed man with short blond hair, wearing a blue shirt with the captain's insignia, appeared by his bed. A broad smile spread across his face as he approached.

'Major Laing. Captain Max Richards,' the man said.

Laing saluted and then shook his hand firmly.

'How are you feeling?'

'Good to meet you, Captain. I'm very well thank you, considering.'

'It looks like you've had a challenging couple of days. We'll leave you to rest for a few hours, and then you'll need to debrief us for the report back to London.'

'Of course. How are you planning to get us back to the UK?'

'It's been taken care of, Major Laing. When you're both ready, one of our Ospreys will fly you to Sardinia, where you'll refuel, courtesy of our Italian colleagues, and then fly on to Gibraltar. In Gib, you'll change to a transporter which has scheduled flights to Brize Norton. All being well, you should be home by this time tomorrow.'

'Excellent. Thank you.'

'One of our cyber analysts has looked at the laptop you brought with you. Bad news, I'm afraid. We think it had a failsafe or remote wipe capability. It won't even boot. However, they've taken out the hard disk, scanned it and our technicians are attempting to get the data off before you go, otherwise we'll give it to you to hand over to the chaps at GCHQ.'

'Very good.' A wave of relief washed over Laing; he was thankful that traces of his financial transaction might have been erased. 'Thanks for getting us out of a tight spot. Your Apache pilot's timing was perfect.'

'Our pleasure. We were lucky they were on board, as we don't normally carry Apaches. Your skirmish allowed us to complete a training exercise with a real-life scenario.' He smiled. 'I'll leave you to rest, Major, and Commander Scott will arrange the debrief. I'll see you before you leave the ship.'

The sound of footsteps echoed in the distance. Laing closed his eyes and surrendered to an overwhelming desire to sleep.

THE BED COVERS felt tight around Laing's feet. He opened his eyes to find Manisha sitting on the end of his bed, frowning over her laptop. 'How are you feeling?'

The sound of Laing's voice made her jump and pulled her focus from the screen. 'I'm good. My head feels sore, but I'm still alive, thanks to you.'

'We had some very close calls, you know.' Laing took a more serious tone. 'We still need to be careful, Manisha. With the number of people killed last night, I know there will be a reprisal. They still want your research, and they will come for it again. You can't go back to your normal life. You can trust no one.'

'I know. I still can't believe Matthew...' Manisha's voice faltered as she said his name. She straightened and continued, regaining her self-control. 'I can't believe so many people who were close to us, betrayed us. I don't know how I can trust anyone again.'

'As I say, trust no one and keep your data secure.'

'I've connected to the VPN in my lab at Beecroft.' She turned the laptop to show Laing. Her screen displayed the CCTV images from cameras in her lab.

Laing pointed to the screen. 'There's another person I wouldn't trust.' Doulton came into view in the top right image, standing outside Manisha's lab.

'I know, which is why I'm doing this.' Manisha switched to a black command prompt window and typed the command: *killquantum -all*. With a decisive strike, she hit enter. 'This script scrubs the disks in my lab, so nobody can recover the data. All backups are being erased too.'

'Do you have the data stored anywhere else?'

'The critical data is in my heart.' Manisha tapped her necklace.

Looking back at the screen, Laing could see Doulton moving frantically from station to station, unable to log in. When he saw the wall of disks lit up like a Christmas tree, he slammed the side of the cabinet and gave a tormented look at one of the CCTV cameras.

Manisha quickly closed her laptop. Laing could see the disappointment and hurt written on her face.

Manisha looked at Laing, seemingly keen to change the subject. 'You shouted in your sleep last night. Did you have a bad dream?'

Laing caught her eyes and looked away. 'Yes, I've had a

recurring nightmare for years. Sometimes I wake up yelling and I'm awake for the rest of the night. Sometimes I get to sleep again. How bad was I?'

'Not too bad. The nurse calmed you down and you drifted off again. Was it a real event that triggers these dreams, or something you imagine?'

Laing laughed. 'Are you psychoanalysing me?'

'Maybe I feel the need to get to know you better. After all, I think you're the only person I can trust.'

'You're a wise woman. Yes, they're from a real event that happened when I was in the Middle East a few years back. I know it's in my past, but when I'm dreaming, it feels so real. My mind and body feel like they are reliving the experience again.'

'I understand,' Manisha nodded. 'Through my research, I'm beginning to see how this can happen.'

'How?'

'We are conditioned from an early age to accept what we see around us as our reality, as if everything we perceive is seen in the same way by everybody else. But the truth is, we all see our own version of the world, our own version of reality. This makes our life experience so unique.'

'You've lost me already.'

'Your brain receives inputs from your senses. Our senses read in streams of electrical impulses from the energy around us, and our brain tries to make sense of them. The reaction you have to this creates your thoughts and feelings about what you're experiencing. Every single moment, since the first spark of energy created your life, your brain has been translating information from your senses, to provide your experience of the world.'

Manisha paused.

'Now, the critical point is, every second of your life is

recorded. What you see, what you hear, and what you feel are recorded and can be recalled later. In layman's terms, we simply call them memories. However, I believe that every split-second of our existence is recorded in precise detail; everything that your senses perceive, as well as your thoughts and feelings. This recording can be accessed at any time if you know how.'

Laing lay back, trying to process what Manisha was explaining.

She continued. 'You've experienced a very vivid and troubling event which has been recorded, just like every other moment in your life. It's your subconscious mind which plays the event back with impeccable clarity while you sleep. The fact it feels so real does not surprise me at all. Because, in effect, it is real. Your brain is re-processing the information as if it were happening in your awake state and this recreates your feelings throughout the event. The fear, sweats, and whatever is making you shout out, is real for you. Your life exists in your brain and nowhere else.'

Laing said, 'It sounds like a hallucination.'

'That's exactly what life is. People think of hallucinations as something a person with a mental illness would experience. They see spiders crawling all over the room and to the person, they are real. They can see the spiders, feel them, smell them,' Manisha shivered in disgust. 'Think of it this way: if a hallucination is an *uncontrolled* perception, then the perception of right here, right now is a *controlled* hallucination. In a controlled hallucination the brain's predictions of what's out there mix with sensory information from the world, helping us make sense of our surroundings. We're hallucinating all the time. It's just when we all agree about our hallucinations, we call it reality.'

Laing shook his head. 'That's a very different way of seeing the world,'

'Most people don't even question the reality in which they live. They exist in a happy oblivion, eking out an existence and content to deal with hard times while looking forward to good times. The truth is our reality only exists in our minds. We create good times and bad times by how we react to a situation with our thoughts and feelings. Humanity has spent thousands of years trying to understand the universe we see all around us, when the strange reality is, we're creating it ourselves. We need to look inside ourselves, inside our minds, to understand the world. Not the other way round.'

'That sounds like God's idea of a sick joke,' Laing said, attempting to make light of Manisha's insight, as he started to feel out of his depth.

Manisha smiled. 'Perhaps it's our creator's way of enabling us to have a human experience. Space and time just enable us to make sense of our environment.'

'So, what happens when we die?' Laing asked.

'Now there's a leading question! You're asking what happened to me in Venice?'

'Yes.'

Manisha's lips curled as she searched for the right words to describe her experience. 'Where do I start?' Excitement shone through her eyes. 'It was amazing. I was in another place, another world, altogether. A world where space and time didn't exist. I met an incredible woman, and we spoke for what seemed like hours. But it can't have been?'

'It can't have been more than ten minutes. If it were any longer, I don't think you'd be here at all.' Laing paused. 'It sounds like you had a near-death experience.'

'I was dead. Although it took me a long time to realise it.

The strange thing is, during this death experience, I've never felt more alive. All my senses were intensified, and I had incredible clarity of thought. I reviewed my whole life in absolute detail, as if I were reliving it. It felt so real, just like you experience in your dreams.'

Laing strained his imagination to try and understand how Manisha had felt.

'Once I understood the truth that I was dead, and the body I was experiencing couldn't be real, it evaporated into bright shards and orbs of light. I was transformed into pure energy—it was ecstasy.'

Laing gave Manisha a sideways glance.

'I know how strange it sounds, but it felt completely real to me. We carry so much baggage in our minds, over-analyse and worry about trivial things. We can't see life on the physical plane for what it really is—an extraordinary experience we must enjoy, cherish, and protect. Live life fully, knowing that death on Earth is not the end.'

Laing thought about those he had lost over the years and hoped they'd had a similar experience. 'It sounds incredible.'

'It was. It's also made me realise the importance of my work.'

'How close are you to making a breakthrough?'

'I've captured thought energy and decoded part of it. An image and location information that shows where the memory happened. But there is so much other information I need to decode. I know it's possible, but it will take more time.'

Laing's brows knitted together. 'This is why Heylel is so keen to get hold of your work, Manisha. The capacity for power and control over people is beyond comprehension. Imagine a world where all thoughts could be read, a world where there are no secrets. It's straight out of the pages of science fiction.'

'I know how it sounds,' Manisha said. 'I can't see how Heylel's vision can be achieved. I haven't seen any evidence in my research that even hints that we can control human consciousness.' Her eyes locked into his. 'However, if our experiences of life are recorded, and can be recalled as single memories, then imagine if my technology were advanced to tap into and capture all memories from the whole of someone's life. If every second of a person's life were captured and decoded, it would be like watching a film of their entire life. Nothing in anyone's life would be a secret.'

Laing's face drained. 'Could this be done without someone even knowing?'

'Possibly,' Manisha said. 'And if Heylel already has scientists following my work, it's only a matter of time before they find the key. That's why it's imperative I continue my work and fully understand how an interface to consciousness would work, before someone less scrupulous does. If I can understand the true nature of consciousness before Heylel, then I can also try and develop the technology to protect it.'

Manisha sat closer to Laing. He felt the warmth of her fingers as she closed them around his hand. 'This is the key to our very existence. No matter what happens, we can't let it fall into Heylel's hands.'

'I won't let that happen,' Laing squeezed her hand.

'When we get back to the UK, I'm going to need your help, Alex.'

'I'm here for you, Manisha. We'll work through this together.'

'We need to find my father.'

Laing looked confused. 'Manisha, your records show your father is dead.'

'That's what I thought. I've known his death was suspicious for a long time. But since my experience, I have no doubt that his death was a lie. Whatever he discovered fifteen years ago was enough for the government to fake his death.'

'Why would they do that?'

Manisha shook her head. 'I don't know. But he must hold the knowledge that they don't want anyone else to have.'

Laing doubted Manisha's vision was real. He was sure it was what she wanted to believe, but that didn't make it true.

'We'll find the truth,' Laing said.

35

'We have learned that we do not see directly, but mediately, and that we have no means of correcting these colored and distorting lenses which we are, or of computing the amount of their errors. Perhaps these subject-lenses have a creative power; perhaps there are no objects.'

Ralph Waldo Emerson – Philosopher (1803–1882)

Laing glanced out the window, his left arm supported by a sling. The barbed wire perimeter fence around Brize Norton appeared through the morning mist. Below him, two black Land Rover SUVs pulled up and sat heavily on the tarmac. The air was fresh with a pleasant spring breeze as he walked beside Manisha down the steps from the Airbus A400M. The sun poured through a break in the mist, catching an orange windsock fluttering in the distance.

A group of five men in dark suits with earpieces stood beside the cars, ready to escort them from the RAF base. A tall man wearing dark glasses stepped forward with an outstretched hand to greet Laing. 'Good flight, Major?' he asked with a broad smile and a hint of an Irish accent.

'Yes, it's great to be back in England.' Laing shook the man's hand firmly.

'How are you, Professor Williams?'

'Good, thank you.'

'My name is Alan Smith. I'll be driving you to London where we'll have a full debrief with the deputy head of MI5. We have additional security with Dave and Gareth in our vehicle, and Paul and Andy in the trailing vehicle. I'm sure you understand we don't want to risk any further incidents. Do you have any questions?'

'No, let's get going,' Laing answered for them both.

Laing and Manisha climbed into the middle row of seats in the lead car, with Alan and Dave in the front and Gareth taking his place in the back seat. The SUV gently pulled away and made its way to the nearest exit. Passing through the security barrier, Alan turned right out of the base and picked up speed. The trailing car followed closely behind.

'It would have been quicker to take a left out of the base and head towards the A40,' Laing said.

'We're under strict instructions to take the least obvious route,' Alan said. 'Intelligence has told us to expect further attacks. So, we're taking no chances.'

'What intelligence?'

'We'll give you a full brief when we get to London, Major.'

Laing sighed, reluctantly accepting that Alan would give

nothing away. He sat back. The atmosphere in the car was heavy and awkward.

Dave looked over his shoulder at Laing and broke the silence. 'I understand you have a hard drive for me?'

'Yes.' Laing pulled the disk from his bag and passed it over.

'Your work has been coming under a lot of scrutiny, Professor Williams,' Dave said. 'When we get to London, we'll need to understand what you have achieved with your research. We'll also be looking for a breakdown on how you've spent the five million pounds of government funds to date.'

'I haven't spent five million!'

Dave looked irritated.

'I received approximately three million pounds of funding for my work and equipment. What makes you think I've received five million?'

Dave stayed silent, grabbed his phone, and sent a message. Laing discreetly glanced over Dave's shoulder at his screen. *Dig deeper into Doulton's finances and bring him in for questioning.*

The prickly silence resumed. Laing looked out at the burgeoning hedgerows and fields as they continued their journey south towards Bampton. The road stretched ahead, empty and quiet.

Alan broke the silence. 'I understand you had a difficult time in Venice.'

'Yes. We were lucky to get out in one piece,' Laing said.

Alan smiled while looking in the rear-view mirror. 'Very true. You're a rare breed, Mr Laing. Not many people can say they've killed so many operatives within the heart of *our* organisation.'

Laing's heart raced as he realised they were in danger again.

'A tooth for a tooth?' Alan said with a wink. The barrel of a silencer slide out from under his arm, followed by the muted crack of two shots. Dave's body jolted with the impact and slumped forward.

Laing attempted to disarm Alan, but the pressure of Gareth's gun in the back of his neck told him to stand down.

'You bastards really are everywhere,' Laing said.

'We run deeper than you can imagine,' Alan said, looking in the rear-view mirror. 'We will succeed. No one can stop us.'

'I would rather die than give you my research,' Manisha seethed through gritted teeth.

'The truth is, you may have to,' Alan smiled. 'But we've got plenty for you to do for us first. Timing is of the essence. You won't be harmed as long as you comply. Now we have everything out in the open, we'll stop at your lab first, Professor Williams, so we can secure your work.'

Manisha and Laing glanced at each other. For the first time, it felt like they were one step ahead.

Laing quietly unzipped the bag beside him and, out of Gareth's sight, removed a pen. Hiding one half in his clenched fist, he dug the end of the pen between his leg and the bag. He looked at Manisha and flicked his gaze downward.

'How long has Doulton been working for you?' Manisha asked, deflecting attention from Laing.

'Not very long. We had to recruit him due to Redfern's untimely death. Every man has his price, and Professor Doulton is very motivated by money. Thanks to Redfern, we've known he's been stealing government funds for years. I'm astonished MI5 have only just cottoned on to the fact,' he said, nodding to the dead man beside him. 'We always knew we could bribe him if needed. It was just a matter of time before we brought him into play. We know a lot about our dear professor and how he's so badly betrayed those close to him.'

Laing caught Alan's mocking look cast towards Manisha in the rear-view mirror and felt a surge of contempt.

The SUVs sped through the Oxfordshire countryside. The mist had cleared, and bright sunlight bounced off the road. Laing saw the rear lights from a vehicle in front flash into life, braking hard and swerving around a lone cyclist. Alan hit the brakes, and they all lurched forward, the seatbelt dug hard into Laing's shoulder. While everyone's attention switched to the road ahead, Laing took his opportunity. He quickly raised the pen, stabbing backward into Gareth's face. Blood spurted from his eye socket as Laing's improvised weapon hit its mark.

Gareth dropped his gun, and it slid onto the footwell behind Manisha. The injured man clutched his face, writhing in pain as blood oozed between his fingers.

Alan swerved the car from side to side, trying to keep his captives off balance.

Manisha tried to reach the gun, her fingertips slipping on the butt, as the car jerked from side to side. In a fluid move, Laing unclipped his seat belt and grabbed the back of Alan's head. His fingers penetrated deep into the soft warmth of Alan's eye sockets.

Screaming out in pain as the car swerved violently, Alan waved his gun towards the back of the vehicle and squeezed the trigger. The shot narrowly missed Manisha and ricocheted off the bulletproof window beside her, embedding itself in Gareth's neck, sealing his fate.

Laing released his grip on Alan's head and took the gun

from his flailing hand, pressing the silencer hard against the man's skull. Removing the sling from around his neck, he reached forward to retrieve Dave's gun from inside the dead man's jacket.

Alan grabbed the steering wheel, regaining control over the vehicle. He rubbed his eyes, trying to recover his blurred vision as he continued down the road at speed. The radio crackled into life as requests for updates came from the trailing car.

'It's amazing how quickly your fortunes can change,' Laing said, as he held the gun to Alan's head.

'Very true.'

Laing saw the flicker of sarcasm on Alan's face too late as he stamped the brakes hard. The screech of tyres, the crunch of metal, and the sound of the rear window shattering reverberated through the car as the chasing vehicle slammed into the boot.

Laing found himself thrown forward through the gap between the two front seats, his head slamming into the dashboard. As Alan pressed the accelerator to the floor, Laing hung on to the front seat to stop himself being thrown back into Manisha. Through the window, he saw the trailing SUV attempt to draw alongside.

Raising his elbow, Laing smacked it hard into the side of Alan's head. He made a grab for the steering wheel, forcing it hard to the right. The SUV slammed into the side of the chasing car, which bounced off the hedgerow and drew back. In a split-second decision, Laing pulled the trigger, sending a bullet through Alan's skull. The slug thudded into the blood-soaked window pillar.

The car lurched from side to side, bouncing from one hedgerow to the next, as Laing fought to keep the vehicle straight. Alan's foot sat heavy on the accelerator, the speed increasing with each second. Laing slid the gearshift into neutral, allowing the car to decelerate. 'We need to get him out.'

As the car started to lose momentum, Laing heard Manisha fiddling with her seatbelt, then the click as it released. She leaned around the driver's seat, holding onto the headrest to steady herself, and opened the door. Laing released the driver's seat belt and pushed Alan's body out of the vehicle. The corpse hit the tarmac and rolled under the chasing car, which lifted onto two wheels before crashing to the road again.

Laing jumped into the driving seat, pulled the flapping door closed, shifted the gearbox into drive and pressed the accelerator to the floor. The sound of the V6 engine roared through the vehicle as it picked up speed. He seized the gun, ready to eliminate the threat from the trailing car.

His eyes flicked between the road in front and the rear-view mirror. He watched as an automatic weapon appeared from the passenger side window of the trailing car. 'Keep your head down!'

Manisha ducked low, and huddled in the footwell, jamming herself tight behind the front seat.

Bullets ricocheted off the roof, flew through the broken rear window, and rebounded off the windscreen.

The cars roared past a sign entering the village of Aston, asking drivers to '*Please drive carefully.*' The thirty miles an hour speed limit sign passed in a blur as the chasing car pulled up alongside Laing and Manisha.

As they entered Aston High Street parked cars along the roadside caused the chasing car to brake hard. It slid in behind them, then accelerated, and Laing braced himself. It smashed into the rear of their SUV for the second time. He had no alternative but to swerve on to the wrong side of the road, smashing wing mirrors off parked cars.

Ahead, he saw horrified faces in the windscreen of an oncoming vehicle. Laing braked hard, and with a heavy pull on the steering wheel, crashed into the side of the chasing car, forcing it down a side road onto a triangular green outside the Red Lion pub. Laing hit the switch to wind down the passenger window and took two shots at the driver across the village green. The rounds hit the driver's door and rebounded off the glass. A barrage of bullets returned from the rear of the vehicle sent chips of stone flying off the village war memorial, then peppered the side of their SUV.

The chasing car weaved its way around the triangular green and caught up with Laing's SUV as it headed down the mail road. The vehicles swerved in and out of parked cars. Oncoming cars were forced off the road as both SUVs sped side by side at ninety miles per hour.

Air rushed around the inside of the vehicle as Laing shouted, 'Stay down and hold on tight!' Manisha complied, hunching behind the back of the passenger seat. Laing fastened his seat belt, watching the driver of the chasing car, waiting for him to yank the steering wheel and force a collision. 'Hang on!' Laing slammed on the brakes. The momentum was too much for the chasing car, and the driver too committed. Laing held his breath as the SUV swept in front of their car and lost control, crashing into the village hall.

Laing pulled in behind the wreckage, leaving his car at an angle. He jumped out, scanning the scene of carnage, gun at arm's length, ready to shoot if there was any sign of a threat.

'Stay in the car, Manisha.' Laing crouched and peered

around the bonnet at the destroyed SUV. The car sat half in and half out of the building, covered in dust, bricks, and mortar. There was no movement. He stepped closer, his gun aimed inside the vehicle, seeking any sign of life. The passenger of the car had taken the brunt of the impact, which had killed him instantly. The driver was alive. As he regained consciousness, he held up his hands, coughing to clear dust from his lungs.

'Throw out your weapon,' Laing said. A gun was dropped through the shattered window onto the tarmac.

'Get out of the car.'

'I can't, my leg is pinned. I can't move,' the driver said through gritted teeth.

Laing opened the door to see the extent of the injuries. Blood gushed from a wound in his leg where the femoral artery had been severed. From the rate of blood loss, Laing judged the man had about three minutes before he would pass out and die.

Manisha jumped out of the car and ran to Laing. Looking in the vehicle, she turned pale at the sight of the blood pooling in the footwell.

'Who are you working for? Who's at the top of the chain?' Laing demanded.

The man looked at them both and gave a low laugh. He coughed blood and winced as his trapped leg shifted. 'I'm not going to betray my leadership in my dying moments. But there is one last thing I can share with you.' He smiled as he held Manisha's gaze. He lifted his wrist to his mouth and spoke into his radio, looking into Manisha's eyes: '*Kill the old man.*'

Manisha's face drained as he started to repeat the words.

Laing trained his gun on the man and pulled the trigger. He was dead before he could finish his sentence.

'They can't kill my father,' Manisha said.

Laing put his arm around Manisha's shoulders, as the truth of the situation hit home. Her father was really alive, and they were using him as punishment for the disruption they had caused Heylel. He kissed her head and hugged her close as she began to sob uncontrollably. He wanted to stay there longer, comforting her, but he knew they had to keep moving. Reluctantly, he left her leaning against the SUV as he dragged Gareth's body from the back of the vehicle and left it on the tarmac. He carefully pulled Dave from the front seat, taking the hard drive from his jacket pocket, and laid him respectfully on the ground.

The sound of approaching police sirens carried on the wind as Laing reversed the car and shifted it into drive. Tyres screeched as they sped away, leaving the carnage behind.

As the countryside sped by, Laing focused on the road ahead. Without looking at Manisha, he reached out and held her shaking hand, keeping one hand firmly on the steering wheel.

'We can't let this happen!' she sobbed. 'I need to see him alive.'

She paused and said, 'We must get to Doulton.'

36

'For more than 200 years, materialists have promised that science will eventually explain everything in terms of physics and chemistry. Believers are sustained by the faith that scientific discoveries will justify their beliefs.'

Rupert Sheldrake – Biochemist (1942–)

Manisha hung on to the grab handle above her seat as the bullet-strewn SUV sped through the gates of the Beecroft Building. Laing mounted the kerb, and parked half on, half off the road. Bewildered students looked on as she ran inside with Laing, taking the most direct path to Doulton's office.

Doulton's PA shot them an indignant look as they barged in. The scene that met them was telling: Doulton's office safe was open, and he was hurriedly stuffing the contents into a large brown leather holdall. Documents were strewn all over his desk. His untidy hair showed where stress-ravaged fingers had ploughed through it time after time.

Now face to face with Doulton, Manisha felt sick. She needed him to tell her the truth. But was he even capable?

'Where's my father?'

Doulton jumped and turned at her voice. She saw the fear etched into his face.

'Manisha, what have you done?' Doulton raked his fingers through his hair. 'All your work has been purged; there's nothing left. You know you're in serious breach of your contract?'

'Nigel, you breached the contract years ago by embezzling funds.'

Doulton looked preoccupied, blinking rapidly, his lips trembling.

'My father is in danger. I need to know where he is, and you're the only one who knows the truth.'

'Your father is dead, Manisha—you know that!'

Manisha clenched her jaw in frustration. 'How can you continue to lie to me after all these years?' Manisha gripped the top of the leather chair. 'This is your opportunity to come clean and put this deception behind you. My father trusted you. Please tell me the truth.'

Doulton gazed at her with watery eyes. His shoulders sagged, as if he were about to admit defeat—but then he set them square again. 'Manisha, he died fifteen years ago. You need to accept it.'

Manisha walked further into the office and picked up some papers from Doulton's desk, passing them to Laing. A cursory glance showed bank statements displaying vast sums of money in Doulton's personal accounts. The shredder under his desk was filled with evidence he'd already destroyed.

'You're in this deep, aren't you?' Laing said.

Doulton stepped towards the desk, grabbing at papers to retrieve the damning evidence.

'Sit down and start talking.' Laing pushed Doulton back into the leather chair. Doulton tried to stand again and gather the paperwork.

'Sit!' An angry look and pointed finger from Laing kept Doulton in his seat.

Doulton's PA looked down her nose at them as Manisha closed the door, shutting out the curious onlookers. Her resolve hardened as anger built up within her.

Laing turned his attention to the desk and continued to search through the papers. 'You're a very wealthy man. How does an Oxford professor have over two million pounds in savings and bonds?'

'That's private information,' Doulton said, thrusting out an arm and quickly withdrawing it again as Laing raised his hand.

'It won't be for long,' Laing said, looking at him from under furrowed brows as he continued to turn the pages.

Manisha stood beside him, scanning documents that included her contract for her research post at Oxford, and her personnel record. Other documents confirmed Doulton's association with the Government and with Redfern—some of it perfectly legitimate, given his role as Science Advisor—but she scanned other papers in disbelief at the double life Doulton had been leading for so many years. Official contracts between Oxford University and the UK government. Statements of work showing what the government expected Doulton to deliver in return for funding her research—and also what benefits Doulton would get for his cooperation. However, the sums of money shown for Doulton's compliance were a fraction of what was in Doulton's accounts.

Laing glanced at Manisha as he tapped a document. She stepped closer—Redfern's instructions on how Doulton was to manage her research, ensuring it served the government's intelligence-gathering efforts.

'All your lies.' She looked up at him, eyebrows knitted, pointing her finger accusingly. 'All the times you called me paranoid when I asked if the government was funding my work. And all the time I was right.'

'I'm sorry, Manisha. I had to do it.'

Manisha saw undiluted fear and shame in Doulton's eyes. The layers of deception ran deep—Doulton was obviously guilty on many levels. However, she realised he was not in control. He was a weak, malleable, self-centred man who wanted the trappings of success and wealth. He was a pawn, not a leader.

'Do you know what you're involved in?' Laing asked, giving Doulton a chance to drop the act.

After several moments of silence, Doulton sat back into his chair and with a blank stare said, 'No, not really.'

'Redfern not only worked for MI5, but she was also a key operative within Heylel. You've been used, Professor. A mole to get Heylel the information they needed about Manisha's research. It wasn't for the UK government at all—although they were funding Manisha's work through Redfern's authority in her role in MI5.'

Manisha looked at Laing, who returned her gaze earnestly. 'All this time I thought it was the UK government driving the urgency,' he explained. 'I was committed to protecting my country's interests.'

Manisha acknowledged this statement of innocence with a small nod.

'I had no idea,' Doulton said, looking stunned as he tried to comprehend the consequences of his actions. 'I've had a strange, threatening, telephone call. They're going to kill me if I don't give them your research, Manisha. You must help me.' The irony of the same situation only a few days earlier, when Simon had sat in the same chair, sharing the same concern, was not lost on anyone in the room.

'Tell me where my father is,' Manisha demanded.

'Some of these documents must provide a trail to him,' Laing said.

Manisha rifled through the papers, watching Doulton's reaction. Nothing. He just stared at the floor, lost in denial.

Laing moved toward the safe. Doulton crossed his arms and, out of the corner of his eye, stole a glance at it, fear and shame written all over his face. Laing flicked through the remaining files inside. He lifted out a folder and sat down in Doulton's high-backed chair. Manisha stood beside him as he opened the thick cardboard folder, which bore a UK Government seal and the words "Quantum—Ref: A-Williams 2002–08".

Doulton sat up, peered at the file—then dropped his head in his hands.

A photo and a brief biography of Professor Andrew Williams filled the first page. Manisha gave a sharp intake of breath as she looked at the image of her father. His silver-grey thinning hair, wide smile and checked short-sleeved shirt he always wore brought memories flooding back. She looked into his eyes and prayed they would get to him in time.

The documents described the professor's research between 2002 and 2008 and his technological advancement that had enabled thought storage and transference. His research was extensive and filled in some gaps Manisha was attempting to resolve. 'Why didn't you give me my father's notes?' Manisha asked. 'This could have saved years of research.'

'I was in debt. I needed the money, Manisha. If you had advanced your research too quickly, then the government funding would have dried up and they would have moved the research to their own facility. I needed to draw out your project, and the funding, for as long as possible.' Doulton slumped back in the chair.

'That's the only good you have done,' Laing said. 'If Manisha had accelerated her research, then Heylel would have intervened way before now.'

Manisha turned to the final pages, hoping this would provide the detail of what had really happened when her father had supposedly died in 2008. Laing read the last page of the folder out loud. 'Entry on 21st April 2008: Professor Andrew Williams has been sectioned under the Mental Health Act. He has been sent to the 'Royal Hospital Haslar' in Gosport, near Portsmouth, following an accident in his laboratory in Oxford.' Doulton's signature sat under the entry.

Doulton squirmed in his chair.

Manisha glared at Doulton. 'My father *is* still alive!'

'I'm sorry.'

Manisha walked towards the door. 'Alex, can we go to him?'

'Wait, Manisha. It's more complicated than it sounds,' Doulton stammered.

'For the first time in your life, tell me the truth! You're one of the last people to see him before his death was faked.'

Doulton was cornered. 'Your father's research was going

well. Better than any of us expected. He had proven the technology to capture thoughts and to translate them into meaningful data. It was in late 2007 that the UK government started showing an interest in what he was doing and how far his research had progressed.'

'Were you in your position as Science Advisor then?' Manisha asked.

'Yes, I was. And yes, it was me who made the government aware of this new technology and how it could be used. I knew it would help with the interrogation of prisoners in wars in the Middle East. Your father was on the verge of preventing the unnecessary deaths of hundreds of troops and thousands of civilians in needless wars. However, he didn't want his technology to be used in a way that compromised a person's privacy. The idea of reading a person's thoughts without their consent was against his principles. He fought the UK government for several months and even threatened to pull out of the research programme and continue his research privately. This was his demise. The government would not allow it, and they lost trust in him. They were afraid, just as you are Manisha, that his work would fall into the wrong hands. That could never be allowed to happen—the consequences are not worth thinking about. This technology was kept secret from even our closest allies. It was the ultimate way of giving UK intelligence services the edge over the rest of the world.

'They also knew the technology discovered by your father was just the tip of the iceberg. He had taken it further forward than any of us dreamed. His reluctance to cooperate caused so many problems, Manisha. The people at the top wanted to take his work and arrange a fatal accident, so the technology would never leak out. I stopped them from doing that. I convinced them that putting him in secure facilities was the best and only approach. I threatened to resign and blow the lid on it all if they did not follow my wishes. Eventually, I got my way. However, they insisted on the cover-up and faked his death and his funeral. I am the only reason your father is still alive.'

Doulton paused for breath.

'Once he was sectioned, the government's top scientists tried to replicate your father's experiments but failed. There was a missing piece of the puzzle, which he had not documented. Something he had told no one. They tried to get this information out of him after he was sectioned, but when they tried to question him, all they found was a blithering wreck. The project was eventually shut down in 2009.'

'Was Redfern your government contact back then?' Laing asked.

'No, she only came along in 2018.'

'So Heylel were not involved back then. The UK government were in control.'

'I guess,' Doulton said. 'I contacted the government about the possibilities for Manisha's research in April 2022, and soon after I was told to work with Redfern.'

'Of course. That's when she had her meteoric rise to the top chair in MI5.' Laing looked lost in thought. 'So, we have the UK government trying to protect its interests up to 2009. Then from 2022, we have Heylel trying to secure Manisha's research. Did you ever tell Redfern about the extent of Andrew Williams's research?'

'No. A part of me understood Andrew's reasons for withholding his research. But I also needed the money. I couldn't let Manisha complete her research too quickly.'

'You just saw an opportunity to take advantage of Manisha and skim off a few million for yourself.'

'How could you,' Manisha's voice was tight with fury. 'You were lying to me all this time.'

'I'm sorry, Manisha. I did my best. I kept your father alive.'

'You betrayed him. You betrayed us both. He was supposed to be your friend! He trusted you to watch out for me. How can you live with yourself?'

Doulton was silent for a moment, lost in his own thoughts. 'What are you going to do with me now?' he asked, turning the attention back to himself.

'We're not going to do anything with you,' Laing answered.

Relief flickered across Doulton's face.

'However, I'm sure these chaps have a few questions for you,' Laing said, nodding to the three government officers standing outside the glass wall.

The door opened, and three women entered the room.

'Professor Doulton, my name is Security Agent Whiteley, and these are my colleagues from the National Fraud Intelligence Bureau,' the woman said as her colleagues approached.

'Professor Doulton, you are under arrest on suspicion of embezzlement of government funds. You have the right to remain silent, but anything you do say may be used as evidence against you in a court of law. Do you understand?' Agent Whiteley said, nodding to her colleagues, who stepped forward to cuff Doulton.

'Yes, I understand,' Doulton looked broken as he looked down at the floor in shame.

'You may want these,' Laing swept the financial papers off the desk into the holdall and handed them over. Manisha picked up her father's 'Quantum' folder and her contract and held them close.

'You should get quite a few years in prison for fraud,' Laing said.

Doulton grimaced.

'Count yourself lucky, as it won't be as long as you've had Manisha's father locked up for.'

As Doulton stood up, his head hung low, his mobile phone on the desk lit up and vibrated with a shrill ringtone.

Manisha read the display—*No Caller ID*—and noted the wave of relief that washed over Doulton's face as the call was diverted to voicemail.

Doulton looked at Manisha. 'How did you know your father was still alive?'

Manisha paused before answering. 'I could feel it.' She looked at the man who had betrayed her family. Emotion had left her; she felt nothing for him.

Doulton looked at her, tears welling in his eyes, his dishevelled hair falling over his forehead. 'You're a brilliant scientist, Manisha. Your father will be proud of you.' He took a step towards the door with the officers—then stopped and looked back at Manisha one final time. 'Manisha, Haslar closed in 2009, soon after your father was taken there. He was moved. You'll find him at Bletchley Residential Nursing Home in Buckinghamshire.

37

'We are living in a culture entirely hypnotised by the illusion of time, in which the so-called present moment is felt as nothing but an infinitesimal hairline between an all-powerfully causative past and an absorbingly important future.'

Alan Watts – Author / Philosopher (1915–1973)

A small, middle-aged man, impeccably dressed in a tailored suit and designer glasses, stared up at the imposing doors to the nursing home. He lifted the cast iron door knocker and let it fall several times. Its impact echoed through the entrance hall beyond the stout oak doors.

An authoritative, full-figured black woman appeared, her white uniform clinging to every curve. 'Can I help you?' she asked. There was a friendly warmth to her voice, and although her deep brown eyes were kind, they were busy weighing up the stranger.

He held up his identification card. 'Hello, my name is Dr Hargreaves. I'm here to assess Andrew Williams.'

She studied the ID, peering between the photo and the man several times. Once satisfied, she opened the door wider. 'You'd better come in.'

The doctor walked into the large entrance hall, and she closed the door behind him. 'Where's his usual doctor?'

'Dr Jones was taken ill. I'm sure he'll be fine. It happens to the best of us, ah...' He peered at the woman's name tag. 'Angela.'

'It sure does. Wait here and I'll check Andrew's okay to see you.'

Dr Hargreaves waited in the entrance hall, beneath the judging gaze of seventeenth-century portraits, mentally preparing himself for what lay ahead.

Under his jacket, the silencer in his gun holster pressed into his side. He hoped he wouldn't have to use it. He quietly took in his surroundings with a buzz of nervous tension at his core.

This should be an easy kill.

'Come on through, Dr Hargreaves.' Angela opened the doors to the old library. The musty, smoky aroma of old books and a slow-burning fire greeted him. The room was quiet, with only a few residents scattered throughout.

'Andrew is very particular about his daily routine. He likes to stay in the same chair, by the large bay window from dawn until dusk. If we try to move him, all hell will break loose. Can you do your assessment here?' she asked as they surveyed the room.

He smiled. 'Of course, this will be fine. It's just a routine check-up for the records. Has he been well lately?'

'No, he hasn't. He's very weak and he's lost a lot of weight over recent weeks,' she whispered. 'He's not eating very much at all.'

Dr Hargreaves kept his smile to himself. 'Thank you. I'll add that detail to his notes.'

Angela grabbed a spare chair and placed it next to Andrew. 'You have a visitor, Andrew. Dr Hargreaves is here to do your assessment today.'

Andrew stared blankly out of the window at the tree-lined drive which swept up to the nursing home.

'Hello, Andrew.' The doctor removed a folder from his briefcase. 'How are you feeling today?'

A steady silence followed, with only Andrew's shallow breath and a small cough filling the void.

Dr Hargreaves reviewed the government folder he'd been given and studied the photograph of his target for the day. *The years haven't been kind to you, have they? How could they ever have thought you'd be of use again?*

The file requested a quiet and peaceful termination —*make it look like natural causes.* For all intents and purposes, the man was already dead. He didn't exist outside of this building, not even on paper.

It was rare the UK government ordered the death of a civilian. However, the tide had changed. The mess stirred up in Oxford meant the risk of keeping Andrew alive was too significant. He and his daughter could not be allowed to work together. The belief was that their collaboration would solve many of the problems they had individually faced with their research. They had both shown they were not prepared to work for the Ministry of Defence, so the risk of Heylel, or any other organisation getting hold of their work, had to be eliminated. The final threat from the '*Quantum*' operation had to be extinguished, as many believed it should have been back in 2008.

Redfern's deception had caused a storm in Whitehall. Anyone in positions of power or in MI5/MI6 was going through additional security checks to weed out the cancer that had grown in the organisation. Alan, Gareth and Paul had only been confirmed as Heylel operatives as the chaos had broken out in Aston. A government risk assessment for the operation had concluded that if there were any incidents while getting Professor Williams to MI5, then Andrew had to die. Both organisations knew Andrew held the key to advancing the technology, and both organisations knew the technology couldn't fall into the other's hands.

ANDREW WAS aware of the man beside him but didn't look in his direction. His eyes still transfixed on the tree-lined drive leading up to the nursing home.

'Would you like some water, Andrew?' Dr Hargreaves offered as he closed the file.

The voice seemed familiar. Like an echo from the past, which pulled Andrew's attention from the view.

'Yes, yes, please,' he said, trying to place where he had heard the man's voice before.

Dr Hargreaves got up and walked to the corner of the old library. He filled a small plastic cup from the water cooler and returned to his seat.

'It's a lovely afternoon out there, not a cloud in the sky.' The doctor removed a small sachet of powder from his briefcase and tipped it into the water. He stirred it with a small wooden spatula and watched it fizz as the powder dissolved.

Confusion swirled in Andrew's mind. The voice he could hear and the dialogue with the doctor seemed so familiar. As if he'd had the same conversation before.

He raised his gaze from the window and looked at the man sitting beside him. He saw a face he knew. A face he hadn't seen for many years. However, he doubted he'd ever met the man in person before. Andrew shook his head as an overwhelming sense of déjà vu consumed him, making him feel dizzy and nauseous. *Could this be the day?* He gently scratched his lips, trying to clear his thoughts.

'Here's your water.' Dr Hargreaves gently put the cup to his lips.

Andrew started to take a sip but stopped. 'No, no, I'll do it myself,' he said, still defying everyone's need to treat him as a child. He turned his watery gaze to the doctor. 'What did you say your name is?'

'I'm Dr Hargreaves. I'm here to do your assessment as Dr Jones is off sick today.'

As the conversation continued, the feeling grew stronger: Andrew had already experienced this encounter. In a previous life, before he'd been interned. Everything he saw, heard, and felt in this moment, he had already experienced. Even the brief smell of the man's cologne added to the recalled memory in his mind.

He gripped the cup, his hand trembling, his mind racing to recall what came next.

'Have I met you before?' Andrew asked, peering at him through narrowing, bloodshot eyes.

'No, I don't recall us having met,' the doctor said. 'Have a drink.'

Andrew's gaze returned to the window. 'You seem very familiar.'

Flashbacks started to fill in pieces of the puzzle. Andrew

closed his eyes and tuned in. He knew what would happen next. Yet he could not see how the meeting would end.

'Angela is coming back.' The sides of Andrew's lips curled up.

Dr Hargreaves looked behind him. 'I can't see her,' he said.

'Look again.' Andrew's confidence was unwavering as the door opened and Angela walked in, making her way towards them.

'How are you getting on, doctor?'

'Yes, fine thank you. I should only be another ten minutes.'

Andrew sat in his chair, smiling—a smile that turned into a chuckle as he started to remember.

'Whatever you're doing, it's having a positive effect,' Angela said, looking between Dr Hargreaves and Andrew. 'He hasn't laughed like this for years.'

Andrew's laugh turned into a weak cough.

'Have some water, Andrew,' Dr Hargreaves encouraged.

Instead, Andrew tried to stand, his frail legs shaking under the strain. The contents of the cup splashed onto the floor, leaving only a mouthful of water left to consume.

Placing his left hand on a table to steady himself, he staggered towards the window.

'They will come for me; I will be free from this place,' he said as he approached the glass.

Andrew slowly lifted the plastic cup to his mouth. The cup shook in his hand as he stared out of the window and started to sip the liquid. He paused—leaning closer to the glass. 'At last!' He dropped the cup, water splashing onto the floor. He placed his palm flat on the glass as a tear rolled down his unshaven face.

The vision he had clung to for fifteen years was finally

unfolding before his eyes—his daughter and a man running up the drive. His daughter stopped in her tracks, staring up at him through the window and throwing her hands to her mouth as a flood of tears poured down her cheeks.

Andrew's synapses fired, a flood of memories from his final experiment filled him. The experiment that had convinced him he could not let his work fall into anyone else's hands, including the government. The experiment had retrieved a collection of memories from a future event —memories which he'd implanted into his mind. He had lived this encounter before, in every detail. What he could see, hear, smell and even how he felt, he had already experienced. The result of the experiment had been a fluke that he hadn't had time to analyse and understand. But the fact that it could happen at all had concerned him deeply. The ability to implant thoughts, to implant memories, was a reality. Quantum theory had always hypothesised that all future possibilities in a person's life had already happened. The past, present and future were just an illusion—all happening at the same time. However, this was tangible evidence that the theory could be correct.

The vision unfolding before him was what he had clung on to so dearly for so many years. The vision that had kept him alive, when all he'd wanted to do was give up and die.

'My daughter, my beautiful, beautiful daughter...'

He felt Angela's arm around him, supporting him as his legs shook from the effort of standing.

'Have a drink, Andrew,' Dr Hargreaves said. 'It looks like this has been quite a shock for you.' The fizz from a new cup of water touched Andrews's face.

'This is the best day of my life,' Andrew said, and drank the cup of water down in one.

Dr Hargreaves smiled at them both. 'My work here is

done,' the doctor said, and packed up his briefcase. 'I'll leave Professor Williams to his visitors.'

'Thank you,' Angela said.

'I'll show myself out.'

MANISHA RAN into the old library. The potent mix of delight and shock on seeing her father, withered and older than she remembered, paralysed her. She stood and stared before running to embrace him, holding him close for the first time in over fifteen years. He felt so small in her arms compared to the strong father of her teenage years.

'My beautiful SagAstar.' Andrew hugged his daughter.

Her heart stopped on hearing her childhood nickname for the first time in so long.

The nurse looked at the dark-haired woman before her. 'Can you prove you're his daughter?'

'Yes,' Manisha said, wiping her tears and showing her driving licence, which bore Andrew's surname. She also found a family photo on her phone from a time long before his internment.

The nurse studied the photo. 'He has the same photo in his possessions.'

'She is my daughter, Angela,' Andrew said with conviction, as he looked at his carer.

'I'll need to contact the government liaison officer and confirm a family member has made contact.'

'I represent the government.' Laing showed his MI5 ID. 'There's no need to contact anyone else,' he said with a smile.

Angela nodded, with a look that said she was happy to bend the rules.

Andrew's face paled. A bead of sweat formed on his upper lip as he coughed and stumbled. Beads of sweat grew on his brow, collecting in a rivulet which ran down his face, mixing with tears. He cried out in pain and clutched his chest.

'Father!' Fear seized Manisha as he dropped to his knees, then collapsed onto the floor. His face slammed into the wooden floorboards as he took a final breath.

Angela frantically searched for a pulse. 'He's gone into cardiac arrest. Get him on his back.'

Laing turned Andrew over and started chest compressions, trying to kick-start his heart while Angela ran for medical equipment.

Manisha knelt by her father's side, holding his hand. 'You can't leave me now.'

Laing continued the chest compressions and started mouth-to-mouth on the lifeless man.

Angela came rushing back with a defibrillator.

Manisha stood back, shaking, holding her face in her hands. A wave of helplessness swamped her as she feared the shock of her sudden appearance in his life had caused his heart to fail.

Laing ripped open Andrew's pyjama top, revealing his thin grey chest and torso, and Angela placed the large sticky pads on his chest.

'Stand clear—analysing now!' the defibrillator's electronic voice commanded as it scanned for a heartbeat. The shrill sound of the device charging filled Manisha's ears.

'Stand clear, push shock button,' the yellow machine prompted. Angela immediately complied.

The shock flew through Andrew, causing his body to jolt as the electricity coursed through his heart. Manisha watched anxiously, but the body remained lifeless.

A QUANTUM OF THOUGHT

'Stand clear, analysing now. Push shock button,' the machine repeated a second and third time.

Manisha knelt on the cold floorboards beside her father's lifeless body. Tears streaming from her eyes, incredulous that he had been taken from her again so quickly.

Angela knelt by her side, her hand on Manisha's shoulder. 'He's gone,' Angela said, as she gently closed his eyes.

38

'Consciousness ... is the phenomenon whereby the universe's very existence is made known.'

Sir Roger Penrose – Mathematician (1931–)

Mark Regan, a Heylel assassin, stood with his phone pressed to his ear as he watched the events unfold through a side window of the old library.

'He's already dead. Miss Williams is kneeling next to the corpse, crying.'

'Was it an accident or has someone beaten us to it?' the well-spoken Englishman on the end of the phone asked.

'It looks like natural causes,' the man said, then relayed the scene he'd just witnessed.

The Englishman paused. 'I don't believe in coincidences. There's something more going on here.'

'Laing is here with Professor Williams. Do you want me to finish them?'

The Heylel second-in-command paused again, as if considering their long-term objectives. 'No. Leave them.'

The assassin shook his head. 'But sir, they stole twenty-five million pounds from us and killed so many of our people in Venice. We can't allow them to get away with it!'

'Yes, we can allow them to get away with it,' the Englishman said, his tone calm and chilling. 'The money taken is pocket change. Professor Williams clearly has a burning passion for her research; otherwise, she wouldn't have progressed this far. With the money they have taken, I fully expect her to build a new lab and continue her work privately. I'd rather fund her research by stealth than have her captive and refusing to cooperate. Consider it a silent investment. Just track where they go next.'

'Do you want me to continue Zarek's work and secure her research?'

'There's no need.'

'Has Doulton delivered?'

'No. However, we've discovered that Zarek had managed to copy Professor Williams's research to his computer's hard drive. A few hours later, Mr Laing kindly connected the PC to the internet and our backup utility automatically kicked in, synchronising the data back to our servers. The fact he made the financial transfer has only helped us. I would have paid double for the data,' the Englishman said with a laugh.

'All evidence of this activity has been removed from Zarek's PC via a remote wipe utility. Since obtaining the data, our scientists have been poring over Professor Williams's brilliant work, and they're beginning to understand how to replicate her experiments. So, the truth is, we have all the data we need.'

'I had no idea, sir.'

'Track them but leave Professor Williams alone to progress her research. We'll bring her back into play when it suits us.'

'Understood.'

The phone went dead.

Regan slipped a tracking device into a bag inside the battered Land Rover, then retraced his steps through the woods.

39

'I shall give you what no eye has seen and what no ear has heard and what no hand has touched and what has not entered into the heart of man.'

Jesus – Gospel of Thomas–17

Kneeling beside her father's body, Manisha felt time stop, as if she were at a crossroads in her life where she was drifting down the wrong path. She felt sick and empty to her core. Continuing her research without her father was inconceivable. 'This can't be right,' she whispered. She thought about what Sarah had said to her. *He will be there to help you. He will stand by your side again.*

Manisha looked at the lifeless shell in front of her and restarted CPR, pushing hard on her father's chest, over and over, before holding his nose and breathing deeply into his lungs.

She sensed Angela and Laing looking on, knowing their eyes would hold mournful disbelief, but ignored them. They didn't know what she knew.

After three cycles, Manisha felt Laing's hands on her shoulders, trying to pull her away gently. She broke free and continued the chest compressions, intent on giving her father one final, long, deep breath into his lungs.

Turning her gaze to her father, she saw his eyes open wide. He coughed and gasped for breath, as if emerging from a deep sea, as his heart started to pump the lifeblood around his body and into his brain. He turned his head and retched, vomiting water.

Manisha felt time snap as her reality shifted her back to her true path. A path that felt intuitively right. A wave of emotion flooded through her. She smiled as she held her father's hand and leaned forward to kiss his forehead. 'Don't leave me again.'

Angela clutched her chest in shock. Snapping out of her stasis, she sprang into action and ran off, returning with a small oxygen bottle. Gently, the nurse placed a mask over Andrew's nose and mouth. 'We need to get him to a hospital.'

Manisha comforted her father, unable to tear her eyes away from the man who had just witnessed life after death.

Angela fumbled with her mobile phone.

'Who was the man who just left?' Laing asked the nurse.

'He was a doctor who came to assess Andrew.'

'Did he give him anything?'

'Only water.' Angela handed over the plastic cup.

Laing smelled the cup. 'He's been drugged. Professor Williams is in danger. We need to move him to a more secure location,' he said, with an urgency which left no room for argument.

Angela breathed in sharply and raised her hand to her mouth. 'I can't believe I've been so stupid. But I insist, he needs hospital treatment now.'

Manisha turned to Angela. 'We can't trust anyone. Give us what you can to help him, and we'll take him somewhere safe.'

Angela looked at them both. 'If you represent the government, you can sign his release forms. And you can sign them on behalf of his family,' Angela said, looking at Manisha.

'We'd be happy to.'

'Wait here. I'll get the release forms and his things.'

Manisha held her father in her arms, unwilling to let him go again. He coughed and breathed heavily, dazed by his experience. His eyes were fixed on hers, like a new-born baby looking into its mother's eyes.

Angela returned with a small pile of clothes and possessions in a clear plastic bag. Manisha laid her father's head gently on a blanket as Angela placed the discharge forms on the table. Manisha signed them without hesitation and returned to her father's side.

Laing signed the form and gently scooped the frail old man into his arms before carrying him to the back of the Land Rover. Manisha ran ahead and levelled the rear seats, hoping she was doing the right thing for her father. It was all happening so fast, but she knew he could not stay in the home any longer.

Laing lay Andrew down and covered him with blankets. Manisha climbed into the space behind the front passenger seat, cradling her father's head on her lap, creating a cushion for his head as she held his hand.

As they slowly headed down the drive, she watched her father's prison disappear behind the trees. 'Where are we going?' she asked, knowing that returning to Oxford was not an option.

She met Laing's eyes in the rear-view mirror. 'The first thing we need to do is get another vehicle. One where your father will be warm and comfortable. Then we'll head down to Sennen Cove in Cornwall. I have a cottage there. It's remote and easy to secure. We'll be safe there and it'll give your father time to recover.'

'Thank you for helping us,' Manisha said.

'Heylel will never stop. You'll constantly need to stay one step ahead and find a way to protect your discovery.'

'I know,' she said with a tone of melancholy as she looked at her father. Sadness ripped through her for all the years they had lost. She thought of the memories that had been stolen and the achievements that might have been—but felt an overwhelming sense of gratitude that they had been brought back together again. She leaned in and kissed his head. 'We'll get you well and make up for lost time.'

'I knew you would come for me,' Andrew said, looking up into her eyes.

'How did you know?'

'I've seen it, experienced it, lived it,' he smiled.

'What do you mean?'

'Manisha, I managed to tap into the source of consciousness. A place where all the memories and possible events in our lives are stored. Years before today, just before they had me interned, I recalled a possible future event. It was you and your friend running up the drive to get me. I've waited and waited for this day to come.'

Manisha shivered as chills ran down her spine. 'You can

recall events that haven't even happened, thoughts from the future, as well as recall thoughts from the past?'

'Yes, Manisha. Early in my research, I found a clue suggesting it was a possibility. Curiosity got the better of me and I felt compelled to follow it. That's why I called my project Janus, the Roman God who could see the future and the past.'

Manisha's mind whirled, extrapolating the consequences of this new information. 'If you can extract a memory that a person has never had, then... is it possible to implant false thoughts or beliefs? Thoughts that are not your own?'

'I don't know, Manisha. My mind isn't what it was—everything feels very hazy. But yes, yes... it may be possible to introduce new habits, thoughts, or beliefs. A belief that could start small and take root in someone's mind.'

Manisha thought back to Heylel's ambition to manipulate human consciousness and her blood ran cold. Their version of reality could unfold unless she worked to stop them.

Laing glanced at her over his shoulder, his face pale with concern. 'You need to control this technology, Manisha. I have the finances for you and your father to continue your research, if that's what you choose to do.'

Manisha didn't need to know how he had that kind of money. She trusted Laing implicitly. She reflected on everything that had happened over the last forty-eight hours. Where her research had taken her, her near-death experience, and what her father experienced all those years ago. Her near-death experience had shown her that nothing was real, yet a part of her doubted—as if it had been a dream, just a chemical reaction in her brain. Looking around her, she questioned everything.

'How can any part of this be real?'

She had always held that question on the tip of her tongue but only in a theoretical, scientific way. However, as the question slipped from her lips, the importance of the words held their own gravity. She looked down at her father's drawn face. His eyes were bright as he looked intently back at her.

'Nothing is real, Manisha. Everything that has ever happened and everything that is going to happen, only exists in our minds.'

She could see the truth in her father's eyes. 'We need to work together to understand how this works and protect it.'

'I can tell you what I remember, but my years in research are long behind me.'

Manisha smiled, knowing that nothing could be further from the truth. 'Just rest,' she said and stroked her father's hair as he drifted off to sleep.

She gazed out of the windscreen as Laing drove them west, towards a new life in Cornwall. In the distance, the sun set behind the clouds, silhouetted against streaks of gold. Manisha felt a tingle of excitement, as though she were on the verge of a new era of human existence. A new dawn of human understanding of reality and our place in the universe. As the last sliver of sunlight dipped below the horizon, Manisha vowed to protect their discovery and keep humanity safe.

www.ingramcontent.com/pod-product-compliance
Ingram Content Group UK Ltd.
Pitfield, Milton Keynes, MK11 3LW, UK
UKHW042010060625